PENGUIN BOOKS

A Room of One's Own
Three Guineas

Virginia Woolf is now recognized as a major twentieth-century author, a great novelist and essayist and a key figure in literary history as a feminist and a modernist. Born in 1882, she was the daughter of the editor and critic Leslie Stephen, and suffered a traumatic adolescence after the deaths of her mother, in 1895, and her step-sister Stella, in 1897, leaving her subject to breakdowns for the rest of her life. Her father died in 1904 and two years later her favourite brother Thoby died suddenly of typhoid. With her sister, the painter Vanessa Bell, she was drawn into the company of writers and artists such as Lytton Strachey and Roger Fry, later known as the Bloomsbury Group. Among them she met Leonard Woolf, whom she married in 1912, and together they founded the Hogarth Press in 1917, which was to publish the work of T. S. Eliot, E. M. Forster and Katherine Mansfield as well as the earliest translations of Freud. Woolf lived an energetic life among friends and family, reviewing and writing, and dividing her time between London and the Sussex Downs. In 1941, fearing another attack of mental illness, she drowned herself.

Her first novel, *The Voyage Out*, appeared in 1915, and she then worked through the transitional *Night and Day* (1919) to the highly experimental and impressionistic *Jacob's Room* (1922). From then on her fiction became a series of brilliant and extraordinarily varied experiments, each one searching for a fresh way of presenting the relationship between individual lives and the forces of society and history. She was particularly concerned with women's experience, not only in her novels but also in her essays and her two books of feminist polemic, *A Room of One's Own* (1929) and *Three Guineas* (1938). Her major novels include *Mrs Dalloway* (1925), the historical fantasy *Orlando* (1928), written for Vita Sackville-West, the extraordinarily poetic vision of *The Waves* (1931), the family saga of *The Years* (1937), and *Between the Acts* (1941). All these are published by Penguin, as are her *Diaries*, Volumes I–V, selections from her essays and short stories, and *Flush* (1933), a reconstruction of the life of Elizabeth Barrett Browning's spaniel.

Michèle Barrett is Professor of Modern Literary and Cultural Theory at Queen Mary and Westfield College, London. In 1979 she edited a collection of Woolf's essays, *Virginia Woolf: Women and Writing*. Michèle Barrett has published widely on feminist, social and cultural questions. Her books include *Women's Oppression Today*, *The Anti-Social Family* (with Mary McIntosh), *The Politics of Diversity: Feminism, Marxism and Nationalism* (co-edited with Roberta Hamilton), *The Politics of Truth: From Marx to Foucault* (1991), *Destabilizing Theory: Contemporary Feminist Debates* (co-edited with Anne Phillips, 1992) and *Imagination in Theory: Essays on Writing and Culture* (1999). She has also edited *The Origin of the Family, Private Property and the State* by Friedrich Engels for Penguin Classics.

Julia Briggs is General Editor for the works of Virginia Woolf in Penguin.

A ROOM OF ONE'S OWN
THREE GUINEAS

VIRGINIA WOOLF

EDITED WITH AN INTRODUCTION AND
NOTES BY MICHÈLE BARRETT

PENGUIN BOOKS

PENGUIN BOOKS

Published by the Penguin Group
Penguin Books Ltd, 80 Strand, London WC2R 0RL, England
Penguin Putnam Inc., 375 Hudson Street, New York, New York 10014, USA
Penguin Books Australia Ltd, 250 Camberwell Road, Camberwell, Victoria 3124, Australia
Penguin Books Canada Ltd, 10 Alcorn Avenue, Toronto, Ontario, Canada M4V 3B2
Penguin Books India (P) Ltd, 11 Community Centre, Panchsheel Park, New Delhi – 110 017, India
Penguin Books (NZ) Ltd, Cnr Rosedale and Airborne Roads, Albany, Auckland, New Zealand
Penguin Books (South Africa) (Pty) Ltd, 24 Sturdee Avenue, Rosebank 2196, South Africa

Penguin Books Ltd, Registered Offices: 80 Strand, London WC2R 0RL, England

www.penguin.com

A Room of One's Own first published by The Hogarth Press 1929
Three Guineas first published by The Hogarth Press 1938
This annotated edition published in Penguin Books 1993
Reprinted in Penguin Classics 2000

16

Introduction and notes copyright © Michèle Barrett, 1993
All rights reserved

The moral right of the author of the Introduction and notes has been asserted

Set in 10.5/12.5 pt Monophoto Garamond
Typeset by Datix International Limited, Bungay, Suffolk
Printed in England by Clays Ltd, St Ives plc

ISBN-13: 978-0-141-18460-9

www.greenpenguin.co.uk

Penguin Books is committed to a sustainable future
for our business, our readers and our planet.
The book in your hands is made from paper
certified by the Forest Stewardship Council.

CONTENTS

Bibliographical Note

The following is a list of abbreviated titles used in this edition.

Diary: *The Diary of Virginia Woolf*, 5 vols., ed. Anne Olivier Bell (Hogarth Press, 1977; Penguin Books, 1979).
Letters: *The Letters of Virginia Woolf*, 6 vols., ed. Nigel Nicolson and Joanne Trautmann (Hogarth Press, 1975–80).
CE: *Collected Essays*, 4 vols., ed. Leonard Woolf (Chatto & Windus, 1966, 1967).
WE: *A Woman's Essays: Selected Essays Vol. 1*, ed. Rachel Bowlby (Penguin Books, 1992).
ROO: *A Room of One's Own*, Virginia Woolf (Hogarth Press, 1929).
TG: *Three Guineas*, Virginia Woolf (Hogarth Press, 1938).

Introduction

'I have collected enough powder to blow up St Pauls'

A Room of One's Own and *Three Guineas* are Virginia Woolf's two major political works. Coming from a writer who was adamant that politics disrupted and unsettled the aesthetic flow of a novel, they are particularly interesting as statements of the deep-seated political passions that can only be glimpsed intermittently in her fiction. One function of this introduction will be to show the relationship between the arguments put forward in these two polemical broadsides against the establishment and the underlying themes of Woolf's fiction. For those readers primarily interested in Woolf as one of this century's most significant modernist writers, the exercise of studying her political essays to illuminate her novels is extremely valuable.

Yet, and this is perhaps more extraordinary when one thinks how powerful the image of Virginia Woolf as a purist aesthete has been in the past, these political works are actually strong enough to stand alone. *A Room of One's Own*, published in 1929, even now remains one of the clearest and most eloquent accounts that we have of women's writing. Certainly many teachers, desperately casting around bulging library shelves of complex treatises on this topic, often decide with relief to go back and recommend *A Room of One's Own*. They can be confident that the students will read it, will enjoy reading it and will extract from it – if not 'a nugget of pure truth' – at least a solid and well-supported argument that can be discussed on its merits. The case of *Three Guineas* is stranger, for here is a book that has now found its time. When it was published in 1938 its audience was by and large uncomprehending and hostile and it isolated Virginia Woolf from her friends and family. Now, its equation between masculinism and war is a topic of heated political debate rather than a cranky eccentricity.

Both of these texts, then, speak to contemporary debates in and around feminism. If, in the interpretation of Woolf's novels, there is room to contest the extent to which she wrote as a 'feminist', this is not really a plausible doubt with regard to these two political works. *A Room of One's Own* and *Three Guineas* are, quite explicitly, feminist polemics. In 1932, as she was starting to work up the material that was to become *Three Guineas*, Virginia Woolf said to her diary:

> And I'm quivering & itching to write my – whats it to be called? – 'Men are like that?' – no thats too patently feminist: the sequel then, for which I have collected enough powder to blow up St Pauls.[1]

Many commentators have noted the prescience of Woolf's ideas and her capacity to anticipate the concerns of feminists in the future. Nowhere is this more fascinatingly clear than if we consider the changes her ideas underwent between the two texts in this volume. Although important continuities in her thought remained, the shifts of emphases and approach from *A Room of One's Own* to *Three Guineas* are very significant. We can find in Woolf's changing ideas a reflection of the central dilemma of feminism now. Sometimes summarized as the 'equality/difference debate', this revolves around whether feminism should press for egalitarian and even 'androgynous' solutions to present iniquities or whether feminism should build on existing differences between women and men in its search for a society and polity with better values. Virginia Woolf's own emphasis moved from upholding an ideal of androgyny in art to a recognition of the power of difference – notably in her insistence that women were social 'outsiders'.

A ROOM OF ONE'S OWN

'It is feminist propaganda, yet it resembles an almond-tree in blossom,' wrote Desmond MacCarthy in the *Sunday Times* when *A Room of One's Own* was published – a review that Virginia

Woolf was later to paste into her scrapbooks for *Three Guineas*.[2] MacCarthy's response captures something of the seductive charm of the essay, the literariness with which bald factual arguments are cloaked, and its intimate appeal to the reader. Although – since the essay retains a sense of the talks to young women that it was based on – it seems most obviously to address women, it was also finely calculated to be attractive to men. An American fan, writing to Woolf on reading it, highlighted this in her comment that '. . . the detachment, tact and grace of *A Room of One's Own*, and the deadly weapons of poetry, wit and irony which compel the male reader to swallow unpalatable truth as if it were sugar are new in feministic writing.'[3] Virginia Woolf herself, in a diary entry about the likely reception of the book, conjured up the same critical response when she noted: 'I am afraid it will not be taken seriously. Mrs Woolf is so accomplished a writer that all she says makes easy reading . . .'[4]

What, we may ask, was the unpalatable truth, the feminist propaganda, that lay beneath the charming conversational style of *A Room of One's Own*? The central argument of the essay is that 'a woman must have money and a room of her own if she is to write fiction.' Woolf argued that the writer was the product of his or her historical circumstances, and that material conditions were crucially important. She also explored the more complex and subtle ways that such material circumstances affected the psychological aspects of writing and the creative process itself. As she puts it, in *A Room of One's Own*:

> . . . these webs are not spun in mid-air by incorporeal creatures, but are the work of suffering human beings, and are attached to grossly material things, like health and money and the houses we live in. (p. 38)

Woolf commented on these material things in her own life, in her essay 'Professions for Women':

> . . . when I came to write, there were very few material obstacles in my way. Writing was a reputable and harmless occupation. The family peace was not broken by the scratching of a pen. No

demand was made on the family purse. For ten and sixpence one can buy paper enough to write all the plays of Shakespeare – if one has a mind that way. Pianos and models, Paris, Vienna and Berlin, masters and mistresses, are not needed by a writer. The cheapness of writing paper is, of course, the reason why women have succeeded as writers before they have succeeded in the other professions.[5]

Woolf's general argument was that women have been constrained from writing by circumstances in which they were deprived of education and denied access to publishing. The passage in *A Room of One's Own* where Virginia Woolf describes how angry she was at being barred from an Oxbridge library, because 'ladies are only admitted to the library if accompanied by a Fellow of the College or furnished with a letter of introduction' (p. 7), is a much-quoted illustration of the general point. More importantly, for Woolf, women were deprived of the right to earn a living from their writing. Prior to the Married Women's Property Acts, in 1870 and 1882, married women's income legally belonged to their husbands. Much of the argument of *A Room of One's Own* concerns the importance of women's financial independence. Woolf's view of writing was one that revolved around 'freedom of mind' as the prerequisite of the writer, since she regarded integrity as the base of good writing and integrity was not to be found where the writer was forced to flatter or appease.

Woolf argued that the material impoverishment of women's lives – including those middle and upper class women who had an affluent lifestyle but no real control over, or ownership of, money – accounted for their lack of creative expression. In a letter to the *New Statesman*, joining a debate about 'the intellectual status of women', she wrote:

> To account for the complete lack not only of good women writers but also of bad women writers I can conceive no reason unless it be that there was some external restraint upon their powers.[6]

In considering the effect of women's social situation on their writing Virginia Woolf stresses the important differences in the opportunities open for women of different social classes and at different periods of history. Up until the end of the seventeenth century it was only eccentric women from the aristocracy, like the Duchess of Newcastle or Lady Winchilsea, who were able – surreptitiously – to 'dabble' in writing. With Aphra Behn, the first woman (albeit not a very respectable one, Woolf notes) actually to earn a living by writing, the field was opened for the middle-class woman who could gain some access to education and through this to the world of literature. Even this hard won education, Woolf emphasizes, was available only to 'the daughters of educated men' and was not open to women – just as it was not open to men – of the working class.

Virginia Woolf was herself extremely conscious of the disadvantages she had suffered in not being formally educated, as her brothers had been as a matter of course given the family's scholarly and upper-middle-class background. In the Stephen family (Virginia Woolf's father was Sir Leslie Stephen, editor of the *Dictionary of National Biography* and a well-known man of letters in late-Victorian society) the boys went to 'public' boarding schools and then to Cambridge while the girls were educated at home. Virginia Woolf wrote an essay entitled 'On Not Knowing Greek',[7] and we find throughout her work a painful awareness of the expense that was lavished on the education of boys while girls languished intellectually under unsatisfactory private tuition or self-taught reading programmes. This theme, as we shall see later, forms the starting point of the argument of *Three Guineas*, where Woolf invokes the shadow of 'Arthur's Education Fund' (from Thackeray's novel *Pendennis*) that lay across the household accounts of the educated classes. The fund was 'a voracious receptacle', as the boys needed not only school and college fees, but also friends, conversation, travel and independent accommodation, and all these were bought at the expense of the girls. Thus 'Arthur's Education Fund' has had the effect that women and men may look at the same things, but see them differently:

So magically does it change the landscape that the noble courts and quadrangles of Oxford and Cambridge often appear to educated men's daughters like petticoats with holes in them, cold legs of mutton, and the boat train starting for abroad while the guard slams the door in their faces. (p. 119)

Woolf's argument about education is a central plank in her general interpretation of women's lack of access to writing. Her argument is a strongly materialist one, although it is very different from the classic Marxist arguments about artists simply 'reflecting' the society in which they lived. In fact, she refers rather disparagingly to the view that – as she put it – 'politicians' have that 'a writer is the product of the society in which he lives, as a screw is the product of a screw machine.'[8] Woolf's own view was materialist, but at the same time less reductive; it was that intellectual freedom depended upon material things. Thus the argument of *A Room of One's Own* is part and parcel of her more general position that the material situation of a writer will determine what she called their 'angle of vision'. In a paper read, in a rare but significant identification of the interests of women with working-class people, to the Brighton Workers' Educational Association in 1940, Woolf linked the vision, or perspective, of writers to their education, and beyond that to their social class background:

> . . . almost every writer who has practised his art successfully had been taught it. He has been taught it by about eleven years of education – at private schools, public schools and universities. He sits upon a tower raised above the rest of us; a tower built first on his parents' station, then on his parents' gold. It is a tower of the utmost importance; it decides his angle of vision; it affects his power of communication.[9]

If Woolf took this position up as a general one, it was developed in far more detail with regard to the specific circumstances, and therefore 'angle of vision', of her own reference group – the daughters of educated men. She was particularly aware of the relegation of such women to the private world of home and family, and the damage that this social isolation and narrowness of experience did to them as writers. Woolf speculated that if Jane Austen had lived longer she would have reaped the social benefits of her fame as a writer, getting away from the quietness of her rural life and being able to meet more people and travel. All this, according to Woolf, would have not only enriched Austen's life, but would have made her novels 'deeper and more suggestive'.[10] Woolf's essays on women writers make the same point – that good writing needs rich experience to emerge – in a variety of different contexts. Another 'case' was Elizabeth Barrett Browning, of whom Woolf said, 'it cannot be doubted that the long years of seclusion had done her irreparable damage as an artist.'[11] For George Eliot, the situation was even more poignant, since her social isolation was the product of a double standard of sexual morality that caused women far more suffering than men. George Eliot, who flouted convention by living with a man whose wife was alive but mentally ill, was painfully aware of her pariah status: 'I wish it to be understood,' she had said, 'that I should never invite anyone to come and see me who did not ask for the invitation.' For a novelist, commented Woolf, to lose the power 'to move on equal terms unnoted among her kind' was a serious loss.[12] Woolf drily draws the comparison with another novelist of the period, a young man by the name of Leo Tolstoy, who was busy philandering around Europe collecting the uncensored social and sexual experience that was later to bring us *Anna Karenina* and *War and Peace* (p. 64).

In its simplest form, then, Virginia Woolf's argument in *A Room of One's Own* concerns the external constraints on women's creativity that were imposed by lack of material resources, lack of education, lack of social experience and lack of access to publishing or other means of communication. There is a second dimension to her analysis, though, and this concerns the nature of the works that do manage to get through these social barriers: she was concerned with the fabric and texture of the writing, psychological aspects of the creative process, and issues of consciousness and identity. Woolf wanted to discuss not only the *production* of literature, but the ways in which the social context of its *reception* influenced the writing itself.

In these concerns Woolf anticipated the interests of what is now a thriving school emphasizing the 'gendered' character of literary criticism. The use of male pseudonyms by women writers is a striking instance of the problem: it was not possible to be 'read' seriously as a writer if you were a woman and hence many aspiring women writers simply decided to publish under male names. Virginia Woolf draws attention to the subtle ways in which the contemptuous and condescending attitude of male critics had influenced women's writing. 'One has only to skim those old forgotten novels and listen to the tone in which they were written,' she writes in *A Room of One's Own*, 'to divine that the writer was saying this by way of aggression, or that by way of conciliation' (p. 67).

In her essay 'Professions for Women' Woolf undertook an interesting account of the main psychological obstacles faced by women writers of her time: challenging norms of self-effacing femininity and resisting the taboo against women speaking about sexuality. In that essay Virginia Woolf invokes the 'angel in the house', whose role entailed sitting in draughts and eating poor cuts of meat so that others would be comfortable, ceaselessly deferring to the wishes and desires of others and never addressing her own. For Woolf, this figure was a writer's nightmare, always getting in the way of that 'integrity' and 'truth' that were the hallmark of her literary creed. Woolf manages, in the essay, to drive out this pallid spectre of domestic femininity (in a typically symbolic move of throwing the inkpot at her whenever she turns up) – but is then confronted by the deeper problem of a femininity that takes root at an unconscious level rather than in social convention. Telling the truth about sexuality – 'telling the truth about my own experiences as a body' – turns out to be still harder to accomplish. For although men have the freedom to write about sexuality and the passions, this is severely controlled in women and (to put it in modern terms) such constraints are internalized.[13] Virginia Woolf maintained that there were thus internal as well as external constraints on the writing that women could produce.

In this context it is important to register that, at the time of writing *A Room of One's Own*, Virginia Woolf was quite adamant that explicit feminist anger had no place in a woman writer's novel. She was insistent that the aesthetic integrity of a novel – its ability to make the reader recognize its truth as 'whole and entire' – was incompatible with the articulation of political anger. This can be most clearly seen in Woolf's curiously unsympathetic treatment of Charlotte Brontë. Chapter IV of *A Room of One's Own* contains an extraordinary passage in which Jane Austen and Emily Brontë are praised and Charlotte Brontë subjected to a criticism that verges on scathing – 'the foolish woman sold the copyright of her novels outright for fifteen hundred pounds' (p. 63). Woolf holds it against Charlotte Brontë that her anger interrupts the flow of the novel – citing an 'awkward break' in *Jane Eyre*, where a lengthy political soliloquy ends with a feeble 'as I was saying' link back to the narrative present. Woolf comments that 'she left her story, to which her entire devotion was due, to attend to some personal grievance.' Charlotte Brontë's books were thus 'deformed and twisted' and the angry jerks that they contain mean that her genius will never get expressed 'whole and entire'. With a rather startling lack of charm and generosity, Woolf concludes, 'How could she help but die young, cramped and thwarted?' (p. 63.) Jane Austen and Emily Brontë, on the other hand, get top marks for walking the impossibly fine Woolf tightrope on this question. They wrote as women but not as women conscious of being women; they did not preach or rage but neither did they give in to the prevailing masculinist values of their time:

> What genius, what integrity it must have required in face of all that criticism, in the midst of that purely patriarchal society, to hold fast to the thing as they saw it without shrinking. (p. 67)

Virginia Woolf's argument on this point is worth looking

into because it illustrates how much she was committed, at this stage, to what we might call an aesthetic of androgyny – which she was later to abandon. At the end of *A Room of One's Own* she invokes Coleridge's conception of the androgynous great mind where male and female qualities live in harmony and thus enable the mind to be fertilized and use all its faculties. Woolf's interpretation of Coleridge's notion of androgyny is interesting; for her, he did not mean that a 'great mind' was likely to have any special sympathy with women, or would take up their cause – on the contrary, 'the androgynous mind is less apt to make these distinctions than the single-sexed mind' (p. 89).

Here we have a classic statement of the so-called 'equality' position within feminism. Woolf's borrowed model of the androgynous mind finds sexual complementarity where others have found sexual difference, and regards the 'creative, incandescent, and undivided' mind as a better model than a mind restricted to the feminine or masculine perspective. In *A Room of One's Own* Woolf complained that the time she lived in was particularly hostile to this androgynous ideal: the suffrage movement had challenged men's assumptions and brought about a state of heightened 'sex consciousness' in both women and men. For writers, she argued, such 'sex consciousness' was disastrous. 'It is fatal for anyone who writes to think of their sex,' she concluded (p. 94).

INTERPRETING A ROOM OF ONE'S OWN

A Room of One's Own was published in October 1929, almost exactly a year after the papers it is based on had been delivered at Cambridge. On her return from Cambridge she had made a characteristic diary entry:

Thank God, my long toil at the women's lecture is this moment ended. I am back from speaking at Girton, in floods of rain. Starved but valiant young women – that's my impression. Intelligent, eager, poor; & destined to become schoolmistresses in shoals. I blandly told them to drink wine & have a room of their own.[14]

In the year that followed, Woolf substantially revised the papers (see the Note on the Text) for publication. In doing so she incorporated a creative rendering of her gastronomic experiences in Cambridge: it seems likely that the lunch she and Leonard Woolf ate in King's College was not as exquisite as the one described in the book, or the fare at the women's colleges as grim.

A Room of One's Own is often regarded as the twentieth century's most important statement on the question of women and writing. It captures a marvellous, rich argument in an immensely pleasurable and entertaining style of writing. It is eloquent as well as elegant, trenchant as well as witty, passionate as well as amusing. It is perhaps because it has all of these differing attributes, because it plays with its own seriousness of purpose, that the book has been such an enormous success. Virginia Woolf articulated her own ambivalence about how seriously the book was to be taken when she said, 'It is a trifle, I shall say; so it is, but I wrote it with ardour & conviction.'[15] This is ostensibly a contradiction, for trifles are not written with conviction, but it gives its readers space to decide for themselves how they want to take it and how they want to read it, and the open-ness of the text in this regard has probably been the key factor in its endurance.

It is not easy to disentangle the author from the text of *A Room of One's Own*. For just as the political credo gives insight into the meaning of her novels, so the meaning and effectiveness of the political statement derives, in part at least, from the literary standing of its author. Had *A Room of One's Own* been written by a much lesser novelist, there would undoubtedly be much less interest in it now. On this point it is tempting to revert to the book's own conclusion: that 'Shakespeare's sister' would come, in another century or so, if we worked for her. As she wrote those lines Virginia Woolf could not have known that, a mere fifty or so years later, many people would regard her as having herself acquired this stature as a writer. Woolf's story of the gifted young woman who committed suicide without writing a word, and the need for us to create the conditions in which 'she shall find it possible to live and write her poetry', is a very moving one in the light of her own subsequent life and death. But our note here should be celebratory: by the time of her death at fifty-nine in 1941 Virginia Woolf had written enough to mark her out as one of the finest modern writers – and even, for some, a writer of the calibre of her own admired Shakespeare. Certainly, one might add, she is now more widely read than Shakespeare.

What, however, might the sceptical reader want to question in *A Room of One's Own*? The argument is certainly not without its weaknesses. For although Woolf may have argued that the majority of writers were cushioned by their parents' money, one can produce many instances of writers being inspired by adversity and overcoming extremely inauspicious circumstances. So the basic thesis of *A Room of One's Own* is not an uncontentious one.

It transpires that, although Woolf was adamant about the room of one's own and the money in this text, she was not consistent in her own life about these issues. In her persona as Mary Beton, the narrator/speaker/protagonist of *A Room of One's Own*, Woolf says that her aunt had left her £500 a year at around the same time as women were enfranchised (i.e. 1918). She comments drily that, 'Of the two – the vote and the money – the money, I own, seemed infinitely the more important' (p. 34). To read this as a straightforward autobiographical fact would, however, be to miss out on a typically complex and contradictory reality. For in her own life, Virginia Woolf had been left £2500 in 1909 by an aunt, Caroline Emelia Stephen – the interest giving her considerably less than £500 a year but none the less a significant amount. Although she must later have come to see this legacy in the terms used in *A Room of One's Own*, she was at the time quite thrown by it. She wrote to her brother-in-law, Clive Bell, describing her aunt's will, in terms that she recognized, even at the time, as distinctly not-feminist:

It is very disappointing. Nessa and Adrian [her sister and brother] each have £100: I have £2500 ... It is miserable for Nessa; still worse for Adrian; I am determined to make him share mine – but there's no need to talk of that act of feminine weakness.[16]

Not only was she inclined to sacrifice her own independence to share her legacy with her brother, but also she was herself aware of the psychological damage that owning capital can do. A younger Virginia Woolf had described in her diary the gist of a conversation, about whether socialists should renounce inherited capital, in which her husband Leonard Woolf had stuck to the traditional Fabian socialist position that such wealth should be kept and spent on worthy political causes. Virginia Woolf, however, had argued that 'psychologically it may be necessary if one is to abolish capitalism', and she reflected that, 'I'm one of those who are hampered by the psychological hindrance of owning capital.'[17] Certainly there is consistency in her understanding that material circumstances have profound psychological effects, but there is also a clear shift from the recognition here to the argument of *A Room of One's Own*. At the very least, one could say that she had decided as a feminist to prioritize the specific needs of (middle-class) women over the more general (socialist) desirability of abolishing capitalism.

Secondly, one might legitimately question Woolf's passionate advocacy of what she calls 'freedom of mind'. In pointing to instances – the education of women for instance – where external constraints hamper freedom of mind, she implies that where such constraints do not exist some absolute mental freedom would exist. This is more doubtful. Certainly there is no essence of mental freedom waiting to be allowed out – and in each social and historical moment the concept and the experience of such liberty may well be very different. Many of the concepts with which Virginia Woolf worked – freedom of mind, freedom of expression, integrity, vision, truth and so on – carry connotations that we might now regard as problematic in terms of what they assume about aesthetic judgement and subjective identity. In her novels Woolf questions assumptions of unitary and uncontradictory identity, and indeed her exploration of shifting, fragmented, divided and multiple consciousnesses has made her a very attractive author to post-structuralist literary critics.

At the same time, however, Woolf had a strongly mystical streak that cut against such tendencies towards fragmentation. It led her to an unproblematic retention of ideas such as 'freedom', 'truth' or 'vision' that we might now understand in more relative terms as the ideas of a particular historical period or intellectual culture. An example can be found in a very interesting passage of Virginia Woolf's 1931 speech, transcribed precisely from her notes (square brackets show Woolf's deletions, angle brackets show Woolf's insertions):

> [But what is a woman?] [So it might appear.] Having rid herself of falsehood, so we might put it, she has now only to be herself ⟨and write⟩. But what is 'herself'? I mean, what is a woman? I assure you, I dont know; I do not believe that you know; I do not believe that anybody can know until she has expressed herself in all the arts and professions open to human skill. [That] ⟨What a woman [is]⟩ is a discovery which you here are in process of making . . .[18]

The hesitations and equivocations of this passage are fascinating. Woolf goes a long way down the road of what has become the preoccupation of a much later feminism – problematizing and destabilizing the notion of 'woman' as a known and predictable category – but she cannot fully accept the consequence: she still regards the essence of woman as something that we shall 'discover' rather than an identity that is built.

Thirdly, Woolf's conception of androgyny and her advocacy of an aesthetic creed in which feminist political anger, and indeed any sex consciousness, should be subordinated to the general vision and narrative of the work are highly contentious from a feminist point of view. *A Room of One's Own* takes up a position that aspires to gender neutrality, though elsewhere in her work Woolf speaks of 'the feminine sentence' and can be lined up in and for a 'woman centred' literary tradition.

Feminists are, of course, divided as to whether, or in what circumstances, one might support gender neutrality, or the so-called 'equality' position, versus an awareness of the distinctive situation or attributes of women and the need to build progress on the recognition of 'difference' between women and men. It must be said that here, in the manifesto that *A Room of One's Own* has become, Woolf's model of androgyny is the nearest she came to the 'equality' position and it is no doubt because she pitched art at the level of general truth – more abstract than sexual difference. Elsewhere in her work, as we shall see clearly in relation to *Three Guineas*, her position was quite different. And even within *A Room of One's Own* there is enough specific address to young women, not least in the call to work for the emergence of Shakespeare's sister, to belie the formal position of advocating androgyny. In any case it is perhaps too simple to plead for the exclusion of overt anger from art, when Virginia Woolf buried feminist insights into the deepest recesses of her own novels. The real debate hangs on how, not whether, feminist ideas interact with the imaginative content of the novels, and for Woolf simply to proscribe intrusiveness is to deal with the problem at a relatively superficial level.

Both *A Room of One's Own* and *Three Guineas* are explicitly feminist texts, but the nature of their 'appropriation' by modern feminism has been contested. In relation to *A Room of One's Own*, there is an interesting debate as to how far the lectures or the book could be seen as a woman-oriented, even homoerotic – rather than a strictly 'feminist' – intervention. Woolf herself had predicted about *A Room of One's Own* that, 'I shall be attacked for a feminist and hinted at for a Sapphist.' It is well known that at the time of the lectures in Cambridge Virginia Woolf had, in the words of her official biographer Quentin Bell, to some extent 'identified herself with the cause of homosexuality'. In September 1928 she had taken a week's holiday in France alone with Vita Sackville-West; Woolf's extraordinary literary tribute to their intense relationship, *Orlando*, was published on 11 October; at the same period Virginia Woolf was willing, if not precisely eager, to testify in the trial for obscenity of Radclyffe Hall's lesbian novel *The Well of Loneliness*. (Both Woolf and Sackville-West felt that a public stand against censorship on the issue should be taken, although both found Radclyffe Hall herself rather irksome in her belief that the novel was of outstanding literary merit.)[19]

The conversational seductiveness of *A Room of One's Own* can be likened to the style of *Orlando*, and the relationship between Vita Sackville-West and Virginia Woolf, with the heightening of private emotion and public awareness that the publication of *Orlando* caused, is an important part of the backdrop to the text. 'I am completely dazzled, bewitched, enchanted . . .' wrote Vita Sackville-West, 'Darling, I don't know and scarcely even like to write, so overwhelmed am I, how you could have hung so splendid a garment on so poor a peg.'[20] As is often the case with Virginia Woolf, there was ambivalence and contradiction in her sexual and emotional involvement with Vita Sackville-West – and her identification with other women in general. *A Room of One's Own* is certainly the high point of this attraction and commitment to women, but even during this period Woolf's diaries and letters show countervailing thoughts and feelings too.[21] Later in her life – with *Three Guineas* the contrasting text to *A Room of One's Own* – Woolf was to become less flirtatious and seductive in her writing about women. *Three Guineas* was also written with ardour and conviction, but was certainly not a 'trifle'.

FROM A ROOM OF ONE'S OWN
TO THREE GUINEAS

Virginia Woolf turned, in the 1930s, to a new type of fiction and a new political identity. Her feminism became more pronounced and overt, her concern with the rise of fascism more and more profound, and her conviction that women had a particular role to play in combating what she saw as a masculine tendency towards militarism more readily argued. These changes underlie the dramatic shift in her novel-writing practice that we see in *The Years* (1938). She referred to this as 'my Arnold Bennett novel', in a wry recognition that the latest experiment she had made (after a decade of triumphs in the modernist idiom – *Mrs Dalloway, To the Lighthouse, The Waves*) was an attempt to go back to the socially relevant novel of the nineteenth century in a deliberate and new way.[22] As John Mepham has noted, this was an 'astonishing turnabout' in her thinking.[23]

It is, then, not perhaps surprising that we find the origins of *Three Guineas* in a speech. Woolf's diary for 20 January 1931 records the moment at which, like Archimedes, she had a brilliant idea:

> I have this moment, while having my bath, conceived an entire new book – a sequel to a Room of Ones Own – about the sexual life of women: to be called Professions for Women perhaps – Lord how exciting! This sprang out of my paper to be read on Wednesday to Pippa's society.[24]

The process of working through this idea was as lengthy and complex as the original idea had been quick and effortless, for Woolf tried to develop a new literary form – she called it a 'Novel-Essay' – to address these questions in ways that were simultaneously politically and aesthetically appropriate. Entitled *The Pargiters*, the book was to alternate scenes of fiction with chapters of historical commentary and analysis, covering the evolution of the middle-class family from 1880 to the present. In the end, Woolf decided that the experiment had failed, and separated the text into a novel, *The Years*, published in 1937, and a work of political polemic, *Three Guineas*, which came out a year later.

It is clear that these were difficult decisions. *The Years* became a bestseller, particularly in the USA, but took a personal toll on its author greater than any other of her books. Both the novel and *Three Guineas* went through various incarnations and the history of these texts shows how vexed their composition was in comparison with some of the earlier novels. Luckily, although

Woolf abandoned the novel-essay, she did not destroy it and we can judge for ourselves this bold experiment. Published under the heading of *The Pargiters* we can now read both the speech that triggered the whole project, and the drafted fictional scenes with their accompanying essays. As the editor comments:

> ... the instances in literature are indeed rare when we find a novelist of Virginia Woolf's stature presenting a fictional specimen and then immediately analysing, explaining and interpreting the scene for us.[25]

The speech that was to form the basis of *Three Guineas* was made to the London branch of the National Society for Women's Service, an organization whose secretary was a friend of Woolf's – Philippa Strachey. Invited to speak about her professional experiences as a woman writer, Virginia Woolf gave a very entertaining speech, airing the problem of 'the angel in the house' who had to be dispatched by the independent writer. Some of the speech has been published in Woolf's essay 'Professions for Women' (reproduced in appendix II), and parts of it found their way into *Three Guineas*. The speech closes with an interesting attempt to talk about the question of women's independence from the point of view of men: an early indication of Woolf's future preoccupation with questions of masculinity and the subconscious sources of men's behaviour. The issue is set up by means of an example – Woolf likens men's response to women earning their own living to that of a man who comes home one evening to find that his servants have suddenly changed.

> He goes into the library – an august apartment which he is accustomed to have all to himself – and finds the kitchen maid curled up in the arm chair reading Plato. He goes into the kitchen and there is the cook engaged in writing a Mass in B flat. He goes into the billiard room and finds the parlourmaid knocking up a fine break at the table. He goes into the bed room and there is the housemaid working out a mathematical problem.[26]

Woolf describes the man's anger and resentment that his role has been usurped and, most importantly, that his function as the breadwinner becomes unnecessary when women can sell their own skills. But this theme, which was to play so central a part in *Three Guineas*, is not at this point dealt with in anger. It was the beginning of 1931 and Virginia Woolf concluded by advising her audience of professional women: 'Do not therefore be angry: be patient; be amused.' She stressed how 'extremely difficult' was the position that 'you have put this man into'. She emphasized 'the tremendous tradition of mastery' that men were used to and would have to overcome. She insisted that there were men who had triumphed, men of generous humanity, 'men with whom women can live in perfect freedom, without any fear'.[27]

The speech of 1931 airs the theme of male resistance to the independence of women, but Woolf is charming and conciliatory to men in her conclusion. By the end of 1932, when she came to revise the speech as the first essay in her proposed novel-essay, there is a significant change in her tone. In the first paragraph she distances herself from the seductive rhetorical style that so characterizes *A Room of One's Own*. Revealingly (and untypically) repeating the crucial words she says, 'acquit me of the desire simply to seduce and to flatter and to bring you round to my own way of thinking by means of flattery and seduction.'[28] This new no-nonsense Virginia Woolf describes herself as an 'outsider' – a key notion for the argument of *Three Guineas*. She claims that 'it is part of a writer's profession to be an outsider'.[29] Finally, introducing the fictional scenes from her new novel, she insists that *The Pargiters* is not a novel of vision, but a novel of fact. 'There is scarcely a statement in it that cannot be . . . verified, if anybody should wish so to misuse their time.' The point is a provocative one. Woolf says that it would be 'easier' to write history, but that 'I prefer, where truth is important, to write fiction.'[30] Here we have three ideas – the rejection of seduction in favour of cold argument, the notion of Woolf (as writer, later as woman) as an outsider, and a new interest in veracity rather than vision – that make a distinctive break with the Virginia

Woolf of the 1920s. Let us now look at *Three Guineas*, where these principles find their clearest expression.

THREE GUINEAS

The title of *Three Guineas* is less of a clue to its contents than some of the earlier ones that Woolf tried out in the course of writing it. *The Next War, On Being Despised, 'Men are like that', Letter to an Englishman, What Are We to Do?*, all indicate the themes and arguments of the book more clearly. It is only when you have finished reading the book that the title *Three Guineas* makes sense, which is unfortunate in the case of a book that has, one fears, been more discussed than it has been read. Woolf's consideration of what women can do to avoid war – the question posed to her by a correspondent – finally closes when she decides to send a guinea each to three societies with particular aims. The first guinea goes to a rebuilding fund for a women's college, the second to an organization helping women's employment in the professions, and the third to her original correspondent, who ran a society aiming to prevent war and (in the 1930s climate of growing fascism) to protect intellectual and cultural freedom. The most important part of Woolf's argument was that these ostensibly separate causes were in fact inseparable, since women's financial independence from men – which could only be brought about by education and employment – was an essential precondition for the fight against war. Why was this? It was because in Woolf's view war in general was a male activity, and fascism in particular was an extreme form of patriarchal dictatorship. Militarism and fascism were bound in with men's insistence that women restrict themselves to serving the needs of fathers, husbands and families, and subject themselves to the often unreasonable demands of men. According to Virginia Woolf, the links between the tyranny of women's domestic servitude and the dictatorship of fascists had not been recognized. In the style of a much later feminism she insisted on the general point that 'the public and the private worlds are inseparably connected . . . the tyrannies and servilities of the one are the tyrannies and servilities of the other' (p. 270).

Virginia Woolf's key problem in *Three Guineas* was to prove, in particular to men, that the political processes of fascism were linked to the political exclusions of petty patriarchalism. The kernel of the argument of the whole book lies in the passage where she moves from a reference to the routine sexism expressed in Britain (she cites many examples from newspapers and from the civil service, for example, of the view that women should not take jobs that men need) to the attitudes of Hitler and Mussolini. Woolf has described her correspondent as a middle-aged barrister. She says to him:

> . . . abroad the monster has come more openly to the surface. There is no mistaking him there. He has widened his scope. He is interfering now with your liberty; he is dictating how you shall live; he is making distinctions not merely between the sexes, but between the races. You are feeling in your own persons what your mothers felt when they were shut out, when they were shut up, because they were women. Now you are being shut out, you are being shut up, because you are Jews, because you are democrats, because of race, because of religion. It is not a photograph that you look upon any longer; there you go, trapesing along in the procession yourselves. And that makes a difference. The whole iniquity of dictatorship, whether in Oxford or Cambridge, in Whitehall or Downing Street, against Jews or against women, in England, or in Germany, in Italy or in Spain is now apparent to you. (p. 228)

Thus Woolf argues that it is not only in women's interests to resist the patriarchal state, and in men's interests to resist the fascist state, for the enemies are the same and the reasons for resistance the same, too.

Although the intellectual centre of gravity of the book is focused on the specific argument about feminism and fascism, *Three Guineas* takes up an extraordinary number of complex related issues. Indeed, the book has a scholarly apparatus of notes which take up in more detail and with examples many of the themes elaborated in the text. Woolf had been amassing data for several years: keeping files, taking press cuttings (some of which are reproduced in appendix I), writing to people for information and so on. Some light is thrown on the diligence with which Virginia Woolf tackled this by her correspondence. To Vita Sackville-West, who didn't like the book and accused her of using 'misleading arguments', she said, 'I took more pains to get up the facts and state them plainly than I ever took with any thing in my life,' and added that, 'all I wanted was to state a very intricate case as plainly and readable as I could.'[31] Posterity is even rewarded with information about why Woolf put the notes at the end of the book rather than at the foot of the page: she told Ethel Smyth that 'I decided for end, thinking people might read them, the most meaty part of the book, separately,' adding, 'I had a mass more and still have. Yes – very hard work that was.'[32] The sheer quantity of facts and arguments mobilized in the text and notes is quite extraordinary, and there can be no doubt that Woolf was trying to make her case as strongly as she possibly could. The notes to *Three Guineas* take up questions subsequently discussed by feminists working in the fields of psychology, history, sociology, anthropology, education, literary criticism, medicine, art history, languages, classics and theology. Some of Woolf's points are real gems that remain eloquent many decades later: one example being the stylish – 'nature . . . is now known to vary greatly in her commands and to be largely under control' (p. 319).

What, then, are the complex and interrelated ideas that Woolf elaborates in this text? Readers are sometimes surprised to find that the first chapter contains a serious discussion of the politics of dress. Men, Woolf argues, use distinctions of dress to symbolize rank and status; like the labels on things in a shop, they advertise the quality of the goods. So much do they differ from women in this that they do not even notice their peculiarity, and here Woolf amuses herself with a note about a judge, preposterously dressed in scarlet, ermine and a vast wig of curls, solemnly pronouncing on the psychology of women's clothes (p. 279).

The function of the photographs in *Three Guineas* is, of course, to ridicule these patriarchal, hierarchical dress codes. But the point is closely drawn into Woolf's underlying theme when she argues that the symbolic function of dress is closely connected to war: 'your finest clothes are those you wear as soldiers' (p. 138).

The first chapter of *Three Guineas* then moves into a critique of the universities, called forth by a letter asking for a contribution to a women's college rebuilding fund (in real life, the same Newnham College, Cambridge, as had featured in *A Room of One's Own*). Woolf believes that she should respond to this letter in the context of the other request she has received – for her to take part in an anti-war society's work. What contribution might the women's college make to an anti-war effort? Woolf suggests that universities have not traditionally done much to avoid war, indeed they have tended to teach people to use rather than to hate force (p. 151). From this observation, which ties in with Virginia Woolf's lifelong loathing of academic institutions (discussed in a more general way later on in this introduction), various speculative arguments are floated. For a university to help in preventing war, what should be taught in it? On this, Woolf is quite clear: 'Not the arts of dominating other people; not the arts of ruling, of killing, of acquiring land and capital' (p. 155). Founded on poverty and youth, the women's college should take advantage of those qualities and be a centre for cooperation rather than competition. But, of course, such an institution will not help its students to get the jobs they need, for which they have to have letters after their names in the approved fashion. In response to this, Woolf floats the more dramatic possibility that she will send a guinea to the college, earmarked 'Rags. Petrol. Matches', so that it can be used to burn the place down (p. 157). But in the end she concedes that the voice of women will only be heard if they can exert an independent influence; if they are restricted to the private realm women's interests will lie in shoring up marriage, the empire and war. And to escape this restriction they will need to be able to earn a living, for which they will need an education. Thus, Woolf reaches the depressing conclusion that, imperfect as the women's college may be, she will send it a guinea – with no strings attached – as a contribution to the prevention of war.

The second chapter takes up this theme, in an exploration of women's employment. Woolf says that she has received a letter, asking not only for money but also for cast-off clothing as a contribution to the work of an organization dedicated to supporting women in the professions. In real life this was the National Society of Women's Service, to whom Woolf had originally made her speech in 1931. Woolf begins by expressing astonishment that professional women should need her help, and this causes her to investigate their situation. Looking at the civil service she tries to square the claim that professional women have difficulty in earning £250 a year with the salaries listed for public administrators, many of which are over £1000. Woolf encounters what sociologists now call 'vertical occupational segregation', the so-called 'glass ceiling' on women's rank and earnings within organizations. As Woolf puts it:

> ... those to whose names the word 'Miss' is attached do not seem to enter the four-figure zone. The sex distinction seems, according to Whitaker [*Whitaker's Almanack*, Woolf's favoured reference book], possessed of a curious leaden quality, liable to keep any name to which it is fastened circling in the lower spheres. (p. 170)

Modern readers may be wondering about the effect of 'Mrs' as a prefix in those days: there was a marriage bar which made their employment impossible. As Woolf put it, 'In Whitehall as in heaven, there is neither marrying nor giving in marriage' (p. 174).

In a typical move, Virginia Woolf sets up in this chapter a shorthand that she will then use to refer back to later in the book. She describes the pattern of segregation at Whitehall in terms of an 'odour' or 'atmosphere', made much stronger when it is explicitly argued in the newspapers that the government should force employers to give work to men rather than women.

Woolf says, 'There! There can be no doubt of the odour now. The cat is out of the bag; and it is a Tom' (p. 174). Reference to 'smells' will now stand in for men, in the interests of men, forcing women out of employment and back into the home. Similarly, this same key passage in the book develops the image of a malign little egg, the poisonous germ of an idea that is shared both by the sexist contributor to the *Daily Telegraph* who wants the government to act in men's interests and by the fascist dictators. Woolf quotes Hitler making an identical point: that man is responsible for his family and the nation, woman for family, husband, children and home (p. 175). She comments that Hitler and Mussolini are recognized as dictators, seen as dangerous, as well as ugly, animals. But when the poison of fascism is spat by a little insect in the heart of England it is not seen as such. In a telling allusion to Blake's *Auguries of Innocence*[33] Woolf describes the dictator at home: 'And he is here among us, raising his ugly head, spitting his poison, small still, curled up like a caterpillar on a leaf, but in the heart of England' (p. 175). The caterpillar, the insect, the egg, the worm are one and the same – metaphors of unrecognized fascism. Woolf's most scathing eloquence is reserved for a man – H. G. Wells – who had criticized feminists in Britain for not protecting women in Germany and Italy from the effects of fascism and Naziism. Woolf's outburst, which she self-deprecatingly describes as having the symptoms of becoming a peroration, is worth quoting in full as the emotional centre of *Three Guineas*:

> And is not the woman who has to breathe that poison and to fight that insect, secretly and without arms, in her office, fighting the Fascist or the Nazi as surely as those who fight him with arms in the limelight of publicity? And must not that fight wear down her strength and exhaust her spirit? Should we not help her to crush him in our own country before we ask her to help us to crush him abroad? And what right have we, Sir, to trumpet our ideals of freedom and justice to other countries when we can shake out from our most respectable newspapers any day of the week eggs like these? (p. 176)

The chapter ends with a plea for women's entry to the professions to be brought about in such a way that women 'remain uncontaminated' by the corrupt structures of that world. Woolf argues that women must adopt various forms of self-denial and self-policing for this goal to be achieved, and she presents these as the conditions under which she is prepared to make a donation to the society for helping women in the professions. These conditions are characteristic of Virginia Woolf: idealistic, unreasonable and romantic at the same time as being insightful, courageous and truthful. The first, and most general, condition is that the society should avoid narrow feminism and 'help all properly qualified people, of whatever sex, class or colour, to enter your profession' (p. 205). Here we see a reflection of Woolf's intense ambivalence about feminism – knowing how fascist dictators discriminate on the bases of sex, race, religion and so on, she found it anathema to recommend a similar form of (positive) discrimination for women. To this painful dilemma we can, perhaps, trace the source of her view that women's political role must be that of 'outsiders'. It is, effectively, an abdication of political agency in the face of the danger of contamination.

Woolf's other conditions are also vexing. Poverty is enjoined: women should earn an independent income but no more. In practice, of course, this is a difficult matter to judge; Virginia and Leonard Woolf's own standard of living rose as she earned more from her writing.[34] Intellectual chastity is recommended: you must refuse to 'sell your brain'. Derision is desirable: when offered bribes such as 'badges, orders, or degrees' they should be flung back with ridicule. And finally, Woolf advocates 'freedom from unreal loyalties': national pride, religious pride, college pride and sex pride are all forms of seduction that should be resisted (p. 203). These conditions, Woolf argues, will enable women to join the professions without taking on their possessiveness, pugnacity and greed. They will enable women to have a mind of their own. Then that independent mind can be used to abolish the horror and folly of war (p. 208).

The chapter ends with an evocation of maternal approval of this act of daughterly authenticity. The daughters will be singing that they have done with tyranny; the mothers will laugh from their graves that it was for this that they suffered in their own times: 'Light up the windows of the new house, daughters! Let them blaze!' (p. 208.) *Three Guineas* is often thought to be more pessimistic about women's solidarity than *A Room of One's Own*, which had celebrated the female tradition and 'thinking back through our mothers', but in this passage we see a flash of Virginia Woolf's earlier optimism.

Many of the points elaborated in the final section of *Three Guineas* have been foreshadowed earlier in the text, but it is none the less an extraordinary culmination of the general argument. Woolf advances an interpretation of how support for war ties in with other more general aspects of men's role and power in society, including subconscious ones; she explains why women's identification with patriotism is less than that of men; she interrogates women's financial dependence within the family and recommends wages for motherhood. She (not surprisingly, given how contentious all these issues are) also engages in a very spiky debate about feminism and concludes by advocating a position of 'outsiders' for women who are opposed to war. To the correspondent who had asked for her support in his campaign to prevent war by fostering cultural and intellectual freedom she offers a guinea – but symbolically refuses to sign up as a member of the society.

The 'real life' antecedents of this letter, which frames the beginning and end of *Three Guineas*, are clear but complex. Woolf devotes a lengthy note to the plethora of manifestos and societies which, during the course of the 1930s, signalled the politicization of intellectuals and others as a result of concern about the rise of fascism (pp. 304–5). She was briefly on the committee of a group entitled 'For Intellectual Liberty', founded in 1935 as a British equivalent to the French anti-fascist organization the *Comité de Vigilance*. In her correspondence she complained to various people about the numbers of letters and meetings she became drawn into, and her increasing irritation and withdrawal becomes evident.

Virginia Woolf saw a parallel between the beliefs and actions of the fascist dictators and those of ordinary men in England. A page of her scrapbooks is reproduced in appendix I where she had juxtaposed a pious political exhortation to stand up to dictators with a divorce court report that showed how dictatorial the husband had been. In *Three Guineas* the same connection is made in Woolf's discussion of the educated and sophisticated Mr Jex-Blake, who was so horrified at the idea of his daughter earning money by teaching that he offered to pay the salary himself if she would refuse it from the college and do the work on a voluntary basis (p. 259ff.). The young Sophia Jex-Blake and Virginia Woolf have a certain amount of fun in their treatment of his patriarchally inflicted agonies. Woolf uses the idea of an 'infantile fixation', very loosely and idiosyncratically drawn from psychoanalysis, as a means of addressing the subconscious desire for control over his daughter that underlies this father's extremely manipulative and coercive behaviour. But it is not only Mr Jex-Blake who has this problem; Woolf maintains that 'society it seems was a father, and afflicted with the infantile fixation too' (p. 263).

A related theme concerns the 'unreal loyalty' of patriotism. For just as the woman has no independent income within the family – a problem which leads Woolf to recommend wages for motherhood and to comment adversely on women's financial position on the dissolution of marriage[35] – so she has no status in her country. More than once in *Three Guineas* Woolf refers to the fact that women lose their citizenship when they marry: where their brothers are England's sons, they are merely her 'step-daughters'. Add to this the little amount of England's land, wealth and property that belong to her and, argues Woolf, the woman will see that she has little to thank the country for. Therefore, Woolf continues, the woman has no interest in a war to protect a country in which she has so small an investment. Virginia Woolf's hypothetical Englishwoman now develops as the full-blown 'outsider', telling her brother that she will not accept that he can be fighting to protect her or 'our country'. Delighting globally minded feminists, Woolf then comes up with the most quotable quote of *Three Guineas*: 'as a woman, I have no country. As a woman I want no country. As a woman my country is the whole world' (p. 234).

THREE GUINEAS:
COMMENTARY AND INTERPRETATION

Interpretation of *Three Guineas* is complicated by the vexed history of its reception. On the favourable side, its anonymous reviewer in the prestigious *Times Literary Supplement* described Virginia Woolf as 'the most brilliant pamphleteer in England', which understandably pleased her.[36] Colleagues on the 'feminist soft left' of those days, such as the Labour Party activist Sheena, Lady Simon, and many others such as Phillipa Strachey and Lady Rhondda, were much in evidence as sympathizers and admirers of Woolf's outspoken essay. In addition, many readers unknown to Woolf wrote to her about the book and these letters have been preserved, making fascinating reading. Among various letters from indignant or genuinely puzzled men are a host of delighted, grateful, surprised women readers. One of these women correspondents – most of whom fully endorsed Woolf's argument – even took it, with some trepidation, a stage further. Belinda Joliffe of New York wrote passionately, hyperbolically and ungrammatically:

> I wouldn't be at all surprised to see even you draw back from me in distaste, if I say to you that I believe the BASE of all such stupidity [i.e. war] begins in the home. It is horrible nauseating FAMILY emotional stuff that clutters people up. Here in America, everyone will Kill, Steal, Sweat, Lie, Anything in order to get money, so THEIR children need not work; that they may Advance Socially . . .[37]

From the vantage point of the 1990s, Woolf's argument

linking masculinism and war is both prescient and uncontentious. A visit to London's reconceptualized Imperial War Museum is enough to make this point: its thoughtful, rather than celebratory, documentation of war results in a museum bookshop with many titles making just the connections that Woolf had seen. The feminist anti-nuclear weapons movement's slogan, 'Take the Toys from the Boys', is another instance of a general recognition of Woolf's point. There is also now considerable awareness of the gendered character of the Hitler and Mussolini regimes which Woolf hated so much. Hence the extent to which the Nazis built a culture on the domestication of women, and the cultural politics of Mussolini's sexualization and domination of Italian women, are now seen as important issues. Similarly, one might note that Woolf's insistence that fascism is not something completely alien and different, but is coterminous with mundane and everyday sexism, is also an insight not heard until comparatively recently.

Yet if a feminist posterity is inclined to a favourable view of *Three Guineas*, this was certainly not the universal reaction when the book was published. Perhaps we can ignore the popular press, although the headline 'WOMAN STARTS NEW SEX-WAR/Says Men's Clothes are "Barbarous"' is not without its charms.[38] Nor was Woolf profoundly affected by the vitriolic attack on the book by Mrs Q. D. ('Queenie') Leavis; she had always regarded the entire Leavis/*Scrutiny* enterprise as priggish and took criticism or praise from them with a certain contempt.[39] Much more importantly, most of Virginia Woolf's own circle of family and friends were ambivalent or critical of the book. She had a difficult correspondence with Vita Sackville-West about it, was disappointed that Leonard was so lukewarm, and in her diary noted the general silence of her friends about it: 'Not one of my friends has mentioned it', and even 'my own friends have sent me to Coventry over it'.[40]

Bloomsbury's collective rejection of *Three Guineas* involved difficult political issues. It must also have involved complex individual responses to Julian Bell's decision to go to the Spanish

Civil War and terrible personal grief at his death there, aged twenty-nine. *Three Guineas* was read by them in this context; Virginia Woolf's writing of the book had, literally, been interrupted by her nephew's death in July 1937. Julian's mother, Vanessa Bell, was utterly devastated and found the presence of her sister Virginia very comforting; hence the tragic death of her adored nephew was a blow that Virginia Woolf experienced as closely and appallingly as could be imagined. It took her some while to resume work, and returning to *Three Guineas* was naturally difficult. Julian Bell's terrible death did not lead Virginia Woolf to change her opinions in deference to his choice to fight; rather it led her to hold them more strongly. She wrote to Vanessa Bell: 'I'm completely stuck on my war pamphlet . . . I'm always wanting to argue it with Julian – in fact I wrote it as an argument with him.'[41]

Julian Bell had wanted to fight in the Spanish Civil War. He went as an ambulance driver, partly because of the distress his decision was causing his mother and family. In March that year Woolf wrote that we 'have to stop him', but they did not succeed.[42] When he died she wrote, to someone outside her immediate circle, using a reflective tone and conceding as much to his decision as she could:

> At the moment the private sorrow is so great one cant get anything clear in one's mind. He was a great joy to us; her children are like my own. But it had become necessary for him to go; and there is a kind of grandeur in that which now and then consoles one. Only – to see what she has to suffer makes one doubt if anything in the world is worth it.[43]

To Vita Sackville-West she wrote she felt nothing but 'varieties of dull anger and despair'. When the cause for which Julian Bell had wanted to fight had been lost, two years later, Woolf noted bitterly in her diary, 'Yesterday, Franco was recognized [by the British Government]. And Julian killed for this.'[44]

Three Guineas was, then, a book that was deeply emotionally charged for the intimate circle of Virginia Woolf's family and friends. She herself wrote out some of her mixed feelings – bewilderment, remorse, anger – about her nephew's decision in a memoir, which was published with Quentin Bell's biography.[45] Looking back on the reception of *Three Guineas*, by Woolf's circle, in 1938, it is plausible to see in their silence and hostility a displaced difficulty that they, by tradition pacifists ('we were all C.O.s in the Great war')[46] had experienced in coming to terms with Julian's decision. Quentin Bell has summarized the criticism that underlay the negative response to *Three Guineas*:

> What really seemed wrong with the book – and I am speaking here of my own reactions at the time – was the attempt to involve a discussion of women's rights with the far more agonizing and immediate question of what we were to do in order to meet the ever-growing menace of Fascism and war. The connections between the two questions seemed tenuous and the positive suggestions wholly inadequate.[47]

One of the ironies is that this view, which does I think represent a more general feeling among Virginia Woolf's family and friends at the time, did not itself offer a better solution than Virginia Woolf's to the menace of fascism. For while many in the Bloomsbury circle did become supporters of the use of military force against fascism, this was not in fact the case for those most intimately affected by Julian Bell's death. In 1938 Clive Bell (Julian's father) was arguing an extreme pacifist position, backed by the Peace Pledge Union.[48] Quentin Bell and Duncan Grant took the classic outsiders' position in the 1939–45 war against fascism: they remained in Sussex and the murals of a beautiful downland church, painted after the original stained glass had been destroyed by bombing in 1941, are a memorial to that decision.[49]

The general argument about fascism and pacifism in the 1930s provides a significant backdrop to *Three Guineas*. If one takes the view, as many erstwhile pacifists did as fascism in Europe grew, that the evils of Hitler's Nazism and Mussolini's fascism were greater than the evil of war, then the arguments of Woolf's essay are as inadequate as any other pacifist statement. (But this is not an objection that pacifists can make to the book.) Underlying this more general debate about pacifism is the vexing question of how Virginia Woolf understood the political agency of women. There is a sense in which Woolf's construction of women as 'outsiders' enables her to exempt women from full participation in difficult decisions. There are many instances in her diary and letters that illustrate this general point, one particularly significant one being the diary entry following the 1935 Labour Party conference at which the leader, George Lansbury, was forced to resign after being attacked by Ernest Bevin for his implacable pacifism. Virginia Woolf, in a rather knowing entry, comments that Lansbury's speech had brought tears to her eyes, that her sympathies were with the speaker who had preached non-resistance and, she added, 'Happily, uneducated & voteless, I am not responsible for the state of society.'[50] The significant word here is 'happily', which links to a more general ambivalence about political agency in Woolf's thinking.

A sense of political powerlessness is present in much of Virginia Woolf's comments on the rise of militarism and fascism in Europe. In 1936 she had written to Julian Bell: 'I have never dreamt so often of war. And what's to be done? Its rather like sitting in a sick room, quite helpless.' Of Hitler's invasion of Prague in March 1939 she wrote in her diary, 'My comment anyhow is superfluous. We sit & watch.'[51] Of course these are natural responses, but in Virginia Woolf's case they were exacerbated by a division of labour between her and Leonard Woolf, often referred to as 'indefatigable' in his political activities. In 1936 she wrote to Ethel Smyth as follows:

> I am badgered by all kinds of politicians at the moment, and have just written a firm letter to resign my only office, on the ground that my husband does all that for two – or even one dozen.

Similarly, she recorded in her diary, apropos of Leonard discussing strategies with regard to refugees: 'I go in, out of courtesy. He is doing a job for me.'[52] Whilst these are not surprising comments, and could even be taken as proof of Virginia Woolf's underlying sense of political responsibility, they do cast a slightly different light on the issue of political agency in relation to her formal advocacy of the position of 'outsider' for women. There is thus an area of unease, an abandonment of agency – possibly even of authenticity – that we should, perhaps, recognize rather than deny. As we shall see later, this is one of a series of ambivalences in Woolf's political attitudes.

Three Guineas poses a number of questions for contemporary feminist politics. Does the argument apply only or specifically to fascism, or to all forms of militarism? What answer does it offer to those debating whether equality should mean the right of women to bear arms rather than act in a merely supporting role? Whilst this question can be brushed aside when speaking of the armed forces of dominant powers, it is less easy to dispose of in relation to the struggles of oppressed peoples against tyrannical rulers – as the debate over the place of women in the Nicaraguan armed forces showed. A second, perhaps more difficult issue, concerns the application of Woolf's argument to a society in which women do now have more of an 'interest' or investment. Given Woolf's inclination towards a materialist line of argument – she was not arguing that women were instinctively pacifist, but that they had no national interest to defend – the increasing financial independence of 'the daughters of educated men' could lead to a profound change in Woolf's argument. Finally, too, one might ask the question as to how far the links Woolf made between the public dictatorship of fascism and the husband who makes his wife call him 'Sir' should be pressed. Certainly, they are both examples of the exercise of power, but we may find it useful to differentiate rather than homogenize these varying forms of power.

FEMINISM AND POLITICS:
VIRGINIA WOOLF AND AMBIVALENCE

However much *Three Guineas* may have been appropriated by feminism, it is none the less the case that Woolf's references in the book to feminism are far from sisterly. On page 227 she refers to feminist as 'a vicious and corrupt word that has done much harm in its day and is now obsolete.' At this point Woolf argues that once the right to earn a living has been won, there are no causes specifically requiring the championing of women's rights – better for men and women to work together in the same cause. On page 246 we find the carefully worded reference to 'the proud boast' that a certain corrupt word might be burnt. Between the two references (on p. 229) Woolf inserts the idea of difference between women and men; we might reasonably conclude that this recognition of difference would necessarily restore the political ground on which feminism operates. Here, again, we find Woolf oscillating on a fundamental point of feminist debate: does she want to support the 'equality' position, seeing differences between men and women as the product of history rather than biology, and thus favouring the participation of men and women in the quest for a more androgynous future? Or does she want to argue a politics based on difference – difference of instinct, difference of experience – that confirms the separate identities of women and men and leads to different futures for them? In a general sense, the political solution of the outsiders' society, and the overall arguments of *Three Guineas*, indicate that Virginia Woolf moved from the androgyny/equality positions of *A Room of One's Own* to a much more 'difference'-oriented stance in *Three Guineas*. There is, however, an incipient tension in the text on this issue. One could take as an example the reference to the woman/outsider's view of men's fighting instinct, which Woolf refers to as 'an instinct which is as foreign to her as centuries of tradition and education can make it' (p. 233). This is no ignorant confusion between instinct and socialization, for Woolf explicitly notes how easily the fighting instinct can, 'if sanctioned', develop in women (p. 311), and differentiates in the text between instinct and reason. No, we may say that Woolf is underscoring the tension and complexities of what is now, in feminism, discussed as the problem of 'essentialism'. And it seems possible that the hostility expressed towards feminism in *Three Guineas* is, in some measure at least, an indication of how difficult – but close to home for Virginia Woolf – were the issues that could not be resolved satisfactorily. Woolf was herself aware of this, noting the different and contradictory emotions that motivated women's fight against patriarchalism. Significantly, this recognition comes in the context of her most extreme attack on the vocabulary of political activism. Woolf counterposes these real (if contradictory) emotions to political tags and labels, dusty lecture halls, damp and dowdy public meetings, saying that 'the emancipation of women' is inexpressive and corrupt and 'anti-Fascism' is fashionable and hideous jargon (p. 265). The violence of her language, attacking causes that she not only believed in but also worked for, might alert us to the possibility of contradictory emotions on the part of the author.

On a range of key issues this text could be said to house and articulate ambiguities that can also be traced through the extensive documentation of Virginia Woolf's life. One such issue is the case of 'contradictory' or 'obstinate' emotion with regard to patriotism. In *Three Guineas* Woolf writes rather poignantly of the outsider who none the less feels 'some love of England' as a drop of pure, if irrational, emotion (p. 234). Woolf's attitude to British royalty might be taken as an example of her irrational emotions. Ostensibly, she was completely critical: 'We are flying for 3 weeks holiday to escape the coronation,' she wrote to Lady Cecil; to Vita Sackville-West (who wasn't a critic at all) she threw out a sparky, 'shan't I be thankful to be in a Courtyard in France, listening to a nightingale, drinking red wine, while you are curtseying and singing God Save the King.'[53] Yet when the abdication of Edward VIII occurred, although her dominant emotion was extremely critical, she yet recognized an odd and contradictory feeling about it:

He has . . . thrown away the kingdom & made us all feel slightly yet perceptibly humiliated. Its odd, but so I even feel it. Walking through Whitehall the other day, I thought what a Kingdom! England! And to put it down the sink . . . Not a very rational feeling.[54]

Virginia Woolf's essay on Mary Wollstonecraft remarks on a political ambivalence comparable to her own. Woolf clearly understood the ambiguity of Wollstonecraft's feelings when – a passionate supporter of the French Revolution – she described being brought to tears and insomnia by the sight of the King conducting himself with dignity. As Woolf comments:

Things were not so simple after all. She could not understand even her own feelings. She saw the most cherished of her convictions put into practice – and her eyes filled with tears. She had won fame and independence and the right to live her own life – and she wanted something different.[55]

It is easy enough to point to other instances of political ambivalence in Virginia Woolf. This issue is important in that the traditional view of Woolf as an élitist aesthete has now been decisively displaced by feminist interpretations stressing both her anti-patriarchal stance and her commitment to a range of radical ideas and politics. Yet – to oversimplify a moment – it would be a big mistake to construct Virginia Woolf as an ideologically simple anarchist, lesbian, ecological, socialist, anti-racist feminist. There were, perhaps, one or two areas where her attitude was consistently and unambiguously critical of society. The award of honours, for example, was anathema to her even when – the point at which opposition frequently melts away – she herself was offered them. Her response to being offered state honours was an immediate and unequivocal refusal; her rejection of honorary degrees equally firm. When Hugh Walpole was knighted, she wrote to a friend, 'What an incredible old ass Hugh is! Think of tagging a title to his quite respectable name! Why?'[56] One 1933 diary entry makes a direct link between life and letters:

It is an utterly corrupt society I have just remarked, speaking in the person of Elvira Pargiter, & I will take nothing that it can give me &c &c: now, as Virginia Woolf, I have to write – oh dear me what a bore – to the Vice Chancellor of Manchester Un[iversi]ty & say that I refuse to be made a Doctor of Letters.[57]

Throughout her life Woolf remained scathingly critical of the academic system: 'How I loathe lectures'; 'I would rather sit in a cellar or watch spiders than listen to an Englishman lecturing.'[58] Yet there was some flexibility in Woolf's attitude. In 1939 she and Leonard talked to a class of book production students in a London polytechnic. She commented, 'No it wasnt formidable. It was rather cheerful. And free & easy. Better much than Oxford & Cambridge.'[59] Towards the end of her life she had reached some sort of accommodation even with the Oxbridge of her male relatives and friends, from which at earlier points she had felt bitterly excluded:

I like outsiders better. Insiders write a colourless English. They are turned out by the University machine. I respect them. Father was one variety. I dont love them. I dont savour them. Insiders are the glory of the 19th century. They do a great service like Roman roads. But they avoid the forests & the will o the wisps.[60]

Honours and academia provide us with Woolf's least complicated political responses; in many other areas there are much greater contradictions. There is no doubt that, notwithstanding her progressive politics on class and colonialism, Virginia Woolf expressed views in her diary and letters that we would now regard as unambiguously snobbish and racist. The flavour of her political ambiguities can be illustrated by the case of her strong views on marriage. The novels, of course, yield many critiques of marriage and family life. Of the abdication crisis, Woolf noted the advice that the King should keep Mrs Simpson as his mistress, commenting, 'But apparently the King's little bourgeois demented mind sticks fast to the marriage service.'[61] Some time later, after attending a wedding, Virginia Woolf typed out for her *Three Guineas* scrapbook the following extreme words:

Marriage service. Savages in tail coats.
The woman has no worldly goods must therefore give
her body; must therefore accept her leader. Must
obey. ⟨Every⟩ [No] woman of any sense breaks her vow
to obey before she had left the church. A form.
But why have forms when you ought to speak the
truth? A solemn moment, really marriage.

Virginia Woolf was, of course, herself married. She regarded the
form of the marriage service as appalling: 'last time I went to
one I had much ado not to stand up and cry out on the
disgusting nature of it.'[62] But there is something bizarrely snobbish in the implication that upper-middle-class intellectuals can
have marriages whose meaning transcends the superficial form,
when the King's desire for marriage is petty or lower middle
class.

Another instance is the case of Woolf's views on homosexuality. Blooomsbury's standard talk of 'bugger boys' is perhaps
much of a muchness with Virginia Woolf's rather offensive use
of the word 'savages'. Probing beneath these relatively superficial
issues we can turn up more vexatious attitudes on Woolf's part.
When the manager of the Hogarth Press died suddenly in 1937,
the ensuing crisis revealed her sexuality. Woolf writes of this
very unsympathetically (note the word 'sordid') in a letter:

Miss West, our manager, died; this led to other complications –
some, as usual, of a sordid though psychologically exciting, kind
(this refers to Sapphism and jealousy and the state of mind of
friends whose hostility is suddenly revealed by death).[63]

More light is shed on this by an extraordinarily unsympathetic
account Woolf gives in her diary of a conversation in which
Hugh Walpole explained to her his sexual preferences ('He only
loves men who dont love men') and practices, and how he could
use none of this experience in his novels. Woolf said to herself:
'They are therefore about lives he hasnt lived wh[ich] explains
their badness. Hasnt the courage to write about his real life.'[64] A
remark which seems extremely harsh when one considers that

these experiences were at the time deemed criminal, and even in modern times the publishers have felt it necessary to omit names from Woolf's account! At least, one might say that it is the response of a securely married woman who is not making any effort to empathize with the experience of those inhabiting the margins of sexual/social life. It is, indeed, another side of Woolf, and one that needs to be set alongside the Virginia Woolf of 1928: publicly exercised about the *Well of Loneliness* trial and semi-publicly seduced by the glamorous Vita Sackville-West.

Finally, we can look at the contradictions of Woolf's own political activity and reflections upon it. The last years of her life show an increasingly irritated commentary on the ways in which she was being drawn into anti-fascist work: '6 letters to sign daily', 'idiotic societies', and so on.[65] Yet when Vita's son Ben Nicolson attacked what he regarded as the political élitism and impotence of Bloomsbury, Woolf rose to an impassioned defence of their politics in a series of carefully argued letters to him on the conflicting duties of artist and political activist and how such issues were to be resolved:

> What puzzles me is that the people who had infinitely greater gifts than any of us had – I mean Keats, Shelley, Wordsworth, Coleridge and so on – were unable to influence society. They didn't have anything like the influence they should have had upon 19th century politics. And so we drifted into imperialism and all the other horrors that led to 1914. Would they have had more influence if they had taken an active part in politics? Or would they only have written worse poetry?[66]

There can be no doubt, however, that towards the end of her life Virginia Woolf was very exercised by the question of how people like her – artists – should act politically. In 1939, when the Woolfs met Sigmund Freud in London, exiled from Nazi Germany and ill with cancer, he had troubled her by tackling her pacifism: 'When we left he took up the stand What are *you* going to do? The English – war.'[67] The next day's diary entry reverts to the conversation with Freud, with Virginia Woolf going over his response to her feelings of guilt about the defeat of Germany in the First World War. By the following day, Woolf has become exercised about the refugees from Spain, trying to escape the fascist regime that Julian Bell had been killed trying to resist. She noted, 'A bitter cold wind. Thought of the refugees from Barcelona walking 40 miles, one with a baby in a parcel.'[68] Significantly, in the month before Julian was killed, eighteen months earlier, Virginia Woolf had been brought to tears by seeing a procession of Spanish refugees from Bilbao – mainly children – walking through Bloomsbury.[69] So, it wasn't perhaps surprising that, when asked to give a manuscript to be sold to raise money for the refugees, Woolf overcame her 'hatred of encouraging writers in their idiotic vanity' and sent them *Three Guineas*.[70] In this gesture it is tempting to see some lasting significance. The manuscript of *Orlando* has reverted to Vita Sackville-West's patriarchal heritage, under the terms of her will, and lies under glass at Knole; Leonard Woolf offered *A Room of One's Own* to the patriarchal Cambridge that Virginia Woolf had so hated and it languished there, misfiled, for nearly half a century. The manuscript of *Three Guineas* has had a more honourable fate and it is empowering that, in her own lifetime, she was able to make some use of it in trying to ameliorate the effects of war. She wrote to Elizabeth Bowen, another writer concerned with the refugees:

> I've a nice letter from someone called something Jones who bought 3 Guineas, I hope for a large sum. Will you thank her, if you see her.[71]

Michèle Barrett   1993

NOTES

1. *Diary*, IV, 16 Feb. 1932, p. 77.
2. Woolf's scrapbooks, in which she collected material for *Three Guineas*, are in the Monks House Papers at the University of Sussex

library. Examples from them can be found in Appendix I of this volume. McCarthy's review is filed as MHP B. 16f1.

3. The letter was from Wanda Neff, located as the wife of a Columbia (New York) professor of English (MHP 18).

4. *Diary*, III, 23 Oct. 1929, p. 262.

5. 'Professions for Women', reprinted in Appendix II, pp. 356–61.

6. The debate on the intellectual status of women is reprinted in *WE*, pp. 30–39.

7. 'On Not Knowing Greek', reprinted in *WE*, pp. 93–106.

8. 'The Leaning Tower', reprinted in *WE*, p. 160.

9. ibid., p. 166.

10. 'Jane Austen', in *Women and Writing* (ed. Michèle Barrett, Women's Press, 1988, p. 120).

11. 'Aurora Leigh' (a review of Elizabeth Barrett-Browning's poem of that name) in *Women and Writing*, p. 139.

12. 'George Eliot', in *Women and Writing*, p. 154.

13. 'Professions for Women', in Appendix II, p. 360.

14. *Diary*, III, 27 Oct. 1928, p. 200.

15. *Diary*, III, 23 Oct. 1929, p. 262.

16. Letter to Clive Bell, 13 April 1909, *Letters*, I, p. 391. In his biography of Virginia Woolf, Quentin Bell comments, 'She tried to persuade Adrian to take a half of this legacy, but I think without success' (Quentin Bell, *Virginia Woolf*, II, Hogarth Press, 1972, p. 39n.).

17. *Diary*, I, 6 Jan. 1918, p. 101.

18. The speech is reproduced in Virginia Woolf, *The Pargiters* (ed. Mitchell A. Leaska, Hogarth Press, 1978, p. xxxiiiff.).

19. Vita Sackville-West had written to Virginia Woolf that they had to protest against the banning of *The Well of Loneliness* as it would have been banned – as she put it – 'even if the W. of L had been a good book', and that this was intolerable. It is clear from various sources that Virginia Woolf and others were taking a principled stand against censorship rather than defending the book as of extraordinary merit. See *The Letters of Vita Sackville-West to Virginia Woolf* (ed. Louise De Salvo and Mitchell A. Leaska, Macmillan, 1984, p. 296).

20. *The Letters of Vita Sackville-West to Virginia Woolf*, p. 305.

21. Jane Marcus has provided an interesting discussion of the lesbian aspects of *A Room of One's Own*, drawing on detailed examination

of the context of the talks in Cambridge, the significance of Oscar Browning, the references to the obscenity trial and so on, and this historical research is invaluable to the interpretation of the text. Whether one would go so far as to agree that 'Much of *A Room* was meant simply to convert her beloved Vita to feminism' is another matter. Marcus emphasizes the fact that Virginia Woolf appeared for her talk at Girton College with Vita Sackville-West, a symbolic statement of lesbian identification that underwrote the conspiratorially female atmosphere and the seductive discursive style ('sapphistry') of Woolf's lectures. Whilst this is true it is, as so often the case with Woolf, only one side of a more complex and ambivalent story. Characteristically balancing her public image as well as her private negotiations, Virginia Woolf had only the week before gone in a very familial mode to Cambridge, with her husband, sister and niece in tow, appearing for a meal at Newnham College with Leonard, who had not, it transpired, been expected. (There is a longer discussion of ambivalence and Woolf later in the introduction.) See Jane Marcus, 'Sapphistry: Narration as Lesbian Seduction in *A Room of One's Own*' in her *Virginia Woolf and the Languages of Patriarchy* (Indiana University Press, 1987).

22. The context for this being a 'wry' remark is that Virginia Woolf had published a very critical account of 'social realist' Edwardian writers such as John Galsworthy and Arnold Bennett: '. . . the Edwardian tools are the wrong ones for us to use. They have laid an enormous stress on the fabric of things. They have given us a house in the hope that we may be able to deduce the human beings who live there' ('Mr Bennett and Mrs Brown', *WE*, p. 82).

23. John Mepham, *Virginia Woolf: A Literary Life*, Macmillan, 1991, p. 151.

24. *Diary*, IV, 20 Jan. 1931, p. 6.

25. *The Pargiters*, p. xx.

26. ibid., p. xlii.

27. ibid., p. xliv.

28. ibid., p. 5.

29. ibid., p. 7.

30. ibid., p. 9.

31. Letter to Vita Sackville-West, 19 June 1938, *Letters*, VI, p. 243.

32. Letter to Ethel Smyth, 7 June 1938, *Letters*, VI, p. 235.

33. William Blake, *Auguries of Innocence*, 'The Catterpiller on the Leaf/ Repeats to thee thy Mother's grief'.

34. See John Mepham, op. cit., which includes discussion of Woolf's sales and income.

35. See *Three Guineas*, p. 236; and Woolf's own Note 17, p. 312.

36. *Diary*, V, 3 June 1938, p. 148.

37. See MHP 18 (University of Sussex).

38. From the *Sunday Referee*, 29 May 1938.

39. On the Leavises, and their journal *Scrutiny*, see *Diary*, IV, 4 Sept. 1935, p. 337; and V, 1 Sept. 1938, p. 165.

40. *Diary*, V, 19 Dec. 1938, p. 193; 22 Nov. 1938, p. 188.

41. Letter to Vanessa Bell, 17 Aug. 1937, *Letters*, VI, p. 159.

42. Letter to Ethel Smyth, 17 March. 1937, ibid., p. 113.

43. Letter to W. A. Robson, 26 July 1937, ibid., p. 150.

44. *Diary*, V, 3 March 1939, p. 206.

45. 'Virginia Woolf and Julian Bell', Appendix C, Bell, op. cit.

46. Woolf noted in her diary, in connection with Julian's desire to go to the war, 'I have never known anyone of my generation have that feeling about a war', ibid., p. 258.

47. Bell, op. cit., p. 205.

48. *Diary*, V, 4 Aug. 1938, p. 159.

49. St Michael and All Angels, Berwick, Sussex, painted by Duncan Grant, Vanessa Bell and Quentin Bell.

50. *Diary*, IV, 2 Oct. 1935, p. 346.

51. Letter to Julian Bell, 2 May 1936, *Letters*, VI, p. 33; *Diary*, V, 16 March 1939, p. 208.

52. Letter to Ethel Smyth, 1 July 1936, *Letters*, VI, p. 51; *Diary*, V, 28 Feb. 1939, p. 205.

53. Letter to Lady Cecil, 28 April 1937, *Letters*, VI, p. 121; Letter to Vita Sackville-West, 3 May 1937, p. 125.

54. *Diary*, V, 10 Dec. 1936, p. 41.

55. Woolf's essay on Mary Wollstonecraft was published as one of 'Four Figures' in *The Common Reader: Second Series* (Hogarth Press, 1932, p. 159).

56. Letter to William Plomer, 30 April 1937, *Letters*, VI, p. 123.

57. *Diary*, IV, 25 March 1933, p. 147.

58. Letter to Janet Case, 26 May 1937; letter to Victoria Ocampo, 2 Sept. 1937, *Letters*, VI, pp. 130, 167.

59. *Diary*, V, 3 March 1939, p. 206.

60. ibid., 26 Oct. 1940, p. 333.

61. ibid., 10 Dec. 1936, p. 41.

62. Letter to Lady Simon, 27 March 1937, *Letters*, VI, p. 115.

63. Letter to Edward Sackville-West, 14 Feb 1937, ibid., p. 107.

64. *Diary*, V, 30 March 1939, p. 211.

65. cf. *Letters*, VI, p. 46, p. 62, p. 64, p. 94.

66. ibid., pp. 413–15, 419–22, 424–5.

67. *Diary*, V, 29 Jan. 1939, p. 202.

68. ibid., 31 Jan. 1939, p. 203.

69. ibid., 23 June 1937, p. 97.

70. Letter to May Sarton, 2 Feb. 1939, *Letters*, VI, p. 314.

71. Letter to Elizabeth Bowen, 28 Feb. 1939, ibid., p. 319.

Acknowledgements

The preparation of this edition has been enormously helped by the fact that so much of the material relating to Virginia Woolf's life and work, particularly her diary and letters, has been published with considerable scholarship and attention to historical context. Quentin and Olivier Bell have set a high standard in the provision of information about Woolf, enabling the myriad interpretations of her writing to rest on a substantial base of shared, publicly available reference. I am very grateful to Quentin Bell for his personal encouragement, and for permission to use material still in copyright. I would also like to endorse the thanks that most Woolf scholars offer to Mrs Bet Inglis, keeper of the Woolf archives at the Sussex University Library; I am particularly grateful to her for the part she played in the reproduction here of pages from the *Three Guineas* scrapbooks. The explanatory notes in this edition draw on many sources; I would like to acknowledge a specific debt to Jane Marcus's research on the political and social background to *A Room of One's Own* and also to Morag Shiach, editor of the Oxford University Press edition, for her work on the literary and other allusions of both texts. I would like to thank Ruthie Petrie for her help with my work on this project. Finally, I am very grateful to Julia Briggs, general editor of the series. She undertook a lot of work on the history and variations of the two texts published here, and gave enthusiasm and encouragement as well as practical advice.

Further Reading

The provenance of these texts is quite complex, as is explained in the Note on the Texts. Readers interested in the process by which these texts emerged may want to look particularly at *The Manuscript Version of A Room of One's Own: 'Women and Fiction'*, (ed. S. P. Rosenbaum, Blackwell, 1991) and the essay-novel that preceded *Three Guineas, The Pargiters* (ed. Mitchell A. Leaska, Hogarth Press, 1978). Readers looking for connections between these political essays and Virginia Woolf's novels will find a fictional exploration of some of the themes of *A Room of One's Own* (gender, androgyny, writing and desire) in *Orlando* (1928; Penguin Books, 1993). The links between *Three Guineas* and *The Years*, originally conceived as a single work, are closer still. It is worth adding, however, that all of Woolf's novels, including those with the greatest abstraction in form, are heavily freighted with the cargo of gender and its meanings.

Many of Virginia Woolf's shorter essays and reviews concern themes related to *A Room of One's Own* and *Three Guineas*. Selections can be found in the two volumes in this series, edited by Rachel Bowlby (*A Woman's Essays*, Penguin Books, 1992; *The Crowded Dance of Modern Life*, Penguin Books, 1993), as well as in *Virginia Woolf: Women and Writing* (ed. Michèle Barrett, Women's Press, 1979, 1992). The complete essays, edited by Andrew McNeillie, are published in six volumes by the Hogarth Press.

The documentation of Woolf's life is now extensive. The edited *Diary* and *Letters* offer a fascinating companion to her political writings as well as to her novels. Woolf's own reading practices have been tracked in Brenda Silver's *The Reading Notebooks of Virginia Woolf* (1983). The secondary literature on Virginia Woolf's life and literature is now so large that book-length publications are required to address it; John Mepham has produced an extremely useful and well-judged discussion of the biographical and critical literature on Woolf in a book in the 'Criticism in Focus' series of Bristol Classical Press (1992).

The secondary literature concerning the interpretations of Woolf's feminism has a particular relevance. See Jane Marcus, *Virginia Woolf and the Languages of Patriarchy* (Indiana University Press, 1987; particularly the essay on *A Room of One's Own*), and the collection edited by Jane Marcus on *Virginia Woolf: A Feminist Slant* (Nebraska University Press, 1983, particularly the essays on *Three Guineas* and Woolf's later work). 'Post-structuralist' treatments of Woolf include Makiko Minow-Pinkney's *Virginia Woolf and the Problem of the Subject* (Harvester Press, 1987) and Elizabeth Abel's *Virginia Woolf and the Fictions of Psychoanalysis* (Chicago University Press, 1989).

A Note on the Texts

A ROOM OF ONE'S OWN

A Room of One's Own began as two lectures that Virginia Woolf gave at Cambridge in October 1928, under the general heading of 'Women and Fiction'. In March 1929 she published an article with that title in the American magazine the *Forum*. It was a general piece on the themes of the lectures and was written – when compared with the later version – in a rather formal and measured style. The essay 'Women and Fiction' was reprinted by Leonard Woolf in the collection of Virginia Woolf's essays entitled *Granite and Rainbow* (1958) and has subsequently been reprinted in *Collected Essays*, vol. II, and other anthologies.

The book that was published as *A Room of One's Own* can be traced through its manuscript and typescript versions. The manuscript is perhaps the most interesting. Virginia Woolf had in fact tried to sell the manuscript, to raise money for the Society for Women's Service, but was unable to do so. After her death the Fitzwilliam Museum in Cambridge asked Leonard Woolf for something by her and he donated this manuscript. Unfortunately it was filed as 'Women in Fiction' and only in 1990 was it discovered to be the missing manuscript of *A Room of One's Own*. S. P. Rosenbaum, who found the manuscript, has now published an annotated transcription, entitled *Women and Fiction: the Manuscript Versions of A Room of One's Own* (Blackwell, 1992). The transcribed manuscript shows that the ideas, images and language of *A Room of One's Own* were subject to considerable revision in the process of writing. Whether Virginia Woolf would have approved of the embargo, imposed between discovery and publication by Professor Rosenbaum, is a matter for ironic speculation.

The typescript of *A Room of One's Own* is in the collection of Monks House Papers at Sussex University (MHP B. 15.1). This provided the basis for the printed text, although a number of passages were cut out during the final stages.

A Room of One's Own was published on 24 October 1929 in England by the Hogarth Press and simultaneously in the United States by Harcourt Brace. These trade editions were of 3,040 and 4,000 copies respectively, preceded by a small signed limited edition. It sold extremely well: Hogarth Press had printed 14,650 copies by March 1930; Harcourt Brace sold 18,640 between November 1929 and February 1953. The first Penguin edition, published in 1945 and priced 9d., was a run of 100,000 copies.

The text used in this edition is a reprint of the first British edition. Later British editions carried virtually no changes, although for some reason in the third impression Woolf altered the sentence on p. 100 about liking women from 'I like their subtlety' to 'I like their completeness'. She also corrected a footnote on p. 18, where the book title of Note 1 had wrongly read *Life of Miss Emily Davies*. This, and the spelling of George Eliot's Mr Casaubon on p. 82 have been corrected in the present edition. The differences between the British and the American texts are (by contrast with the novels of this period) minimal; none could clearly be shown to be authorial. The largest number of differences occur in the placing of commas. A list of the more substantive variants, and particularly of all those adopted in this edition, follows. The British version is given first, followed by the American. An asterisk after the American text indicates that that variant has been adopted in this edition (the adoption of variant readings has been made taking the typescript into account).

21.22 provided us with any thing comparable] provided us with anything comparable*

35.29 so speculating I found my way] so speculating, I found my way*

40.25 Cassandra Atossa and Antigone,] Cassandra, Atossa and Antigone*

53.28 And if someone would soar above the rest,] And if some one would soar above the rest*

55.1   whose mind was tuned to nature and reflection,]
        whose mind was turned to nature and reflection,*

75.11 Hence, perhaps, the peculiar nature of women in
        fiction;] Hence, perhaps, the peculiar nature of
        woman in fiction;*

85.11 there was fence beyond that] there was a fence
        beyond that*

91.9   (I said turning the pages)] (I said, turning the
        pages)*

93.23 and so were Keats and Sterne] and so was Keats and
        Sterne

94.13 before the art of creation] before the act of creation

97.29 curiously enough to two wars] curiously enough, to
        two wars*

99.8   now a daffodil in the sun] now in a daffodil in the
        sun*

THREE GUINEAS

The origins of *Three Guineas* lie in a speech given by Virginia
Woolf on 21 January 1931 to the London branch of the National
Society for Women's Service. An essay, based on a shortened
and revised version of the speech, was published in *The Death of
the Moth* (1942) entitled 'Professions for Women' (reprinted as
appendix II of this edition). A full transcription of the manuscript
of the speech itself has now been published in *The Pargiters: The
Novel-Essay Portion of The Years* (ed. Mitchell A. Leaska, Hogarth
Press, 1978).

Following on from this speech, Virginia Woolf attempted the
ambitious project documented in the work published much later
as *The Pargiters*. As is discussed in more length in the introduction, Woolf intended to develop a new literary form – the
'Novel-Essay' – which would interleave fictional scenes and
social interpretation using the development of a family group
over three generations. In the end, she abandoned this plan,
publishing the fiction as *The Years* and the political argument as

Three Guineas. It is, none the less, important to consider the linked history of the two texts, and the publication of *The Pargiters* enables this to be done.

The manuscript of *Three Guineas* is now in the Berg Collection of the New York Public Library, having originally been sold by Virginia Woolf herself (in 1939) to an individual buyer to raise funds for the refugees from the Spanish Civil War.[1] At the time of publication of *Three Guineas* a summary was published in *Atlantic Monthly* in May and June 1938, under the title 'Women Must Weep'.

Three Guineas was published in Britain by the Hogarth Press on 2 June 1938; 16,250 copies were printed. It was published in the United States on 25 August 1938, by Harcourt Brace, in a run of 7,500 copies. A second British issue followed in 1943 and a second American edition in 1963. In 1977 and 1978 a Penguin edition was published in Britain, the two printings totalling 31,000 copies.[2]

Early editions of *Three Guineas* carried photograph illustrations, which were dropped from some of the later editions. The present edition reproduces the photographs, in their original placing in the text. Where Virginia Woolf obtained these illustrations, and what became of the originals, is not known. (This is also the case for the photographs of war damage that Woolf refers to at the beginning of the text.) Photographic illustrations of the *Three Guineas* scrapbooks (reproduced as appendix I of this edition) have been supplied by the University of Sussex from material in the Monks House Papers in the Library there.

The text of this edition is based on the British first edition. There are a number of minor variants between the British and American first editions, and some new sentences and a new paragraph added to the American footnotes. These, plus a number of minor emendations made from the American text, are listed in appendix III.

Virginia Woolf's notes to *Three Guineas* are indicated in the text by superscript arabic numerals. Michèle Barrett's editorial notes are indicated by superscript italic letters.

NOTES

1. Letter to May Sarton, 2 Feb. 1939; Letter to Elizabeth Bowen, 28 Feb. 1939, *Letters*, VI, pp. 314, 319.
2. Bibliographical data is taken from B. J. Kirkpatrick, *A Bibliography of Virginia Woolf* (3rd edn, OUP, 1980, pp. 40–42).

A ROOM OF ONE'S OWN

A ROOM OF ONE'S OWN*

Chapter I

But, you may say, we asked you to speak about women and fiction – what has that got to do with a room of one's own? I will try to explain. When you asked me to speak about women and fiction I sat down on the banks of a river and began to wonder what the words meant. They might mean simply a few remarks about Fanny Burney; a few more about Jane Austen; a tribute to the Brontës and a sketch of Haworth Parsonage under snow; some witticisms if possible about Miss Mitford; a respectful allusion to George Eliot; a reference to Mrs Gaskell and one would have done. But at second sight the words seemed not so simple. The title women and fiction might mean, and you may have meant it to mean, women and what they are like; or it might mean women and the fiction that they write; or it might mean women and the fiction that is written about them; or it might mean that somehow all three are inextricably mixed together and you want me to consider them in that light. But when I began to consider the subject in this last way, which seemed the most interesting, I soon saw that it had one fatal drawback. I should never be able to come to a conclusion. I should never be able to fulfil what is, I understand, the first duty of a lecturer – to hand you after an hour's discourse a nugget of pure truth to wrap up between the pages of your notebooks and keep on the mantelpiece for ever. All I could do was to offer you an opinion upon one minor point – a woman must have money and a room of her own if she is to write fiction; and that, as you will see, leaves the great problem of the true nature of woman and the true nature of fiction unsolved. I have shirked the duty of coming to a conclusion upon these two questions – women

* This essay is based upon two papers read to the Arts Society at Newnham and the Odtaa¹ at Girton in October 1928. The papers were too long to be read in full, and have since been altered and expanded.

and fiction remain, so far as I am concerned, unsolved problems. But in order to make some amends I am going to do what I can to show you how I arrived at this opinion about the room and the money. I am going to develop in your presence as fully and freely as I can the train of thought which led me to think this. Perhaps if I lay bare the ideas, the prejudices, that lie behind this statement you will find that they have some bearing upon women and some upon fiction. At any rate, when a subject is highly controversial – and any question about sex is that – one cannot hope to tell the truth. One can only show how one came to hold whatever opinion one does hold. One can only give one's audience the chance of drawing their own conclusions as they observe the limitations, the prejudices, the idiosyncrasies of the speaker. Fiction here is likely to contain more truth than fact. Therefore I propose, making use of all the liberties and licences of a novelist, to tell you the story of the two days that preceded my coming here – how, bowed down by the weight of the subject which you have laid upon my shoulders, I pondered it, and made it work in and out of my daily life. I need not say that what I am about to describe has no existence; Oxbridge is an invention; so is Fernham;[2] 'I' is only a convenient term for somebody who has no real being. Lies will flow from my lips, but there may perhaps be some truth mixed up with them; it is for you to seek out this truth and to decide whether any part of it is worth keeping. If not, you will of course throw the whole of it into the waste-paper basket and forget all about it.

Here then was I (call me Mary Beton, Mary Seton, Mary Carmichael[3] or by any name you please – it is not a matter of any importance) sitting on the banks of a river a week or two ago in fine October weather, lost in thought. That collar I have spoken of, women and fiction, the need of coming to some conclusion on a subject that raises all sorts of prejudices and passions, bowed my head to the ground. To the right and left bushes of some sort, golden and crimson, glowed with the colour, even it seemed burnt with the heat, of fire. On the further bank the willows wept in perpetual lamentation, their hair about their shoulders. The river reflected whatever it chose of sky and bridge and burning tree, and when the undergraduate had oared his boat through the reflections they closed again, completely, as if he had never been. There one might have sat the clock round lost in thought. Thought — to call it by a prouder name than it deserved — had let its line down into the stream.[4] It swayed, minute after minute, hither and thither among the reflections and the weeds, letting the water lift it and sink it, until — you know the little tug — the sudden conglomeration of an idea at the end of one's line: and then the cautious hauling of it in, and the careful laying of it out? Alas, laid on the grass how small, how insignificant this thought of mine looked; the sort of fish that a good fisherman puts back into the water so that it may grow fatter and be one day worth cooking and eating. I will not trouble you with that thought now, though if you look carefully you may find it for yourselves in the course of what I am going to say.

But however small it was, it had, nevertheless, the mysterious property of its kind — put back into the mind, it became at once very exciting, and important; and as it darted and sank, and flashed hither and thither, set up such a wash and tumult of ideas that it was impossible to sit still. It was thus that I found myself walking with extreme rapidity across a grass plot. Instantly a man's figure rose to intercept me. Nor did I at first understand that the gesticulations of a curious-looking object, in a cut-away coat and evening shirt, were aimed at me. His face expressed horror and indignation. Instinct rather than reason came to my help; he was a Beadle;[5] I was a woman. This was the turf; there was the path. Only the Fellows and Scholars are allowed here; the gravel is the place for me. Such thoughts were the work of a moment. As I regained the path the arms of the Beadle sank, his face assumed its usual repose, and though turf is better walking than gravel, no very great harm was done. The only charge I could bring against the Fellows and Scholars of whatever the college might happen to be was that in protection of their turf, which has been rolled for 300 years in succession, they had sent my little fish into hiding.

What idea it had been that had sent me so audaciously trespassing I could not now remember. The spirit of peace descended like a cloud from heaven, for if the spirit of peace dwells anywhere, it is in the courts and quadrangles of Oxbridge on a fine October morning. Strolling through those colleges past those ancient halls the roughness of the present seemed smoothed away; the body seemed contained in a miraculous glass cabinet through which no sound could penetrate, and the mind, freed from any contact with facts (unless one trespassed on the turf again), was at liberty to settle down upon whatever meditation was in harmony with the moment. As chance would have it, some stray memory of some old essay about revisiting Oxbridge in the long vacation brought Charles Lamb to mind – Saint Charles, said Thackeray, putting a letter of Lamb's to his forehead. Indeed, among all the dead (I give you my thoughts as they came to me), Lamb is one of the most congenial; one to whom one would have liked to say, Tell me then how you wrote your essays? For his essays are superior even to Max Beerbohm's, I thought, with all their perfection, because of that wild flash of imagination, that lightning crack of genius in the middle of them which leaves them flawed and imperfect, but starred with poetry. Lamb then came to Oxbridge perhaps a hundred years ago. Certainly he wrote an essay – the name escapes me[6] – about the manuscript of one of Milton's poems which he saw here. It was *Lycidas* perhaps, and Lamb wrote how it shocked him to think it possible that any word in *Lycidas* would have been different from what it is. To think of Milton changing the words in that poem seemed to him a sort of sacrilege. This led me to remember what I could of *Lycidas* and to amuse myself with guessing which word it could have been that Milton had altered, and why. It then occurred to me that the very manuscript itself which Lamb had looked at was only a few hundred yards away, so that one could follow Lamb's footsteps across the quadrangle to that famous library where the treasure is kept. Moreover, I recollected, as I put this plan into execution, it is in this famous library[7] that the manuscript of Thackeray's *Esmond* is also preserved. The critics often say that *Esmond* is Thackeray's most perfect novel. But the affectation of the style, with its imitation of the eighteenth century, hampers one, so far as I remember; unless indeed the eighteenth-century style was natural to Thackeray – a fact that one might prove by looking at the manuscript and seeing whether the alterations were for the benefit of the style or of the sense. But then one would have to decide what is style and what is meaning, a question which – but here I was actually at the door which leads into the library itself. I must have opened it, for instantly there issued, like a guardian angel barring the way with a flutter of black gown instead of white wings, a deprecating, silvery, kindly gentleman, who regretted in a low voice as he waved me back that ladies are only admitted to the library if accompanied by a Fellow of the College or furnished with a letter of introduction.

That a famous library has been cursed by a woman is a matter of complete indifference to a famous library. Venerable and calm, with all its treasures safe locked within its breast, it sleeps complacently and will, so far as I am concerned, so sleep for ever. Never will I wake those echoes, never will I ask for that hospitality again, I vowed as I descended the steps in anger. Still an hour remained before luncheon, and what was one to do? Stroll on the meadows? sit by the river? Certainly it was a lovely autumn morning; the leaves were fluttering red to the ground; there was no great hardship in doing either. But the sound of music reached my ear. Some service or celebration was going forward. The organ complained magnificently as I passed the chapel door. Even the sorrow of Christianity sounded in that serene air more like the recollection of sorrow than sorrow itself; even the groanings of the ancient organ seemed lapped in peace. I had no wish to enter had I the right, and this time the verger might have stopped me, demanding perhaps my baptismal certificate, or a letter of introduction from the Dean. But the outside of these magnificent buildings is often as beautiful as the inside. Moreover, it was amusing enough to watch the congregation assembling, coming in and going out again, busying themselves at the door of the chapel like bees at the mouth of a hive. Many were in cap and gown; some had tufts of fur[8] on their shoulders; others were wheeled in bath-chairs; others, though not past middle age, seemed creased and crushed into shapes so singular that one was reminded of those giant crabs and crayfish who heave with difficulty across the sand of an aquarium. As I leant against the wall the University indeed seemed a sanctuary in which are preserved rare types which would soon be obsolete if left to fight for existence on the pavement of the Strand. Old stories of old deans and old dons came back to mind, but before I had summoned up courage to whistle – it used to be said that at the sound of a whistle old Professor — instantly broke into a gallop – the venerable congregation had gone inside. The outside of the chapel remained. As you know, its high domes and pinnacles can be seen, like a sailing-ship[9] always voyaging never arriving, lit up at night and visible for miles, far away across the hills. Once, presumably, this quadrangle with its smooth lawns, its massive buildings and the chapel itself was marsh too, where the grasses waved and the swine rootled. Teams of horses and oxen, I thought, must have hauled the stone in wagons from far counties, and then with infinite labour the grey blocks in whose shade I was now standing were poised in order one on top of another, and then the painters brought their glass for the windows, and the masons were busy for centuries up on that roof with putty and cement, spade and trowel. Every Saturday somebody must have poured gold and silver out of a leathern purse into their ancient fists, for they had their beer and skittles presumably of an evening. An unending stream of gold and silver, I thought, must have flowed into this court perpetually to keep the stones coming and the masons working; to level, to ditch, to dig and to drain. But it was then the age of faith, and money was poured liberally to set these stones on a deep foundation, and when the stones were raised, still more money was poured in from the coffers of kings and queens and great nobles to ensure that hymns should be sung here and scholars taught. Lands were granted; tithes were paid. And when the age of faith was over and the age of reason had come, still the same flow of gold and silver went on; fellowships were founded; lectureships endowed; only the gold and silver flowed now, not from the coffers of the king, but from the chests of merchants and manufacturers, from the purses of men who had made, say, a fortune from industry, and returned, in their wills, a bounteous share of it to endow more chairs, more lectureships, more fellowships in the university where they had learnt their craft. Hence the libraries and laboratories; the observatories; the splendid equipment of costly and delicate instruments which now stands on glass shelves, where centuries ago the grasses waved and the swine rooted. Certainly, as I strolled round the court, the foundation of gold and silver seemed deep enough; the pavement laid solidly over the wild grasses. Men with trays on their heads went busily from staircase to staircase. Gaudy blossoms flowered in window-boxes. The strains of the gramophone blared out from the rooms within. It was impossible not to reflect – the reflection whatever it may have been was cut short. The clock struck. It was time to find one's way to luncheon.

It is a curious fact that novelists have a way of making us believe that luncheon parties are invariably memorable for something very witty that was said, or for something very wise that was done. But they seldom spare a word for what was eaten. It is part of the novelist's convention not to mention soup and salmon and ducklings, as if soup and salmon and ducklings were of no importance whatsoever, as if nobody ever smoked a cigar or drank a glass of wine. Here, however, I shall take the liberty to defy that convention and to tell you that the lunch on this occasion[10] began with soles, sunk in a deep dish, over which the college cook had spread a counterpane of the whitest cream, save that it was branded here and there with brown spots like the spots on the flanks of a doe. After that came the partridges, but if this suggests a couple of bald, brown birds on a plate you are mistaken. The partridges, many and various, came with all their retinue of sauces and salads, the sharp and the sweet, each in its order; their potatoes, thin as coins but not so hard; their sprouts, foliated as rosebuds but more succulent. And no sooner had the roast and its retinue been done with than the silent serving-man, the Beadle himself perhaps in a milder manifestation, set before us, wreathed in napkins, a confection which rose all sugar from the waves. To call it pudding and so relate it to rice and tapioca would be an insult. Meanwhile the wineglasses had flushed yellow and flushed crimson; had been emptied; had been filled. And thus by degrees was lit, half-way down the spine, which is the seat of the soul, not that hard little electric light which we call brilliance, as it pops in and out upon our lips, but the more profound, subtle and subterranean glow which is the rich yellow flame of rational intercourse. No need to hurry. No need to sparkle. No need to be anybody but oneself. We are all going to heaven and Vandyck is of the company [11] – in other words, how good life seemed, how sweet its rewards, how trivial this grudge or that grievance, how admirable friendship and the society of one's kind, as, lighting a good cigarette, one sunk among the cushions in the window-seat.

If by good luck there had been an ash-tray handy, if one had not knocked the ash out of the window in default, if things had been a little different from what they were, one would not have seen, presumably, a cat without a tail. The sight of that abrupt and truncated animal padding softly across the quadrangle changed by some fluke of the subconscious intelligence the emotional light for me. It was as if someone had let fall a shade. Perhaps the excellent hock was relinquishing its hold. Certainly, as I watched the Manx cat pause in the middle of the lawn as if it too questioned the universe, something seemed lacking, something seemed different. But what was lacking, what was different, I asked myself, listening to the talk? And to answer that question I had to think myself out of the room, back into the past, before the war indeed, and to set before my eyes the model of another luncheon party held in rooms not very far distant from these; but different. Everything was different. Meanwhile the talk went on among the guests, who were many and young, some of this sex, some of that; it went on swimmingly, it went on agreeably, freely, amusingly. And as it went on I set it against the background of that other talk, and as I matched the two together I had no doubt that one was the descendant, the legitimate heir of the other. Nothing was changed; nothing was different save only – here I listened with all my ears not entirely to what was being said, but to the murmur or current behind it. Yes, that was it – the change was there. Before the war[12] at a luncheon party like this people would have said precisely the same things but they would have sounded different, because in those days they were accompanied by a sort of humming noise, not articulate, but musical, exciting, which changed the value of the words themselves. Could one set that humming noise to words? Perhaps with the help of the poets one could. A book lay beside me and, opening it, I turned casually enough to Tennyson. And here I found Tennyson was singing:

> There has fallen a splendid tear
>   From the passion-flower at the gate.
> She is coming, my dove, my dear;
>   She is coming, my life, my fate;
> The red rose cries, 'She is near, she is near';
>   And the white rose weeps, 'She is late';
> The larkspur listens, 'I hear, I hear',
>   And the lily whispers, 'I wait.'[13]

Was that what men hummed at luncheon parties before the war? And the women?

> My heart is like a singing bird
>   Whose nest is in a water'd shoot;
> My heart is like an apple tree
>   Whose boughs are bent with thick-set fruit;
> My heart is like a rainbow shell
>   That paddles in a halcyon sea;
> My heart is gladder than all these
>   Because my love is come to me.[14]

Was that what women hummed at luncheon parties before the war?

There was something so ludicrous in thinking of people humming such things even under their breath at luncheon parties before the war that I burst out laughing, and had to explain my laughter by pointing at the Manx cat, who did look a little absurd, poor beast, without a tail, in the middle of the lawn. Was he really born so, or had he lost his tail in an accident? The tailless cat, though some are said to exist in the Isle of Man, is rarer than one thinks. It is a queer animal, quaint rather than beautiful. It is strange what a difference a tail makes – you know the sort of things one says as a lunch party breaks up and people are finding their coats and hats.

This one, thanks to the hospitality of the host, had lasted far into the afternoon. The beautiful October day was fading and the leaves were falling from the trees in the avenue as I walked through it. Gate after gate seemed to close with gentle finality behind me. Innumerable beadles were fitting innumerable keys into well-oiled locks; the treasure-house was being made secure for another night. After the avenue one comes out upon a road – I forget its name – which leads you, if you take the right turning, along to Fernham. But there was plenty of time. Dinner was not till half-past seven. One could almost do without dinner after such a luncheon. It is strange how a scrap of poetry works in the mind and makes the legs move in time to it along the road. Those words –

> There has fallen a splendid tear
>   From the passion-flower at the gate.
> She is coming, my dove, my dear –

sang in my blood as I stepped quickly along towards Headingley. And then, switching off into the other measure, I sang, where the waters are churned up by the weir:

> My heart is like a singing bird
>   Whose nest is in a water'd shoot;
> My heart is like an apple tree . . .

What poets, I cried aloud, as one does in the dusk, what poets they were!

In a sort of jealousy, I suppose, for our own age, silly and absurd though these comparisons are, I went on to wonder if honestly one could name two living poets now as great as Tennyson and Christina Rossetti were then. Obviously it is impossible, I thought, looking into those foaming waters, to compare them. The very reason why that poetry excites one to such abandonment, such rapture, is that it celebrates some feeling that one used to have (at luncheon parties before the war perhaps), so that one responds easily, familiarly, without troubling to check the feeling, or to compare it with any that one has now. But the living poets express a feeling that is actually being made and torn out of us at the moment. One does not recognize it in the first place; often for some reason one fears it; one watches it with keenness and compares it jealously and suspiciously with the old feeling that one knew. Hence the difficulty of modern poetry; and it is because of this difficulty that one cannot remember more than two consecutive lines of any good modern poet. For this reason – that my memory failed me – the argument flagged for want of material. But why, I continued, moving on towards Headingley, have we stopped humming under our breath at luncheon parties? Why has Alfred ceased to sing

> She is coming, my dove, my dear.

Why has Christina ceased to respond

> My heart is gladder than all these
> Because my love is come to me?

Shall we lay the blame on the war? When the guns fired in August 1914, did the faces of men and women show so plain in each other's eyes that romance was killed? Certainly it was a shock (to women in particular with their illusions about education, and so on) to see the faces of our rulers in the light of the shell-fire. So ugly they looked – German, English, French – so stupid. But lay the blame where one will, on whom one will, the illusion which inspired Tennyson and Christina Rossetti to sing so passionately about the coming of their loves is far rarer now than then. One has only to read, to look, to listen, to remember. But why say 'blame'? Why, if it was an illusion, not praise the catastrophe, whatever it was, that destroyed illusion and put truth in its place? For truth . . . those dots mark the spot where, in search of truth, I missed the turning up to Fernham. Yes indeed, which was truth and which was illusion, I asked myself? What was the truth about these houses, for example, dim and festive now with their red windows in the dusk, but raw and red and squalid, with their sweets and their bootlaces, at nine o'clock in the morning? And the willows and the river and the gardens that run down to the river, vague now with the mist stealing over them, but gold and red in the sunlight – which was the truth, which was the illusion about them? I spare you the twists and turns of my cogitations, for no conclusion was found on the road to Headingley, and I ask you to suppose that I soon found out my mistake about the turning and retraced my steps to Fernham.

As I have said already that it was an October day, I dare not forfeit your respect and imperil the fair name of fiction by changing the season and describing lilacs hanging over garden walls, crocuses, tulips and other flowers of spring. Fiction must stick to facts, and the truer the facts the better the fiction – so we are told. Therefore it was still autumn and the leaves were still yellow and falling, if anything, a little faster than before, because it was now evening (seven twenty-three to be precise) and a breeze (from the south-west to be exact) had risen. But for all that there was something odd at work:

> My heart is like a singing bird
>   Whose nest is in a water'd shoot;
> My heart is like an apple tree
>   Whose boughs are bent with thick-set fruit –

perhaps the words of Christina Rossetti were partly responsible for the folly of the fancy – it was nothing of course but a fancy –

that the lilac was shaking its flowers over the garden walls, and the brimstone butterflies were scudding hither and thither, and the dust of the pollen was in the air. A wind blew, from what quarter I know not, but it lifted the half-grown leaves so that there was a flash of silver grey in the air. It was the time between the lights when colours undergo their intensification and purples and golds burn in window-panes like the beat of an excitable heart; when for some reason the beauty of the world revealed and yet soon to perish (here I pushed into the garden, for, unwisely, the door was left open and no beadles seemed about), the beauty of the world which is so soon to perish, has two edges, one of laughter, one of anguish, cutting the heart asunder. The gardens of Fernham lay before me in the spring twilight, wild and open, and in the long grass, sprinkled and carelessly flung, were daffodils and bluebells, not orderly perhaps at the best of times, and now wind-blown and waving as they tugged at their roots. The windows of the building, curved like ships' windows among generous waves of red brick, changed from lemon to silver under the flight of the quick spring clouds. Somebody was in a hammock, somebody, but in this light they were phantoms, only, half guessed, half seen, raced across the grass – would no one stop her? – and then on the terrace, as if popping out to breathe the air, to glance at the garden, came a bent figure, formidable yet humble, with her great forehead and her shabby dress – could it be the famous scholar, could it be J— H— herself?[15] All was dim, yet intense too, as if the scarf which the dusk had flung over the garden were torn asunder by star or sword – the flash of some terrible reality leaping, as its way is, out of the heart of the spring. For youth—

Here was my soup. Dinner was being served in the great dining-hall. Far from being spring it was in fact an evening in October. Everybody was assembled in the big dining-room. Dinner was ready. Here was the soup. It was a plain gravy soup. There was nothing to stir the fancy in that. One could have seen through the transparent liquid any pattern that there might have been on the plate itself. But there was no pattern. The plate was plain. Next came beef with its attendant greens and potatoes – a homely trinity, suggesting the rumps of cattle in a muddy market, and sprouts curled and yellowed at the edge, and bargaining and cheapening, and women with string bags on Monday morning. There was no reason to complain of human nature's daily food, seeing that the supply was sufficient and coal-miners doubtless were sitting down to less. Prunes and custard followed. And if anyone complains that prunes, even when mitigated by custard, are an uncharitable vegetable (fruit they are not), stringy as a miser's heart and exuding a fluid such as might run in misers' veins who have denied themselves wine and warmth for eighty years and yet not given to the poor, he should reflect that there are people whose charity embraces even the prune. Biscuits and cheese came next, and here the water-jug was liberally passed round, for it is the nature of biscuits to be dry, and these were biscuits to the core. That was all. The meal was over. Everybody scraped their chairs back; the swing-doors swung violently to and fro; soon the hall was emptied of every sign of food and made ready no doubt for breakfast next morning. Down corridors and up staircases the youth of England went banging and singing. And was it for a guest, a stranger (for I had no more right here in Fernham than in Trinity or Somerville or Girton or Newnham or Christchurch), to say, 'The dinner was not good,' or to say (we were now, Mary Seton and I, in her sitting-room), 'Could we not have dined up here alone?' for if I had said anything of the kind I should have been prying and searching into the secret economies of a house which to the stranger wears so fine a front of gaiety and courage. No, one could say nothing of the sort. Indeed, conversation for a moment flagged. The human frame being what it is, heart, body and brain all mixed together, and not contained in separate compartments as they will be no doubt in another million years, a good dinner is of great importance to good talk. One cannot think well, love well, sleep well, if one has not dined well. The lamp in the spine does not light on beef and prunes. We are all *probably* going to heaven, and Vandyck is, we *hope*, to meet us round the next corner – that is the dubious and qualifying state of mind that beef and prunes at the end of the day's work breed between them. Happily my friend, who taught science, had a cupboard where there was a squat bottle and little glasses – (but there should have been sole and partridge to begin with) – so that we were able to draw up to the fire and repair some of the damages of the day's living. In a minute or so we were slipping freely in and out among all those objects of curiosity and interest which form in the mind in the absence of a particular person, and are naturally to be discussed on coming together again – how somebody has married, another has not; one thinks this, another that; one has improved out of all knowledge, the other most amazingly gone to the bad – with all those speculations upon human nature and the character of the amazing world we live in which spring naturally from such beginnings. While these things were being said, however, I became shamefacedly aware of a current setting in of its own accord and carrying everything forward to an end of its own. One might be talking of Spain or Portugal, of book or racehorse, but the real interest of whatever was said was none of those things, but a scene of masons on a high roof some five centuries ago. Kings and nobles brought treasure in huge sacks and poured it under the earth. This scene was for ever coming alive in my mind and placing itself by another of lean cows and a muddy market and withered greens and the stringy hearts of old men – these two pictures, disjointed and disconnected and nonsensical as they were, were for ever coming together and combating each other and had me entirely at their mercy. The best course, unless the whole talk was to be distorted, was to expose what was in my mind to the air, when with good luck it would fade and crumble like the head of the dead king when they opened the coffin at Windsor. Briefly, then, I told Miss Seton about the masons who had been all those years on the roof of the chapel, and about the kings and queens and nobles bearing sacks of gold and silver on their shoulders, which they shovelled into the earth; and then how the great financial magnates of our own time came and laid cheques and bonds, I suppose, where the others had laid ingots and rough lumps of gold. All that lies beneath the colleges down there, I said; but this college, where we are now sitting, what lies beneath its gallant red brick and the wild unkempt grasses of the garden? What force is behind that plain china off which we dined, and (here it popped out of my mouth before I could stop it) the beef, the custard and the prunes?

Well, said Mary Seton, about the year 1860 – Oh, but you know the story, she said, bored, I suppose, by the recital. And she told me – rooms were hired. Committees met. Envelopes were addressed. Circulars were drawn up. Meetings were held; letters were read out; so-and-so has promised so much; on the contrary, Mr — won't give a penny. The *Saturday Review* has been very rude. How can we raise a fund to pay for offices? Shall we hold a bazaar? Can't we find a pretty girl to sit in the front row? Let us look up what John Stuart Mill[16] said on the subject. Can anyone persuade the editor of the — to print a letter? Can we get Lady — to sign it? Lady — is out of town. That was the way it was done, presumably, sixty years ago, and it was a prodigious effort, and a great deal of time was spent on it. And it was only after a long struggle and with the utmost difficulty that they got thirty thousand pounds together.* So obviously we cannot have wine and partridges and servants carrying tin dishes on their heads, she said. We cannot have sofas and separate rooms. 'The amenities,' she said, quoting from some book or other, 'will have to wait.'†

At the thought of all those women working year after year and finding it hard to get two thousand pounds together, and as

---

* 'We are told that we ought to ask for £30,000 at least . . . It is not a large sum, considering that there is to be but one college of this sort for Great Britain, Ireland and the Colonies, and considering how easy it is to raise immense sums for boys' schools. But considering how few people really wish women to be educated, it is a good deal.' – Lady Stephen, *Life of Miss Emily Davies and Girton College.*

† 'Every penny which could be scraped together was set aside for building, and the amenities had to be postponed.' – R. Strachey, *The Cause.*

much as they could do to get thirty thousand pounds, we burst out in scorn at the reprehensible poverty of our sex. What had our mothers been doing then that they had no wealth to leave us? Powdering their noses? Looking in at shop windows? Flaunting in the sun at Monte Carlo? There were some photographs on the mantelpiece. Mary's mother – if that was her picture – may have been a wastrel in her spare time (she had thirteen children by a minister of the church), but if so her gay and dissipated life had left too few traces of its pleasures on her face. She was a homely body; an old lady in a plaid shawl which was fastened by a large cameo; and she sat in a basket-chair, encouraging a spaniel to look at the camera, with the amused, yet strained expression of one who is sure that the dog will move directly the bulb is pressed. Now if she had gone into business; had become a manufacturer of artificial silk or a magnate on the Stock Exchange; if she had left two or three hundred thousand pounds to Fernham, we could have been sitting at our ease to-night and the subject of our talk might have been archaeology, botany, anthropology, physics, the nature of the atom, mathematics, astronomy, relativity, geography. If only Mrs Seton and her mother and her mother before her had learnt the great art of making money and had left their money, like their fathers and their grandfathers before them, to found fellowships and lectureships and prizes and scholarships appropriated to the use of their own sex, we might have dined very tolerably up here alone off a bird and a bottle of wine; we might have looked forward without undue confidence to a pleasant and honourable lifetime spent in the shelter of one of the liberally endowed professions. We might have been exploring or writing; mooning about the venerable places of the earth; sitting contemplative on the steps of the Parthenon, or going at ten to an office and coming home comfortably at half-past four to write a little poetry. Only, if Mrs Seton and her like had gone into business at the age of fifteen, there would have been – that was the snag in the argument – no Mary. What, I asked, did Mary think of that? There between the curtains was the October night, calm and lovely, with a star or two caught in the yellowing trees. Was she ready to resign her share of it and her memories (for they had been a happy family, though a large one) of games and quarrels up in Scotland, which she is never tired of praising for the fineness of its air and the quality of its cakes, in order that Fernham might have been endowed with fifty thousand pounds or so by a stroke of the pen? For, to endow a college would necessitate the suppression of families altogether. Making a fortune and bearing thirteen children – no human being could stand it. Consider the facts, we said. First there are nine months before the baby is born. Then the baby is born. Then there are three or four months spent in feeding the baby. After the baby is fed there are certainly five years spent in playing with the baby. You cannot, it seems, let children run about the streets. People who have seen them running wild in Russia say that the sight is not a pleasant one. People say, too, that human nature takes its shape in the years between one and five. If Mrs Seton, I said, had been making money, what sort of memories would you have had of games and quarrels? What would you have known of Scotland, and its fine air and cakes and all the rest of it? But it is useless to ask these questions, because you would never have come into existence at all. Moreover, it is equally useless to ask what might have happened if Mrs Seton and her mother and her mother before her had amassed great wealth and laid it under the foundations of college and library, because, in the first place, to earn money was impossible for them, and in the second, had it been possible, the law denied them the right to possess what money they earned. It is only for the last forty-eight years that Mrs Seton has had a penny of her own.[17] For all the centuries before that it would have been her husband's property – a thought which, perhaps, may have had its share in keeping Mrs Seton and her mothers off the Stock Exchange. Every penny I earn, they may have said, will be taken from me and disposed of according to my husband's wisdom – perhaps to found a scholarship or to endow a fellowship in Balliol or King's,[18] so that to earn money, even if I could earn money, is not a matter that interests me very greatly. I had better leave it to my husband.

At any rate, whether or not the blame rested on the old lady who was looking at the spaniel, there could be no doubt that for some reason or other our mothers had mismanaged their affairs very gravely. Not a penny could be spared for 'amenities'; for partridges and wine, beadles and turf, books and cigars, libraries and leisure. To raise bare walls out of the bare earth was the utmost they could do.

So we talked standing at the window and looking, as so many thousands look every night, down on the domes and towers of the famous city beneath us. It was very beautiful, very mysterious in the autumn moonlight. The old stone looked very white and venerable. One thought of all the books that were assembled down there; of the pictures of old prelates and worthies hanging in the panelled rooms; of the painted windows that would be throwing strange globes and crescents on the pavement; of the tablets and memorials and inscriptions; of the fountains and the grass; of the quiet rooms looking across the quiet quadrangles. And (pardon me the thought) I thought, too, of the admirable smoke and drink and the deep arm-chairs and the pleasant carpets: of the urbanity, the geniality, the dignity which are the offspring of luxury and privacy and space. Certainly our mothers had not provided us with anything comparable to all this – our mothers who found it difficult to scrape together thirty thousand pounds, our mothers who bore thirteen children to ministers of religion at St Andrews.

So I went back to my inn, and as I walked through the dark streets I pondered this and that, as one does at the end of the day's work. I pondered why it was that Mrs Seton had no money to leave us; and what effect poverty has on the mind; and what effect wealth has on the mind; and I thought of the queer old gentlemen I had seen that morning with tufts of fur upon their shoulders; and I remembered how if one whistled one of them ran; and I thought of the organ booming in the chapel and of the shut doors of the library; and I thought how unpleasant it is to be locked out; and I thought how it is worse perhaps to be locked in; and, thinking of the safety and prosperity of the one sex and of the poverty and insecurity of the other and of the effect of tradition and of the lack of tradition upon the mind of a writer, I thought at last that it was time to roll up the crumpled skin of the day, with its arguments and its impressions and its anger and its laughter, and cast it into the hedge. A thousand stars were flashing across the blue wastes of the sky. One seemed alone with an inscrutable society. All human beings were laid asleep – prone, horizontal, dumb. Nobody seemed stirring in the streets of Oxbridge. Even the door of the hotel sprang open at the touch of an invisible hand – not a boots was sitting up to light me to bed, it was so late.

Chapter II

The scene, if I may ask you to follow me, was now changed.
The leaves were still falling, but in London now, not Oxbridge;
and I must ask you to imagine a room, like many thousands,
with a window looking across people's hats and vans and motor-
cars to other windows, and on the table inside the room a blank
sheet of paper on which was written in large letters WOMEN
AND FICTION, but no more. The inevitable sequel to lunching
and dining at Oxbridge seemed, unfortunately, to be a visit to
the British Museum. One must strain off what was personal and
accidental in all these impressions and so reach the pure fluid,
the essential oil of truth. For that visit to Oxbridge and the
luncheon and the dinner had started a swarm of questions. Why
did men drink wine and women water? Why was one sex so
prosperous and the other so poor? What effect has poverty on
fiction? What conditions are necessary for the creation of works
of art? – a thousand questions at once suggested themselves. But
one needed answers, not questions; and an answer was only to
be had by consulting the learned and the unprejudiced, who
have removed themselves above the strife of tongue and the
confusion of body and issued the result of their reasoning and
research in books which are to be found in the British Museum.
If truth is not to be found on the shelves of the British Museum,
where, I asked myself, picking up a notebook and a pencil, is
truth?

Thus provided, thus confident and enquiring, I set out in the
pursuit of truth. The day, though not actually wet, was dismal,
and the streets in the neighbourhood of the Museum were full
of open coal-holes, down which sacks were showering; four-
wheeled cabs were drawing up and depositing on the pavement
corded boxes containing, presumably, the entire wardrobe of
some Swiss or Italian family seeking fortune or refuge or some

other desirable commodity which is to be found in the boarding-houses of Bloomsbury in the winter. The usual hoarse-voiced men paraded the streets with plants on barrows. Some shouted; others sang. London was like a workshop. London was like a machine. We were all being shot backwards and forwards on this plain foundation to make some pattern. The British Museum was another department of the factory. The swing-doors swung open; and there one stood under the vast dome, as if one were a thought in the huge bald forehead which is so splendidly encircled by a band of famous names.[1] One went to the counter; one took a slip of paper; one opened a volume of the catalogue, and . . . . . the five dots here indicate five separate minutes of stupefaction, wonder and bewilderment. Have you any notion how many books are written about women in the course of one year? Have you any notion how many are written by men? Are you aware that you are, perhaps, the most discussed animal in the universe? Here had I come with a notebook and a pencil proposing to spend a morning reading, supposing that at the end of the morning I should have transferred the truth to my notebook. But I should need to be a herd of elephants, I thought, and a wilderness of spiders, desperately referring to the animals that are reputed longest lived and most multitudinously eyed, to cope with all this. I should need claws of steel and beak of brass even to penetrate the husk. How shall I ever find the grains of truth embedded in all this mass of paper? I asked myself, and in despair began running my eye up and down the long list of titles. Even the names of the books gave me food for thought. Sex and its nature might well attract doctors and biologists; but what was surprising and difficult of explanation was the fact that sex – woman, that is to say – also attracts agreeable essayists, light-fingered novelists, young men who have taken the M.A. degree; men who have taken no degree; men who have no apparent qualification save that they are not women. Some of these books were, on the face of it, frivolous and facetious; but many, on the other hand, were serious and prophetic, moral and hortatory. Merely to read the titles suggested innumerable schoolmasters, innumerable clergymen mounting their platforms and pulpits and holding forth with a loquacity which far exceeded the hour usually allotted to such discourse on this one subject. It was a most strange phenomenon; and apparently – here I consulted the letter M – one confined to the male sex. Women do not write books about men – a fact that I could not help welcoming with relief, for if I had first to read all that men have written about women, then all that women have written about men, the aloe that flowers once in a hundred years would flower twice before I could set pen to paper. So, making a perfectly arbitrary choice of a dozen volumes or so, I sent my slips of paper to lie in the wire tray, and waited in my stall, among the other seekers for the essential oil of truth.

What could be the reason, then, of this curious disparity, I wondered, drawing cart-wheels on the slips of paper provided by the British taxpayer for other purposes. Why are women, judging from this catalogue, so much more interesting to men than men are to women? A very curious fact it seemed, and my mind wandered to picture the lives of men who spend their time in writing books about women; whether they were old or young, married or unmarried, red-nosed or hump-backed – anyhow, it was flattering, vaguely, to feel oneself the object of such attention, provided that it was not entirely bestowed by the crippled and the infirm – so I pondered until all such frivolous thoughts were ended by an avalanche of books sliding down on to the desk in front of me. Now the trouble began. The student who has been trained in research at Oxbridge has no doubt some method of shepherding his question past all distractions till it runs into its answer as a sheep runs into its pen. The student by my side, for instance, who was copying assiduously from a scientific manual, was, I felt sure, extracting pure nuggets of the essential ore every ten minutes or so. His little grunts of satisfaction indicated so much. But if, unfortunately, one has had no training in a university, the question far from being shepherded to its pen flies like a frightened flock hither and thither, helter-skelter, pursued by a whole pack of hounds. Professors,

schoolmasters, sociologists, clergymen, novelists, essayists, journalists, men who had no qualification save that they were not
women, chased my simple and single question – Why are women
poor? – until it became fifty questions; until the fifty questions
leapt frantically into mid-stream and were carried away. Every
page in my notebook was scribbled over with notes. To show
the state of mind I was in, I will read you a few of them,
explaining that the page was headed quite simply, WOMEN AND
POVERTY, in block letters; but what followed was something
like this:

> Condition in Middle Ages of,
> Habits in the Fiji Islands of,
> Worshipped as goddesses by,
> Weaker in moral sense than,
> Idealism of,
> Greater conscientiousness of,
> South Sea Islanders, age of puberty among,
> Attractiveness of,
> Offered as sacrifice to,
> Small size of brain of,
> Profounder sub-consciousness of,
> Less hair on the body of,
> Mental, moral and physical inferiority of,
> Love of children of,
> Greater length of life of,
> Weaker muscles of,
> Strength of affections of,
> Vanity of,
> Higher education of,
> Shakespeare's opinion of,
> Lord Birkenhead's opinion of,
> Dean Inge's opinion of,
> La Bruyère's opinion of,
> Dr Johnson's opinion of,
> Mr Oscar Browning's opinion of . . .

Here I drew breath and added, indeed, in the margin, Why does
Samuel Butler say, 'Wise men never say what they think of

women?' Wise men never say anything else apparently. But, I continued, leaning back in my chair and looking at the vast dome in which I was a single but by now somewhat harassed thought, what is so unfortunate is that wise men never think the same thing about women. Here is Pope:

> Most women have no character at all.[2]

And here is La Bruyère:

> Les femmes sont extrêmes; elles sont meilleures ou pires que les hommes —[3]

a direct contradiction by keen observers who were contemporary. Are they capable of education or incapable? Napoleon thought them incapable. Dr Johnson thought the opposite.* Have they souls or have they not souls? Some savages[4] say they have none. Others, on the contrary, maintain that women are half divine and worship them on that account.† Some sages hold that they are shallower in the brain; others that they are deeper in the consciousness. Goethe honoured them; Mussolini despises them. Wherever one looked men thought about women and thought differently. It was impossible to make head or tail of it all, I decided, glancing with envy at the reader next door who was making the neatest abstracts, headed often with an A or a B or a C, while my own notebook rioted with the wildest scribble of contradictory jottings. It was distressing, it was bewildering, it was humiliating. Truth had run through my fingers. Every drop had escaped

I could not possibly go home, I reflected, and add as a serious contribution to the study of women and fiction that women

---

* '"Men know that women are an overmatch for them, and therefore they choose the weakest or the most ignorant. If they did not think so, they never could be afraid of women knowing as much as themselves." ... In justice to the sex, I think it but candid to acknowledge that, in a subsequent conversation, he told me that he was serious in what he said.' – Boswell, *The Journal of a Tour to the Hebrides*.

† 'The ancient Germans believed that there was something holy in women, and accordingly consulted them as oracles.' – Frazer, *Golden Bough*.

have less hair on their bodies than men, or that the age of puberty among the South Sea Islanders is nine – or is it ninety? – even the handwriting had become in its distraction indecipherable. It was disgraceful to have nothing more weighty or respectable to show after a whole morning's work. And if I could not grasp the truth about W. (as for brevity's sake I had come to call her) in the past, why bother about W. in the future? It seemed pure waste of time to consult all those gentlemen who specialize in woman and her effect on whatever it may be – politics, children, wages, morality – numerous and learned as they are. One might as well leave their books unopened.

But while I pondered I had unconsciously, in my listlessness, in my desperation, been drawing a picture where I should, like my neighbour, have been writing a conclusion. I had been drawing a face, a figure. It was the face and the figure of Professor von X. engaged in writing his monumental work entitled *The Mental, Moral, and Physical Inferiority of the Female Sex*. He was not in my picture a man attractive to women. He was heavily built; he had a great jowl; to balance that he had very small eyes; he was very red in the face. His expression suggested that he was labouring under some emotion that made him jab his pen on the paper as if he were killing some noxious insect as he wrote, but even when he had killed it that did not satisfy him; he must go on killing it; and even so, some cause for anger and irritation remained. Could it be his wife, I asked, looking at my picture? Was she in love with a cavalry officer? Was the cavalry officer slim and elegant and dressed in astrachan? Had he been laughed at, to adopt the Freudian theory,[5] in his cradle by a pretty girl? For even in his cradle the professor, I thought, could not have been an attractive child. Whatever the reason, the professor was made to look very angry and very ugly in my sketch, as he wrote his great book upon the mental, moral and physical inferiority of women. Drawing pictures was an idle way of finishing an unprofitable morning's work. Yet it is in our idleness, in our dreams, that the submerged truth sometimes comes to the top. A very elementary exercise in psychology, not to be dignified by the name of psycho-analysis, showed me, on looking at my notebook, that the sketch of the angry professor had been made in anger. Anger had snatched my pencil while I dreamt. But what was anger doing there? Interest, confusion, amusement, boredom – all these emotions I could trace and name as they succeeded each other throughout the morning. Had anger, the black snake, been lurking among them? Yes, said the sketch, anger had. It referred me unmistakably to the one book, to the one phrase, which had roused the demon; it was the professor's statement about the mental, moral and physical inferiority of women. My heart had leapt. My cheeks had burnt. I had flushed with anger. There was nothing specially remarkable, however foolish, in that. One does not like to be told that one is naturally the inferior of a little man – I looked at the student next me – who breathes hard, wears a ready-made tie, and has not shaved this fortnight. One has certain foolish vanities. It is only human nature, I reflected, and began drawing cartwheels and circles over the angry professor's face till he looked like a burning bush or a flaming comet – anyhow, an apparition without human semblance or significance. The professor was nothing now but a faggot burning on the top of Hampstead Heath. Soon my own anger was explained and done with; but curiosity remained. How explain the anger of the professors? Why were they angry? For when it came to analysing the impression left by these books there was always an element of heat. This heat took many forms; it showed itself in satire, in sentiment, in curiosity, in reprobation. But there was another element which was often present and could not immediately be identified. Anger, I called it. But it was anger that had gone underground and mixed itself with all kinds of other emotions. To judge from its odd effects, it was anger disguised and complex, not anger simple and open.

Whatever the reason, all these books, I thought, surveying the pile on the desk, are worthless for my purposes. They were worthless scientifically, that is to say, though humanly they were full of instruction, interest, boredom, and very queer facts about

the habits of the Fiji Islanders. They had been written in the red
light of emotion and not in the white light of truth. Therefore
they must be returned to the central desk and restored each to
his own cell in the enormous honeycomb. All that I had retrieved
from that morning's work had been the one fact of anger. The
professors – I lumped them together thus – were angry. But
why, I asked myself, having returned the books, why, I repeated,
standing under the colonnade among the pigeons and the prehis-
toric canoes, why are they angry? And, asking myself this
question, I strolled off to find a place for luncheon. What is the
real nature of what I call for the moment their anger? I asked.
Here was a puzzle that would last all the time that it takes to be
served with food in a small restaurant somewhere near the
British Museum. Some previous luncher had left the lunch
edition of the evening paper on a chair, and, waiting to be
served, I began idly reading the headlines. A ribbon of very
large letters ran across the page. Somebody had made a big score
in South Africa. Lesser ribbons announced that Sir Austen
Chamberlain[6] was at Geneva. A meat axe with human hair on it
had been found in a cellar. Mr Justice — commented in the
Divorce Courts upon the Shamelessness of Women. Sprinkled
about the paper were other pieces of news. A film actress had
been lowered from a peak in California and hung suspended in
mid-air. The weather was going to be foggy. The most transient
visitor to this planet, I thought, who picked up this paper could
not fail to be aware, even from this scattered testimony, that
England is under the rule of a patriarchy. Nobody in their senses
could fail to detect the dominance of the professor. His was the
power and the money and the influence. He was the proprietor of
the paper and its editor and sub-editor. He was the Foreign
Secretary and the Judge. He was the cricketer; he owned the
racehorses and the yachts. He was the director of the company
that pays two hundred per cent to its shareholders. He left
millions to charities and colleges that were ruled by himself. He
suspended the film actress in mid-air. He will decide if the hair
on the meat axe is human; he it is who will acquit or convict the

murderer, and hang him, or let him go free. With the exception of the fog he seemed to control everything. Yet he was angry. I knew that he was angry by this token. When I read what he wrote about women I thought, not of what he was saying, but of himself. When an arguer argues dispassionately he thinks only of the argument; and the reader cannot help thinking of the argument too. If he had written dispassionately about women, had used indisputable proofs to establish his argument and had shown no trace of wishing that the result should be one thing rather than another, one would not have been angry either. One would have accepted the fact, as one accepts the fact that a pea is green or a canary yellow. So be it, I should have said. But I had been angry because he was angry. Yet it seemed absurd, I thought, turning over the evening paper, that a man with all this power should be angry. Or is anger, I wondered, somehow, the familiar, the attendant sprite on power? Rich people, for example, are often angry because they suspect that the poor want to seize their wealth. The professors, or patriarchs, as it might be more accurate to call them, might be angry for that reason partly, but partly for one that lies a little less obviously on the surface. Possibly they were not 'angry' at all; often, indeed, they were admiring, devoted, exemplary in the relations of private life. Possibly when the professor insisted a little too emphatically upon the inferiority of women, he was concerned not with their inferiority, but with his own superiority. That was what he was protecting rather hot-headedly and with too much emphasis, because it was a jewel to him of the rarest price. Life for both sexes – and I looked at them, shouldering their way along the pavement – is arduous, difficult, a perpetual struggle. It calls for gigantic courage and strength. More than anything, perhaps, creatures of illusion as we are, it calls for confidence in oneself. Without self-confidence we are as babes in the cradle. And how can we generate this imponderable quality, which is yet so invaluable, most quickly? By thinking that other people are inferior to oneself. By feeling that one has some innate superiority – it may be wealth, or rank, a straight nose, or the portrait of a grandfather by Romney – for there is no end to the pathetic devices of the human imagination – over other people. Hence the enormous importance to a patriarch who has to conquer, who has to rule, of feeling that great numbers of people, half the human race indeed, are by nature inferior to himself. It must indeed be one of the chief sources of his power. But let me turn the light of this observation on to real life, I thought. Does it help to explain some of those psychological puzzles that one notes in the margin of daily life? Does it explain my astonishment the other day when Z, most humane, most modest of men, taking up some book by Rebecca West[7] and reading a passage in it, exclaimed, 'The arrant feminist! She says that men are snobs!' The exclamation, to me so surprising – for why was Miss West an arrant feminist for making a possibly true if uncomplimentary statement about the other sex? – was not merely the cry of wounded vanity; it was a protest against some infringement of his power to believe in himself. Women have served all these centuries as looking-glasses possessing the magic and delicious power of reflecting the figure of man at twice its natural size. Without that power probably the earth would still be swamp and jungle. The glories of all our wars would be unknown. We should still be scratching the outlines of deer on the remains of mutton bones and bartering flints for sheep skins or whatever simple ornament took our unsophisticated taste. Supermen and Fingers of Destiny would never have existed. The Czar and the Kaiser would never have worn crowns or lost them. Whatever may be their use in civilized societies, mirrors are essential to all violent and heroic action. That is why Napoleon and Mussolini[8] both insist so emphatically upon the inferiority of women, for if they were not inferior, they would cease to enlarge. That serves to explain in part the necessity that women so often are to men. And it serves to explain how restless they are under her criticism; how impossible it is for her to say to them this book is bad, this picture is feeble, or whatever it may be, without giving far more pain and rousing far more anger than a man would do who gave the same criticism. For if she begins to tell the truth, the figure in the looking-glass shrinks; his fitness for life is diminished. How is he to go on giving judgement, civilizing natives, making laws, writing books, dressing up and speechifying at banquets, unless he can see himself at breakfast and at dinner at least twice the size he really is? So I reflected, crumbling my bread and stirring my coffee and now and again looking at the people in the street. The looking-glass vision is of supreme importance because it charges the vitality; it stimulates the nervous system. Take it away and man may die, like the drug fiend deprived of his cocaine. Under the spell of that illusion, I thought, looking out of the window, half the people on the pavement are striding to work. They put on their hats and coats in the morning under its agreeable rays. They start the day confident, braced, believing themselves desired at Miss Smith's tea party; they say to themselves as they go into the room, I am the superior of half the people here, and it is thus that they speak with that self-confidence, that self-assurance, which have had such profound consequences in public life and lead to such curious notes in the margin of the private mind.

But these contributions to the dangerous and fascinating subject of the psychology of the other sex – it is one, I hope, that you will investigate when you have five hundred a year of your own – were interrupted by the necessity of paying the bill. It came to five shillings and ninepence. I gave the waiter a ten-shilling note and he went to bring me change. There was another ten-shilling note in my purse; I noticed it, because it is a fact that still takes my breath away – the power of my purse to breed ten-shilling notes automatically. I open it and there they are. Society gives me chicken and coffee, bed and lodging, in return for a certain number of pieces of paper which were left me by an aunt, for no other reason than that I share her name.

My aunt, Mary Beton, I must tell you, died by a fall from her horse when she was riding out to take the air in Bombay. The news of my legacy reached me one night about the same time that the act was passed that gave votes to women. A solicitor's letter fell into the post-box and when I opened it I found that

she had left me five hundred pounds a year for ever.[9] Of the two
– the vote and the money – the money, I own, seemed infinitely
the more important. Before that I had made my living by
cadging odd jobs from newspapers, by reporting a donkey show
here or a wedding there; I had earned a few pounds by addressing
envelopes, reading to old ladies, making artificial flowers, teaching the alphabet to small children in a kindergarten. Such were
the chief occupations that were open to women before 1918. I
need not, I am afraid, describe in any detail the hardness of the
work, for you know perhaps women who have done it; nor the
difficulty of living on the money when it was earned, for you
may have tried. But what still remains with me as a worse
infliction than either was the poison of fear and bitterness which
those days bred in me. To begin with, always to be doing work
that one did not wish to do, and to do it like a slave, flattering
and fawning, not always necessarily perhaps, but it seemed
necessary and the stakes were too great to run risks; and then the
thought of that one gift which it was death to hide – a small one
but dear to the possessor – perishing and with it my self, my
soul – all this became like a rust eating away the bloom of the
spring, destroying the tree at its heart. However, as I say, my
aunt died; and whenever I change a ten-shilling note a little of
that rust and corrosion is rubbed off; fear and bitterness go.
Indeed, I thought, slipping the silver into my purse, it is
remarkable, remembering the bitterness of those days, what a
change of temper a fixed income will bring about. No force in
the world can take from me my five hundred pounds. Food,
house and clothing are mine for ever. Therefore not merely do
effort and labour cease, but also hatred and bitterness. I need not
hate any man; he cannot hurt me. I need not flatter any man; he
has nothing to give me. So imperceptibly I found myself adopting a new attitude towards the other half of the human race. It
was absurd to blame any class or any sex, as a whole. Great
bodies of people are never responsible for what they do. They
are driven by instincts which are not within their control. They
too, the patriarchs, the professors, had endless difficulties, terrible

drawbacks to contend with. Their education had been in some ways as faulty as my own. It had bred in them defects as great. True, they had money and power, but only at the cost of harbouring in their breasts an eagle, a vulture, for ever tearing the liver out and plucking at the lungs – the instinct for possession, the rage for acquisition which drives them to desire other people's fields and goods perpetually; to make frontiers and flags; battleships and poison gas; to offer up their own lives and their children's lives. Walk through the Admiralty Arch (I had reached that monument), or any other avenue given up to trophies and cannon, and reflect upon the kind of glory celebrated there. Or watch in the spring sunshine the stockbroker and the great barrister going indoors to make money and more money and more money when it is a fact that five hundred pounds a year will keep one alive in the sunshine. These are unpleasant instincts to harbour, I reflected. They are bred of the conditions of life; of the lack of civilization, I thought, looking at the statue of the Duke of Cambridge, and in particular at the feathers in his cocked hat, with a fixity that they have scarcely ever received before. And, as I realised these drawbacks, by degrees fear and bitterness modified themselves into pity and toleration; and then in a year or two, pity and toleration went, and the greatest release of all came, which is freedom to think of things in themselves. That building, for example, do I like it or not? Is that picture beautiful or not? Is that in my opinion a good book or a bad? Indeed my aunt's legacy unveiled the sky to me, and substituted for the large and imposing figure of a gentleman, which Milton recommended for my perpetual adoration, a view of the open sky.

So thinking, so speculating, I found my way back to my house by the river. Lamps were being lit and an indescribable change had come over London since the morning hour. It was as if the great machine after labouring all day had made with our help a few yards of something very exciting and beautiful – a fiery fabric flashing with red eyes, a tawny monster roaring with hot breath. Even the wind seemed flung like a flag as it lashed the houses and rattled the hoardings.

In my little street, however, domesticity prevailed. The house painter was descending his ladder; the nursemaid was wheeling the perambulator carefully in and out back to nursery tea; the coal-heaver was folding his empty sacks on top of each other; the woman who keeps the greengrocer's shop was adding up the day's takings with her hands in red mittens. But so engrossed was I with the problem you have laid upon my shoulders that I could not see even these usual sights without referring them to one centre. I thought how much harder it is now than it must have been even a century ago to say which of these employments is the higher, the more necessary. Is it better to be a coal-heaver or a nursemaid; is the charwoman who has brought up eight children of less value to the world than the barrister who has made a hundred thousand pounds? It is useless to ask such questions; for nobody can answer them. Not only do the comparative values of charwomen and lawyers rise and fall from decade to decade, but we have no rods with which to measure them even as they are at the moment. I had been foolish to ask my professor to furnish me with 'indisputable proofs' of this or that in his argument about women. Even if one could state the value of any one gift at the moment, those values will change; in a century's time very possibly they will have changed completely. Moreover, in a hundred years, I thought, reaching my own doorstep, women will have ceased to be the protected sex. Logically they will take part in all the activities and exertions that were once denied them. The nursemaid will heave coal. The shopwoman will drive an engine. All assumptions founded on the facts observed when women were the protected sex will have disappeared − as, for example (here a squad of soldiers marched down the street), that women and clergymen and gardeners live longer than other people. Remove that protection, expose them to the same exertions and activities, make them soldiers and sailors and engine-drivers and dock labourers, and will not women die off so much younger, so much quicker, than men that one will say, 'I saw a woman to-day', as one used to say, 'I saw an aeroplane'. Anything may happen when womanhood has ceased to be a protected occupation, I thought, opening the door. But what bearing has all this upon the subject of my paper, Women and Fiction? I asked, going indoors.

Chapter III

It was disappointing not to have brought back in the evening some important statement, some authentic fact. Women are poorer than men because – this or that. Perhaps now it would be better to give up seeking for the truth, and receiving on one's head an avalanche of opinion hot as lava, discoloured as dishwater. It would be better to draw the curtains; to shut out distractions; to light the lamp; to narrow the enquiry and to ask the historian, who records not opinions but facts, to describe under what conditions women lived, not throughout the ages, but in England, say in the time of Elizabeth.

For it is a perennial puzzle why no woman wrote a word of that extraordinary literature when every other man, it seemed, was capable of song or sonnet. What were the conditions in which women lived, I asked myself; for fiction, imaginative work that is, is not dropped like a pebble upon the ground, as science may be; fiction is like a spider's web, attached ever so lightly perhaps, but still attached to life at all four corners. Often the attachment is scarcely perceptible; Shakespeare's plays, for instance, seem to hang there complete by themselves. But when the web is pulled askew, hooked up at the edge, torn in the middle, one remembers that these webs are not spun in mid-air by incorporeal creatures, but are the work of suffering human beings, and are attached to grossly material things, like health and money and the houses we live in.

I went, therefore, to the shelf where the histories stand and took down one of the latest, Professor Trevelyan's *History of England*. Once more I looked up Women, found 'position of' and turned to the pages indicated. 'Wife-beating', I read, 'was a recognized right of man, and was practised without shame by high as well as low ... Similarly,' the historian goes on, 'the daughter who refused to marry the gentleman of her parents' choice was liable to be locked up, beaten and flung about the room, without any shock being inflicted on public opinion. Marriage was not an affair of personal affection, but of family avarice, particularly in the "chivalrous" upper classes ... Betrothal often took place while one or both of the parties was in the cradle, and marriage when they were scarcely out of the nurses' charge.' That was about 1470, soon after Chaucer's time. The next reference to the position of women is some two hundred years later, in the time of the Stuarts. 'It was still the exception for women of the upper and middle class to choose their own husbands, and when the husband had been assigned, he was lord and master, so far at least as law and custom could make him. Yet even so,' Professor Trevelyan concludes, 'neither Shakespeare's women nor those of authentic seventeenth-century memoirs, like the Verneys and the Hutchinsons, seem wanting in personality and character.' Certainly, if we consider it, Cleopatra must have had a way with her; Lady Macbeth, one would suppose, had a will of her own; Rosalind, one might conclude, was an attractive girl. Professor Trevelyan is speaking no more than the truth when he remarks that Shakespeare's women do not seem wanting in personality and character. Not being a historian, one might go even further and say that women have burnt like beacons in all the works of all the poets from the beginning of time – Clytemnestra, Antigone, Cleopatra, Lady Macbeth, Phèdre, Cressida, Rosalind, Desdemona, the Duchess of Malfi, among the dramatists; then among the prose writers: Millamant, Clarissa, Becky Sharp, Anna Karenine, Emma Bovary, Madame de Guermantes – the names flock to mind, nor do they recall women 'lacking in personality and character'. Indeed, if woman had no existence save in the fiction written by men, one would imagine her a person of the utmost importance; very various; heroic and mean; splendid and sordid; infinitely beautiful and hideous in the extreme; as great as a man, some think even greater.* But this is woman in fiction. In fact, as—

* 'It remains a strange and almost inexplicable fact that in Athena's city, where women were kept in almost Oriental suppression as odalisques or drudges, the

Professor Trevelyan points out, she was locked up, beaten and flung about the room.

A very queer, composite being thus emerges. Imaginatively she is of the highest importance; practically she is completely insignificant. She pervades poetry from cover to cover; she is all but absent from history. She dominates the lives of kings and conquerors in fiction; in fact she was the slave of any boy whose parents forced a ring upon her finger. Some of the most inspired words, some of the most profound thoughts in literature fall from her lips; in real life she could hardly read, could scarcely spell, and was the property of her husband.

It was certainly an odd monster that one made up by reading the historians first and the poets afterwards – a worm winged like an eagle; the spirit of life and beauty in a kitchen chopping up suet. But these monsters, however amusing to the imagination, have no existence in fact. What one must do to bring her to life was to think poetically and prosaically at one and the same moment, thus keeping in touch with fact – that she is Mrs Martin, aged thirty-six, dressed in blue, wearing a black hat and brown shoes; but not losing sight of fiction either – that she is a vessel in which all sorts of spirits and forces are coursing and flashing perpetually. The moment, however, that one tries this method with the Elizabethan woman, one branch of illumination fails; one is held up by the scarcity of facts. One knows nothing

---

stage should yet have produced figures like Clytemnestra and Cassandra, Atossa and Antigone, Phèdre and Medea, and all the other heroines who dominate play after play of the "misogynist" Euripides. But the paradox of this world where in real life a respectable woman could hardly show her face alone in the street, and yet on the stage woman equals or surpasses man, has never been satisfactorily explained. In modern tragedy the same predominance exists. At all events, a very cursory survey of Shakespeare's work (similarly with Webster, though not with Marlowe or Jonson) suffices to reveal how this dominance, this initiative of women, persists from Rosalind to Lady Macbeth. So too in Racine; six of his tragedies bear their heroines' names; and what male characters of his shall we set against Hermione and Andromaque, Bérénice and Roxane, Phèdre and Athalie? So again with Ibsen; what men shall we match with Solveig and Nora, Heda and Hilda Wangel and Rebecca West?' – F. L. Lucas, *Tragedy*, pp. 114–15.

detailed, nothing perfectly true and substantial about her. History scarcely mentions her. And I turned to Professor Trevelyan again to see what history meant to him. I found by looking at his chapter headings that it meant –

'The Manor Court and the Methods of Open-field Agriculture ... The Cistercians and Sheep-farming ... The Crusades ... The University ... The House of Commons ... The Hundred Years' War ... The Wars of the Roses ... The Renaissance Scholars ... The Dissolution of the Monasteries ... Agrarian and Religious Strife ... The Origin of English Sea-power ... The Armada ...' and so on. Occasionally an individual woman is mentioned, an Elizabeth, or a Mary; a queen or a great lady. But by no possible means could middle-class women with nothing but brains and character at their command have taken part in any one of the great movements which, brought together, constitute the historian's view of the past. Nor shall we find her in any collection of anecdotes. Aubrey[1] hardly mentions her. She never writes her own life and scarcely keeps a diary; there are only a handful of her letters in existence. She left no plays or poems by which we can judge her. What one wants, I thought – and why does not some brilliant student at Newnham or Girton supply it? – is a mass of information; at what age did she marry; how many children had she as a rule; what was her house like; had she a room to herself; did she do the cooking; would she be likely to have a servant? All these facts lie somewhere, presumably, in parish registers and account books; the life of the average Elizabethan woman must be scattered about somewhere, could one collect it and make a book of it. It would be ambitious beyond my daring, I thought, looking about the shelves for books that were not there, to suggest to the students of those famous colleges that they should rewrite history, though I own that it often seems a little queer as it is, unreal, lop-sided; but why should they not add a supplement to history? calling it, of course, by some inconspicuous name so that women might figure there without impropriety? For one often catches a glimpse of them in the lives of the great, whisking away into the background, concealing, I sometimes think, a wink, a laugh, perhaps a tear. And, after all, we have lives enough of Jane Austen; it scarcely seems necessary to consider again the influence of the tragedies of Joanna Baillie[2] upon the poetry of Edgar Allan Poe; as for myself, I should not mind if the homes and haunts of Mary Russell Mitford were closed to the public for a century at least. But what I find deplorable, I continued, looking about the bookshelves again, is that nothing is known about women before the eighteenth century. I have no model in my mind to turn about this way and that. Here am I asking why women did not write poetry in the Elizabethan age, and I am not sure how they were educated; whether they were taught to write; whether they had sitting-rooms to themselves; how many women had children before they were twenty-one; what, in short, they did from eight in the morning till eight at night. They had no money evidently; according to Professor Trevelyan they were married whether they liked it or not before they were out of the nursery, at fifteen or sixteen very likely. It would have been extremely odd, even upon this showing, had one of them suddenly written the plays of Shakespeare, I concluded, and I thought of that old gentleman, who is dead now, but was a bishop, I think, who declared that it was impossible for any woman, past, present, or to come, to have the genius of Shakespeare. He wrote to the papers about it. He also told a lady who applied to him for information that cats do not as a matter of fact go to heaven, though they have, he added, souls of a sort. How much thinking those old gentlemen used to save one! How the borders of ignorance shrank back at their approach! Cats do not go to heaven. Women cannot write the plays of Shakespeare.

3.

Be that as it may, I could not help thinking, as I looked at the works of Shakespeare on the shelf, that the bishop was right at least in this; it would have been impossible, completely and entirely, for any woman to have written the plays of Shakespeare in the age of Shakespeare. Let me imagine, since facts are so hard to come by, what would have happened had Shakespeare had a wonderfully gifted sister, called Judith, let us say. Shakespeare himself went, very probably – his mother was an heiress[3] – to the grammar school, where he may have learnt Latin – Ovid, Virgil and Horace – and the elements of grammar and logic. He was, it is well-known, a wild boy who poached rabbits, perhaps shot a deer, and had, rather sooner than he should have done, to marry a woman in the neighbourhood, who bore him a child rather quicker than was right. That escapade sent him to seek his fortune in London. He had, it seemed, a taste for the theatre; he began by holding horses at the stage door. Very soon he got work in the theatre, became a successful actor, and lived at the hub of the universe, meeting everybody, knowing everybody, practising his art on the boards, exercising his wits in the streets, and even getting access to the palace of the queen. Meanwhile his extraordinarily gifted sister, let us suppose, remained at home. She was as adventurous, as imaginative, as agog to see the world as he was. But she was not sent to school. She had no chance of learning grammar and logic, let alone of reading Horace and Virgil. She picked up a book now and then, one of her brother's perhaps, and read a few pages. But then her parents came in and told her to mend the stockings or mind the stew and not moon about with books and papers. They would have spoken sharply but kindly, for they were substantial people who knew the conditions of life for a woman and loved their daughter – indeed, more likely than not she was the apple of her father's eye. Perhaps she scribbled some pages up in an apple loft on the sly, but was careful to hide them or set fire to them. Soon, however, before she was out of her teens, she was to be betrothed to the son of a neighbouring wool-stapler. She cried out that marriage was hateful to her, and for that she was severely beaten by her father. Then he ceased to scold her. He begged her instead not to hurt him, not to shame him in this matter of her marriage. He would give her a chain of beads or a fine petticoat, he said; and there were tears in his eyes. How could she disobey him? How could she break his heart? The force of her own gift alone drove her to it. She made up a small parcel of her belongings, let herself down by a rope one summer's night and took the road to London. She was not seventeen. The birds that sang in the hedge were not more musical than she was. She had the quickest fancy, a gift like her brother's, for the tune of words. Like him, she had a taste for the theatre. She stood at the stage door; she wanted to act, she said. Men laughed in her face. The manager – a fat, loose-lipped man – guffawed. He bellowed something about poodles dancing and women acting[4] – no woman, he said, could possibly be an actress. He hinted – you can imagine what. She could get no training in her craft. Could she even seek her dinner in a tavern or roam the streets at midnight? Yet her genius was for fiction and lusted to feed abundantly upon the lives of men and women and the study of their ways. At last – for she was very young, oddly like Shakespeare the poet in her face, with the same grey eyes and rounded brows – at last Nick Greene[5] the actor-manager took pity on her; she found herself with child by that gentleman and so – who shall measure the heat and violence of the poet's heart when caught and tangled in a woman's body? – killed herself one winter's night and lies buried at some cross-roads where the omnibuses now stop outside the Elephant and Castle.

That, more or less, is how the story would run, I think, if a woman in Shakespeare's day had had Shakespeare's genius. But for my part, I agree with the deceased bishop, if such he was – it is unthinkable that any woman in Shakespeare's day should have had Shakespeare's genius. For genius like Shakespeare's is not born among labouring, uneducated, servile people. It was not born in England among the Saxons and the Britons. It is not born to-day among the working classes. How, then, could it have been born among women whose work began, according to Professor Trevelyan, almost before they were out of the nursery, who were forced to it by their parents and held to it by all the power of law and custom? Yet genius of a sort must have existed among women as it must have existed among the working classes. Now and again an Emily Brontë or a Robert Burns blazes out and proves its presence. But certainly it never got itself on to paper. When, however, one reads of a witch being ducked, of a woman possessed by devils, of a wise woman selling herbs, or even of a very remarkable man who had a mother, then I think we are on the track of a lost novelist, a suppressed poet, of some mute and inglorious[6] Jane Austen, some Emily Brontë who dashed her brains out on the moor or mopped and mowed about the highways crazed with the torture that her gift had put her to. Indeed, I would venture to guess that Anon, who wrote so many poems without signing them, was often a woman. It was a woman Edward Fitzgerald,[7] I think, suggested who made the ballads and the folk-songs, crooning them to her children, beguiling her spinning with them, or the length of the winter's night.

This may be true or it may be false – who can say? – but what is true in it, so it seemed to me, reviewing the story of Shakespeare's sister as I had made it, is that any woman born with a great gift in the sixteenth century would certainly have gone crazed, shot herself, or ended her days in some lonely cottage outside the village, half witch, half wizard, feared and mocked at. For it needs little skill in psychology to be sure that a highly gifted girl who had tried to use her gift for poetry would have been so thwarted and hindered by other people, so tortured and pulled asunder by her own contrary instincts, that she must have lost her health and sanity to a certainty. No girl could have walked to London and stood at a stage door and forced her way into the presence of actor-managers without doing herself a violence and suffering an anguish which may have been irrational – for chastity may be a fetish invented by certain societies for unknown reasons – but were none the less inevitable. Chastity had then, it has even now, a religious importance in a woman's life, and has so wrapped itself round with nerves and instincts that to cut it free and bring it to the light of day demands courage of the rarest. To have lived a free life in London in the sixteenth century would have meant for a woman who was poet and playwright a nervous stress and dilemma which might well have killed her. Had she survived, whatever she had written would have been twisted and deformed, issuing from a strained and morbid imagination. And undoubtedly, I thought, looking at the shelf where there are no plays by women, her work would have gone unsigned. That refuge she would have sought certainly. It was the relic of the sense of chastity that dictated anonymity to women even so late as the nineteenth century. Currer Bell, George Eliot, George Sand,[8] all the victims of inner strife as their writings prove, sought ineffectively to veil themselves by using the name of a man. Thus they did homage to the convention, which if not implanted by the other sex was liberally encouraged by them (the chief glory of a woman is not to be talked of, said Pericles, himself a much-talked-of man) that publicity in women is detestable. Anonymity runs in their blood. The desire to be veiled still possesses them. They are not even now as concerned about the health of their fame as men are, and, speaking generally, will pass a tombstone or a signpost without feeling an irresistible desire to cut their names on it, as Alf, Bert or Chas. must do in obedience to their instinct, which murmurs if it sees a fine woman go by, or even a dog, Ce chien est à moi. And, of course, it may not be a dog, I thought, remembering Parliament Square, the Sieges Allee[9] and other avenues; it may be a piece of land or a man with curly black hair. It is one of the great advantages of being a woman that one can pass even a very fine negress[10] without wishing to make an Englishwoman of her.

That woman, then, who was born with a gift of poetry in the sixteenth century, was an unhappy woman, a woman at strife against herself. All the conditions of her life, all her own instincts, were hostile to the state of mind which is needed to set free whatever is in the brain. But what is the state of mind that is most propitious to the act of creation, I asked? Can one come by any notion of the state that furthers and makes possible that strange activity? Here I opened the volume containing the Tragedies of Shakespeare. What was Shakespeare's state of mind, for instance, when he wrote Lear and Antony and Cleopatra? It was certainly the state of mind most favourable to poetry that there has ever existed. But Shakespeare himself said nothing about it. We only know casually and by chance that he 'never blotted a line'. Nothing indeed was ever said by the artist himself about his state of mind until the eighteenth century perhaps. Rousseau[11] perhaps began it. At any rate, by the nineteenth century self-consciousness had developed so far that it was the habit for men of letters to describe their minds in confessions and autobiographies. Their lives also were written, and their letters were printed after their deaths. Thus, though we do not know what Shakespeare went through when he wrote *Lear*, we do know what Carlyle went through when he wrote the *French Revolution*; what Flaubert went through when he wrote *Madame Bovary*; what Keats[12] was going through when he tried to write poetry against the coming of death and the indifference of the world.

And one gathers from this enormous modern literature of confession and self-analysis that to write a work of genius is almost always a feat of prodigious difficulty. Everything is against the likelihood that it will come from the writer's mind whole and entire. Generally material circumstances are against it. Dogs will bark; people will interrupt; money must be made; health will break down. Further, accentuating all these difficulties and making them harder to bear is the world's notorious indifference. It does not ask people to write poems and novels and histories; it does not need them. It does not care whether Flaubert finds the right word or whether Carlyle scrupulously verifies this or that fact. Naturally, it will not pay for what it does not want. And so the writer, Keats, Flaubert, Carlyle, suffers, especially in the creative years of youth, every form of distraction and discouragement. A curse, a cry of agony, rises from those books of analysis and confession. 'Mighty poets in their misery dead'[13] – that is the burden of their song. If anything comes through in spite of all this, it is a miracle, and probably no book is born entire and uncrippled as it was conceived.

But for women, I thought, looking at the empty shelves, these difficulties were infinitely more formidable. In the first place, to have a room of her own, let alone a quiet room or a sound-proof room, was out of the question, unless her parents were exceptionally rich or very noble, even up to the beginning of the nineteenth century. Since her pin money, which depended on the goodwill of her father, was only enough to keep her clothed, she was debarred from such alleviations as came even to Keats or Tennyson or Carlyle, all poor men, from a walking tour, a little journey to France, from the separate lodging which, even if it were miserable enough, sheltered them from the claims and tyrannies of their families. Such material difficulties were formidable; but much worse were the immaterial. The indifference of the world which Keats and Flaubert and other men of genius have found so hard to bear was in her case not indifference but hostility. The world did not say to her as it said to them, Write if you choose; it makes no difference to me. The world said with a guffaw, Write? What's the good of your writing? Here the psychologists of Newnham and Girton might come to our help, I thought, looking again at the blank spaces on the shelves. For surely it is time that the effect of discouragement upon the mind of the artist should be measured, as I have seen a dairy company measure the effect of ordinary milk and Grade A milk upon the body of the rat. They set two rats in cages side by side, and of the two one was furtive, timid and small, and the other was glossy, bold and big. Now what food do we feed women as artists upon? I asked, remembering, I suppose, that dinner of prunes and custard. To answer that question I had only to open the evening paper and to read that Lord Birkenhead is of opinion – but really I am not going to trouble to copy out Lord Birkenhead's opinion upon the writing of women. What Dean Inge says I will leave in peace. The Harley Street[14] specialist may be allowed to rouse the echoes of Harley Street with his vociferations without raising a hair on my head. I will quote, however, Mr Oscar Browning, because Mr Oscar Browning was a great figure in Cambridge at one time, and used to examine the students at Girton and Newnham. Mr Oscar Browning was wont to declare 'that the impression left on his mind, after looking over any set of examination papers, was that, irrespective of the marks he might give, the best woman was intellectually the inferior of the worst man.' After saying that Mr Browning went back to his rooms – and it is this sequel that endears him and makes him a human figure of some bulk and majesty – he went back to his rooms and found a stable-boy lying on the sofa – 'a mere skeleton, his cheeks were cavernous and sallow, his teeth were black, and he did not appear to have the full use of his limbs . . . "That's Arthur" [said Mr Browning]. "He's a dear boy really and most high-minded." '[15] The two pictures always seem to me to complete each other. And happily in this age of biography the two pictures often do complete each other, so that we are able to interpret the opinions of great men not only by what they say, but by what they do.

But though this is possible now, such opinions coming from the lips of important people must have been formidable enough even fifty years ago. Let us suppose that a father from the highest motives did not wish his daughter to leave home and become writer, painter or scholar. 'See what Mr Oscar Browning says,' he would say; and there was not only Mr Oscar Browning; there was the *Saturday Review*; there was Mr Greg – the 'essentials of a woman's being', said Mr Greg emphatically, 'are that *they are supported by, and they minister to, men*'[16] – there was an enormous body of masculine opinion to the effect that nothing could be expected of women intellectually. Even if her father did not read out loud these opinions, any girl could read them for herself; and the reading, even in the nineteenth century, must have lowered her vitality, and told profoundly upon her work. There would always have been that assertion – you cannot do this, you are incapable of doing that – to protest against, to overcome. Probably for a novelist this germ is no longer of much effect; for there have been women novelists of merit. But for painters it must still have some sting in it; and for musicians, I imagine, is even now active and poisonous in the extreme. The woman composer stands where the actress stood in the time of Shakespeare. Nick Greene, I thought, remembering the story I had

made about Shakespeare's sister, said that a woman acting put
him in mind of a dog dancing. Johnson repeated the phrase two
hundred years later of women preaching. And here, I said,
opening a book about music, we have the very words used again
in this year of grace, 1928, of women who try to write music.
'Of Mlle Germaine Tailleferre one can only repeat Dr Johnson's
dictum concerning a woman preacher, transposed into terms of
music. "Sir, a woman's composing is like a dog's walking on his
hind legs. It is not done well, but you are surprised to find it
done at all."'* So accurately does history repeat itself.

Thus, I concluded, shutting Mr Oscar Browning's life and
pushing away the rest, it is fairly evident that even in the
nineteenth century a woman was not encouraged to be an artist.
On the contrary, she was snubbed, slapped, lectured and ex-
horted. Her mind must have been strained and her vitality
lowered by the need of opposing this, of disproving that. For
here again we come within range of that very interesting and
obscure masculine complex which has had so much influence
upon the woman's movement; that deep-seated desire, not so
much that *she* shall be inferior as that *he* shall be superior, which
plants him wherever one looks, not only in front of the arts, but
barring the way to politics too, even when the risk to himself
seems infinitesimal and the suppliant humble and devoted. Even
Lady Bessborough, I remembered, with all her passion for
politics, must humbly bow herself and write to Lord Granville
Leveson-Gower: '. . . notwithstanding all my violence in politicks
and talking so much on that subject, I perfectly agree with you
that no woman has any business to meddle with that or any
other serious business, farther than giving her opinion (if she is
ask'd).'[17] And so she goes on to spend her enthusiasm where it
meets with no obstacle whatsoever, upon that immensely important subject, Lord Granville's maiden speech in the House of
Commons. The spectacle is certainly a strange one, I thought.
The history of men's opposition to women's emancipation is

* *A Survey of Contemporary Music*, Cecil Gray, p. 246.

more interesting perhaps than the story of that emancipation itself. An amusing book might be made of it if some young student at Girton or Newnham would collect examples and deduce a theory – but she would need thick gloves on her hands, and bars to protect her of solid gold.

But what is amusing now, I recollected, shutting Lady Bessborough, had to be taken in desperate earnest once. Opinions that one now pastes in a book labelled cock-a-doodle-dum and keeps for reading to select audiences on summer nights once drew tears, I can assure you. Among your grandmothers and great-grandmothers there were many that wept their eyes out. Florence Nightingale shrieked aloud in her agony.* Moreover, it is all very well for you, who have got yourselves to college and enjoy sitting-rooms – or is it only bed-sitting-rooms? – of your own to say that genius should disregard such opinions; that genius should be above caring what is said of it. Unfortunately, it is precisely the men or women of genius who mind most what is said of them. Remember Keats. Remember the words he had cut on his tombstone.[18] Think of Tennyson; think – but I need hardly multiply instances of the undeniable, if very unfortunate, fact that it is the nature of the artist to mind excessively what is said about him. Literature is strewn with the wreckage of men who have minded beyond reason the opinions of others.

And this susceptibility of theirs is doubly unfortunate, I thought, returning again to my original enquiry into what state of mind is most propitious for creative work, because the mind of an artist, in order to achieve the prodigious effort of freeing whole and entire the work that is in him, must be incandescent, like Shakespeare's mind, I conjectured, looking at the book which lay open at *Antony and Cleopatra*. There must be no obstacle in it, no foreign matter unconsumed.

For though we say that we know nothing about Shakespeare's state of mind, even as we say that, we are saying something about Shakespeare's state of mind. The reason perhaps why we

* See Florence Nightingale, *Cassandra*, printed in R. Strachey, *The Cause*.

know so little of Shakespeare – compared with Donne or Ben Jonson or Milton – is that his grudges and spites and antipathies are hidden from us. We are not held up by some 'revelation' which reminds us of the writer. All desire to protest, to preach, to proclaim an injury, to pay off a score, to make the world the witness of some hardship or grievance was fired out of him and consumed. Therefore his poetry flows from him free and unimpeded. If ever a human being got his work expressed completely, it was Shakespeare. If ever a mind was incandescent, unimpeded, I thought, turning again to the bookcase, it was Shakespeare's mind.

Chapter IV

That one would find any woman in that state of mind in the sixteenth century was obviously impossible. One has only to think of the Elizabethan tombstones with all those children kneeling with clasped hands; and their early deaths; and to see their houses with their dark, cramped rooms, to realize that no woman could have written poetry then. What one would expect to find would be that rather later perhaps some great lady would take advantage of her comparative freedom and comfort to publish something with her name to it and risk being thought a monster. Men, of course, are not snobs, I continued, carefully eschewing 'the arrant feminism' of Miss Rebecca West; but they appreciate with sympathy for the most part the efforts of a countess to write verse. One would expect to find a lady of title meeting with far greater encouragement than an unknown Miss Austen or a Miss Brontë at that time would have met with. But one would also expect to find that her mind was disturbed by alien emotions like fear and hatred and that her poems showed traces of that disturbance. Here is Lady Winchilsea, for example, I thought, taking down her poems. She was born in the year 1661; she was noble both by birth and by marriage; she was childless; she wrote poetry, and one has only to open her poetry to find her bursting out in indignation against the position of women:

> How are we fallen! fallen by mistaken rules,
> And Education's more than Nature's fools;
> Debarred from all improvements of the mind,
> And to be dull, expected and designed;
> And if some one would soar above the rest,
> With warmer fancy, and ambition pressed,
> So strong the opposing faction still appears,
> The hopes to thrive can ne'er outweigh the fears.

Clearly her mind has by no means 'consumed all impediments and become incandescent'. On the contrary, it is harassed and distracted with hates and grievances. The human race is split up for her into two parties. Men are the 'opposing faction'; men are hated and feared, because they have the power to bar her way to what she wants to do – which is to write.

> Alas! a woman that attempts the pen,
> Such a presumptuous creature is esteemed,
> The fault can by no virtue be redeemed.
> They tell us we mistake our sex and way;
> Good breeding, fashion, dancing, dressing, play,
> Are the accomplishments we should desire;
> To write, or read, or think, or to enquire,
> Would cloud our beauty, and exhaust our time,
> And interrupt the conquests of our prime,
> Whilst the dull manage of a servile house
> Is held by some our utmost art and use.

Indeed she has to encourage herself to write by supposing that what she writes will never be published; to soothe herself with the sad chant:

> To some few friends, and to thy sorrows sing,
> For groves of laurel thou wert never meant;
> Be dark enough thy shades, and be thou there content.

Yet it is clear that could she have freed her mind from hate and fear and not heaped it with bitterness and resentment, the fire was hot within her. Now and again words issue of pure poetry:

> Nor will in fading silks compose,
> Faintly the inimitable rose.

– they are rightly praised by Mr Murry, and Pope, it is thought, remembered and appropriated those others:

> Now the jonquille o'ercomes the feeble brain;
> We faint beneath the aromatic pain.[1]

It was a thousand pities that the woman who could write like that, whose mind was turned to nature and reflection, should have been forced to anger and bitterness. But how could she have helped herself? I asked, imagining the sneers and the laughter, the adulation of the toadies, the scepticism of the professional poet. She must have shut herself up in a room in the country to write, and been torn asunder by bitterness and scruples perhaps, though her husband was of the kindest, and their married life perfection. She 'must have', I say, because when one comes to seek out the facts about Lady Winchilsea, one finds, as usual, that almost nothing is known about her. She suffered terribly from melancholy, which we can explain at least to some extent when we find her telling us how in the grip of it she would imagine:

> My lines decried, and my employment thought
> An useless folly or presumptuous fault:

The employment, which was thus censured, was, as far as one can see, the harmless one of rambling about the fields and dreaming:

> My hand delights to trace unusual things,
> And deviates from the known and common way,
> Nor will in fading silks compose,
> Faintly the inimitable rose.

Naturally, if that was her habit and that was her delight, she could only expect to be laughed at; and, accordingly, Pope or Gay[2] is said to have satirized her 'as a blue-stocking with an itch for scribbling'. Also it is thought that she offended Gay by laughing at him. She said that his *Trivia* showed that 'he was more proper to walk before a chair than to ride in one.' But this is all 'dubious gossip' and, says Mr Murry, 'uninteresting'. But there I do not agree with him, for I should have liked to have had more even of dubious gossip so that I might have found out or made up some image of this melancholy lady, who loved wandering in the fields and thinking about unusual things and scorned, so rashly, so unwisely, 'the dull manage of a servile house'. But she became diffuse, Mr Murry says. Her gift is all grown about with weeds and bound with briars. It had no chance of showing itself for the fine distinguished gift it was. And so, putting her back on the shelf, I turned to the other great lady, the Duchess whom Lamb loved, hare-brained, fantastical Margaret of Newcastle,[3] her elder, but her contemporary. They were very different, but alike in this that both were noble and both childless, and both were married to the best of husbands. In both burnt the same passion for poetry and both are disfigured and deformed by the same causes. Open the Duchess and one finds the same outburst of rage, 'Women live like Bats or Owls, labour like Beasts, and die like Worms . . .' Margaret too might have been a poet; in our day all that activity would have turned a wheel of some sort. As it was, what could bind, tame or civilize for human use that wild, generous, untutored intelligence? It poured itself out, higgledy-piggledy, in torrents of rhyme and prose, poetry and philosophy which stand congealed in quartos and folios that nobody ever reads. She should have had a microscope put in her hand. She should have been taught to look at the stars and reason scientifically. Her wits were turned with solitude and freedom. No one checked her. No one taught her. The professors fawned on her. At Court they jeered at her. Sir Egerton Brydges complained of her coarseness – 'as flowing from a female of high rank brought up in the Courts'. She shut herself up at Welbeck alone.[4]

What a vision of loneliness and riot the thought of Margaret Cavendish brings to mind! as if some giant cucumber had spread itself over all the roses and carnations in the garden and choked them to death. What a waste that the woman who wrote 'the best bred women are those whose minds are civilest' should have frittered her time away scribbling nonsense and plunging ever deeper into obscurity and folly till the people crowded round her coach when she issued out. Evidently the crazy Duchess became a bogey to frighten clever girls with. Here, I remembered, putting away the Duchess and opening Dorothy Osborne's letters,[5] is Dorothy writing to Temple about the

Duchess's new book. 'Sure the poore woman is a little distracted, shee could never bee soe rediculous else as to venture at writeing book's and in verse too, if I should not sleep this fortnight I should not come to that.'

And so, since no woman of sense and modesty could write books, Dorothy, who was sensitive and melancholy, the very opposite of the Duchess in temper, wrote nothing. Letters did not count. A woman might write letters while she was sitting by her father's sick-bed. She could write them by the fire whilst the men talked without disturbing them. The strange thing is, I thought, turning over the pages of Dorothy's letters, what a gift that untaught and solitary girl had for the framing of a sentence, for the fashioning of a scene. Listen to her running on:

'After dinner wee sitt and talk till Mr B. com's in question and then I am gon. the heat of the day is spent in reading or working and about sixe or seven a Clock, I walke out into a Common that lyes hard by the house where a great many young wenches keep Sheep and Cow's and sitt in the shades singing of Ballads; I goe to them and compare their voyces and Beauty's to some Ancient Shepherdesses that I have read of and finde a vaste difference there, but trust mee I think these are as innocent as those could bee. I talke to them, and finde they want nothing to make them the happiest People in the world, but the knoledge that they are soe. most commonly when we are in the middest of our discourse one looks aboute her and spyes her Cow's goeing into the Corne and then away they all run, as if they had wing's at theire heels. I that am not soe nimble stay behinde, and when I see them driveing home theire Cattle I think tis time for mee to retyre too. when I have supped I goe into the Garden and soe to the syde of a small River that runs by it where I sitt downe and wish you with mee . . .'

One could have sworn that she had the makings of a writer in her. But 'if I should not sleep this fortnight I should not come to that' – one can measure the opposition that was in the air to a woman writing when one finds that even a woman with a great turn for writing has brought herself to believe that to write a book was to be ridiculous, even to show oneself distracted. And so we come, I continued, replacing the single short volume of Dorothy Osborne's letters upon the shelf, to Mrs Behn.[6]

And with Mrs Behn we turn a very important corner on the road. We leave behind, shut up in their parks among their folios, those solitary great ladies who wrote without audience or criticism, for their own delight alone. We come to town and rub shoulders with ordinary people in the streets. Mrs Behn was a middle-class woman with all the plebeian virtues of humour, vitality and courage; a woman forced by the death of her husband and some unfortunate adventures of her own to make her living by her wits. She had to work on equal terms with men. She made, by working very hard, enough to live on. The importance of that fact outweighs anything that she actually wrote, even the splendid 'A Thousand Martyrs I have made', or 'Love in Fantastic Triumph sat', for here begins the freedom of the mind, or rather the possibility that in the course of time the mind will be free to write what it likes. For now that Aphra Behn had done it, girls could go to their parents and say, You need not give me an allowance; I can make money by my pen. Of course the answer for many years to come was, Yes, by living the life of Aphra Behn! Death would be better! and the door was slammed faster than ever. That profoundly interesting subject, the value that men set upon women's chastity and its effect upon their education, here suggests itself for discussion, and might provide an interesting book if any student at Girton or Newnham cared to go into the matter. Lady Dudley, sitting in diamonds among the midges of a Scottish moor, might serve for frontispiece. Lord Dudley, *The Times* said when Lady Dudley died the other day, 'a man of cultivated taste and many accomplishments, was benevolent and bountiful, but whimsically despotic. He insisted upon his wife's wearing full dress, even at the remotest shooting-lodge in the Highlands; he loaded her with gorgeous jewels', and so on, 'he gave her everything – always excepting any measure of responsibility'. Then Lord Dudley had a stroke and she nursed him and ruled his estates with supreme competence for ever after. That whimsical despotism was in the nineteenth century too.

But to return. Aphra Behn proved that money could be made by writing at the sacrifice, perhaps, of certain agreeable qualities; and so by degrees writing became not merely a sign of folly and a distracted mind, but was of practical importance. A husband might die, or some disaster overtake the family. Hundreds of women began as the eighteenth century drew on to add to their pin money, or to come to the rescue of their families by making translations or writing the innumerable bad novels which have ceased to be recorded even in text-books, but are to be picked up in the fourpenny boxes in the Charing Cross Road.[7] The extreme activity of mind which showed itself in the later eighteenth century among women – the talking, and the meeting, the writing of essays on Shakespeare, the translating of the classics – was founded on the solid fact that women could make money by writing. Money dignifies what is frivolous if unpaid for. It might still be well to sneer at 'blue stockings with an itch for scribbling', but it could not be denied that they could put money in their purses. Thus, towards the end of the eighteenth century a change came about which, if I were rewriting history, I should describe more fully and think of greater importance than the Crusades or the Wars of the Roses. The middle-class woman began to write. For if *Pride and Prejudice* matters, and *Middlemarch* and *Villette* and *Wuthering Heights* matter, then it matters far more than I can prove in an hour's discourse that women generally, and not merely the lonely aristocrat shut up in her country house among her folios and her flatterers, took to writing. Without those forerunners, Jane Austen and the Brontës and George Eliot could no more have written than Shakespeare could have written without Marlowe, or Marlowe without Chaucer, or Chaucer without those forgotten poets who paved the ways and tamed the natural savagery of the tongue. For masterpieces are not single and solitary births; they are the outcome of many years of thinking in common, of thinking by the body of the people, so that the experience of the mass is behind the single voice. Jane Austen should have laid a wreath upon the grave of Fanny Burney, and George Eliot done homage to the robust shade of Eliza Carter[8] – the valiant old woman who tied a bell to her bedstead in order that she might wake early and learn Greek. All women together ought to let flowers fall upon the tomb of Aphra Behn, which is, most scandalously but rather appropriately, in Westminster Abbey, for it was she who earned them the right to speak their minds. It is she – shady and amorous as she was – who makes it not quite fantastic for me to say to you to-night: Earn five hundred a year by your wits.

Here, then, one had reached the early nineteenth century. And here, for the first time, I found several shelves given up entirely to the works of women. But why, I could not help asking, as I ran my eyes over them, were they, with very few exceptions, all novels? The original impulse was to poetry. The 'supreme head of song'[9] was a poetess. Both in France and in England the women poets precede the women novelists. Moreover, I thought, looking at the four famous names, what had George Eliot in common with Emily Brontë? Did not Charlotte Brontë fail entirely to understand Jane Austen? Save for the possibly relevant fact that not one of them had a child, four more incongruous characters could not have met together in a room – so much so that it is tempting to invent a meeting and a dialogue between them. Yet by some strange force they were all compelled when they wrote, to write novels. Had it something to do with being born of the middle class, I asked; and with the fact, which Miss Emily Davies a little later was so strikingly to demonstrate, that the middle-class family in the early nineteenth century was possessed only of a single sitting-room between them? If a woman wrote, she would have to write in the common sitting-room. And, as Miss Nightingale was so vehemently to complain – 'women never have an half hour . . . that they can call their own' – she was always interrupted. Still it would be easier to write prose and fiction there than to write poetry or a play. Less concentration is required. Jane Austen wrote like that to the end of her days. 'How she was able to effect all this', her nephew writes in his Memoir, 'is surprising, for she had no separate study to repair to, and most of the work must have been done in the general sitting-room, subject to all kinds of casual interruptions. She was careful that her occupation should not be suspected by servants or visitors or any persons beyond her own family party'.* Jane Austen hid her manuscripts or covered them with a piece of blotting-paper. Then, again, all the literary training that a woman had in the early nineteenth century was training in the observation of character, in the analysis of emotion. Her sensibility had been educated for centuries by the influences of the common sitting-room. People's feelings were impressed on her; personal relations were always before her eyes. Therefore, when the middle-class woman took to writing, she naturally wrote novels, even though, as seems evident enough, two of the four famous women here named were not by nature novelists. Emily Brontë should have written poetic plays; the overflow of George Eliot's capacious mind should have spread itself when the creative impulse was spent upon history or biography. They wrote novels, however; one may even go further, I said, taking *Pride and Prejudice* from the shelf, and say that they wrote good novels. Without boasting or giving pain to the opposite sex, one may say that *Pride and Prejudice* is a good book. At any rate, one would not have been ashamed to have been caught in the act of writing *Pride and Prejudice*. Yet Jane Austen was glad that a hinge creaked, so that she might hide her manuscript before anyone came in. To Jane Austen there was something discreditable in writing *Pride and Prejudice*. And, I wondered, would *Pride and Prejudice* have been a better novel if Jane Austen had not thought it necessary to hide her manuscript from visitors? I read a page or two to see; but I could not find any signs that her circumstances had harmed her work in the slightest. That, perhaps, was the chief miracle about it. Here was a woman about the year 1800 writing without hate, without bitterness, without fear, without protest, without preaching.

* *Memoir of Jane Austen*, by her nephew, James Edward Austen-Leigh.

That was how Shakespeare wrote, I thought, looking at *Antony and Cleopatra*; and when people compare Shakespeare and Jane Austen, they may mean that the minds of both had consumed all impediments; and for that reason we do not know Jane Austen and we do not know Shakespeare, and for that reason Jane Austen pervades every word that she wrote, and so does Shakespeare. If Jane Austen suffered in any way from her circumstances it was in the narrowness of life that was imposed upon her. It was impossible for a woman to go about alone. She never travelled; she never drove through London in an omnibus or had luncheon in a shop by herself. But perhaps it was the nature of Jane Austen not to want what she had not. Her gift and her circumstances matched each other completely. But I doubt whether that was true of Charlotte Brontë, I said, opening *Jane Eyre* and laying it beside *Pride and Prejudice*.

I opened it at chapter twelve and my eye was caught by the phrase 'Anybody may blame me who likes'. What were they blaming Charlotte Brontë for? I wondered. And I read how Jane Eyre used to go up on to the roof when Mrs Fairfax was making jellies and looked over the fields at the distant view. And then she longed – and it was for this that they blamed her – that 'then I longed for a power of vision which might overpass that limit; which might reach the busy world, towns, regions full of life I had heard of but never seen: that then I desired more of practical experience than I possessed; more of intercourse with my kind, of acquaintance with variety of character than was here within my reach. I valued what was good in Mrs Fairfax, and what was good in Adèle; but I believed in the existence of other and more vivid kinds of goodness, and what I believed in I wished to behold.

'Who blames me? Many, no doubt, and I shall be called discontented. I could not help it: the restlessness was in my nature; it agitated me to pain sometimes . . .

'It is vain to say human beings ought to be satisfied with tranquillity: they must have action; and they will make it if they cannot find it. Millions are condemned to a stiller doom than mine, and millions are in silent revolt against their lot. Nobody knows how many rebellions ferment in the masses of life which people earth. Women are supposed to be very calm generally: but women feel just as men feel; they need exercise for their faculties and a field for their efforts as much as their brothers do; they suffer from too rigid a restraint, too absolute a stagnation, precisely as men would suffer; and it is narrow-minded in their more privileged fellow-creatures to say that they ought to confine themselves to making puddings and knitting stockings, to playing on the piano and embroidering bags. It is thoughtless to condemn them, or laugh at them, if they seek to do more or learn more than custom has pronounced necessary for their sex.

'When thus alone I not unfrequently heard Grace Poole's laugh . . .'

That is an awkward break, I thought.[10] It is upsetting to come upon Grace Poole all of a sudden. The continuity is disturbed. One might say, I continued, laying the book down beside *Pride and Prejudice*, that the woman who wrote those pages had more genius in her than Jane Austen; but if one reads them over and marks that jerk in them, that indignation, one sees that she will never get her genius expressed whole and entire. Her books will be deformed and twisted. She will write in a rage where she should write calmly. She will write foolishly where she should write wisely. She will write of herself where she should write of her characters. She is at war with her lot. How could she help but die young, cramped and thwarted?

One could not but play for a moment with the thought of what might have happened if Charlotte Brontë had possessed say three hundred a year – but the foolish woman sold the copyright of her novels outright for fifteen hundred pounds; had somehow possessed more knowledge of the busy world, and towns and regions full of life; more practical experience, and intercourse with her kind and acquaintance with a variety of character. In those words she puts her finger exactly not only upon her own defects as a novelist but upon those of her sex at that time. She knew, no one better, how enormously her genius would have profited if it had not spent itself in solitary visions over distant fields; if experience and intercourse and travel had been granted her. But they were not granted; they were withheld; and we must accept the fact that all those good novels, *Villette, Emma, Wuthering Heights, Middlemarch*, were written by women without more experience of life than could enter the house of a respectable clergyman; written too in the common sitting-room of that respectable house and by women so poor that they could not afford to buy more than a few quires of paper at a time upon which to write *Wuthering Heights* or *Jane Eyre*. One of them, it is true, George Eliot, escaped after much tribulation, but only to a secluded villa in St John's Wood. And there she settled down in the shadow of the world's disapproval. 'I wish it to be understood', she wrote, 'that I should never invite anyone to come and see me who did not ask for the invitation'; for was she not living in sin with a married man and might not the sight of her damage the chastity of Mrs Smith or whoever it might be that chanced to call? One must submit to the social convention, and be 'cut off from what is called the world'. [11] At the same time, on the other side of Europe, there was a young man living freely with this gipsy or with that great lady; going to the wars; picking up unhindered and uncensored all that varied experience of human life which served him so splendidly later when he came to write his books. Had Tolstoi lived at the Priory in seclusion with a married lady 'cut off from what is called the world', however edifying the moral lesson, he could scarcely, I thought, have written *War and Peace*.

But one could perhaps go a little deeper into the question of novel-writing and the effect of sex upon the novelist. If one shuts one's eyes and thinks of the novel as a whole, it would seem to be a creation owning a certain looking-glass likeness to life, though of course with simplifications and distortions innumerable. At any rate, it is a structure leaving a shape on the mind's eye, built now in squares, now pagoda shaped, now throwing out wings and arcades, now solidly compact and domed like the Cathedral of Saint Sofia at Constantinople. This shape, I thought, thinking back over certain famous novels, starts in one the kind of emotion that is appropriate to it. But that emotion at once blends itself with others, for the 'shape' is not made by the relation of stone to stone, but by the relation of human being to human being. Thus a novel starts in us all sorts of antagonistic and opposed emotions. Life conflicts with something that is not life. Hence the difficulty of coming to any agreement about novels, and the immense sway that our private prejudices have upon us. On the one hand, we feel You – John the hero – must live, or I shall be in the depths of despair. On the other, we feel, Alas, John, you must die, because the shape of the book requires it. Life conflicts with something that is not life. Then since life it is in part, we judge it as life. James is the sort of man I most detest, one says. Or, This is a farrago of absurdity. I could never feel anything of the sort myself. The whole structure, it is obvious, thinking back on any famous novel, is one of infinite complexity, because it is thus made up of so many different judgements, of so many different kinds of emotion. The wonder is that any book so composed holds together for more than a year or two, or can possibly mean to the English reader what it means for the Russian or the Chinese. But they do hold together occasionally very remarkably. And what holds them together in these rare instances of survival (I was thinking of *War and Peace*) is something that one calls integrity, though it has nothing to do with paying one's bills or behaving honourably in an emergency. What one means by integrity, in the case of the novelist, is the conviction that he gives one that this is the truth. Yes, one feels, I should never have thought that this could be so; I have never known people behaving like that. But you have convinced me that so it is, so it happens. One holds every phrase, every scene to the light as one reads – for Nature seems, very oddly, to have provided us with an inner light by which to judge of the novelist's integrity or disintegrity. Or perhaps it is rather that Nature, in her most irrational mood, has traced in invisible ink on the walls of the mind a premonition which these great artists confirm; a sketch which only needs to be held to the fire of genius to become visible. When one so exposes it and sees it come to life one exclaims in rapture, But this is what I have always felt and known and desired! And one boils over with excitement, and, shutting the book even with a kind of reverence as if it were something very precious, a stand-by to return to as long as one lives, one puts it back on the shelf, I said, taking *War and Peace* and putting it back in its place. If, on the other hand, these poor sentences that one takes and tests rouse first a quick and eager response with their bright colouring and their dashing gestures but there they stop: something seems to check them in their development: or if they bring to light only a faint scribble in that corner and a blot over there, and nothing appears whole and entire, then one heaves a sigh of disappointment and says, Another failure. This novel has come to grief somewhere.

And for the most part, of course, novels do come to grief somewhere. The imagination falters under the enormous strain. The insight is confused; it can no longer distinguish between the true and the false; it has no longer the strength to go on with the vast labour that calls at every moment for the use of so many different faculties. But how would all this be affected by the sex of the novelist, I wondered, looking at *Jane Eyre* and the others. Would the fact of her sex in any way interfere with the integrity of a woman novelist – that integrity which I take to be the backbone of the writer? Now, in the passages I have quoted from *Jane Eyre*, it is clear that anger was tampering with the integrity of Charlotte Brontë the novelist. She left her story, to which her entire devotion was due, to attend to some personal grievance. She remembered that she had been starved of her proper due of experience – she had been made to stagnate in a parsonage mending stockings when she wanted to wander free over the world. Her imagination swerved from indignation and we feel it swerve. But there were many more influences than anger tugging at her imagination and deflecting it from its path. Ignorance, for instance. The portrait of Rochester is drawn in the dark. We feel the influence of fear in it; just as we constantly feel an acidity which is the result of oppression, a buried suffering smouldering beneath her passion, a rancour which contracts those books, splendid as they are, with a spasm of pain.

And since a novel has this correspondence to real life, its values are to some extent those of real life. But it is obvious that the values of women differ very often from the values which have been made by the other sex; naturally, this is so. Yet it is the masculine values that prevail. Speaking crudely, football and sport are 'important'; the worship of fashion, the buying of clothes 'trivial'. And these values are inevitably transferred from life to fiction. This is an important book, the critic assumes, because it deals with war. This is an insignificant book because it deals with the feelings of women in a drawing-room. A scene in a battle-field is more important than a scene in a shop – everywhere and much more subtly the difference of value persists. The whole structure, therefore, of the early nineteenth-century novel was raised, if one was a woman, by a mind which was slightly pulled from the straight, and made to alter its clear vision in deference to external authority. One has only to skim those old forgotten novels and listen to the tone of voice in which they are written to divine that the writer was meeting criticism; she was saying this by way of aggression, or that by way of conciliation. She was admitting that she was 'only a woman', or protesting that she was 'as good as a man'. She met that criticism as her temperament dictated, with docility and diffidence, or with anger and emphasis. It does not matter which it was; she was thinking of something other than the thing itself. Down comes her book upon our heads. There was a flaw in the centre of it. And I thought of all the women's novels that lie scattered, like small pock-marked apples in an orchard, about the second-hand book shops of London. It was the flaw in the centre that had rotted them. She had altered her values in deference to the opinion of others.

But how impossible it must have been for them not to budge either to the right or to the left. What genius, what integrity it must have required in face of all that criticism, in the midst of that purely patriarchal society, to hold fast to the thing as they saw it without shrinking. Only Jane Austen did it and Emily Brontë. It is another feather, perhaps the finest, in their caps. They wrote as women write, not as men write.[12] Of all the thousand women who wrote novels then, they alone entirely ignored the perpetual admonitions of the eternal pedagogue – write this, think that. They alone were deaf to that persistent voice, now grumbling, now patronising, now domineering, now grieved, now shocked, now angry, now avuncular, that voice which cannot let women alone, but must be at them, like some too conscientious governess, adjuring them, like Sir Egerton Brydges, to be refined; dragging even into the criticism of poetry criticism of sex;* admonishing them, if they would be good and win, as I suppose, some shiny prize, to keep within certain limits which the gentleman in question thinks suitable – '. . . female novelists should only aspire to excellence by coura- geously acknowledging the limitations of their sex'.† That puts the matter in a nutshell, and when I tell you, rather to your surprise, that this sentence was written not in August 1828 but in August 1928, you will agree, I think, that however delightful it is to us now, it represents a vast body of opinion – I am not going to stir those old pools; I take only what chance has floated to my feet – that was far more vigorous and far more vocal a century ago. It would have needed a very stalwart young woman in 1828 to disregard all those snubs and chidings and promises of prizes. One must have been something of a firebrand to say to oneself, Oh, but they can't buy literature too. Literature is open

* '[She] has a metaphysical purpose, and that is a dangerous obsession, especially with a woman, for women rarely possess men's healthy love of rhetoric. It is a strange lack in the sex which is in other things more primitive and more materialistic.' – *New Criterion*, June 1928.
† 'If, like the reporter, you believe that female novelists should only aspire to excellence by courageously acknowledging the limitations of their sex (Jane Austen [has] demonstrated how gracefully this gesture can be accomplished . . .)' – *Life and Letters*, August 1928.[13]

to everybody. I refuse to allow you, Beadle though you are, to turn me off the grass. Lock up your libraries if you like; but there is no gate, no lock, no bolt that you can set upon the freedom of my mind.

But whatever effect discouragement and criticism had upon their writing – and I believe that they had a very great effect – that was unimportant compared with the other difficulty which faced them (I was still considering those early nineteenth-century novelists) when they came to set their thoughts on paper – that is that they had no tradition behind them, or one so short and partial that it was of little help. For we think back through our mothers if we are women.[14] It is useless to go to the great men writers for help, however much one may go to them for pleasure. Lamb, Browne, Thackeray, Newman, Sterne, Dickens, De Quincey – whoever it may be – never helped a woman yet, though she may have learnt a few tricks of them and adapted them to her use. The weight, the pace, the stride of a man's mind are too unlike her own for her to lift anything substantial from him successfully. The ape is too distant to be sedulous. Perhaps the first thing she would find, setting pen to paper, was that there was no common sentence ready for her use. All the great novelists like Thackeray and Dickens and Balzac have written a natural prose, swift but not slovenly, expressive but not precious, taking their own tint without ceasing to be common property. They have based it on the sentence that was current at the time. The sentence that was current at the beginning of the nineteenth century ran something like this perhaps: 'The grandeur of their works was an argument with them, not to stop short, but to proceed. They could have no higher excitement or satisfaction than in the exercise of their art and endless generations of truth and beauty. Success prompts to exertion; and habit facilitates success.' That is a man's sentence; behind it one can see Johnson, Gibbon[15] and the rest. It was a sentence that was unsuited for a woman's use. Charlotte Brontë, with all her splendid gift for prose, stumbled and fell with that clumsy weapon in her hands. George Eliot committed atrocities with it that beggar description. Jane Austen looked at it and laughed at it and devised a perfectly natural, shapely sentence proper for her own use and never departed from it. Thus, with less genius for writing than Charlotte Brontë, she got infinitely more said. Indeed, since freedom and fullness of expression are of the essence of the art, such a lack of tradition, such a scarcity and inadequacy of tools, must have told enormously upon the writing of women. Moreover, a book is not made of sentences laid end to end, but of sentences built, if an image helps, into arcades or domes. And this shape too has been made by men out of their own needs for their own uses. There is no reason to think that the form of the epic or of the poetic play suit a woman any more than the sentence suits her. But all the older forms of literature were hardened and set by the time she became a writer. The novel alone was young enough to be soft in her hands – another reason, perhaps, why she wrote novels. Yet who shall say that even now 'the novel' (I give it inverted commas to mark my sense of the words' inadequacy), who shall say that even this most pliable of all forms is rightly shaped for her use? No doubt we shall find her knocking that into shape for herself when she has the free use of her limbs; and providing some new vehicle, not necessarily in verse, for the poetry in her. For it is the poetry that is still denied outlet. And I went on to ponder how a woman nowadays would write a poetic tragedy in five acts. Would she use verse? – would she not use prose rather?

But these are difficult questions which lie in the twilight of the future. I must leave them, if only because they stimulate me to wander from my subject into trackless forests where I shall be lost and, very likely, devoured by wild beasts. I do not want, and I am sure that you do not want me, to broach that very dismal subject, the future of fiction, so that I will only pause here one moment to draw your attention to the great part which must be played in that future so far as women are concerned by physical conditions. The book has somehow to be adapted to the body, and at a venture one would say that women's books should be shorter, more concentrated, than those of men, and framed so that they do not need long hours of steady and uninterrupted work. For interruptions there will always be. Again, the nerves that feed the brain would seem to differ in men and women, and if you are going to make them work their best and hardest, you must find out what treatment suits them – whether these hours of lectures, for instance, which the monks devised, presumably, hundreds of years ago, suit them – what alternations of work and rest they need, interpreting rest not as doing nothing but as doing something but something that is different; and what should that difference be? All this should be discussed and discovered; all this is part of the question of women and fiction. And yet, I continued, approaching the bookcase again, where shall I find that elaborate study of the psychology of women by a woman? If through their incapacity to play football women are not going to be allowed to practise medicine –

Happily my thoughts were now given another turn.

Chapter V

I had come at last, in the course of this rambling, to the shelves which hold books by the living; by women and by men; for there are almost as many books written by women now as by men. Or if that is not yet quite true, if the male is still the voluble sex, it is certainly true that women no longer write novels solely. There are Jane Harrison's books on Greek archaeology; Vernon Lee's books on aesthetics; Gertrude Bell's books on Persia. There are books on all sorts of subjects which a generation ago no woman could have touched. There are poems and plays and criticism; there are histories and biographies, books of travel and books of scholarship and research; there are even a few philosophies and books about science and economics. And though novels predominate, novels themselves may very well have changed from association with books of a different feather. The natural simplicity, the epic age of women's writing, may have gone. Reading and criticism may have given her a wider range, a greater subtlety. The impulse towards autobiography may be spent. She may be beginning to use writing as an art, not as a method of self-expression. Among these new novels one might find an answer to several such questions.

I took down one of them at random. It stood at the very end of the shelf, was called *Life's Adventure*, or some such title, by Mary Carmichael,[1] and was published in this very month of October. It seems to be her first book, I said to myself, but one must read it as if it were the last volume in a fairly long series, continuing all those other books that I have been glancing at – Lady Winchilsea's poems and Aphra Behn's plays and the novels of the four great novelists. For books continue each other, in spite of our habit of judging them separately. And I must also consider her – this unknown woman – as the descendant of all those other women whose circumstances I have been glancing at and see what she inherits of their characteristics and restrictions. So, with a sigh, because novels so often provide an anodyne and not an antidote, glide one into torpid slumbers instead of rousing one with a burning brand, I settled down with a notebook and a pencil to make what I could of Mary Carmichael's first novel, *Life's Adventure*.

To begin with, I ran my eye up and down the page. I am going to get the hang of her sentences first, I said, before I load my memory with blue eyes and brown and the relationship that there may be between Chloe and Roger. There will be time for that when I have decided whether she has a pen in her hand or a pickaxe. So I tried a sentence or two on my tongue. Soon it was obvious that something was not quite in order. The smooth gliding of sentence after sentence was interrupted. Something tore, something scratched; a single word here and there flashed its torch in my eyes. She was 'unhanding' herself as they say in the old plays. She is like a person striking a match that will not light, I thought. But why, I asked her as if she were present, are Jane Austen's sentences not of the right shape for you? Must they all be scrapped because Emma and Mr Woodhouse are dead? Alas, I sighed, that it should be so. For while Jane Austen breaks from melody to melody as Mozart from song to song, to read this writing was like being out at sea in an open boat. Up one went, down one sank. This terseness, this short-windedness, might mean that she was afraid of something; afraid of being called 'sentimental' perhaps; or she remembers that women's writing has been called flowery and so provides a superfluity of thorns; but until I have read a scene with some care, I cannot be sure whether she is being herself or someone else. At any rate, she does not lower one's vitality, I thought, reading more carefully. But she is heaping up too many facts. She will not be able to use half of them in a book of this size. (It was about half the length of *Jane Eyre*.) However, by some means or other she succeeded in getting us all – Roger, Chloe, Olivia, Tony and Mr Bigham – in a canoe up the river. Wait a moment, I said, leaning back in my chair, I must consider the whole thing more carefully before I go any further.

I am almost sure, I said to myself, that Mary Carmichael is playing a trick on us. For I feel as one feels on a switchback railway when the car, instead of sinking, as one has been led to expect, swerves up again. Mary is tampering with the expected sequence. First she broke the sentence; now she has broken the sequence. Very well, she has every right to do both these things if she does them not for the sake of breaking, but for the sake of creating. Which of the two it is I cannot be sure until she has faced herself with a situation. I will give her every liberty, I said, to choose what that situation shall be; she shall make it of tin cans and old kettles if she likes; but she must convince me that she believes it to be a situation; and then when she has made it she must face it. She must jump. And, determined to do my duty by her as reader if she would do her duty by me as writer, I turned the page and read . . . I am sorry to break off so abruptly. Are there no men present? Do you promise me that behind that red curtain over there the figure of Sir Chartres Biron[2] is not concealed? We are all women you assure me? Then I may tell you that the very next words I read were these – 'Chloe liked Olivia . . .' Do not start. Do not blush. Let us admit in the privacy of our own society that these things sometimes happen. Sometimes women do like women.

'Chloe liked Olivia,' I read. And then it struck me how immense a change was there. Chloe liked Olivia perhaps for the first time in literature. Cleopatra did not like Octavia. And how completely *Antony and Cleopatra* would have been altered had she done so! As it is, I thought, letting my mind, I am afraid, wander a little from *Life's Adventure*, the whole thing is simplified, conventionalized, if one dared say it, absurdly. Cleopatra's only feeling about Octavia is one of jealousy. Is she taller than I am? How does she do her hair? The play, perhaps, required no more. But how interesting it would have been if the relationship between the two women had been more complicated. All these relationships between women, I thought, rapidly recalling the splendid gallery of fictitious women, are too simple. So much has been left out, unattempted. And I tried to remember any

case in the course of my reading where two women are represented as friends. There is an attempt at it in *Diana of the
Crossways*.[3] They are confidantes, of course, in Racine and the
Greek tragedies. They are now and then mothers and daughters.
But almost without exception they are shown in their relation to
men. It was strange to think that all the great women of fiction
were, until Jane Austen's day, not only seen by the other sex,
but seen only in relation to the other sex. And how small a part
of a woman's life is that; and how little can a man know even of
that when he observes it through the black or rosy spectacles
which sex puts upon his nose. Hence, perhaps, the peculiar
nature of women in fiction; the astonishing extremes of her
beauty and horror; her alternations between heavenly goodness
and hellish depravity – for so a lover would see her as his love
rose or sank, was prosperous or unhappy. This is not so true of
the nineteenth-century novelists, of course. Woman becomes
much more various and complicated there. Indeed it was the
desire to write about women perhaps that led men by degrees to
abandon the poetic drama which, with its violence, could make
so little use of them, and to devise the novel as a more fitting
receptacle. Even so it remains obvious, even in the writing of
Proust, that a man is terribly hampered and partial in his
knowledge of women, as a woman in her knowledge of men.

Also, I continued, looking down at the page again, it is
becoming evident that women, like men, have other interests
besides the perennial interests of domesticity. 'Chloe liked Olivia.
They shared a laboratory together . . .'[4] I read on and discovered
that these two young women were engaged in mincing liver,
which is, it seems, a cure for pernicious anæmia; although one of
them was married and had – I think I am right in stating – two
small children. Now all that, of course, has had to be left out,
and thus the splendid portrait of the fictitious woman is much
too simple and much too monotonous. Suppose, for instance,
that men were only represented in literature as the lovers of
women, and were never the friends of men, soldiers, thinkers,
dreamers; how few parts in the plays of Shakespeare could be

allotted to them; how literature would suffer! We might perhaps have most of Othello; and a good deal of Antony; but no Caesar, no Brutus, no Hamlet, no Lear, no Jaques – literature would be incredibly impoverished, as indeed literature is impoverished beyond our counting by the doors that have been shut upon women. Married against their will, kept in one room, and to one occupation, how could a dramatist give a full or interesting or truthful account of them? Love was the only possible interpreter. The poet was forced to be passionate or bitter, unless indeed he chose to 'hate women', which meant more often than not that he was unattractive to them.

Now if Chloe likes Olivia and they share a laboratory, which of itself will make their friendship more varied and lasting because it will be less personal; if Mary Carmichael knows how to write, and I was beginning to enjoy some quality in her style; if she has a room to herself, of which I am not quite sure; if she has five hundred a year of her own – but that remains to be proved – then I think that something of great importance has happened.

For if Chloe likes Olivia and Mary Carmichael knows how to express it she will light a torch in that vast chamber where nobody has yet been. It is all half lights and profound shadows like those serpentine caves where one goes with a candle peering up and down, not knowing where one is stepping. And I began to read the book again, and read how Chloe watched Olivia put a jar on a shelf and say how it was time to go home to her children. That is a sight that has never been seen since the world began, I exclaimed. And I watched too, very curiously. For I wanted to see how Mary Carmichael set to work to catch those unrecorded gestures, those unsaid or half-said words, which form themselves, no more palpably than the shadows of moths on the ceiling, when women are alone, unlit by the capricious and coloured light of the other sex. She will need to hold her breath, I said, reading on, if she is to do it; for women are so suspicious of any interest that has not some obvious motive behind it, so terribly accustomed to concealment and suppression, that they are off at the flicker of an eye turned observingly in their direction. The only way for you to do it, I thought, addressing Mary Carmichael as if she were there, would be to talk of something else, looking steadily out of the window, and thus note, not with a pencil in a notebook, but in the shortest of shorthand, in words that are hardly syllabled yet, what happens when Olivia – this organism that has been under the shadow of the rock these million years – feels the light fall on it, and sees coming her way a piece of strange food – knowledge, adventure, art. And she reaches out for it, I thought, again raising my eyes from the page, and has to devise some entirely new combination of her resources, so highly developed for other purposes, so as to absorb the new into the old without disturbing the infinitely intricate and elaborate balance of the whole.

But, alas, I had done what I had determined not to do; I had slipped unthinkingly into praise of my own sex. 'Highly developed' – 'infinitely intricate' – such are undeniably terms of praise, and to praise one's own sex is always suspect, often silly; moreover, in this case, how could one justify it? One could not go to the map and say Columbus discovered America and Columbus was a woman; or take an apple and remark, Newton discovered the laws of gravitation and Newton was a woman; or look into the sky and say aeroplanes are flying overhead and aeroplanes were invented by women. There is no mark on the wall to measure the precise height of women. There are no yard measures, neatly divided into the fractions of an inch, that one can lay against the qualities of a good mother or the devotion of a daughter, or the fidelity of a sister, or the capacity of a housekeeper. Few women even now have been graded at the universities; the great trials of the professions, army and navy, trade, politics and diplomacy have hardly tested them. They remain even at this moment almost unclassified. But if I want to know all that a human being can tell me about Sir Hawley Butts, for instance, I have only to open Burke or Debrett[5] and I shall find that he took such and such a degree; owns a hall; has an heir; was Secretary to a Board; represented Great Britain in

Canada; and has received a certain number of degrees, offices, medals and other distinctions by which his merits are stamped upon him indelibly. Only Providence can know more about Sir Hawley Butts than that.

When, therefore, I say 'highly developed', 'infinitely intricate' of women, I am unable to verify my words either in Whitaker, Debrett or the University Calendar. In this predicament what can I do? And I looked at the bookcase again. There were the biographies: Johnson and Goethe and Carlyle and Sterne and Cowper and Shelley and Voltaire and Browning and many others. And I began thinking of all those great men who have for one reason or another admired, sought out, lived with, confided in, made love to, written of, trusted in, and shown what can only be described as some need of and dependence upon certain persons of the opposite sex. That all these relation-ships were absolutely Platonic I would not affirm, and Sir William Joynson Hicks[6] would probably deny. But we should wrong these illustrious men very greatly if we insisted that they got nothing from these alliances but comfort, flattery and the pleasures of the body. What they got, it is obvious, was some-thing that their own sex was unable to supply; and it would not be rash, perhaps, to define it further, without quoting the doubtless rhapsodical words of the poets, as some stimulus, some renewal of creative power which is in the gift only of the opposite sex to bestow. He would open the door of drawing-room or nursery, I thought, and find her among her children perhaps, or with a piece of embroidery on her knee – at any rate, the centre of some different order and system of life, and the contrast between this world and his own, which might be the law courts or the House of Commons, would at once refresh and invigorate; and there would follow, even in the simplest talk, such a natural difference of opinion that the dried ideas in him would be fertilized anew; and the sight of her creating in a different medium from his own would so quicken his creative power that insensibly his sterile mind would begin to plot again, and he would find the phrase or the scene which was lacking when he put on his hat to visit her. Every Johnson has his Thrale, and holds fast to her for some such reasons as these, and when the Thrale marries[7] her Italian music master Johnson goes half mad with rage and disgust, not merely that he will miss his pleasant evenings at Streatham, but that the light of his life will be 'as if gone out'.

And without being Dr Johnson or Goethe or Carlyle or Voltaire, one may feel, though very differently from these great men, the nature of this intricacy and the power of this highly developed creative faculty among women. One goes into the room – but the resources of the English language would be much put to the stretch, and whole flights of words would need to wing their way illegitimately into existence before a woman could say what happens when she goes into a room. The rooms differ so completely; they are calm or thunderous; open on to the sea, or, on the contrary, give on to a prison yard; are hung with washing; or alive with opals and silks; are hard as horsehair or soft as feathers – one has only to go into any room in any street for the whole of that extremely complex force of femininity to fly in one's face. How should it be otherwise? For women have sat indoors all these millions of years, so that by this time the very walls are permeated by their creative force, which has, indeed, so overcharged the capacity of bricks and mortar that it must needs harness itself to pens and brushes and business and politics. But this creative power differs greatly from the creative power of men. And one must conclude that it would be a thousand pities if it were hindered or wasted, for it was won by centuries of the most drastic discipline, and there is nothing to take its place. It would be a thousand pities if women wrote like men, or lived like men, or looked like men, for if two sexes are quite inadequate, considering the vastness and variety of the world, how should we manage with one only? Ought not education to bring out and fortify the differences rather than the similarities? For we have too much likeness as it is, and if an explorer should come back and bring word of other sexes looking through the branches of other trees at other skies, nothing would be of greater service to humanity; and we should have the immense pleasure into the bargain of watching Professor X rush for his measuring-rods to prove himself 'superior'.

Mary Carmichael, I thought, still hovering at a little distance above the page, will have her work cut out for her merely as an observer. I am afraid indeed that she will be tempted to become, what I think the less interesting branch of the species – the naturalist-novelist, and not the contemplative. There are so many new facts for her to observe. She will not need to limit herself any longer to the respectable houses of the upper middle classes. She will go without kindness or condescension, but in the spirit of fellowship, into those small, scented rooms where sit the courtesan, the harlot and the lady with the pug dog. There they still sit in the rough and ready-made clothes that the male writer has had perforce to clap upon their shoulders. But Mary Carmichael will have out her scissors and fit them close to every hollow and angle. It will be a curious sight, when it comes, to see these women as they are, but we must wait a little, for Mary Carmichael will still be encumbered with that self-consciousness in the presence of 'sin' which is the legacy of our sexual barbarity. She will still wear the shoddy old fetters of class on her feet.

However, the majority of women are neither harlots nor courtesans; nor do they sit clasping pug dogs to dusty velvet all through the summer afternoon. But what do they do then? and there came to my mind's eye one of those long streets somewhere south of the river whose infinite rows are innumerably populated. With the eye of the imagination I saw a very ancient lady crossing the street on the arm of a middle-aged woman, her daughter, perhaps, both so respectably booted and furred that their dressing in the afternoon must be a ritual, and the clothes themselves put away in cupboards with camphor, year after year, throughout the summer months. They cross the road when the lamps are being lit (for the dusk is their favourite hour), as they must have done year after year. The elder is close on eighty; but if one asked her what her life has meant to her, she would say that she remembered the streets lit for the battle of Balaclava, or had heard the guns fire in Hyde Park for the birth of King Edward the Seventh.[8] And if one asked her, longing to pin down the moment with date and season, but what were you doing on the fifth of April 1868, or the second of November 1875, she would look vague and say that she could remember nothing. For all the dinners are cooked; the plates and cups washed; the children sent to school and gone out into the world. Nothing remains of it all. All has vanished. No biography or history has a word to say about it. And the novels, without meaning to, inevitably lie.

All these infinitely obscure lives remain to be recorded, I said, addressing Mary Carmichael as if she were present; and went on in thought through the streets of London feeling in imagination the pressure of dumbness, the accumulation of unrecorded life, whether from the women at the street corners with their arms akimbo, and the rings embedded in their fat swollen fingers, talking with a gesticulation like the swing of Shakespeare's words; or from the violet-sellers and match-sellers and old crones stationed under doorways; or from drifting girls whose faces, like waves in sun and cloud, signal the coming of men and women and the flickering lights of shop windows. All that you will have to explore, I said to Mary Carmichael, holding your torch firm in your hand. Above all, you must illumine your own soul with its profundities and its shallows, and its vanities and its generosities, and say what your beauty means to you or your plainness, and what is your relation to the ever-changing and turning world of gloves and shoes and stuffs swaying up and down among the faint scents that come through chemists' bottles down arcades of dress material over a floor of pseudo-marble. For in imagination I had gone into a shop; it was laid with black and white paving; it was hung, astonishingly beautifully, with coloured ribbons. Mary Carmichael might well have a look at that in passing, I thought, for it is a sight that would lend itself to the pen as fittingly as any snowy peak or rocky gorge in the Andes. And there is the girl behind the counter too – I would as

soon have her true history as the hundred and fiftieth life of
Napoleon or seventieth study of Keats and his use of Miltonic
inversion which old Professor Z and his like are now inditing.
And then I went on very warily, on the very tips of my toes (so
cowardly am I, so afraid of the lash that was once almost laid on
my own shoulders), to murmur that she should also learn to
laugh, without bitterness, at the vanities – say rather at the
peculiarities, for it is a less offensive word – of the other sex. For
there is a spot the size of a shilling at the back of the head which
one can never see for oneself. It is one of the good offices that
sex can discharge for sex – to describe that spot the size of a
shilling at the back of the head. Think how much women have
profited by the comments of Juvenal; by the criticism of Strindberg.[9] Think with what humanity and brilliancy men, from the
earliest ages, have pointed out to women that dark place at the
back of the head! And if Mary were very brave and very honest,
she would go behind the other sex and tell us what she found
there. A true picture of man as a whole can never be painted
until a woman has described that spot the size of a shilling. Mr
Woodhouse and Mr Casaubon[10] are spots of that size and nature.
Not of course that anyone in their senses would counsel her to
hold up to scorn and ridicule of set purpose – literature shows
the futility of what is written in that spirit. Be truthful, one
would say, and the result is bound to be amazingly interesting.
Comedy is bound to be enriched. New facts are bound to be discovered.

However, it was high time to lower my eyes to the page
again. It would be better, instead of speculating what Mary
Carmichael might write and should write, to see what in fact
Mary Carmichael did write. So I began to read again. I remembered that I had certain grievances against her. She had broken
up Jane Austen's sentence, and thus given me no chance of
pluming myself upon my impeccable taste, my fastidious ear.
For it was useless to say, 'Yes, yes, this is very nice; but Jane
Austen wrote much better than you do', when I had to admit
that there was no point of likeness between them. Then she had

gone further and broken the sequence – the expected order. Perhaps she had done this unconsciously, merely giving things their natural order, as a woman would, if she wrote like a woman. But the effect was somehow baffling; one could not see a wave heaping itself, a crisis coming round the next corner. Therefore I could not plume myself either upon the depths of my feelings and my profound knowledge of the human heart. For whenever I was about to feel the usual things in the usual places, about love, about death, the annoying creature twitched me away, as if the important point were just a little further on. And thus she made it impossible for me to roll out my sonorous phrases about 'elemental feelings', the 'common stuff of humanity', 'the depths of the human heart', and all those other phrases which support us in our belief that, however clever we may be on top, we are very serious, very profound and very humane underneath. She made me feel, on the contrary, that instead of being serious and profound and humane, one might be – and the thought was far less seductive – merely lazy minded and conventional into the bargain.

But I read on, and noted certain other facts. She was no 'genius' – that was evident. She had nothing like the love of Nature, the fiery imagination, the wild poetry, the brilliant wit, the brooding wisdom of her great predecessors, Lady Winchilsea, Charlotte Brontë, Emily Brontë, Jane Austen and George Eliot; she could not write with the melody and the dignity of Dorothy Osborne – indeed she was no more than a clever girl whose books will no doubt be pulped by the publishers in ten years' time. But, nevertheless, she had certain advantages which women of far greater gift lacked even half a century ago. Men were no longer to her 'the opposing faction'; she need not waste her time railing against them; she need not climb on to the roof and ruin her peace of mind longing for travel, experience and a knowledge of the world and character that were denied her. Fear and hatred were almost gone, or traces of them showed only in a slight exaggeration of the joy of freedom, a tendency to the caustic and satirical, rather than to the romantic, in her treatment of the other sex. Then there could be no doubt that as a novelist she enjoyed some natural advantages of a high order. She had a sensibility that was very wide, eager and free. It responded to an almost imperceptible touch on it. It feasted like a plant newly stood in the air on every sight and sound that came its way. It ranged, too, very subtly and curiously, among almost unknown or unrecorded things; it lighted on small things and showed that perhaps they were not small after all. It brought buried things to light and made one wonder what need there had been to bury them. Awkward though she was and without the unconscious bearing of long descent which makes the least turn of the pen of a Thackeray or a Lamb delightful to the ear, she had – I began to think – mastered the first great lesson; she wrote as a woman, but as a woman who has forgotten that she is a woman, so that her pages were full of that curious sexual quality which comes only when sex is unconscious of itself.

All this was to the good. But no abundance of sensation or fineness of perception would avail unless she could build up out of the fleeting and the personal the lasting edifice which remains unthrown. I had said that I would wait until she faced herself with 'a situation'. And I meant by that until she proved by summoning, beckoning and getting together that she was not a skimmer of surfaces merely, but had looked beneath into the depths. Now is the time, she would say to herself at a certain moment, when without doing anything violent I can show the meaning of all this. And she would begin – how unmistakable that quickening is! – beckoning and summoning, and there would rise up in memory, half forgotten, perhaps quite trivial things in other chapters dropped by the way. And she would make their presence felt while someone sewed or smoked a pipe as naturally as possible, and one would feel, as she went on writing, as if one had gone to the top of the world and seen it laid out, very majestically, beneath.

At any rate, she was making the attempt. And as I watched her lengthening out for the test, I saw, but hoped that she did not see, the bishops and the deans, the doctors and the professors,

the patriarchs and the pedagogues all at her shouting warning
and advice. You can't do this and you shan't do that! Fellows
and scholars only allowed on the grass! Ladies not admitted
without a letter of introduction! Aspiring and graceful female
novelists this way! So they kept at her like the crowd at a fence
on the race-course, and it was her trial to take her fence without
looking to right or to left. If you stop to curse you are lost, I
said to her; equally, if you stop to laugh. Hesitate or fumble and
you are done for. Think only of the jump, I implored her, as if I
had put the whole of my money on her back; and she went over
it like a bird. But there was a fence beyond that and a fence
beyond that. Whether she had the staying power I was doubtful,
for the clapping and the crying were fraying to the nerves. But
she did her best. Considering that Mary Carmichael was no
genius, but an unknown girl writing her first novel in a bed-
sitting-room, without enough of those desirable things, time,
money and idleness, she did not do so badly, I thought.

Give her another hundred years, I concluded, reading the last
chapter – people's noses and bare shoulders showed naked
against a starry sky, for someone had twitched the curtain in the
drawing-room – give her a room of her own and five hundred a
year, let her speak her mind and leave out half that she now puts
in, and she will write a better book one of these days. She will
be a poet, I said, putting *Life's Adventure*, by Mary Carmichael,
at the end of the shelf, in another hundred years' time.

Chapter VI

Next day the light of the October morning was falling in dusty shafts through the uncurtained windows, and the hum of traffic rose from the street. London then was winding itself up again; the factory was astir; the machines were beginning. It was tempting, after all this reading, to look out of the window and see what London was doing on the morning of the 26th of October 1928. And what was London doing? Nobody, it seemed, was reading *Antony and Cleopatra*. London was wholly indifferent, it appeared, to Shakespeare's plays. Nobody cared a straw – and I do not blame them – for the future of fiction, the death of poetry or the development by the average woman of a prose style completely expressive of her mind. If opinions upon any of these matters had been chalked on the pavement, nobody would have stooped to read them. The nonchalance of the hurrying feet would have rubbed them out in half an hour. Here came an errand-boy; here a woman with a dog on a lead. The fascination of the London street is that no two people are ever alike; each seems bound on some private affair of his own. There were the business-like, with their little bags; there were the drifters rattling sticks upon area railings; there were affable characters to whom the streets serve for clubroom, hailing men in carts and giving information without being asked for it. Also there were funerals to which men, thus suddenly reminded of the passing of their own bodies, lifted their hats. And then a very distinguished gentleman came slowly down a doorstep and paused to avoid collision with a bustling lady who had, by some means or other, acquired a splendid fur coat and a bunch of Parma violets. They all seemed separate, self-absorbed, on business of their own.

At this moment, as so often happens in London, there was a complete lull and suspension of traffic. Nothing came down the street; nobody passed. A single leaf detached itself from the plane tree at the end of the street, and in that pause and suspension fell. Somehow it was like a signal falling, a signal pointing to a force in things which one had overlooked. It seemed to point to a river, which flowed past, invisibly, round the corner, down the street, and took people and eddied them along, as the stream at Oxbridge had taken the undergraduate in his boat and the dead leaves. Now it was bringing from one side of the street to the other diagonally a girl in patent leather boots, and then a young man in a maroon overcoat; it was also bringing a taxi-cab; and it brought all three together at a point directly beneath my window; where the taxi stopped; and the girl and the young man stopped; and they got into the taxi; and then the cab glided off as if it were swept on by the current elsewhere.

The sight was ordinary enough; what was strange was the rhythmical order with which my imagination had invested it; and the fact that the ordinary sight of two people getting into a cab had the power to communicate something of their own seeming satisfaction. The sight of two people coming down the street and meeting at the corner seems to ease the mind of some strain, I thought, watching the taxi turn and make off. Perhaps to think, as I had been thinking these two days, of one sex as distinct from the other is an effort. It interferes with the unity of the mind. Now that effort had ceased and that unity had been restored by seeing two people come together and get into a taxi-cab. The mind is certainly a very mysterious organ, I reflected, drawing my head in from the window, about which nothing whatever is known, though we depend upon it so completely. Why do I feel that there are severances and oppositions in the mind, as there are strains from obvious causes on the body? What does one mean by 'the unity of the mind'? I pondered, for clearly the mind has so great a power of concentrating at any point at any moment that it seems to have no single state of being. It can separate itself from the people in the street, for example, and think of itself as apart from them, at an upper window looking down on them. Or it can think with other people spontaneously, as, for instance, in a crowd waiting to hear some piece of news read out. It can think back through its fathers or through its mothers, as I have said that a woman writing thinks back through her mothers. Again if one is a woman one is often surprised by a sudden splitting off of consciousness, say in walking down Whitehall, when from being the natural inheritor of that civilization, she becomes, on the contrary, outside of it, alien and critical. Clearly the mind is always altering its focus, and bringing the world into different perspectives. But some of these states of mind seem, even if adopted spontaneously, to be less comfortable than others. In order to keep oneself continuing in them one is unconsciously holding something back, and gradually the repression becomes an effort. But there may be some state of mind in which one could continue without effort because nothing is required to be held back. And this perhaps, I thought, coming in from the window, is one of them. For certainly when I saw the couple get into the taxi-cab the mind felt as if, after being divided, it had come together again in a natural fusion. The obvious reason would be that it is natural for the sexes to co-operate. One has a profound, if irrational, instinct in favour of the theory that the union of man and woman makes for the greatest satisfaction, the most complete happiness. But the sight of the two people getting into the taxi and the satisfaction it gave me made me also ask whether there are two sexes in the mind corresponding to the two sexes in the body, and whether they also require to be united in order to get complete satisfaction and happiness? And I went on amateurishly to sketch a plan of the soul so that in each of us two powers preside, one male, one female; and in the man's brain the man predominates over the woman, and in the woman's brain the woman predominates over the man. The normal and comfortable state of being is that when the two live in harmony together, spiritually co-operating. If one is a man, still the woman part of the brain must have effect; and a woman also must have intercourse with the man in her. Coleridge[1] perhaps meant this when he said that a great mind is androgynous. It is when this fusion takes place that the mind is fully fertilized and uses all its faculties. Perhaps a mind that is purely masculine cannot create any more than a mind that is purely feminine, I thought. But it would be well to test what one meant by man-womanly, and conversely by woman-manly, by pausing and looking at a book or two.

Coleridge certainly did not mean, when he said that a great mind is androgynous, that it is a mind that has any special sympathy with women; a mind that takes up their cause or devotes itself to their interpretation. Perhaps the androgynous mind is less apt to make these distinctions than the single-sexed mind. He meant, perhaps, that the androgynous mind is resonant and porous; that it transmits emotion without impediment; that it is naturally creative, incandescent and undivided. In fact one goes back to Shakespeare's mind as the type of the androgynous, of the man-womanly mind, though it would be impossible to say what Shakespeare thought of women. And if it be true that it is one of the tokens of the fully developed mind that it does not think specially or separately of sex, how much harder it is to attain that condition now than ever before. Here I came to the books by living writers, and there paused and wondered if this fact were not at the root of something that had long puzzled me. No age can ever have been as stridently sex-conscious as our own; those innumerable books by men about women in the British Museum are a proof of it. The Suffrage campaign was no doubt to blame. It must have roused in men an extraordinary desire for self-assertion; it must have made them lay an emphasis upon their own sex and its characteristics which they would not have troubled to think about had they not been challenged. And when one is challenged, even by a few women in black bonnets, one retaliates, if one has never been challenged before, rather excessively. That perhaps accounts for some of the characteristics that I remember to have found here, I thought, taking down a new novel by Mr A, who is in the prime of life and very well thought of, apparently, by the reviewers. I opened it. Indeed, it was delightful to read a man's writing again. It was so direct, so straightforward after the writing of women. It indicated such freedom of mind, such liberty of person, such confidence in himself. One had a sense of physical well-being in the presence of this well-nourished, well-educated, free mind, which had never been thwarted or opposed, but had had full liberty from birth to stretch itself in whatever way it liked. All this was admirable. But after reading a chapter or two a shadow seemed to lie across the page. It was a straight dark bar, a shadow shaped something like the letter 'I'. One began dodging this way and that to catch a glimpse of the landscape behind it. Whether that was indeed a tree or a woman walking I was not quite sure. Back one was always hailed to the letter 'I'. One began to be tired of 'I'. Not but what this 'I' was a most respectable 'I'; honest and logical; as hard as a nut, and polished for centuries by good teaching and good feeding. I respect and admire that 'I' from the bottom of my heart. But – here I turned a page or two, looking for something or other – the worst of it is that in the shadow of the letter 'I' all is shapeless as mist. Is that a tree? No, it is a woman. But . . . she has not a bone in her body, I thought, watching Phoebe, for that was her name, coming across the beach. Then Alan got up and the shadow of Alan at once obliterated Phoebe. For Alan had views and Phoebe was quenched in the flood of his views. And then Alan, I thought, has passions; and here I turned page after page very fast, feeling that the crisis was approaching, and so it was. It took place on the beach under the sun. It was done very openly. It was done very vigorously. Nothing could have been more indecent. But . . . I had said 'but' too often. One cannot go on saying 'but'. One must finish the sentence somehow, I rebuked myself. Shall I finish it, 'But – I am bored!' But why was I bored? Partly because of the dominance of the letter 'I' and the aridity, which, like the giant beech tree, it casts within its shade. Nothing will grow there. And partly for some more obscure reason. There seemed to be some obstacle, some impediment in Mr A's mind which blocked the fountain of creative energy and shored it within narrow limits. And remembering the lunch party at

Oxbridge, and the cigarette ash and the Manx cat and Tennyson and Christina Rossetti all in a bunch, it seemed possible that the impediment lay there. As he no longer hums under his breath, 'There has fallen a splendid tear from the passion-flower at the gate', when Phoebe crosses the beach, and she no longer replies, 'My heart is like a singing bird whose nest is in a water'd shoot', when Alan approaches what can he do? Being honest as the day and logical as the sun, there is only one thing he can do. And that he does, to do him justice, over and over (I said, turning the pages) and over again. And that, I added, aware of the awful nature of the confession, seems somehow dull. Shakespeare's indecency uproots a thousand other things in one's mind, and is far from being dull. But Shakespeare does it for pleasure; Mr A, as the nurses say, does it on purpose. He does it in protest. He is protesting against the equality of the other sex by asserting his own superiority. He is therefore impeded and inhibited and self-conscious as Shakespeare might have been if he too had known Miss Clough and Miss Davies.² Doubtless Elizabethan literature would have been very different from what it is if the woman's movement had begun in the sixteenth century and not in the nineteenth.

What, then, it amounts to, if this theory of the two sides of the mind holds good, is that virility has now become self-conscious – men, that is to say, are now writing only with the male side of their brains. It is a mistake for a woman to read them, for she will inevitably look for something that she will not find. It is the power of suggestion that one most misses, I thought, taking Mr B the critic in my hand and reading, very carefully and very dutifully, his remarks upon the art of poetry. Very able they were, acute and full of learning; but the trouble was that his feelings no longer communicated; his mind seemed separated into different chambers; not a sound carried from one to the other. Thus, when one takes a sentence of Mr B into the mind it falls plump to the ground – dead; but when one takes a sentence of Coleridge into the mind, it explodes and gives birth to all kinds of other ideas, and that is the only sort of writing of which one can say that it has the secret of perpetual life.

But whatever the reason may be, it is a fact that one must deplore. For it means – here I had come to rows of books by Mr Galsworthy and Mr Kipling – that some of the finest works of our greatest living writers fall upon deaf ears. Do what she will a woman cannot find in them that fountain of perpetual life which the critics assure her is there. It is not only that they celebrate male virtues, enforce male values and describe the world of men; it is that the emotion with which these books are permeated is to a woman incomprehensible. It is coming, it is gathering, it is about to burst on one's head, one begins saying long before the end. That picture will fall on old Jolyon's head;[3] he will die of the shock; the old clerk will speak over him two or three obituary words; and all the swans on the Thames will simultaneously burst out singing. But one will rush away before that happens and hide in the gooseberry bushes, for the emotion which is so deep, so subtle, so symbolical to a man moves a woman to wonder. So with Mr Kipling's officers who turn their backs; and his Sowers who sow the Seed; and his Men who are alone with their Work; and the Flag – one blushes at all these capital letters as if one had been caught eavesdropping at some purely masculine orgy. The fact is that neither Mr Galsworthy nor Mr Kipling has a spark of the woman in him. Thus all their qualities seem to a woman, if one may generalize, crude and immature. They lack suggestive power. And when a book lacks suggestive power, however hard it hits the surface of the mind it cannot penetrate within.

And in that restless mood in which one takes books out and puts them back again without looking at them I began to envisage an age to come of pure, of self-assertive virility,[4] such as the letters of professors (take Sir Walter Raleigh's letters, for instance) seem to forebode, and the rulers of Italy have already brought into being. For one can hardly fail to be impressed in Rome by the sense of unmitigated masculinity; and whatever the value of unmitigated masculinity upon the state, one may question the effect of it upon the art of poetry. At any rate, according to the newspapers, there is a certain anxiety about fiction in

Italy. There has been a meeting of academicians whose object it is 'to develop the Italian novel'. 'Men famous by birth, or in finance, industry or the Fascist corporations' came together the other day and discussed the matter, and a telegram was sent to the Duce expressing the hope 'that the Fascist era would soon give birth to a poet worthy of it'. We may all join in that pious hope, but it is doubtful whether poetry can come out of an incubator. Poetry ought to have a mother as well as a father. The Fascist poem, one may fear, will be a horrid little abortion such as one sees in a glass jar in the museum of some county town. Such monsters never live long, it is said; one has never seen a prodigy of that sort cropping grass in a field. Two heads on one body do not make for length of life.

However, the blame for all this, if one is anxious to lay blame, rests no more upon one sex than upon the other. All seducers and reformers are responsible: Lady Bessborough when she lied to Lord Granville; Miss Davies when she told the truth to Mr Greg. All who have brought about a state of sex-consciousness are to blame, and it is they who drive me, when I want to stretch my faculties on a book, to seek it in that happy age, before Miss Davies and Miss Clough were born, when the writer used both sides of his mind equally. One must turn back to Shakespeare then, for Shakespeare was androgynous; and so were Keats and Sterne and Cowper and Lamb and Coleridge. Shelley perhaps was sexless. Milton and Ben Jonson had a dash too much of the male in them. So had Wordsworth and Tolstoi. In our time Proust was wholly androgynous, if not perhaps a little too much of a woman. But that failing is too rare for one to complain of it, since without some mixture of the kind the intellect seems to predominate and the other faculties of the mind harden and become barren. However, I consoled myself with the reflection that this is perhaps a passing phase; much of what I have said in obedience to my promise to give you the course of my thoughts will seem out of date; much of what flames in my eyes will seem dubious to you who have not yet come of age.

Even so, the very first sentence that I would write here, I said,

crossing over to the writing-table and taking up the page headed
Women and Fiction, is that it is fatal for anyone who writes to
think of their sex. It is fatal to be a man or woman pure and
simple; one must be woman-manly or man-womanly. It is fatal
for a woman to lay the least stress on any grievance; to plead
even with justice any cause; in any way to speak consciously as a
woman. And fatal is no figure of speech; for anything written
with that conscious bias is doomed to death. It ceases to be
fertilized. Brilliant and effective, powerful and masterly, as it
may appear for a day or two, it must wither at nightfall; it
cannot grow in the minds of others. Some collaboration has to
take place in the mind between the woman and the man before
the art of creation can be accomplished. Some marriage of oppo-
sites has to be consummated. The whole of the mind must lie
wide open if we are to get the sense that the writer is communicat-
ing his experience with perfect fullness. There must be freedom
and there must be peace. Not a wheel must grate, not a light
glimmer. The curtains must be close drawn. The writer, I
thought, once his experience is over, must lie back and let his
mind celebrate its nuptials in darkness. He must not look or
question what is being done. Rather, he must pluck the petals
from a rose or watch the swans float calmly down the river. And
I saw again the current which took the boat and the undergraduate and the dead leaves; and the taxi took the man and the
woman, I thought, seeing them come together across the street,
and the current swept them away, I thought, hearing far off the
roar of London's traffic, into that tremendous stream.

Here, then, Mary Beton ceases to speak. She has told you how
she reached the conclusion – the prosaic conclusion – that it is
necessary to have five hundred a year and a room with a lock on
the door if you are to write fiction or poetry. She has tried to lay
bare the thoughts and impressions that led her to think this. She
has asked you to follow her flying into the arms of a Beadle,
lunching here, dining there, drawing pictures in the British
Museum, taking books from the shelf, looking out of the

window. While she has been doing all these things, you no doubt have been observing her failings and foibles and deciding what effect they have had on her opinions. You have been contradicting her and making whatever additions and deductions seem good to you. That is all as it should be, for in a question like this truth is only to be had by laying together many varieties of error. And I will end now in my own person by anticipating two criticisms, so obvious that you can hardly fail to make them.

No opinion has been expressed, you may say, upon the comparative merits of the sexes even as writers. That was done purposely, because, even if the time had come for such a valuation – and it is far more important at the moment to know how much money women had and how many rooms than to theorise about their capacities – even if the time had come I do not believe that gifts, whether of mind or character, can be weighed like sugar and butter, not even in Cambridge, where they are so adept at putting people into classes and fixing caps on their heads and letters after their names. I do not believe that even the Table of Precedency which you will find in Whitaker's *Almanac* represents a final order of values, or that there is any sound reason to suppose that a Commander of the Bath will ultimately walk into dinner behind a Master in Lunacy. All this pitting of sex against sex, of quality against quality; all this claiming of superiority and imputing of inferiority, belong to the private-school stage of human existence where there are 'sides', and it is necessary for one side to beat another side, and of the utmost importance to walk up to a platform and receive from the hands of the Headmaster himself a highly ornamental pot. As people mature they cease to believe in sides or in Headmasters or in highly ornamental pots. At any rate, where books are concerned, it is notoriously difficult to fix labels of merit in such a way that they do not come off. Are not reviews of current literature a perpetual illustration of the difficulty of judgement? 'This great book', 'this worthless book', the same book is called by both names. Praise and blame alike mean nothing. No, delightful as the pastime of measuring may be, it is the most futile of all occupations, and to submit to the decrees of the measurers the most servile of attitudes. So long as you write what you wish to write, that is all that matters; and whether it matters for ages or only for hours, nobody can say. But to sacrifice a hair of the head of your vision, a shade of its colour, in deference to some Headmaster with a silver pot in his hand or to some professor with a measuring-rod up his sleeve, is the most abject treachery, and the sacrifice of wealth and chastity which used to be said to be the greatest of human disasters, a mere flea-bite in comparison.

Next I think that you may object that in all this I have made too much of the importance of material things. Even allowing a generous margin for symbolism, that five hundred a year stands for the power to contemplate, that a lock on the door means the power to think for oneself, still you may say that the mind should rise above such things; and that great poets have often been poor men. Let me then quote to you the words of your own Professor of Literature, who knows better than I do what goes to the making of a poet. Sir Arthur Quiller-Couch writes:*

'What are the great poetical names of the last hundred years or so? Coleridge, Wordsworth, Byron, Shelley, Landor, Keats, Tennyson, Browning, Arnold, Morris, Rossetti, Swinburne – we may stop there. Of these, all but Keats, Browning, Rossetti were University men; and of these three, Keats, who died young, cut off in his prime, was the only one not fairly well to do. It may seem a brutal thing to say, and it is a sad thing to say: but, as a matter of hard fact, the theory that poetical genius bloweth where it listeth, and equally in poor and rich, holds little truth. As a matter of hard fact, nine out of those twelve were University men: which means that somehow or other they procured the means to get the best education England can give. As a matter of hard fact, of the remaining three you know that Browning was well to do, and I challenge you that, if he had not been well to do, he would no more have attained to write *Saul* or *The Ring*

* *The Art of Writing*, by Sir Arthur Quiller-Couch.

and the Book than Ruskin would have attained to writing *Modern Painters* if his father had not dealt prosperously in business. Rossetti had a small private income; and, moreover, he painted. There remains but Keats; whom Atropos[5] slew young, as she slew John Clare in a mad-house, and James Thomson by the laudanum he took to drug disappointment. These are dreadful facts, but let us face them. It is – however dishonouring to us as a nation – certain that, by some fault in our commonwealth, the poor poet has not in these days, nor has had for two hundred years, a dog's chance. Believe me – and I have spent a great part of ten years in watching some three hundred and twenty elementary schools – we may prate of democracy, but actually, a poor child in England has little more hope than had the son of an Athenian slave to be emancipated into that intellectual freedom of which great writings are born.'

Nobody could put the point more plainly. 'The poor poet has not in these days, nor has had for two hundred years, a dog's chance . . . a poor child in England has little more hope than had the son of an Athenian slave to be emancipated into that intellectual freedom of which great writings are born.' That is it. Intellectual freedom depends upon material things. Poetry depends upon intellectual freedom. And women have always been poor, not for two hundred years merely, but from the beginning of time. Women have had less intellectual freedom than the sons of Athenian slaves. Women, then, have not had a dog's chance of writing poetry. That is why I have laid so much stress on money and a room of one's own. However, thanks to the toils of those obscure women in the past, of whom I wish we knew more, thanks, curiously enough, to two wars, the Crimean which let Florence Nightingale out of her drawing-room, and the European War which opened the doors to the average woman some sixty years later, these evils are in the way to be bettered. Otherwise you would not be here to-night, and your chance of earning five hundred pounds a year, precarious as I am afraid that it still is, would be minute in the extreme.

Still, you may object, why do you attach so much importance

to this writing of books by women when, according to you, it requires so much effort, leads perhaps to the murder of one's aunts, will make one almost certainly late for luncheon, and may bring one into very grave disputes with certain very good fellows? My motives, let me admit, are partly selfish. Like most uneducated Englishwomen, I like reading – I like reading books in the bulk. Lately my diet has become a trifle monotonous; history is too much about wars; biography too much about great men; poetry has shown, I think, a tendency to sterility, and fiction – but I have sufficiently exposed my disabilities as a critic of modern fiction and will say no more about it. Therefore I would ask you to write all kinds of books, hesitating at no subject however trivial or however vast. By hook or by crook, I hope that you will possess yourselves of money enough to travel and to idle, to contemplate the future or the past of the world, to dream over books and loiter at street corners and let the line of thought dip deep into the stream. For I am by no means confining you to fiction. If you would please me – and there are thousands like me – you would write books of travel and adventure, and research and scholarship, and history and biography, and criticism and philosophy and science. By so doing you will certainly profit the art of fiction. For books have a way of influencing each other. Fiction will be much the better for standing cheek by jowl with poetry and philosophy. Moreover, if you consider any great figure of the past, like Sappho, like the Lady Murasaki,[6] like Emily Brontë, you will find that she is an inheritor as well as an originator, and has come into existence because women have come to have the habit of writing naturally; so that even as a prelude to poetry such activity on your part would be invaluable.

But when I look back through these notes and criticize my own train of thought as I made them, I find that my motives were not altogether selfish. There runs through these comments and discursions the conviction – or is it the instinct? – that good books are desirable and that good writers, even if they show every variety of human depravity, are still good human beings.

Thus when I ask you to write more books I am urging you to do what will be for your good and for the good of the world at large. How to justify this instinct or belief I do not know, for philosophic words, if one has not been educated at a university, are apt to play one false. What is meant by 'reality'? It would seem to be something very erratic, very undependable – now to be found in a dusty road, now in a scrap of newspaper in the street, now in a daffodil in the sun. It lights up a group in a room and stamps some casual saying. It overwhelms one walking home beneath the stars and makes the silent world more real than the world of speech – and then there it is again in an omnibus in the uproar of Piccadilly. Sometimes, too, it seems to dwell in shapes too far away for us to discern what their nature is. But whatever it touches, it fixes and makes permanent. That is what remains over when the skin of the day has been cast into the hedge; that is what is left of past time and of our loves and hates. Now the writer, as I think, has the chance to live more than other people in the presence of this reality. It is his business to find it and collect it and communicate it to the rest of us. So at least I infer from reading *Lear* or *Emma* or *La Recherche du Temps Perdu*. For the reading of these books seems to perform a curious couching operation on the senses; one sees more intensely afterwards; the world seems bared of its covering and given an intenser life. Those are the enviable people who live at enmity with unreality; and those are the pitiable who are knocked on the head by the thing done without knowing or caring. So that when I ask you to earn money and have a room of your own, I am asking you to live in the presence of reality, an invigorating life, it would appear, whether one can impart it or not.

Here I would stop, but the pressure of convention decrees that every speech must end with a peroration. And a peroration addressed to women should have something, you will agree, particularly exalting and ennobling about it. I should implore you to remember your responsibilities, to be higher, more spiritual; I should remind you how much depends upon you, and what an influence you can exert upon the future. But those exhortations can safely, I think, be left to the other sex, who will put them, and indeed have put them, with far greater eloquence than I can compass. When I rummage in my own mind I find no noble sentiments about being companions and equals and influencing the world to higher ends. I find myself saying briefly and prosaically that it is much more important to be oneself than anything else. Do not dream of influencing other people, I would say, if I knew how to make it sound exalted. Think of things in themselves.

And again I am reminded by dipping into newspapers and novels and biographies that when a woman speaks to women she should have something very unpleasant up her sleeve. Women are hard on women. Women dislike women. Women – but are you not sick to death of the word? I can assure you that I am. Let us agree, then, that a paper read by a woman to women should end with something particularly disagreeable.

But how does it go? What can I think of? The truth is, I often like women. I like their unconventionality. I like their subtlety. I like their anonymity. I like – but I must not run on in this way. That cupboard there – you say it holds clean table-napkins only; but what if Sir Archibald Bodkin[7] were concealed among them? Let me then adopt a sterner tone. Have I, in the preceding words, conveyed to you sufficiently the warnings and reprobation of mankind? I have told you the very low opinion in which you were held by Mr Oscar Browning. I have indicated what Napoleon once thought of you and what Mussolini thinks now. Then, in case any of you aspire to fiction, I have copied out for your benefit the advice of the critic about courageously acknowledging the limitations of your sex. I have referred to Professor X and given prominence to his statement that women are intellectually, morally and physically inferior to men. I have handed on all that has come my way without going in search of it, and here is a final warning – from Mr John Langdon Davies.* Mr John Langdon Davies warns women 'that when

* *A Short History of Women*, by John Langdon Davies.

children cease to be altogether desirable, women cease to be altogether necessary'.[8] I hope you will make a note of it.

How can I further encourage you to go about the business of life? Young women, I would say, and please attend, for the peroration is beginning, you are, in my opinion, disgracefully ignorant. You have never made a discovery of any sort of importance. You have never shaken an empire or led an army into battle. The plays of Shakespeare are not by you, and you have never introduced a barbarous race to the blessings of civilization. What is your excuse? It is all very well for you to say, pointing to the streets and squares and forests of the globe swarming with black and white and coffee-coloured inhabitants, all busily engaged in traffic and enterprise and love-making, we have had other work on our hands. Without our doing, those seas would be unsailed and those fertile lands a desert. We have borne and bred and washed and taught, perhaps to the age of six or seven years, the one thousand six hundred and twenty-three million human beings who are, according to statistics, at present in existence, and that, allowing that some had help, takes time.

There is truth in what you say – I will not deny it. But at the same time may I remind you that there have been at least two colleges for women in existence in England since the year 1866; that after the year 1880 a married woman was allowed by law to possess her own property; and that in 1919 – which is a whole nine years ago – she was given a vote? May I also remind you that the most of the professions have been open to you for close on ten years now? When you reflect upon these immense privileges and the length of time during which they have been enjoyed, and the fact that there must be at this moment some two thousand women capable of earning over five hundred a year in one way or another, you will agree that the excuse of lack of opportunity, training, encouragement, leisure and money no longer holds good. Moreover, the economists are telling us that Mrs Seton has had too many children. You must, of course, go on bearing children, but, so they say, in twos and threes, not in tens and twelves.

Thus, with some time on your hands and with some book learning in your brains – you have had enough of the other kind, and are sent to college partly, I suspect, to be un-educated – surely you should embark upon another stage of your very long, very laborious and highly obscure career. A thousand pens are ready to suggest what you should do and what effect you will have. My own suggestion is a little fantastic, I admit; I prefer, therefore, to put it in the form of fiction.

I told you in the course of this paper that Shakespeare had a sister; but do not look for her in Sir Sidney Lee's life of the poet. She died young – alas, she never wrote a word. She lies buried where the omnibuses now stop, opposite the Elephant and Castle. Now my belief is that this poet who never wrote a word and was buried at the cross-roads still lives. She lives in you and in me, and in many other women who are not here to-night, for they are washing up the dishes and putting the children to bed. But she lives; for great poets do not die; they are continuing presences; they need only the opportunity to walk among us in the flesh. This opportunity, as I think, it is now coming within your power to give her. For my belief is that if we live another century or so – I am talking of the common life which is the real life and not of the little separate lives which we live as individuals – and have five hundred a year each of us and rooms of our own; if we have the habit of freedom and the courage to write exactly what we think; if we escape a little from the common sitting-room and see human beings not always in their relation to each other but in relation to reality; and the sky, too, and the trees or whatever it may be in themselves; if we look past Milton's bogey,[9] for no human being should shut out the view; if we face the fact, for it is a fact, that there is no arm to cling to, but that we go alone and that our relation is to the world of reality and not only to the world of men and women, then the opportunity will come and the dead poet who was Shakespeare's sister will put on the body which she has so often laid down. Drawing her life from the lives of the unknown who were her forerunners, as her brother did before her, she will be born. As for her coming without that preparation, without that effort on our part, without that determination that when she is born again she shall find it possible to live and write her poetry, that we cannot expect, for that would be impossible. But I maintain that she would come if we worked for her, and that so to work, even in poverty and obscurity, is worth while.

THE END

Editor's Notes

CHAPTER I

1. *Odtaa*: the Girton *Odtaa* took its name from John Masefield's 1926 novel *Odtaa* ('one damn thing after another').
2. *Fernham*: Woolf has amalgamated Girton and Newnham Colleges, Cambridge.
3. *Mary Beton ... Mary Carmichael*: Woolf alludes to the well-known 'Ballad of Mary Hamilton' ('There was Mary Beaton and Mary Seaton/Mary Carmichael and me'), taken to refer to the companions of the ill-fated Mary, Queen of Scots. Later in *A ROO* these names appear again, attached to the Principal of the college, an aunt of the writer, a young novelist and so on.
4. *into the stream*: this fishing metaphor is employed in Woolf's essay 'Professions for Women' (reprinted in Appendix II), where it is used to show how female creativity can be hampered by the conventions barring women from writing honestly about their sexual experiences.
5. *a Beadle*: a university official.
6. *the name escapes me*: Charles Lamb (1775–1834); the essay is 'Oxford in the Vacation', first published in the *London Magazine*, 1820. Lamb's disillusion over the manuscript is described in a footnote.
7. *this famous library*: the manuscript of John Milton's poem *Lycidas* is in the library of Trinity College, Cambridge; Woolf's father, Sir Leslie Stephen, had given the manuscript of Thackeray's *Esmond* to the same library.
8. *cap and gown ... tufts of fur*: academic dress at Cambridge includes mortarboards (hats), gowns and hoods edged with rabbit fur.
9. *like a sailing-ship*: Woolf is presumably referring to the chapel of King's College, Cambridge.
10. *lunch on this occasion*: this celebrated description of lunch was thought to be much elaborated for artistic purposes. Leonard and Virginia Woolf did, however, have lunch in George Ryland's rooms in King's College (with Maynard Keynes and Lytton Strachey) on 21 October 1928.

11. *We are all going to . . . the company*: 'We are all going to heaven and Vandyck is of the company', were supposedly the last words of the painter Thomas Gainsborough (1727–88).

12. *before the war*: this is the first reference to the First World War in *A ROO*. Woolf was intensely affected by it and became preoccupied with how to prevent war – a central theme of *TG*. See discussion in the introduction.

13. *There . . . 'I wait'*: Alfred, Lord Tennyson (1809–92), *Maud*, Part 1, XXII, x.

14. *My heart . . . is come to me*: the opening stanzas of Christina Rossetti's (1830–94) best-known poem 'A Birthday'. Both these verses were reprinted in *The Oxford Book of English Verse* (1912).

15. *J—H— herself*: Jane Harrison (1850–1928), cultural anthropologist, classical scholar and popularizer of Freudian psychoanalysis, and much admired by Woolf, had died in April 1928.

16. *John Stuart Mill*: (1806–73) English philosopher, economist and early feminist, the author of *The Subjection of Women* (1869).

17. *a penny of her own*: Woolf refers to the passing of the Married Women's Property Acts in 1870 and 1882, which enabled married women to keep their own earnings.

18. *Balliol or King's*: Balliol College, Oxford, and King's College, Cambridge.

CHAPTER II

1. *vast dome . . . famous names*: Woolf is describing the famous reading room of the British Museum. The names of great men of letters are engraved in a band round the dome, causing one of Woolf's fictional characters to reflect bitterly: 'Oh damn . . . why didn't they leave room for an Eliot or a Brontë?' (*Jacob's Room*, 1922; Penguin Books, 1992, p. 91.)

2. *Most women . . . at all*: Alexander Pope (1688–1744), poet and satirist. His second *Moral Essay*, 'To a Lady', opens:

> Nothing so true as what you once let fall,
> Most women have no character at all.

3. *Les femmes . . . les hommes*: Jean de la Bruyère (1645–96), French writer and novelist. *Les Caracteres: des femmes*: 'Women go to extremes: they are better or worse than men.'

4. *savages*: Woolf's first use in the text of a vocabulary now regarded as offensive and racist, but common among liberals of her time.

5. *Freudian theory*: the question of Woolf's attitude to psychoanalysis is much debated. She was familiar with the basic ideas of Freud as early as 1918 (e.g. *Diary*, I, 21 Jan. 1918, p. 110), and she and Leonard Woolf, in publishing Freud at the Hogarth Press, were influential in the general introduction of psychoanalytic work to Britain. Here, however, as in her discussion of 'infantile fixation' in *TG*, her use of the theory is very loose. For a detailed discussion see Elizabeth Abel, *Virginia Woolf and the Fictions of Psychoanalysis* (Chicago University Press, 1989).

6. *Sir Austen Chamberlain*: (1863–1937) the Foreign Secretary at the time.

7. *Z . . . Rebecca West*: 'Z' seems to be the critic Desmond MacCarthy: 'I was amused to find that when Rebecca West says "men are snobs" she gets an instant rise out of Desmond' (*Diary*, III, 10 Sept. 1928, p. 195); see below, chapter IV, Note 13; and *WE*, p. 30. Rebecca West (1892–1983) was a novelist, critic and essayist, and, as a young woman, a committed feminist and social reformer.

8. *Mussolini*: Benito Mussolini (1883–1945), Italian fascist leader who subsequently formed an alliance with Adolf Hitler's National Socialist (Nazi) Party in Germany. Woolf here introduces one of the arguments to be developed in *Three Guineas*.

9. *five hundred pounds a year for ever*: see the introduction (p. xx) for discussion of the lack of correspondence between this account and Woolf's own legacy.

CHAPTER III

1. *Aubrey*: John Aubrey (1626–97), collector of gossip and anecdotes, best known for his *Brief Lives* (1690).

2. *Joanna Baillie*: (1762–1851) dramatist, poet and close friend of Sir Walter Scott. (In the manuscript Woolf had written '. . . further consideration of the claims of Joanna Baillie to have influenced Scott'.)

3. *his mother was an heiress*: in the manuscript version Woolf originally named Shakespeare's sister after his mother: 'Let us call her Mary Arden', she wrote. She was an extraordinary child, born around 1564. 'Her father was a small tradesman, perhaps a butcher or a dealer in wool.' See *Women and Fiction*, p. 73.

4. *poodles dancing and women acting*: the reference here is to Samuel Johnson's much-quoted view that a woman preaching was like a dog walking on its hind legs: 'It is not done well; but you are surprised to find it done at all' (from Boswell's *Life of Samuel Johnson*, 31 July 1763).

5. *Nick Greene*: the character of Nicholas Greene, an imaginary poet and critic, had been elaborated in *Orlando* (1928; Penguin Books, 1993, p. 59ff).

6. *some mute and inglorious*: Woolf refers to Thomas Gray's 'Elegy Written in a Country Church-Yard' (1751) ('Some mute inglorious Milton here may rest'). There are both direct and oblique references to John Milton (1608–74) throughout *A ROO*, who can be understood as representing, for Woolf, the masculine appropriation of writing.

7. *Edward Fitzgerald*: (1809–83) translator of *The Rubáiyát of Omar Khayyám* and Victorian man of letters.

8. *Currer Bell . . . George Sand*: Currer Bell was Charlotte Brontë's (1816–55) pseudonym, under which her early work was published; George Eliot and George Sand were the names under which Mary Ann Evans (1819–80) and Amandine Dupin (1804–76) published.

9. *Ce chien . . . the Sieges Allee*: 'This dog is mine', from Blaise Pascal's (1623–62) *Pensées*. The Siegesallee (Victory Avenue) is in Berlin.

10. *a very fine negress*: Woolf's remark is rather disturbing now. It demonstrates the rare, exoticized status of black women in England at that time, and many years were to pass before an identity of 'black British' people would be accepted. More positively, Woolf's belief that 'as a woman I have no country' (elaborated in *TG*) enables her here to recognize cultural and 'racial' differences without harnessing them to nationalistic dogmas.

11. *Rousseau*: Jean Jacques Rousseau (1712–78), Swiss-born French philosopher and author, and social theorist in his *Confessions*.

12. *Carlyle . . . Keats*: Thomas Carlyle (1795–1881), Scottish philosopher and historian. His posthumous *Reminiscences* appeared in 1881, followed by several volumes of letters and a biography, edited or written by J. A. Froude; Gustave Flaubert (1821–80), French novelist and author of *Madame Bovary* (1857); he and the English romantic poet John Keats (1795–1821) recorded their writing labours in their letters.

13. *Mighty poets in their misery dead*: the quotation is from Wordsworth's 'Resolution and Independence' (1807).

14. *Lord Birkenhead ... Harley Street*: Lord Birkenhead (F. E. Smith, 1872–1930) was the current (Conservative) Lord Chancellor; Dean Inge (1860–1954) was the Dean of St Paul's Cathedral in London; Harley Street is the centre of London's most exclusive medical practices.

15. *He's a dear boy really and most high-minded*: Oscar Browning was a Fellow of King's College, Cambridge; the reference to 'high-minded' Arthur implies a link between misogyny and homosexuality and might thus be seen as somewhat homophobic on Woolf's part. Jane Marcus has interpreted this in terms of a history in which Sir Leslie Stephen had acted to protect Browning and his nephew, J. K. Stephen, from scandal. Browning had been sacked from Eton, with an implication of sexual scandal, and J. K. Stephen was a favoured pupil there who followed him to Cambridge. Marcus reads Woolf's scorching remarks on Browning as, to some extent at least, a displacement of her anger at the patriarchalism of her father and male relatives. See Jane Marcus, *Virginia Woolf and the Languages of Patriarchy* (Indiana University Press, 1987, pp. 181ff.). Browning recorded his own *Memories of Sixty Years* (1910) and his nephew H. E. Wortham published a biography of him in 1927 (the source of Woolf's anecdote).

16. *they are supported by, and they minister to, men*: Woolf encountered this remark in Barbara Stephen's *Emily Davies and Girton College*, published in 1927. *Two Women*, her review of the book, is reprinted in *WE*, pp. 115–20.

17. *she is ask'd ...*: Lady Bessborough's letters to Lord Granville Leveson Gower were included in the two volumes of his *Private Correspondence* (ed. Countess Granville, 1916).

18. *Keats ... on his tombstone*: Keats had instructed that the words 'here lies one whose name was writ in water' be carved on his tombstone.

CHAPTER IV

1. *Lady Winchilsea ... the aromatic pain*: Anne Finch, Countess of Winchilsea, described by the 1967 *Oxford Companion to English Literature* as 'a writer of pleasant occasional verse', none the less influenced both Pope and Shelley. Her poems were introduced by the well-known critic John Middleton Murry, in a 1928 edition. The first three quotations are taken from her poem 'The Introduction',

the next four from 'The Spleen'. In 'An Essay on Man' (1733) Pope wrote the line 'Die of a rose in aromatic pain', which echoes her line 'We faint beneath the aromatic pain'.

2. *Gay*: John Gay (1685–1732), the playwright, poet and author. His *Trivia* describes a walk through the streets of London.

3. *Margaret of Newcastle*: Margaret Cavendish, Duchess of Newcastle (1624?–74). Woolf's essay on her, which first appeared in *The Common Reader*, is reprinted in *WE*, pp. 107–14.

4. *Sir Egerton Brydges . . . Welbeck*: Sir Egerton Brydges had written a preface to the *Memoirs* (1914) of the Duchess of Newcastle; Welbeck was their country house.

5. *Dorothy Osborne's letters*: Dorothy Osborne (1627–95). An edition of her letters to Sir William Temple, whom she married in 1655, was published in 1928. Woolf's review is reprinted in *WE*, pp. 126–32.

6. *Mrs Behn*: Aphra Behn (1640–89), the playwright, poet, novelist and spy for Charles II, had been the subject of a biography by Vita Sackville-West (*Aphra Behn: The Incomparable Astraea*) in 1927.

7. *Charing Cross Road*: in London, a centre for second-hand bookshops.

8. *Eliza Carter*: Elizabeth Carter (1717–1806), translator of Epictetus, letter-writer, friend of Dr Johnson and an original 'blue stocking'. The 'blue stockings' were a group of women who hosted evening parties in the 1750s. Eschewing card games and evening dress in favour of literary conversation, they invited eminent men of letters to take part in their discussions. One member of the group, Benjamin Stillingfleet, regularly attended wearing blue worsted stockings instead of black evening clothes, giving rise to the nickname 'blue stocking' for a woman with literary tastes.

9. *supreme head of song*: Woolf quotes Swinburne's *Ave Atque Vale*, for the early Greek woman poet Sappho (b. 612 BC). She wrote hymns and love poems, some of which Swinburne translated.

10. *That is an awkward break, I thought*: Woolf's discussion here of Charlotte Brontë is unsympathetic (see discussion in the introduction), as required by her argument. Elsewhere she was far more generous. Likening Charlotte Brontë to Thomas Hardy, she said that they had both 'forged for themselves a prose which takes the mould of their minds entire; which has, into the bargain, a beauty, a power, a swiftness of its own'. See Woolf's essays 'Jane Eyre' and 'Wuthering Heights' in *The Common Reader* (1925); reprinted in

Virginia Woolf, *Women and Writing*, ed. Michèle Barrett (The Women's Press, 1979).

11. *cut off from what is called the world*: Mary Ann Evans (George Eliot) had set up home with George Henry Lewes, a writer, philosopher and editor who was not free to marry as he had a (mentally ill) wife. Their relationship illustrated the prevailing double standard of sexual morality, according to which Lewes was free to move in the public world while Evans was forced into social retirement.

12. *They wrote as women write, not as men write*: Woolf is here taking a position that is more subtle than a simple claim that women write differently from men. Taking her work as a whole, it is more likely she would emphasize the different experiences that give rise to what is written. Later in *A ROO* she argues that writers should try to banish consciousness of their sex as they write (pp. 94 ff.).

13. *If, like the reporter . . .*: Woolf has reproduced this quotation from *Life and Letters* in such a way as to obscure two important facts: that it was written by a friend of hers, Desmond MacCarthy (the journal's editor), and that she *herself* was cited in his original remarks. The offending sentence read in full:

> If, like the reporter, you believe that female novelists should only aspire to excellence by courageously acknowledging the limitations of their sex (Jane Austen and, in our own time, Mrs Virginia Woolf, have demonstrated how gracefully this gesture can be accomplished), Miss du Coudray's first novel may at the outset prove a little disappointing, since here is a writer definitely bent upon the attainment of masculine standards.

Woolf recorded in her diary that she had taxed MacCarthy over his 'condescending phrase', adding rather surprisingly, 'But there was no acrimony in this' (*Diary*, III, 10 Sept. 1928, pp. 195–6).

14. *we think back through our mothers if we are women*: Woolf's argument has become enormously influential for a new generation of feminist critics, particularly in the USA where the re-appropriation of the mother/daughter relationship has been highly significant for feminism.

15. *Johnson, Gibbon*: Samuel Johnson (1709–84), English lexicographer, essayist, poet and moralist; Edward Gibbon (1737–94), author of *History of the Decline and Fall of the Roman Empire* (1776–88).

CHAPTER V

1. *Mary Carmichael*: in 1928 Marie Stopes (pioneer of birth control) published a novel entitled *Love's Creation* under the name Marie Carmichael.

2. *Sir Chartres Biron*: Sir Chartres Biron was the magistrate in the obscenity trial, taking place at the time of Woolf's lectures, of Radclyffe Hall's lesbian novel *The Well of Loneliness*. (See the introduction for discussion of this issue.)

3. *Diana of the Crossways*: (1885) a novel by George Meredith (1828–1909), often thought of as depicting a 'modern' woman.

4. *They shared a laboratory together* . . .: the manuscript contains the following passage, showing that Woolf originally intended to allude directly to the trial of *The Well of Loneliness*. It reads in its unfinished state as follows:

   'Chloe liked Olivia: they shared a –' the words came at the bottom of the page; the pages had stuck; while fumbling to open them there flashed into my mind the inevitable police-man; the summons; the order to attend the court; the dreary waiting; the Magistrate coming in with little bow; the glass of water; the counsel for the prosecution; for the defense; the verdict; this book is obscene; & flames rising, perhaps on Tower Hill, as they consumed masses of paper. Here the pages came apart. Heaven be praised! It was only a laboratory. Chloe and Olivia. They were engaged in mincing liver which is apparently a cure for pernicious anaemia. (See *Women and Fiction*, p. 114)

5. *Burke or Debrett*: reference books about the British aristocracy and gentry. Sir Hawley Butts appears to be imaginary.

6. *Sir William Joynson Hicks*: the Home Secretary at the time. Woolf knew his name well as she had used it in a letter she and E. M. Forster (novelist and closeted homosexual) had written to the *Nation*. Protesting at the Home Secretary's banning of *The Well of Loneliness*, they had satirized his attempts at literary censorship:

   The subject of the book exists as a fact among the many other facts of life . . . novelists in England have now been forbidden to mention it by Sir W. Joynson Hicks. May they mention it incidentally? Although it is forbidden as a main theme, may it be alluded to, or ascribed to subsidiary characters? Perhaps the Home Secretary will issue further orders on this point.

7. *Thrale marries*: Samuel Johnson's close friendship with Mrs Hester Thrale came to an end when she married the musician Gabriel Piozzi.

8. *Balaclava ... Edward the Seventh*: the Battle of Balaclava (Crimean War), 1854; the birth of Edward VII was in 1841.

9. *Juvenal ... Strindberg*: Juvenal (AD 60?–140?) attacked women in his sixth satire; the Swedish playwright and author August Strindberg (1849–1912) was a misogynist.

10. *Mr Woodhouse and Mr Casaubon*: Mr Woodhouse is the father of Jane Austen's *Emma* (1816); Mr Casaubon is in George Eliot's *Middlemarch* (1872).

CHAPTER VI

1. *Coleridge*: Samuel Taylor Coleridge (1772–1834), poet and essayist. See *Table Talk*, 1 Sept. 1832.

2. *Miss Clough and Miss Davies*: campaigners for women's education who became, respectively, principal of Newnham College and mistress of Girton College, Cambridge.

3. *old Jolyon's head*: the dynastic head in John Galsworthy's novel sequence *The Forsyte Saga*.

4. *an age to come of ... self-assertive virility*: See *Three Guineas* for elaboration of this point

5. *Atropos*: one of the three fates in Greek mythology, she cut the thread of human life with her shears.

6. *Lady Murasaki*: Japanese novelist (978?–1015?) whose *Tale of Genji* was currently being translated by Arthur Waley.

7. *Sir Archibald Bodkin*: the Director of Public Prosecutions at the time, and thus involved in the trial of *The Well of Loneliness*. This is the third such reference, following on from the presiding magistrate, Sir Chartres Biron, and the Home Secretary, Sir William Joynson-Hicks (see Notes 2 and 6, chapter V).

8. *Mr John Langdon Davies ... altogether necessary*: Woolf has exaggerated a little. The quotation should actually read: 'And if children cease to be altogether desirable, women cease to be altogether necessary.'

9. *Milton's bogey*: cf. Note 6, chapter III. Woolf appears to be referring

back to the passage on p. 35, where, walking home from the British Museum, she evokes a sequence of patriarchal London sights with military connotations (Whitehall, Admiralty Arch and so on). At that point, as now, she preferred a view of the open sky to the large figure of a gentleman (probably metaphorical – the text is not clear) that Milton had 'recommended for my perpetual adoration.'

THREE GUINEAS

List of Illustrations

One

Three years is a long time to leave a letter unanswered, and
your letter has been lying without an answer even longer than
that. I had hoped that it would answer itself, or that other
people would answer it for me. But there it is with its question
– How in your opinion are we to prevent war? – still unanswered.

It is true that many answers have suggested themselves, but
none that would not need explanation, and explanations take
time. In this case, too, there are reasons why it is particularly
difficult to avoid misunderstanding. A whole page could be
filled with excuses and apologies; declarations of unfitness, in-
competence, lack of knowledge, and experience: and they would
be true. But even when they were said there would still remain
some difficulties so fundamental that it may well prove impossible for you to understand or for us to explain. But one does not
like to leave so remarkable a letter as yours – a letter perhaps
unique in the history of human correspondence, since when
before has an educated man asked a woman how in her opinion
war can be prevented? – unanswered. Therefore let us make the
attempt; even if it is doomed to failure.

In the first place let us draw what all letter-writers instinctively
draw, a sketch of the person to whom the letter is addressed.
Without someone warm and breathing on the other side of
the page, letters are worthless. You, then, who ask the question, are a little grey on the temples; the hair is no longer
thick on the top of your head. You have reached the middle
years of life not without effort, at the Bar; but on the whole
your journey has been prosperous. There is nothing parched,
mean or dissatisfied in your expression. And without wishing
to flatter you, your prosperity – wife, children, house – has
been deserved. You have never sunk into the contented apathy

of middle life, for, as your letter from an office in the heart of London shows, instead of turning on your pillow and prodding your pigs, pruning your pear trees – you have a few acres in Norfolk – you are writing letters, attending meetings, presiding over this and that, asking questions, with the sound of the guns in your ears. For the rest, you began your education at one of the great public schools and finished it at the university.

It is now that the first difficulty of communication between us appears. Let us rapidly indicate the reason. We both come of what, in this hybrid age when, though birth is mixed, classes still remain fixed, it is convenient to call the educated class. When we meet in the flesh we speak with the same accent; use knives and forks in the same way; expect maids to cook dinner and wash up after dinner; and can talk during dinner without much difficulty about politics and people; war and peace; barbarism and civilization – all the questions indeed suggested by your letter. Moreover, we both earn our livings. But . . . those three dots mark a precipice, a gulf so deeply cut between us that for three years and more I have been sitting on my side of it wondering whether it is any use to try to speak across it. Let us then ask someone else – it is Mary Kingsley – to speak for us. 'I don't know if I ever revealed to you the fact that being allowed to learn German was *all* the paid-for education I ever had. Two thousand pounds was spent on my brother's, I still hope not in vain.'[1] Mary Kingsley is not speaking for herself alone;[a] she is speaking, still, for many of the daughters of educated men. And she is not merely speaking for them; she is also pointing to a very important fact about them, a fact that must profoundly influence all that follows: the fact of Arthur's Education Fund. You, who have read *Pendennis*, will remember how the mysterious letters A.E.F. figured in household ledgers. Ever since the thirteenth century English families have been paying money into that account. From the Pastons to the Pendennises,[b] all educated families from the thirteenth century to the present moment have paid money into that account. It is a voracious receptacle. Where there were many sons to educate it required a great effort on the part of the family to keep it full. For your education was not merely in book-learning; games educated your body; friends taught you more than books or games. Talk with them broadened your outlook and enriched your mind. In the holidays you travelled; acquired a taste for art; a knowledge of foreign politics; and then, before you could earn your own living, your father made you an allowance upon which it was possible for you to live while you learnt the profession which now entitles you to add the letters K.C.ᶜ to your name. All this came out of Arthur's Education Fund. And to this your sisters, as Mary Kingsley indicates, made their contribution. Not only did their own education, save for such small sums as paid the German teacher, go into it; but many of those luxuries and trimmings which are, after all, an essential part of education – travel, society, solitude, a lodging apart from the family house – they were paid into it too. It was a voracious receptacle, a solid fact – Arthur's Education Fund – a fact so solid indeed that it cast a shadow over the entire landscape. And the result is that though we look at the same things, we see them differently. What is that congregation of buildings there, with a semi-monastic look, with chapels and halls and green playing-fields? To you it is your old school; Eton or Harrow; your old university, Oxford or Cambridge; the source of memories and of traditions innumerable. But to us, who see it through the shadow of Arthur's Education Fund, it is a schoolroom table; an omnibus going to a class; a little woman with a red nose who is not well educated herself but has an invalid mother to support; an allowance of £50 a year with which to buy clothes, give presents and take journeys on coming to maturity. Such is the effect that Arthur's Education Fund has had upon us. So magically does it change the landscape that the noble courts and quadrangles of Oxford and Cambridge often appear to educated men's daughters[2] like petticoats with holes in them, cold legs of mutton, and the boat train starting for abroad while the guard slams the door in their faces.

The fact that Arthur's Education Fund changes the landscape – the halls, the playing grounds, the sacred edifices – is an important one; but that aspect must be left for future discussion. Here we are only concerned with the obvious fact, when it comes to considering this important question – how we are to help you prevent war – that education makes a difference. Some knowledge of politics, of international relations, of economics, is obviously necessary in order to understand the causes which lead to war. Philosophy, theology even, might come in usefully. Now you the uneducated, you with an untrained mind, could not possibly deal with such questions satisfactorily. War, as the result of impersonal forces, is you will agree beyond the grasp of the untrained mind. But war as the result of human nature is another thing. Had you not believed that human nature, the reasons, the emotions of the ordinary man and woman, lead to war, you would not have written asking for our help. You must have argued, men and women, here and now, are able to exert their wills; they are not pawns and puppets dancing on a string held by invisible hands. They can act, and think for themselves. Perhaps even they can influence other people's thoughts and actions. Some such reasoning must have led you to apply to us; and with justification. For happily there is one branch of education which comes under the heading 'unpaid-for education' – that understanding of human beings and their motives which, if the word is rid of its scientific associations, might be called psychology. Marriage, the one great profession open to our class since the dawn of time until the year 1919;[d] marriage, the art of choosing the human being with whom to live life successfully, should have taught us some skill in that. But here again another difficulty confronts us. For though many instincts are held more or less in common by both sexes, to fight has always been the man's habit, not the woman's. Law and practice have developed that difference, whether innate or accidental. Scarcely a human being in the course of history has fallen to a woman's rifle; the vast majority of birds and beasts have been killed by you, not by us; and it is difficult to judge what we do not share.[3]

How then are we to understand your problem, and if we cannot, how can we answer your question, how to prevent war? The answer based upon our experience and our psychology – Why fight? – is not an answer of any value. Obviously there is for you some glory, some necessity, some satisfaction in fighting which we have never felt or enjoyed. Complete understanding could only be achieved by blood transfusion and memory transfusion – a miracle still beyond the reach of science. But we who live now have a substitute for blood transfusion and memory transfusion which must serve at a pinch. There is that marvellous, perpetually renewed, and as yet largely untapped aid to the understanding of human motives which is provided in our age by biography and autobiography. Also there is the daily paper, history in the raw. There is thus no longer any reason to be confined to the minute span of actual experience which is still, for us, so narrow, so circumscribed. We can supplement it by looking at the picture of the lives of others. It is of course only a picture at present, but as such it must serve. It is to biography then that we will turn first, quickly and briefly, in order to attempt to understand what war means to you. Let us extract a few sentences from a biography.

First, this from a soldier's life:

I have had the happiest possible life, and have always been working for war, and have now got into the biggest in the prime of life for a soldier . . . Thank God, we are off in an hour. Such a magnificent regiment! Such men, such horses! Within ten days I hope Francis and I will be riding side by side straight at the Germans.[4]

To which the biographer adds:

From the first hour he had been supremely happy, for he had found his true calling.

To that let us add this from an airman's life:

> We talked of the League of Nations and the prospects of peace
> and disarmament. On this subject he was not so much militarist as
> martial. The difficulty to which he could find no answer was that
> if permanent peace were ever achieved, and armies and navies
> ceased to exist, there would be no outlet for the manly qualities
> which fighting developed, and that human physique and human
> character would deteriorate.[5]

Here, immediately, are three reasons which lead your sex to
fight; war is a profession; a source of happiness and excitement;
and it is also an outlet for manly qualities, without which men
would deteriorate. But that these feelings and opinions are by no
means universally held by your sex is proved by the following
extract from another biography, the life of a poet who was killed
in the European war:[e] Wilfred Owen.

> Already I have comprehended a light which never will filter into
> the dogma of any national church: namely, that one of Christ's
> essential commands was: Passivity at any price! Suffer dishonour
> and disgrace, but never resort to arms. Be bullied, be outraged, be
> killed; but do not kill . . . Thus you see how pure Christianity will
> not fit in with pure patriotism.

And among some notes for poems that he did not live to
write are these:

> The unnaturalness of weapons . . . Inhumanity of war . . . The
> insupportability of war . . . Horrible beastliness of war . . . Foolish-
> ness of war.[6]

From these quotations it is obvious that the same sex holds
very different opinions about the same thing. But also it is
obvious, from to-day's newspaper, that however many dissen-
tients there are, the great majority of your sex are to-day in

favour of war. The Scarborough Conference of educated men, the Bournemouth Conference of working men⁰ are both agreed that to spend £300,000,000 annually upon arms is a necessity. They are of opinion that Wilfred Owen was wrong; that it is better to kill than to be killed. Yet since biography shows that differences of opinion are many, it is plain that there must be some one reason which prevails in order to bring about this overpowering unanimity. Shall we call it, for the sake of brevity, 'patriotism'? What then, we must ask next, is this 'patriotism' which leads you to go to war? Let the Lord Chief Justice of England interpret it for us:

> Englishmen are proud of England. For those who have been trained in English schools and universities, and who have done the work of their lives in England, there are few loves stronger than the love we have for our country. When we consider other nations, when we judge the merits of the policy of this country or of that, it is the standard of our own country that we apply ... Liberty has made her abode in England. England is the home of democratic institutions ... It is true that in our midst there are many enemies of liberty – some of them, perhaps, in rather unexpected quarters. But we are standing firm. It has been said that an Englishman's Home is his Castle. The home of Liberty is in England. And it is a castle indeed – a castle that will be defended to the last ... Yes, we are greatly blessed, we English-men.⁷

That is a fair general statement of what patriotism means to an educated man and what duties it imposes upon him. But the educated man's sister – what does 'patriotism' mean to her? Has she the same reasons for being proud of England, for loving England, for defending England? Has she been 'greatly blessed' in England? History and biography when questioned would seem to show that her position in the home of freedom has been different from her brother's; and psychology would seem to hint that history is not without its effect upon mind and body. Therefore her interpretation of the word 'patriotism' may well differ from his. And that difference may make it extremely difficult for her to understand his definition of patriotism and the duties it imposes. If then our answer to your question, 'How in your opinion are we to prevent war?' depends upon understanding the reasons, the emotions, the loyalties which lead men to go to war, this letter had better be torn across and thrown into the waste-paper basket. For it seems plain that we cannot understand each other because of these differences. It seems plain that we think differently according as we are born differently; there is a Grenfell point of view; a Knebworth point of view; a Wilfred Owen point of view; a Lord Chief Justice's point of view and the point of view of an educated man's daughter. All differ. But is there no absolute point of view? Can we not find somewhere written up in letters of fire or gold, 'This is right. This wrong'? – a moral judgement which we must all, whatever our differences, accept? Let us then refer the question of the rightness or wrongness of war to those who make morality their profession – the clergy. Surely if we ask the clergy the simple question: 'Is war right or is war wrong?' they will give us a plain answer which we cannot deny. But no – the Church of England, which might be supposed able to abstract the question from its worldly confusions, is of two minds also. The bishops themselves are at loggerheads. The Bishop of London maintained that 'the real danger to the peace of the world to-day were the pacifists. Bad as war was dishonour was far worse.'[8] On the other hand, the Bishop of Birmingham[9] described himself as an 'extreme pacifist ... I cannot see myself that war can be regarded as consonant with the spirit of Christ.' So the Church itself gives us divided counsel – in some circumstances it is right to fight; in no circumstances is it right to fight. It is distressing, baffling, confusing, but the fact must be faced; there is no certainty in heaven above or on earth below. Indeed the more lives we read, the more speeches we listen to, the more opinions we consult, the greater the confusion becomes and the less possible it seems, since we cannot understand the impulses, the motives, or the morality which lead you to go to war, to make any suggestion that will help you to prevent war.

But besides these pictures of other people's lives and minds – these biographies and histories – there are also other pictures – pictures of actual facts; photographs. Photographs, of course, are not arguments addressed to the reason; they are simply statements of fact addressed to the eye. But in that very simplicity there may be some help. Let us see then whether when we look at the same photographs we feel the same things. Here then on the table before us are photographs. The Spanish Government⁸ sends them with patient pertinacity about twice a week.* They are not pleasant photographs to look upon. They are photographs of dead bodies for the most part. This morning's collection contains the photograph of what might be a man's body, or a woman's; it is so mutilated that it might, on the other hand, be the body of a pig. But those certainly are dead children, and that undoubtedly is the section of a house. A bomb has torn open the side; there is still a bird-cage hanging in what was presumably the sitting-room, but the rest of the house looks like nothing so much as a bunch of spillikins suspended in mid air.

Those photographs are not an argument; they are simply a crude statement of fact addressed to the eye. But the eye is connected with the brain; the brain with the nervous system. That system sends its messages in a flash through every past memory and present feeling. When we look at those photographs some fusion takes place within us; however different the education, the traditions behind us, our sensations are the same; and they are violent. You, Sir, call them 'horror and disgust'. We also call them horror and disgust. And the same words rise to our lips. War, you say, is an abomination; a barbarity; war must be stopped at whatever cost. And we echo your words. War is an abomination; a barbarity; war must be stopped. For now at last we are looking at the same

* Written in the winter of 1936–7.

picture; we are seeing with you the same dead bodies, the same ruined houses.

Let us then give up, for the moment, the effort to answer your question, how we can help you to prevent war, by discussing the political, the patriotic or the psychological reasons which lead you to go to war. The emotion is too positive to suffer patient analysis. Let us concentrate upon the practical suggestions which you bring forward for our consideration. There are three of them. The first is to sign a letter to the newspapers; the second is to join a certain society; the third is to subscribe to its funds. Nothing on the face of it could sound simpler. To scribble a name on a sheet of paper is easy; to attend a meeting where pacific opinions are more or less rhetorically reiterated to people who already believe in them is also easy; and to write a cheque in support of those vaguely acceptable opinions, though not so easy, is a cheap way of quieting what may conveniently be called one's conscience. Yet there are reasons which make us hesitate; reasons into which we must enter, less superficially, later on. Here it is enough to say that though the three measures you suggest seem plausible, yet it also seems that, if we did what you ask, the emotion caused by the photographs would still remain unappeased. That emotion, that very positive emotion, demands something more positive than a name written on a sheet of paper; an hour spent listening to speeches; a cheque written for whatever sum we can afford – say one guinea.[b] Some more energetic, some more active method of expressing our belief that war is barbarous, that war is inhuman, that war, as Wilfred Owen put it, is insupportable, horrible and beastly seems to be required. But, rhetoric apart, what active method is open to us? Let us consider and compare. You, of course, could once more take up arms – in Spain, as before in France[i] – in defence of peace. But that presumably is a method that having tried you have rejected. At any rate that method is not open to us; both the Army and the Navy are closed to our sex. We are not allowed to fight. Nor again are we allowed to be members of the Stock Exchange. Thus we can use neither the pressure of force nor the pressure of money. The less direct but still effective weapons which our brothers, as educated men, possess in the diplomatic service, in the Church, are also denied to us. We cannot preach sermons or negotiate treaties. Then again although it is true that we can write articles or send letters to the Press, the control of the Press – the decision what to print, what not to print – is entirely in the hands of your sex. It is true that for the past twenty years we have been admitted to the Civil Service and to the Bar; but our position there is still very precarious and our authority of the slightest.*j* Thus all the weapons with which an educated man can enforce his opinion are either beyond our grasp or so nearly beyond it that even if we used them we could scarcely inflict one scratch. If the men in your profession were to unite in any demand and were to say: 'If it is not granted we will stop work', the laws of England would cease to be administered. If the women in your profession said the same thing it would make no difference to the laws of England whatever. Not only are we incomparably weaker than the men of our own class; we are weaker than the women of the working class. If the working women of the country were to say: 'If you go to war, we will refuse to make munitions or to help in the production of goods,' the difficulty of war-making would be seriously increased. But if all the daughters of educated men were to down tools to-morrow, nothing essential either to the life or to the war-making of the community would be embarrassed. Our class is the weakest of all the classes in the state. We have no weapon with which to enforce our will.[10]

The answer to that is so familiar that we can easily anticipate it. The daughters of educated men have no direct influence, it is true; but they possess the greatest power of all; that is, the influence that they can exert upon educated men. If this is true, if, that is, influence is still the strongest of our weapons and the only one that can be effective in helping you to prevent war, let us, before we sign your manifesto or join your society, consider what that influence amounts to. Clearly it is of such immense importance that it deserves profound and prolonged scrutiny. Ours cannot be profound; nor can it be prolonged; it must be rapid and imperfect – still, let us attempt it.

What influence then have we had in the past upon the profession that is most closely connected with war – upon politics? There again are the innumerable, the invaluable biographies, but it would puzzle an alchemist to extract from the massed lives of politicians that particular strain which is the influence upon them of women. Our analysis can only be slight and superficial; still if we narrow our enquiry to manageable limits, and run over the memoirs of a century and a half we can hardly deny that there have been women who have influenced politics. The famous Duchess of Devonshire, Lady Palmerston, Lady Melbourne, Madame de Lieven, Lady Holland, Lady Ashburton – to skip from one famous name to another – were all undoubtedly possessed of great political influence. Their famous houses and the parties that met in them play so large a part in the political memoirs of the time that we can hardly deny that English politics, even perhaps English wars, would have been different had those houses and those parties never existed. But there is one characteristic that all those memoirs possess in common; the names of the great political leaders – Pitt, Fox, Burke, Sheridan, Peel, Canning, Palmerston, Disraeli, Gladstone – are sprinkled on every page; but you will not find either at the head of the stairs receiving the guests, or in the more private apartments of the house, any daughter of an educated man. It may be that they were deficient in charm, in wit, in rank, or in clothing. Whatever the reason, you may turn page after page, volume after volume, and though you will find their brothers and husbands – Sheridan at Devonshire House, Macaulay at Holland House, Matthew Arnold at Lansdowne House, Carlyle even at Bath House, the names of Jane Austen, Charlotte Brontë, and George Eliot do not occur; and though Mrs Carlyle* went,

Mrs Carlyle seems on her own showing to have found herself ill at ease.

But, as you will point out, the daughters of educated men may have possessed another kind of influence – one that was independent of wealth and rank, of wine, food, dress and all the other amenities that make the great houses of the great ladies so seductive. Here indeed we are on firmer ground, for there was of course one political cause which the daughters of educated men had much at heart during the past 150 years: the franchise.¹ But when we consider how long it took them to win that cause, and what labour, we can only conclude that influence has to be combined with wealth in order to be effective as a political weapon, and that influence of the kind that can be exerted by the daughters of educated men is very low in power, very slow in action, and very painful in use.¹¹ Certainly the one great political achievement of the educated man's daughter cost her over a century of the most exhausting and menial labour; kept her trudging in processions, working in offices, speaking at street corners; finally, because she used force, sent her to prison, and would very likely still keep her there, had it not been, paradoxically enough, that the help she gave her brothers when they used force at last gave her the right to call herself, if not a full daughter, still a stepdaughter of England.¹²

Influence then when put to the test would seem to be only fully effective when combined with rank, wealth and great houses. The influential are the daughters of noblemen, not the daughters of educated men. And that influence is of the kind described by a distinguished member of your own profession, the late Sir Ernest Wild.

He claimed that the great influence which women exerted over men always had been, and always ought to be, an indirect influence. Man liked to think he was doing his job himself when, in fact, he was doing just what the woman wanted, but the wise woman always let him think he was running the show when he was not. Any woman who chose to take an interest in politics had an immensely greater power without the vote than with it, because she could influence many voters. His feeling was that it was not right to bring women down to the level of men. He looked up to women, and wanted to continue to do so. He desired that the age of chivalry should not pass, because every man who had a woman to care about him liked to shine in her eyes.[13]

And so on.

If such is the real nature of our influence, and we all recognize the description and have noted the effects, it is either beyond our reach, for many of us are plain, poor and old; or beneath our contempt, for many of us would prefer to call ourselves prostitutes simply and to take our stand openly under the lamps of Piccadilly Circus[m] rather than use it. If such is the real nature, the indirect nature, of this celebrated weapon, we must do without it; add our pigmy impetus to your more substantial forces, and have recourse, as you suggest, to letter signing, society joining and the drawing of an occasional exiguous cheque. Such would seem to be the inevitable, though depressing, conclusion of our enquiry into the nature of influence, were it not that for some reason, never satisfactorily explained, the right to vote, in itself by no means negligible,[14] was mysteriously connected with another right of such immense value to the daughters of educated men that almost every word in the dictionary has been changed by it, including the word 'influence'. You will not think these words exaggerated if we explain that they refer to the right to earn one's living.

That, Sir, was the right that was conferred upon us less than twenty years ago, in the year 1919, by an Act which unbarred the professions.[n] The door of the private house was thrown open. In every purse there was, or might be, one bright new sixpence[o] in whose light every thought, every sight, every action looked different. Twenty years is not, as time goes, a long time; nor is a sixpenny bit a very important coin; nor can we yet draw upon biography to supply us with a picture of the lives and minds of the new-sixpenny owners. But in imagination perhaps we can see the educated man's daughter, as she issues from the shadow of the private house, and stands on the bridge which lies between the old world and the new, and asks, as she twirls the sacred coin in her hand, 'What shall I do with it? What do I see with it?' Through that light we may guess everything she saw looked different – men and women, cars and churches. The moon even, scarred as it is in fact with forgotten craters, seemed to her a white sixpence, a chaste sixpence, an altar upon which she vowed never to side with the servile, the signers-on, since it was hers to do what she liked with – the sacred sixpence that she had earned with her own hands herself. And if, checking imagination with prosaic good sense, you object that to depend upon a profession is only another form of slavery, you will admit from your own experience that to depend upon a profession is a less odious form of slavery than to depend upon a father. Recall the joy with which you received your first guinea for your first brief,^{p} and the deep breath of freedom that you drew when you realized that your days of dependence upon Arthur's Education Fund were over. From that guinea, as from one of the magic pellets to which children set fire and a tree rises, all that you most value – wife, children, home – and above all that influence which now enables you to influence other men, have sprung. What would that influence be if you were still drawing £40 a year from the family purse, and for any addition to that income were dependent even upon the most benevolent of fathers? But it is needless to expatiate. Whatever the reason, whether pride, or love of freedom, or hatred of hypocrisy, you will understand the excitement with which in 1919 your sisters began to earn not a guinea but a sixpenny bit, and will not scorn that pride, or deny that it was justly based, since it meant that they need no longer use the influence described by Sir Ernest Wild.

The word 'influence' then has changed. The educated man's daughter has now at her disposal an influence which is different from any influence that she has possessed before. It is not the influence which the great lady, the Siren, possesses; nor is it the influence which the educated man's daughter possessed when she had no vote; nor is it the influence which she possessed when she had a vote but was debarred from the right to earn her living. It differs, because it is an influence from which the charm element has been removed; it is an influence from which the money element has been removed. She need no longer use her charm to procure money from her father or brother. Since it is beyond the power of her family to punish her financially she can express her own opinions. In place of the admirations and antipathies which were often unconsciously dictated by the need of money she can declare her genuine likes and dislikes. In short, she need not acquiesce; she can criticize. At last she is in possession of an influence that is disinterested.

Such in rough and rapid outlines is the nature of our new weapon, the influence which the educated man's daughter can exert now that she is able to earn her own living. The question that has next to be discussed, therefore, is how can she use this new weapon to help you to prevent war? And it is immediately plain that if there is no difference between men who earn their livings in the professions and women who earn their livings, then this letter can end; for if our point of view is the same as yours then we must add our sixpence to your guinea; follow your methods and repeat your words. But, whether fortunately or unfortunately, that is not true. The two classes still differ enormously. And to prove this, we need not have recourse to the dangerous and uncertain theories of psychologists and biologists; we can appeal to facts. Take the fact of education. Your class has been educated at public schools and universities for five or six hundred years, ours for sixty. Take the fact of property.[15] Your class possesses in its own right and not through marriage practically all the capital, all the land, all the valuables, and all the patronage in England. Our class possesses in its own right and not through marriage practically none of the capital, none of the land, none of the valuables, and none of the patronage in England. That such differences make for very considerable differences in mind and body, no psychologist or biologist would deny. It would seem to follow then as an indisputable fact that 'we' – meaning by 'we' a whole made up of body, brain and spirit, influenced by memory and tradition – must still differ in some essential respects from 'you', whose body, brain and spirit have been so differently trained and are so differently influenced by memory and tradition. Though we see the same world, we see it through different eyes. Any help we can give you must be different from that you can give yourselves, and perhaps the value of that help may lie in the fact of that difference. Therefore before we agree to sign your manifesto or join your society, it might be well to discover where the difference lies, because then we may discover where the help lies also. Let us then by way of a very elementary beginning lay before you a photograph – a crudely coloured photograph – of your world as it appears to us who see it from the threshold of the private house; through the shadow of the veil that St Paul[9] still lays upon our eyes; from the bridge which connects the private house with the world of public life.

Your world, then, the world of professional, of public life, seen from this angle undoubtedly looks queer. At first sight it is enormously impressive. Within quite a small space are crowded together St Paul's, the Bank of England, the Mansion House, the massive if funereal battlements of the Law Courts; and on the other side, Westminster Abbey and the Houses of Parliament. There, we say to ourselves, pausing, in this moment of transition on the bridge, our fathers and brothers have spent their lives. All these hundreds of years they have been mounting those steps, passing in and out of those doors, ascending those pulpits, preaching, money-making, administering justice. It is from this world that the private house (somewhere, roughly speaking, in the West End) has derived its creeds, its laws, its clothes and carpets, its beef and mutton. And then, as is now permissible, cautiously pushing aside the swing doors of one of these temples, we enter on tiptoe and survey the scene in greater detail. The first sensation of colossal size, of majestic masonry is broken up into a myriad points of amazement mixed with interrogation. Your clothes in the first place make us gape with astonishment.[16] How many, how splendid, how extremely ornate they are – the clothes worn by the educated man in his public capacity! Now you dress in violet; a jewelled crucifix swings on your breast; now your shoulders are covered with lace; now furred with ermine; now slung with many linked chains set with precious stones. Now you wear wigs on your heads; rows of graduated curls descend to your necks. Now your hats are boat-shaped, or cocked; now they mount in cones of black fur; now they are made of brass and scuttle shaped; now plumes of red, now of blue hair surmount them. Sometimes gowns cover your legs; sometimes gaiters. Tabards embroidered with lions and unicorns swing from your shoulders; metal objects cut in star shapes or in circles glitter and twinkle upon your breasts. Ribbons of all colours – blue, purple, crimson – cross from shoulder to shoulder. After the comparative simplicity of your dress at home, the splendour of your public attire is dazzling.

But far stranger are two other facts that gradually reveal themselves when our eyes have recovered from their first amazement. Not only are whole bodies of men dressed alike summer and winter – a strange characteristic to a sex which changes its clothes according to the season, and for reasons of private taste and comfort – but every button, rosette and stripe seems to have some symbolical meaning. Some have the right to wear plain buttons only; others rosettes; some may wear a single stripe; others three, four, five or six. And each curl or stripe is sewn on at precisely the right distance apart; it may be one inch for one man, one inch and a quarter for another. Rules again regulate the gold wire on the shoulders, the braid on the trousers, the cockades on the hats – but no single pair of eyes can observe all these distinctions, let alone account for them accurately.

Even stranger, however, than the symbolic splendour of your clothes are the ceremonies that take place when you wear them. Here you kneel; there you bow; here you advance in procession behind a man carrying a silver poker; here you mount a carved chair; here you appear to do homage to a piece of painted wood; here you abase yourselves before tables covered with richly

worked tapestry. And whatever these ceremonies may mean you perform them always together, always in step, always in the uniform proper to the man and the occasion.

Apart from the ceremonies, such decorative apparel appears to us at first sight strange in the extreme. For dress, as we use it, is comparatively simple. Besides the prime function of covering the body, it has two other offices – that it creates beauty for the eye, and that it attracts the admiration of your sex. Since marriage until the year 1919 – less than twenty years ago – was the only profession open to us, the enormous importance of dress to a woman can hardly be exaggerated. It was to her what clients are to you – dress was her chief, perhaps her only, method of becoming Lord Chancellor. But your dress in its immense elaboration has obviously another function. It not only covers naked-ness, gratifies vanity, and creates pleasure for the eye, but it serves to advertise the social, professional, or intellectual standing of the wearer. If you will excuse the humble illustration, your dress fulfils the same function as the tickets in a grocer's shop. But, here, instead of saying 'This is margarine; this pure butter; this is the finest butter in the market,' it says, 'This man is a clever man – he is Master of Arts; this man is a very clever man – he is Doctor of Letters; this man is a most clever man – he is a Member of the Order of Merit.' It is this function – the advertise-ment function – of your dress that seems to us most singular. In the opinion of St Paul, such advertisement, at any rate for our sex, was unbecoming and immodest; until a very few years ago we were denied the use of it. And still the tradition, or belief, lingers among us that to express worth of any kind, whether intellectual or moral, by wearing pieces of metal, or ribbon, coloured hoods or gowns, is a barbarity which deserves the ridicule which we bestow upon the rites of savages. A woman who advertised her motherhood by a tuft of horsehair on the left shoulder would scarcely, you will agree, be a venerable object.

But what light does our difference here throw upon the prob-lem before us? What connection is there between the sartorial splendours of the educated man and the photograph of ruined houses and dead bodies? Obviously the connection between dress and war is not far to seek; your finest clothes are those that you wear as soldiers.ʳ Since the red and the gold, the brass and the feathers are discarded upon active service, it is plain that their expensive and not, one might suppose, hygienic splendour is invented partly in order to impress the beholder with the majesty of the military office, partly in order through their vanity to induce young men to become soldiers. Here, then, our influence and our difference might have some effect; we, who are forbidden to wear such clothes ourselves, can express the opinion that the wearer is not to us a pleasing or an impressive spectacle. He is on the contrary a ridiculous, a barbarous, a displeasing spectacle. But as the daughters of educated men we can use our influence more effectively in another direction, upon our own class – the class of educated men. For there, in courts and universities, we find the same love of dress. There, too, are velvet and silk, fur and ermine. We can say that for educated men to emphasize their superiority over other people, either in birth or intellect, by dressing differently, or by adding titles before, or letters after, their names are acts that rouse competition and jealousy – emotions which, as we need scarcely draw upon biography to prove, nor ask psychology to show, have their share in encouraging a disposition towards war. If then we express the opinion that such distinctions make those who possess them ridiculous and learning contemptible we should do something, indirectly, to discourage the feelings that lead to war. Happily we can now do more than express an opinion; we can refuse all such distinctionsˢ and all such uniforms for ourselves. This would be a slight but definite contribution to the problem before us – how to prevent war; and one that a different training and a different tradition puts more easily within our reach than within yours.[17]

But our bird's-eye view of the outside of things is not altogether encouraging. The coloured photograph that we have been looking at presents some remarkable features, it is true; but

it serves to remind us that there are many inner and secret chambers that we cannot enter. What real influence can we bring to bear upon law or business, religion or politics – we to whom many doors are still locked, or at best ajar, we who have neither capital nor force behind us? It seems as if our influence must stop short at the surface. When we have expressed an opinion upon the surface we have done all that we can do. It is true that the surface may have some connection with the depths, but if we are to help you to prevent war we must try to penetrate deeper beneath the skin. Let us then look in another direction – in a direction natural to educated men's daughters, in the direction of education itself.

Here, fortunately, the year, the sacred year 1919, comes to our help. Since that year put it into the power of educated men's daughters to earn their livings they have at last some real influence upon education. They have money. They have money to subscribe to causes. Honorary treasurers invoke their help. To prove it, here, opportunely, cheek by jowl with your letter, is a letter from one such treasurer asking for money with which to rebuild a women's college.[1] And when honorary treasurers invoke help, it stands to reason that they can be bargained with. We have the right to say to her, 'You shall only have our guinea with which to help you to rebuild your college if you will help this gentleman whose letter also lies before us to prevent war.' We can say to her, 'You must educate the young to hate war. You must teach them to feel the inhumanity, the beastliness, the insupportability of war.' But what kind of education shall we bargain for? What sort of education will teach the young to hate war?

That is a question that is difficult enough in itself; and may well seem unanswerable by those who are of Mary Kingsley's persuasion – those who have had no direct experience of university education themselves. Yet the part that education plays in human life is so important, and the part that it might play in answering your question is so considerable that to shirk any attempt to see how we can influence the young through education against war would be craven. Let us therefore turn from our station on the bridge across the Thames to another bridge over another river, this time in one of the great universities; for both have rivers, and both have bridges, too, for us to stand upon. Once more, how strange it looks, this world of domes and spires, of lecture rooms and laboratories, from our vantage point! How different it looks to us from what it must look to you! To those who behold it from Mary Kingsley's angle – 'being allowed to learn German was *all* the paid education I ever had' – it may well appear a world so remote, so formidable, so intricate in its ceremonies and traditions that any criticism or comment may well seem futile. Here, too, we marvel at the brilliance of your clothes; here, too, we watch maces erect themselves and processions form, and note with eyes too dazzled to record the differences, let alone to explain them, the subtle distinctions of hats and hoods, of purples and crimsons, of velvet and cloth, of cap and gown. It is a solemn spectacle. The words of Arthur's song in *Pendennis* rise to our lips:

> Although I enter not,
> Yet round about the spot
>   Sometimes I hover,
> And at the sacred gate,
> With longing eyes I wait,
>   Expectant . . .

and again,

> I will not enter there,
> To sully your pure prayer
>   With thoughts unruly.
>
> But suffer me to pace
> Round the forbidden place,
>   Lingering a minute,
> Like outcast spirits, who wait
> And see through Heaven's gate
>   Angels within it.

But, since both you, Sir, and the honorary treasurer of the college rebuilding fund are waiting for answers to your letters we must cease to hang over old bridges humming old songs; we must attempt to deal with the question of education, however imperfectly.

What, then, is this 'university education' of which Mary Kingsley's sisterhood have heard so much and to which they have contributed so painfully? What is this mysterious process that takes about three years to accomplish, costs a round sum in hard cash, and turns the crude and raw human being into the finished product – an educated man or woman? There can be no doubt in the first place of its supreme value. The witness of biography – that witness which any one who can read English can consult on the shelves of any public library – is unanimous upon this point; the value of education is among the greatest of all human values. Biography proves this in two ways. First, there is the fact that the great majority of the men who have ruled England for the past 500 years, who are now ruling England in Parliament and the Civil Service, have received a university education. Second, there is the fact which is even more impressive if you consider what toil, what privation it implies – and of this, too, there is ample proof in biography – the fact of the immense sum of money that has been spent upon education in the past 500 years. The income of Oxford University is £435,656 (1933–4), the income of Cambridge University is £212,000 (1930). In addition to the university income each college has its own separate income, which, judging only from the gifts and bequests announced from time to time in the newspapers, must in some cases be of fabulous proportions.[18] If we add further the incomes enjoyed by the great public schools – Eton, Harrow, Winchester, Rugby, to name the largest only – so huge a sum of money is reached that there can be no doubt of the enormous value that human beings place upon education. And the study of biography – the lives of the poor, of the obscure, of the uneducated – proves that they will make any effort, any

sacrifice to procure an education at one of the great universities.[19]

But perhaps the greatest testimony to the value of education
with which biography provides us is the fact that the sisters of
educated men not only made the sacrifices of comfort and
pleasure, which were needed in order to educate their brothers,
but actually desired to be educated themselves. When we consider
the ruling of the Church on this subject, a ruling which we learn
from biography was in force only a few years ago – '. . . I was
told that desire for learning in women was against the will of
God . . .'[20] – we must allow that their desire must have been
strong. And if we reflect that all the professions for which a
university education fitted her brothers were closed to her, her
belief in the value of education must appear still stronger, since
she must have believed in education for itself. And if we reflect
further that the one profession that was open to her – marriage –
was held to need no education, and indeed was of such a nature
that education unfitted women to practise it, then it would have
been no surprise to find that she had renounced any wish or
attempt to be educated herself, but had contented herself with
providing education for her brothers – the vast majority of
women, the nameless, the poor, by cutting down household
expenses; the minute minority, the titled, the rich, by founding
or endowing colleges for men. This indeed they did. But so
innate in human nature is the desire for education that you will
find, if you consult biography, that the same desire, in spite
of all the impediments that tradition, poverty and ridicule
could put in its way, existed too among women. To prove
this let us examine one life only – the life of Mary Astell.[21]
Little is known about her, but enough to show that almost
250 years ago this obstinate and perhaps irreligious desire was
alive in her; she actually proposed to found a college for women.
What is almost as remarkable, the Princess Ann was ready to
give her £10,000 – a very considerable sum then, and, indeed,
now, for any woman to have at her disposal – towards the
expenses. And then – then we meet with a fact which is of

extreme interest, both historically and psychologically: the Church intervened. Bishop Burnet was of opinion that to educate the sisters of educated men would be to encourage the wrong branch, that is to say, the Roman Catholic branch, of the Christian faith. The money went elsewhere; the college was never founded.

But these facts, as facts so often do, prove double-faced; for though they establish the value of education, they also prove that education is by no means a positive value; it is not good in all circumstances, and good for all people; it is only good for some people and for some purposes. It is good if it produces a belief in the Church of England; bad if it produces a belief in the Church of Rome; it is good for one sex and for some professions, but bad for another sex and for another profession.

Such at least would seem to be the answer of biography – the oracle is not dumb, but it is dubious. As, however, it is of great importance that we should use our influence through education to affect the young against war we must not be baffled by the evasions of biography or seduced by its charm. We must try to see what kind of education an educated man's sister receives at present, in order that we may do our utmost to use our influence in the universities where it properly belongs, and where it will have most chance of penetrating beneath the skin. Now happily we need no longer depend upon biography, which inevitably, since it is concerned with the private life, bristles with innumerable conflicts of private opinion. We have now to help us that record of the public life which is history. Even outsiders can consult the annals of those public bodies which record not the day-to-day opinions of private people, but use a larger accent and convey through the mouths of Parliaments and Senates the considered opinions of bodies of educated men.

History at once informs us that there are now, and have been since about 1870, colleges for the sisters of educated men both at Oxford and at Cambridge. But history also informs us of facts of such a nature about those colleges that all attempt to influence the young against war through the education they receive there must be abandoned. In face of them it is mere waste of time and breath to talk of 'influencing the young'; useless to lay down terms, before allowing the honorary treasurer to have her guinea; better to take the first train to London than to haunt the sacred gates. But, you will interpose, what are these facts? these historical but deplorable facts? Therefore let us place them before you, warning you that they are taken only from such records as are available to an outsider" and from the annals of the university which is not your own – Cambridge. Your judgement, therefore, will be undistorted by loyalty to old ties, or gratitude for benefits received, but it will be impartial and disinterested.

To begin then where we left off: Queen Anne died and Bishop Burnet died and Mary Astell died; but the desire to found a college for her own sex did not die. Indeed, it became stronger and stronger. By the middle of the nineteenth century it became so strong that a house was taken at Cambridge to lodge the students. It was not a nice house; it was a house without a garden in the middle of a noisy street. Then a second house was taken, a better house this time, though it is true that the water rushed through the dining-room in stormy weather and there was no playground. But that house was not sufficient; the desire for education was so urgent that more rooms were needed, a garden to walk in, a playground to play in. Therefore another house was needed. Now history tells us that in order to build this house, money was needed. You will not question that fact but you may well question the next – that the money was borrowed. It will seem to you more probable that the money was given. The other colleges, you will say, were rich; all derived their incomes indirectly, some directly, from their sisters. There is Gray's *Ode* to prove it. And you will quote the song with which he hails the benefactors: the Countess of Pembroke who founded Pembroke; the Countess of Clare who founded Clare; Margaret of Anjou who founded Queens'; the Countess of Richmond and Derby who founded St John's and Christ's.

What is grandeur, what is power?
Heavier toil, superior pain.
What the bright reward we gain?
The grateful memory of the good.
Sweet is the breath of vernal shower,
The bee's collected treasures sweet,
Sweet music's melting fall, but sweeter yet
The still small voice of gratitude.[22]

Here, you will say in sober prose, was an opportunity to repay the debt. For what sum was needed? A beggarly £10,000 – the very sum that the bishop intercepted about two centuries previously. That £10,000 surely was disgorged by the Church that had swallowed it? But churches do not easily disgorge what they have swallowed. Then the colleges, you will say, which had benefited, they must have given it gladly in memory of their noble benefactresses? What could £10,000 mean to St John's, or Clare, or Christ's? And the land belonged to St John's. But the land, history says, was leased; and the £10,000 was not given; it was collected laboriously from private purses. Among them one lady must be for ever remembered because she gave £1,000; and Anon. must receive whatever thanks Anon. will consent to receive, because she gave sums ranging from £20 to £100. And another lady was able, owing to a legacy from her mother, to give her services as mistress without salary. And the students themselves subscribed – so far as students can – by making beds and washing dishes, by forgoing amenities and living on simple fare. Ten thousand pounds is not at all a beggarly sum when it has to be collected from the purses of the poor, from the bodies of the young. It takes time, energy, brains, to collect it; sacrifice to give it. Of course, several educated men were very kind; they lectured to their sisters; others were not so kind; they refused to lecture to their sisters. Some educated men were very kind and encouraged their sisters; others were not so kind, they discouraged their sisters.[23] Nevertheless, by hook or by crook, the day came at last, history tells us, when somebody passed an examination. And then the mistresses, principals or whatever they called themselves – for the title that should be worn by a woman who will not take a salary must be a matter of doubt – asked the Chancellors and the Masters about whose titles there need be no doubt, at any rate upon that score, whether the girls who had passed examinations might advertise the fact as those gentlemen themselves did by putting letters after their names. This was advisable, because, as the present Master of Trinity, Sir J. J. Thomson, O.M., F.R.S., after poking a little justifiable fun at the 'pardonable vanity' of those who put letters after their names, informs us, 'the general public who have not taken a degree themselves attach much more importance to B.A. after a person's name than those who have. Head mistresses of schools therefore prefer a belettered staff, so that students of Newnham and Girton, since they could not put B.A. after their names, were at a disadvantage in obtaining appointments.' And in Heaven's name, we may both ask, what conceivable reason could there be for preventing them from putting the letters B.A. after their names if it helped them to obtain appointments? To that question history supplies no answer; we must look for it in psychology, in biography; but history supplies us with the fact. 'The proposal, however,' the Master of Trinity continues – the proposal, that is, that those who had passed examinations might call themselves B.A. – 'met with the most determined opposition . . . On the day of the voting there was a great influx of non-residents and the proposal was thrown out by the crushing majority of 1707 to 661. I believe the number of voters has never been equalled . . . The behaviour of some of the undergraduates after the poll was declared in the Senate House was exceptionally deplorable and disgraceful. A large band of them left the Senate House, proceeded to Newnham and damaged the bronze gates which had been put up as a memorial to Miss Clough, the first Principal.'[24]

Is that not enough? Need we collect more facts from history and biography to prove our statement that all attempt to influence the young against war through the education they receive at the universities must be abandoned? For do they not prove that education, the finest education in the world, does not teach people to hate force, but to use it? Do they not prove that education, far from teaching the educated generosity and magnanimity, makes them on the contrary so anxious to keep their possessions, that 'grandeur and power' of which the poet speaks, in their own hands, that they will use not force but much subtler methods than force when they are asked to share them? And are not force and possessiveness very closely connected with war? Of what use then is a university education in influencing people to prevent war? But history goes on of course; year succeeds to year. The years change things; slightly but imperceptibly they change them. And history tells us that at last, after spending time and strength whose value is immeasurable in repeatedly soliciting the authorities with the humility expected of our sex and proper to suppliants the right to impress head mistresses by putting the letters B.A. after the name was granted. But that right, history tells us, was only a titular right. At Cambridge, in the year 1937, the women's colleges – you will scarcely believe it, Sir, but once more it is the voice of fact that is speaking, not of fiction – the women's colleges are not allowed to be members of the university;[25] and the number of educated men's daughters who are allowed to receive a university education is still strictly limited; though both sexes contribute to the university funds.[26] As for poverty, *The Times* newspaper supplies us with figures; any ironmonger will provide us with a foot-rule; if we measure the money available for scholarships at the men's colleges with the money available for their sisters at the women's colleges, we shall save ourselves the trouble of adding up; and come to the conclusion that the colleges for the sisters of educated men are, compared with their brothers' colleges, unbelievably and shamefully poor.[27]

Proof of that last fact comes pat to hand in the honorary treasurer's letter, asking for money with which to rebuild her college. She has been asking for some time; she is still asking, it seems. But there is nothing, after what has been said above, that need puzzle us, either in the fact that she is poor, or in the fact that her college needs rebuilding. What is puzzling, and has become still more puzzling, in view of the facts given above, is this: What answer ought we to make her when she asks us to help her to rebuild her college? History, biography, and the daily paper between them make it difficult either to answer her letter or to dictate terms. For between them they have raised many questions. In the first place, what reason is there to think that a university education makes the educated against war? Again, if we help an educated man's daughter to go to Cambridge are we not forcing her to think not about education but about war? – not how she can learn, but how she can fight in order that she may win the same advantages as her brothers? Further, since the daughters of educated men are not members of Cambridge University they have no say in that education, therefore how can they alter that education, even if we ask them to? And then, of course, other questions arise – questions of a practical nature, which will easily be understood by a busy man, an honorary treasurer, like yourself, Sir. You will be the first to agree that to ask people who are so largely occupied in raising funds with which to rebuild a college to consider the nature of education and what effect it can have upon war is to heap another straw upon an already overburdened back. From an outsider, moreover, who has no right to speak, such a request may well deserve, and perhaps receive, a reply too forcible to be quoted. But we have sworn that we will do all we can to help you to prevent war by using our influence – our earned money influence. And education is the obvious way. Since she is poor, since she is asking for money, and since the giver of money is entitled to dictate terms, let us risk it and draft a letter to her, laying down the terms upon which she shall have our money to help to rebuild her college. Here, then, is an attempt:

'Your letter, Madam, has been waiting some time without an answer. But certain doubts and questions have arisen. May we put them to you, ignorantly as an outsider must, but frankly as an outsider should when asked to contribute money? You say, then, that you are asking for £100,000 with which to rebuild your college. But how can you be so foolish? Or are you so secluded among the nightingales and the willows, or so busy with profound questions of caps and gowns, and which is to walk first into the Provost's drawing-room – the Master's pug or the Mistress's pom – that you have no time to read the daily papers? Or are you so harassed with the problem of drawing £100,000 gracefully from an indifferent public that you can only think of appeals and committees, bazaars and ices, strawberries and cream?

'Let us then inform you: we are spending three hundred millions annually upon the army and navy; for, according to a letter that lies cheek by jowl with your own, there is grave danger of war. How then can you seriously ask us to provide you with money with which to rebuild your college? If you reply that the college was built on the cheap, and that the college needs rebuilding, that may be true. But when you go on to say that the public is generous, and that the public is still capable of providing large sums for rebuilding colleges, let us draw your attention to a significant passage in the Master of Trinity's memoirs. It is this: "Fortunately, however, soon after the beginning of this century the University began to receive a succession of very handsome bequests and donations, and these, aided by a liberal grant from the Government, have put the finances of the University in such a good position that it has been quite unnecessary to ask for any increase in the contribution from the Colleges. The income of the University from all sources has increased from about £60,000 in 1900 to £212,000 in 1930. It is not a very wild hypothesis to suppose that this has been to a large extent due to the important and very interesting discoveries which have been made in the University, and Cambridge may be quoted as an example of the practical results which come from Research for its own sake."

'Consider only that last sentence. ". . . Cambridge may be quoted as an example of the practical results which come from Research for its own sake." What has your college done to stimulate great manufacturers to endow it? Have you taken a leading part in the invention of the implements of war? How far have your students succeeded in business as capitalists? How then can you expect "very handsome bequests and donations" to come your way? Again, are you a member of Cambridge University? You are not. How then can you fairly ask for any say in their distribution? You can not. Therefore, Madam, it is plain that you must stand at the door, cap in hand, giving parties, spending your strength and your time in soliciting subscriptions. That is plain. But it is also plain that outsiders who find you thus occupied must ask themselves, when they receive a request for a contribution towards rebuilding your college, Shall I send it or shan't I? If I send it, what shall I ask them to do with it? Shall I ask them to rebuild the college on the old lines? Or shall I ask them to rebuild it, but differently? Or shall I ask them to buy rags and petrol and Bryant & May's matches and burn the college to the ground?

'These are the questions, Madam, that have kept your letter so long unanswered. They are questions of great difficulty and perhaps they are useless questions. But can we leave them unasked in view of this gentleman's questions? He is asking us how can we help him to prevent war? He is asking us how can we help him to defend liberty; to defend culture? Also consider these photographs: they are pictures of dead bodies and ruined houses. Surely in view of these questions and pictures you must consider very carefully before you begin to rebuild your college what is the aim of education, what kind of society, what kind of human being it should seek to produce. At any rate I will only send you a guinea with which to rebuild your college if you can satisfy me that you will use it to produce the kind of society, the kind of people that will help to prevent war.

'Let us then discuss as quickly as we can the sort of education that is needed. Now since history and biography – the only evidence available to an outsider – seem to prove that the old education of the old colleges breeds neither a particular respect for liberty nor a particular hatred of war it is clear that you must rebuild your college differently. It is young and poor; let it therefore take advantage of those qualities and be founded on poverty and youth. Obviously, then, it must be an experimental college, an adventurous college. Let it be built on lines of its own. It must be built not of carved stone and stained glass, but of some cheap, easily combustible material which does not hoard dust and perpetrate traditions. Do not have chapels.[28] Do not have museums and libraries with chained books and first editions under glass cases. Let the pictures and the books be new and always changing. Let it be decorated afresh by each generation with their own hands cheaply. The work of the living is cheap; often they will give it for the sake of being allowed to do it. Next, what should be taught in the new college, the poor college? Not the arts of dominating other people; not the arts of ruling, of killing, of acquiring land and capital. They require too many overhead expenses; salaries and uniforms and ceremonies. The poor college must teach only the arts that can be taught cheaply and practised by poor people; such as medicine, mathematics, music, painting and literature. It should teach the arts of human intercourse; the art of understanding other people's lives and minds, and the little arts of talk, of dress, of cookery that are allied with them. The aim of the new college, the cheap college, should be not to segregate and specialize, but to combine. It should explore the ways in which mind and body can be made to co-operate; discover what new combinations make good wholes in human life. The teachers should be drawn from the good livers as well as from the good thinkers. There should be no difficulty in attracting them. For there would be none of the barriers of wealth and ceremony, of advertisement and competition which now make the old and rich universities such uneasy dwelling-places – cities of strife, cities where this is locked up and that is chained down; where nobody can walk freely or talk freely for fear of transgressing some chalk mark, of displeasing some dignitary. But if the college were poor it would have nothing to offer; competition would be abolished. Life would be open and easy. People who love learning for itself would gladly come there. Musicians, painters, writers, would teach there, because they would learn. What could be of greater help to a writer than to discuss the art of writing with people who were thinking not of examinations or degrees or of what honour or profit they could make literature give them but of the art itself?

'And so with the other arts and artists. They would come to the poor college and practise their arts there because it would be a place where society was free; not parcelled out into the miserable distinctions of rich and poor, of clever and stupid; but where all the different degrees and kinds of mind, body and soul merit co-operated. Let us then found this new college; this poor college; in which learning is sought for itself; where advertisement is abolished; and there are no degrees; and lectures are not given, and sermons are not preached, and the old poisoned vanities and parades which breed competition and jealousy . . .'

The letter broke off there. It was not from lack of things to say; the peroration indeed was only just beginning. It was because the face on the other side of the page – the face that a letter-writer always sees – appeared to be fixed with a certain melancholy, upon a passage in the book from which quotation has already been made. 'Head mistresses of schools therefore prefer a belettered staff, so that students of Newnham and Girton, since they could not put B.A. after their name, were at a disadvantage in obtaining appointments.' The honorary treasurer of the Rebuilding Fund had her eyes fixed on that. 'What is the use of thinking how a college can be different,' she seemed to say, 'when it must be a place where students are taught to obtain appointments?' 'Dream your dreams,' she seemed to add, turning, rather wearily, to the table which she was arranging for some festival, a bazaar presumably, 'but we have to face realities.'

That then was the 'reality' on which her eyes were fixed; students must be taught to earn their livings. And since that reality meant that she must rebuild her college on the same lines as the others, it followed that the college for the daughters of educated men must also make Research produce practical results which will induce bequests and donations from rich men; it must encourage competition; it must accept degrees and coloured hoods; it must accumulate great wealth; it must exclude other people from a share of its wealth; and, therefore, in 500 years or so, that college, too, must ask the same question that you, Sir, are asking now: 'How in your opinion are we to prevent war?'

An undesirable result that seemed; why then subscribe a guinea to procure it? That question at any rate was answered. No guinea of earned money should go to rebuilding the college on the old plan; just as certainly none could be spent upon building a college upon a new plan; therefore the guinea should be earmarked 'Rags. Petrol. Matches'. And this note should be attached to it. 'Take this guinea and with it burn the college to the ground. Set fire to the old hypocrisies. Let the light of the burning building scare the nightingales and incarnadine the willows. And let the daughters of educated men dance round the fire and heap armful upon armful of dead leaves upon the flames. And let their mothers lean from the upper windows and cry "Let it blaze! Let it blaze! For we have done with this 'education'"!'

That passage, Sir, is not empty rhetoric, for it is based upon the respectable opinion of the late head master of Eton, the present Dean of Durham.[29] Nevertheless, there is something hollow about it, as is shown by a moment's conflict with fact. We have said that the only influence which the daughters of educated men can at present exert against war is the disinterested influence that they possess through earning their livings. If there were no means of training them to earn their livings, there would be an end of that influence. They could not obtain appointments. If they could not obtain appointments they would again be dependent upon their fathers and brothers; and if they were again dependent upon their fathers and brothers they would again be consciously and unconsciously in favour of war. History would seem to put that beyond doubt. Therefore we must send a guinea to the honorary treasurer of the college rebuilding fund, and let her do what she can with it. It is useless as things are to attach conditions as to the way in which that guinea is to be spent.

Such then is the rather lame and depressing answer to our question whether we can ask the authorities of the colleges for the daughters of educated men to use their influence through education to prevent war. It appears that we can ask them to do nothing; they must follow the old road to the old end; our own influence as outsiders can only be of the most indirect sort. If we are asked to teach, we can examine very carefully into the aim of such teaching, and refuse to teach any art or science that encourages war. Further, we can pour mild scorn upon chapels, upon degrees, and upon the value of examinations. We can intimate that a prize poem can still have merit in spite of the fact that it has won a prize; and maintain that a book may still be worth reading in spite of the fact that its author took a first class with honours in the English tripos.[v] If we are asked to lecture we can refuse to bolster up the vain and vicious system of lecturing by refusing to lecture.[30] And, of course, if we are offered offices and honours for ourselves we can refuse them – how, indeed, in view of the facts, could we possibly do otherwise? But there is no blinking the fact that in the present state of things the most effective way in which we can help you through education to prevent war is to subscribe as generously as possible to the colleges for the daughters of educated men. For, to repeat, if those daughters are not going to be educated they are not going to earn their livings; if they are not going to earn their livings, they are going once more to be restricted to the education of the private house; and if they are going to be restricted to the education of the private house they are going, once more, to exert all their influence both consciously and unconsciously in favour of war. Of that there can be little doubt. Should you doubt it, should you ask proof, let us once more consult biography. Its testimony upon this point is so conclusive, but so voluminous, that we must try to condense many volumes into one story. Here, then, is the narrative of the life of an educated man's daughter who was dependent upon father and brother in the private house of the nineteenth century.

The day was hot, but she could not go out. 'How many a long dull summer's day have I passed immured indoors because there was no room for me in the family carriage and no lady's maid who had time to walk out with me.' The sun set; and out she went at last, dressed as well as could be managed upon an allowance of from £40 to £100 a year.[31] But 'to any sort of entertainment she must be accompanied by father or mother or by some married woman.' Whom did she meet at those entertainments thus dressed, thus accompanied? Educated men – 'cabinet ministers, ambassadors, famous soldiers and the like, all splendidly dressed, wearing decorations.' What did they talk about? Whatever refreshed the minds of busy men who wanted to forget their own work – 'the gossip of the dancing world' did very well. The days passed. Saturday came. On Saturday 'M.P.s and other busy men had leisure to enjoy society'; they came to tea and they came to dinner. Next day was Sunday. On Sundays 'the great majority of us went as a matter of course to morning church.' The seasons changed. It was summer. In the summer they entertained visitors, 'mostly relatives' in the country. Now it was winter. In the winter 'they studied history and literature and music, and tried to draw and paint. If they did not produce anything remarkable they learnt much in the process.' And so with some visiting the sick and teaching the poor, the years passed. And what was the great end and aim of these years, of that education? Marriage, of course. '. . . it was not a question of *whether* we should marry, but simply of *whom* we should marry,' says one of them. It was with a view to marriage that her mind was taught. It was with a view to marriage that she tinkled on the piano, but was not allowed to join an orchestra; sketched innocent domestic scenes, but was not allowed to study from the nude; read this book, but was not allowed to read that, charmed, and talked. It was with a view to marriage that her body was educated; a maid was provided for her; that the streets were shut to her; that the fields were shut to her; that solitude was denied her – all this was enforced upon her in order that she might preserve her body intact for her husband. In short, the thought of marriage influenced what she said, what she thought, what she did. How could it be otherwise? Marriage was the only profession open to her.[32]

The sight is so curious for what it shows of the educated man as well as of his daughter that it is tempting to linger. The influence of the pheasant upon love alone deserves a chapter to itself.[33] But we are not asking now the interesting question, what was the effect of that education upon the race? We are asking why did such an education make the person so educated consciously and unconsciously in favour of war? Because consciously, it is obvious, she was forced to use whatever influence she possessed to bolster up the system which provided her with maids; with carriages; with fine clothes; with fine parties – it was by these means that she achieved marriage. Consciously she must use whatever charm or beauty she possessed to flatter and cajole the busy men, the soldiers, the lawyers, the ambassadors, the cabinet ministers who wanted recreation after their day's work. Consciously she must accept their views, and fall in with their decrees because it was only so that she could wheedle them into giving her the means to marry or marriage itself.[34] In short, all her conscious effort must be in favour of what Lady Lovelace called 'our splendid Empire' . . . 'the price of which,' she added, 'is mainly paid by women.' And who can doubt her, or that the price was heavy?

But her unconscious influence was even more strongly perhaps in favour of war. How else can we explain that amazing outburst in August 1914, when the daughters of educated men who had been educated thus rushed into hospitals, some still attended by their maids, drove lorries, worked in fields and munition factories, and used all their immense stores of charm, of sympathy, to persuade young men that to fight was heroic, and that the wounded in battle deserved all her care and all her praise? The reason lies in that same education. So profound was her unconscious loathing for the education of the private house with its cruelty, its poverty, its hypocrisy, its immorality, its inanity that she would undertake any task however menial, exercise any fascination however fatal that enabled her to escape. Thus consciously she desired 'our splendid Empire'; unconsciously she desired our splendid war.

So, Sir, if you want us to help you to prevent war the conclusion seems to be inevitable; we must help to rebuild the college which, imperfect as it may be, is the only alternative to the education of the private house. We must hope that in time that education may be altered. That guinea must be given before we give you the guinea that you ask for your own society. But it is contributing to the same cause – the prevention of war. Guineas are rare; guineas are valuable, but let us send one without any condition attached to the honorary treasurer of the building fund, because by so doing we are making a positive contribution to the prevention of war.

Two

Now that we have given one guinea towards rebuilding a college we must consider whether there is not more that we can do to help you to prevent war. And it is at once obvious, if what we have said about influence is true, that we must turn to the professions, because if we could persuade those who can earn their livings, and thus actually hold in their hands this new weapon, our only weapon, the weapon of independent opinion based upon independent income, to use that weapon against war, we should do more to help you than by appealing to those who must teach the young to earn their livings; or by lingering, however long, round the forbidden places and sacred gates of the universities where they are thus taught. This, therefore, is a more important question than the other.

Let us then lay your letter asking for help to prevent war, before the independent, the mature, those who are earning their livings in the professions. There is no need of rhetoric; hardly, one would suppose, of argument. 'Here is a man,' one has only to say, 'whom we all have reason to respect; he tells us that war is possible; perhaps probable; he asks us, who can earn our livings, to help him in any way we can to prevent war.' That surely will be enough without pointing to the photographs that are all this time piling up on the table – photographs of more dead bodies, of more ruined houses, to call forth an answer, and an answer that will give you, Sir, the very help that you require. But . . . it seems that there is some hesitation, some doubt – not certainly that war is horrible, that war is beastly, that war is insupportable and that war is inhuman, as Wilfred Owen said, or that we wish to do all we can to help you to prevent war. Nevertheless, doubts and hesitations there are; and the quickest way to understand them is to place before you another letter, a letter as genuine as your own, a letter that happens to lie beside it on the table.[1]

It is a letter from another honorary treasurer, and it is again asking for money. 'Will you,' she writes, 'send a subscription to' [a society to help the daughters of educated men to obtain employment in the professions]*a* 'in order to help us to earn our livings? Failing money,' she goes on, 'any gift will be acceptable – books, fruit or cast-off clothing that can be sold in a bazaar.' Now that letter has so much bearing upon the doubts and hesitations referred to above, and upon the help we can give you, that it seems impossible either to send her a guinea or to send you a guinea until we have considered the questions which it raises.

The first question is obviously, Why is she asking for money? Why is she so poor, this representative of professional women, that she must beg for cast-off clothing for a bazaar? That is the first point to clear up, because if she is as poor as this letter indicates, then the weapon of independent opinion upon which we have been counting to help you to prevent war is not, to put it mildly, a very powerful weapon. On the other hand, poverty has its advantages; for if she is poor, as poor as she pretends to be, then we can bargain with her, as we bargained with her sister at Cambridge,*b* and exercise the right of potential givers to impose terms. Let us then question her about her financial position and certain other facts before we give her a guinea, or lay down the terms upon which she is to have it. Here is the draft of such a letter:

'Accept a thousand apologies, Madam, for keeping you waiting so long for an answer to your letter. The fact is, certain questions have arisen, to which we must ask you to reply before we send you a subscription. In the first place you are asking for money – money with which to pay your rent. But how can it be, how can it possibly be, my dear Madam, that you are so terribly poor? The professions have been open to the daughters of educated men for almost 20 years. Therefore, how can it be, that you, whom we take to be their representative, are standing, like your sister at Cambridge, hat in hand, pleading for money, or failing money, for fruit, books, or cast-off clothing to sell at a bazaar?

How can it be, we repeat? Surely there must be some very grave defect, of common humanity, of common justice, or of common sense. Or can it simply be that you are pulling a long face and telling a tall story like the beggar at the street corner who has a stocking full of guineas safely hoarded under her bed at home? In any case, this perpetual asking for money and pleading of poverty is laying you open to very grave rebukes, not only from indolent outsiders who dislike thinking about practical affairs almost as much as they dislike signing cheques, but from educated men. You are drawing upon yourselves the censure and contempt of men of established reputation as philosophers and novelists – of men like Mr Joad and Mr Wells.[c] Not only do they deny your poverty, but they accuse you of apathy and indifference. Let me draw your attention to the charges that they bring against you. Listen, in the first place, to what Mr C. E. M. Joad has to say of you. He says: "I doubt whether at any time during the last fifty years young women have been more politically apathetic, more socially indifferent than at the present time." That is how he begins. And he goes on to say, very rightly, that it is not his business to tell you what you ought to do; but he adds, very kindly, that he will give you an example of what you might do. You might imitate your sisters in America. You might found "a society for the advertisement of peace". He gives an example. This society explained, "I know not with what truth, that the number of pounds spent by the world on armaments in the current year was exactly equal to the number of minutes (or was it seconds?) which had elapsed since the death of Christ, who taught that war is unchristian . . ." Now why should not you, too, follow their example and create such a society in England? It would need money, of course; but – and this is the point that I wish particularly to emphasize – there can be no doubt that you have the money. Mr Joad provides the proof. "Before the war money poured into the coffers of the W.S.P.U.[d] in order that women might win the vote which, it was hoped, would enable them to make war a thing of the past. The vote is won," Mr Joad continues, "but war is very far from being a thing of the past." That I can corroborate myself – witness this letter from a gentleman asking for help to prevent war, and there are certain photographs of dead bodies and ruined houses – but let Mr Joad continue. "Is it unreasonable," he goes on, "to ask that contemporary women should be prepared to give as much energy and money, to suffer as much obloquy and insult in the cause of peace, as their mothers gave and suffered in the cause of equality?" And again, I cannot help but echo, is it unreasonable to ask women to go on, from generation to generation, suffering obloquy and insult first from their brothers and then for their brothers? Is it not both perfectly reasonable and on the whole for their physical, moral and spiritual welfare? But let us not interrupt Mr Joad. "If it is, then the sooner they give up the pretence of playing with public affairs and return to private life the better. If they cannot make a job of the House of Commons, let them at least make something of their own houses. If they cannot learn to save men from the destruction which incurable male mischievousness bids fair to bring upon them, let women at least learn to feed them, before they destroy themselves."[2] Let us not pause to ask how even with a vote they can cure what Mr Joad himself admits to be incurable, for the point is how, in the face of that statement, you have the effrontery to ask me for a guinea towards your rent? According to Mr Joad you are not only extremely rich; you are also extremely idle; and so given over to the eating of peanuts and ice cream that you have not learnt how to cook him a dinner before he destroys himself, let alone how to prevent that fatal act. But more serious charges are to follow. Your lethargy is such that you will not fight even to protect the freedom which your mothers won for you. That charge is made against you by the most famous of living English novelists – Mr H. G. Wells. Mr H. G. Wells says, "There has been no perceptible woman's movement to resist the practical obliteration of their freedom by Fascists or Nazis."[3] Rich, idle, greedy and lethargic as you are, how have you the effrontery to ask me to subscribe to a society which helps the daughters of educated men to make their livings in the professions? For as these gentlemen prove in spite of the vote and the wealth which that vote must have brought with it, you have not ended war; in spite of the vote and the power which that vote must have brought with it, you have not resisted the practical obliteration of your freedom by Fascists or Nazis. What other conclusion then can one come to but that the whole of what was called "the woman's movement" has proved itself a failure; and the guinea which I am sending you herewith is to be devoted not to paying your rent but to burning your building. And when that is burnt, retire once more to the kitchen, Madam, and learn, if you can, to cook the dinner which you may not share . . .'[4]

There, Sir, the letter stopped; for on the face at the other side of the letter – the face that a letter-writer always sees – was an expression, of boredom was it, or was it of fatigue? The honorary treasurer's glance seemed to rest upon a little scrap of paper upon which were written two dull little facts which, since they have some bearing upon the question we are discussing, how the daughters of educated men who are earning their livings in the professions can help you to prevent war, may be copied here. The first fact was that the income of the W.S.P.U. upon which Mr Joad has based his estimate of their wealth was (in the year 1912 at the height of their activity) £42,000.[5] The second fact was that: 'To earn £250 a year is quite an achievement even for a highly qualified woman with years of experience.'[6] The date of that statement is 1934.

Both facts are interesting; and since both have a direct bearing upon the question before us, let us examine them. To take the first fact first – that is interesting because it shows that one of the greatest political changes of our times was accomplished upon the incredibly minute income of £42,000 a year. 'Incredibly minute' is, of course, a comparative term; it is incredibly minute, that is to say, compared with the income which the Conservative party, or the Liberal party – the parties to which the educated woman's brother belonged – had at their disposal for their political causes. It is considerably less than the income which the

Labour party – the party to which the working woman's brother belongs – has at their disposal.[7] It is incredibly minute compared with the sums that a society like the Society for the Abolition of Slavery for example had at its disposal for the abolition of that slavery. It is incredibly minute compared with the sums which the educated man spends annually, not upon political causes, but upon sports and pleasure. But our amazement, whether at the poverty of educated men's daughters or at their economy, is a decidedly unpleasant emotion in this case, for it forces us to suspect that the honorary treasurer is telling the sober truth; she is poor; and it forces us to ask once more how, if £42,000 was all that the daughters of educated men could collect after many years of indefatigable labour for their own cause, they can help you to win yours? How much peace will £42,000 a year buy at the present moment when we are spending £300,000,000 annually upon arms?

But the second fact is the more startling and the more depressing of the two – the fact that now, almost 20 years, that is, after they have been admitted to the money-making professions 'to earn £250 a year is quite an achievement even for a highly qualified woman with years of experience.' Indeed, that fact, if it is a fact, is so startling and has so much bearing upon the question before us that we must pause for a moment to examine it. It is so important that it must be examined, moreover, by the white light of facts, not by the coloured light of biography. Let us have recourse then to some impersonal and impartial authority who has no more axe to grind or dinner to cook than Cleopatra's needle[e] – Whitaker's Almanack, for example.

Whitaker, needless to say, is not only one of the most dispassionate of authors, but one of the most methodical. There, in his Almanack he has collected all the facts about all, or almost all, of the professions that have been opened to the daughters of educated men. In a section called 'Government and Public Offices' he provides us with a plain statement of whom the Government employs professionally, and of what the Government pays those whom it employs. Since Whitaker adopts the alphabetical system, let us follow his lead and examine the first six letters of the alphabet. Under A there are the Admiralty, the Air Ministry, and Ministry of Agriculture. Under B there is the British Broadcasting Corporation; under C the Colonial Office and the Charity Commissioners; under D the Dominions Office and Development Commission; under E there are the Ecclesiastical Commissioners and the Board of Education; and so we come to the sixth letter F under which we find the Ministry of Fisheries, the Foreign Office, the Friendly Societies and the Fine Arts. These then are some of the professions which are now, as we are frequently reminded, open to both men and women equally. And the salaries paid to those employed in them come out of public money which is supplied by both sexes equally. And the income tax which supplies those salaries (among other things) now stands at about five shillings in the pound. ∫ We have all, therefore, an interest in asking how that money is spent, and upon whom. Let us look at the salary list of the Board of Education, since that is the class to which we both, Sir, though in very different degrees, have the honour to belong. The President, Whitaker says, of the Board of Education, gets £2,000; his principal Private Secretary gets from £847 to £1,058; his Assistant Private Secretary gets from £277 to £634. Then there is the Permanent Secretary of the Board of Education. He gets £3,000; his Private Secretary gets from £277 to £634. The Parliamentary Secretary gets £1,200; his Private Secretary gets from £277 to £634. The Deputy Secretary gets £2,200. The Permanent Secretary of the Welsh Department gets £1,650. And then there are Principal Assistant Secretaries and Assistant Secretaries, there are Directors of Establishments, Accountants-General, principal Finance Officers, Finance Officers, Legal Advisers, Assistant Legal Advisers – all these ladies and gentlemen, the impeccable and impartial Whitaker informs us, get incomes which run into four figures or over. Now an income which is over or about a thousand a year is a nice round sum when it is paid yearly and paid punctually; but when we consider that the work is a whole-time job and a skilled job we shall not grudge these ladies and gentlemen their salaries, even though our income tax does stand at five shillings in the pound, and our incomes are by no means paid punctually or paid annually. Men and women who spend every day and all day in an office from the age of about 23 to the age of 60 or so deserve every penny they get. Only, the reflection will intrude itself, if these ladies are drawing £1,000, £2,000 and £3,000 a year, not only in the Board of Education, but in all the other boards and offices which are now open to them, from the Admiralty at the beginning of the alphabet to the Board of Works at the end, the statement that '£250 is quite an achievement, even for a highly qualified woman with years of experience' must be, to put it plainly, an unmitigated lie. Why, we have only to walk down Whitehall; consider how many boards and offices are housed there; reflect that each is staffed and officered by a flock of secretaries and under-secretaries so many and so nicely graded that their very names make our heads spin; and remember that each has his or her own sufficient salary, to exclaim that the statement is impossible, inexplicable. How can we explain it? Only by putting on a stronger pair of glasses. Let us read down the list, further and further and further down. At last we come to a name to which the prefix 'Miss' is attached. Can it be that all the names on top of hers, all the names to which the big salaries are attached, are the names of gentlemen? It seems so. So then it is not the salaries that are lacking; it is the daughters of educated men.

Now three good reasons for this curious deficiency or disparity lie upon the surface. Dr Robson supplies us with the first – 'The Administrative Class, which occupies all the controlling positions in the Home Civil Service, consists to an over-whelming extent of the fortunate few who can manage to get to Oxford and Cambridge; and the entrance examination has always been expressly designed for that purpose.'⁸ The fortunate few in our class, the daughters of educated men class, are very, very few. Oxford and Cambridge, as we have seen, strictly limit the number of educated men's daughters who are allowed to receive a university education. Secondly, many more daughters stay at home to look after old mothers than sons stay at home to look after old fathers. The private house, we must remember, is still a going concern. Hence fewer daughters than sons enter for the Civil Service Examination. In the third place, we may fairly assume that 60 years of examination passing are not so effective as 500. The Civil Service Examination is a stiff one; we may reasonably expect more sons to pass it than daughters. We have nevertheless to explain the curious fact that though a certain number of daughters enter for the examination and pass the examination those to whose names the word 'Miss' is attached do not seem to enter the four-figure zone. The sex distinction seems, according to Whitaker, possessed of a curious leaden quality, liable to keep any name to which it is fastened circling in the lower spheres. Plainly the reason for this may lie not upon the surface, but within. It may be, to speak bluntly, that the daughters are in themselves deficient; that they have proved themselves untrustworthy; unsatisfactory; so lacking in the necessary ability that it is to the public interest to keep them to the lower grades where, if they are paid less, they have less chance of impeding the transaction of public business. This solution would be easy but, unfortunately, it is denied to us. It is denied to us by the Prime Minister himself. Women in the Civil Services are not untrustworthy, Mr Baldwin*ᵍ informed us the other day. 'Many of them,' he said, 'are in positions in the course of their daily work to amass secret information. Secret information has a way of leaking very often, as we politicians know to our cost. I have never known a case of such a leakage being due to a woman, and I have known cases of leakage coming from men who should have known a great deal better.' So they are not so loose-lipped and fond of gossip as the tradition would have it? A useful contribution in its way to psychology and a hint to novelists; but still there may be other objections to women's employment as Civil Servants.

* Since these words were written Mr Baldwin has ceased to be Prime Minister and become an Earl.

Intellectually, they may not be so able as their brothers. But here again the Prime Minister will not help us out. 'He was not prepared to say that any conclusion had been formed – or was even necessary – whether women were as good as, or better than, men, but he believed that women had worked in the Civil Service to their own content, and certainly to the complete satisfaction of everybody who had anything to do with them.' Finally, as if to cap what must necessarily be an inconclusive statement by expressing a personal opinion which might rightly be more positive he said, 'I should like to pay my personal tribute to the industry, capacity, ability and loyalty of the women I have come across in Civil Service positions.' And he went on to express the hope that business men would make more use of those very valuable qualities.[9]

Now if anyone is in a position to know the facts it is the Prime Minister; and if anyone is able to speak the truth about them it is the same gentleman. Yet Mr Baldwin says one thing; Mr Whitaker says another. If Mr Baldwin is well-informed, so is Mr Whitaker. Nevertheless, they contradict each other. The issue is joined; Mr Baldwin says that women are first-class civil servants; Mr Whitaker says that they are third-class civil servants. It is, in short, a case of *Baldwin* v. *Whitaker*, and since it is a very important case, for upon it depends the answer to many questions which puzzle us, not only about the poverty of educated men's daughters but about the psychology of educated men's sons, let us try the case of the *Prime Minister* v. *the Almanack*.

For such a trial you, Sir, have definite qualifications; as a barrister you have first-hand knowledge of one profession, and as an educated man second-hand knowledge of many more. And if it is true that the daughters of educated men who are of Mary Kingsley's persuasion have no direct knowledge, still through fathers and uncles, cousins and brothers they may claim some indirect knowledge of professional life – it is a photograph that they have often looked upon – and this indirect knowledge they can improve, if they have a mind, by peeping through doors, taking notes, and asking questions discreetly. If, then, we pool our first-hand, second-hand, direct and indirect knowledge of the professions with a view to trying the important case of *Baldwin* v. *Whitaker* we shall agree at the outset that professions are very queer things. It by no means follows that a clever man gets to the top or that a stupid man stays at the bottom. This rising and falling is by no means a cut-and-dried clear-cut rational process, we shall both agree. After all, as we both have reason to know, Judges are fathers; and Permanent Secretaries have sons. Judges require marshals; Permanent Secretaries, private secretaries. What is more natural than that a nephew should be a marshal or the son of an old school friend a private secretary? To have such perquisites in their gift is as much the due of the public servant as a cigar now and then or a cast-off dress here and there are perquisites of the private servant. But the giving of such perquisites, the exercise of such influence, queers the professions. Success is easier for some, harder for others, however equal the brain power may be, so that some rise unexpectedly; some fall unexpectedly; some remain strangely stationary; with the result that the professions are queered. Often indeed it is the public advantage that they should be queered. Since nobody, from the Master of Trinity downwards (bating, presumably, a few head mistresses), believes in the infallibility of examiners, a certain degree of elasticity is to the public advantage; since the impersonal is fallible, it is well that it should be supplemented by the personal. Happily for us all, therefore, we may conclude, a board is not made literally of oak, nor a division of iron. Both boards and divisions[b] transmit human sympathies, and reflect human antipathies with the result that the imperfections of the examination system are rectified; the public interest is served; and the ties of blood and friendship are recognized. Thus it is quite possible that the name 'Miss' transmits through the board or division some vibration which is not registered in the examination room. 'Miss' transmits sex; and sex may carry with it an aroma. 'Miss' may carry with it the swish of petticoats, the savour of scent or other odour perceptible to the nose on the further side of the partition and obnoxious to it. What charms and consoles in the private house may distract and exacerbate in the public office. The Archbishops' Commission assures us that this is so in the pulpit.[10] Whitehall may be equally susceptible. At any rate since Miss is a woman, Miss was not educated at Eton or Christ Church. Since Miss is a woman, Miss is not a son or a nephew. We are hazarding our way among imponderables. We can scarcely proceed too much on tiptoe. We are trying, remember, to discover what flavour attaches itself to sex in a public office; we are sniffing most delicately not facts but savours. And therefore it would be well not to depend on our own private noses, but to call in evidence from outside. Let us turn to the public press and see if we can discover from the opinions aired there any hint that will guide us in our attempt to decide the delicate and difficult question as to the aroma, the atmosphere that surrounds the word 'Miss' in Whitehall. We will consult the newspapers.

First:

I think your correspondent . . . correctly sums up this discussion in the observation that woman has too much liberty. It is probable that this so-called liberty came with the war, when women assumed responsibilities so far unknown to them. They did splendid service during those days. Unfortunately, they were praised and petted out of all proportion to the value of their performances.[11]

That does very well for a beginning. But let us proceed:

I am of the opinion that a considerable amount of the distress which is prevalent in this section of the community [the clerical] could be relieved by the policy of employing men instead of women, wherever possible. There are to-day in Government offices, post offices, insurance companies, banks and other offices, thousands of women doing work which men could do. At the same time there are thousands of qualified men, young and middle-aged, who cannot get a job of any sort. There is a large demand for woman labour in the domestic arts, and in the process of re-grading a large number of women who have drifted into clerical service would become available for domestic service.[12]

The odour thickens, you will agree.

Then once more:

> I am certain I voice the opinion of thousands of young men when I say that if men were doing the work that thousands of young women are now doing the men would be able to keep those same women in decent homes. Homes are the real places of the women who are now compelling men to be idle. It is time the Government insisted upon employers giving work to more men, thus enabling them to marry the women they cannot now approach.[13]

There! There can be no doubt of the odour now. The cat is out of the bag; and it is a Tom.

After considering the evidence contained in those three quotations, you will agree that there is good reason to think that the word 'Miss', however delicious its scent in the private house, has a certain odour attached to it in Whitehall which is disagreeable to the noses on the other side of the partition; and that it is likely that a name to which 'Miss' is attached will, because of this odour, circle in the lower spheres where the salaries are small rather than mount to the higher spheres where the salaries are substantial. As for 'Mrs', it is a contaminated word; an obscene word. The less said about that word the better. Such is the smell of it, so rank does it stink in the nostrils of Whitehall, that Whitehall excludes it entirely.[i] In Whitehall as in heaven, there is neither marrying nor giving in marriage.[14]

Odour then – or shall we call it 'atmosphere'? – is a very important element in professional life; in spite of the fact that like other important elements it is impalpable. It can escape the noses of examiners in examination rooms, yet penetrate boards and divisions and affect the senses of those within. Its bearing upon the case before us is undeniable. For it allows us to decide in the case of *Baldwin* v. *Whitaker* that both the Prime Minister and the Almanack are telling the truth. It is true that women civil servants deserve to be paid as much as men; but it is also true that they are not paid as much as men. The discrepancy is due to atmosphere.

Atmosphere plainly is a very mighty power. Atmosphere not only changes the sizes and shapes of things; it affects solid bodies, like salaries, which might have been thought impervious to atmosphere. An epic poem might be written about atmosphere, or a novel in ten or fifteen volumes. But since this is only a letter, and you are pressed for time, let us confine ourselves to the plain statement that atmosphere is one of the most powerful, partly because it is one of the most impalpable, of the enemies with which the daughters of educated men have to fight. If you think that statement exaggerated, look once more at the samples of atmosphere contained in those three quotations. We shall find there not only the reason why the pay of the professional woman is still so small, but something more dangerous, something which, if it spreads, may poison both sexes equally. There, in those quotations, is the egg of the very same worm that we know under other names in other countries. There we have in embryo the creature, Dictator as we call him when he is Italian or German, who believes that he has the right whether given by God, Nature, sex or race is immaterial, to dictate to other human beings how they shall live; what they shall do. Let us quote again: 'Homes are the real places of the women who are now compelling men to be idle. It is time the Government insisted upon employers giving work to more men, thus enabling them to marry the women they cannot now approach.' Place beside it another quotation: 'There are two worlds in the life of the nation, the world of men and the world of women. Nature has done well to entrust the man with the care of his family and the nation. The woman's world is her family, her husband, her children, and her home.' One is written in English, the other in German.*ʲ* But where is the difference? Are they not both saying the same thing? Are they not both the voices of Dictators, whether they speak English or German, and are we not all agreed that the dictator when we meet him abroad is a very dangerous as well as a very ugly animal? And he is here among us, raising his ugly head, spitting his poison, small still, curled up like a caterpillar on a leaf, but in the heart of England. Is it not from this egg, to quote Mr Wells again, that 'the practical obliteration of [our] freedom by Fascists or Nazis' will spring? And is not the woman who has to breathe that poison and to fight that insect, secretly and without arms, in her office, fighting the Fascist or the Nazi as surely as those who fight him with arms in the limelight of publicity? And must not that fight wear down her strength and exhaust her spirit? Should we not help her to crush him in our own country before we ask her to help us to crush him abroad? And what right have we, Sir, to trumpet our ideals of freedom and justice to other countries when we can shake out from our most respectable newspapers any day of the week eggs like these?

Here, rightly, you will check what has all the symptoms of becoming a peroration by pointing out that though the opinions expressed in these letters are not altogether agreeable to our national self-esteem they are the natural expression of a fear and a jealousy which we must understand before we condemn them. It is true, you will say, that these gentlemen seem a little unduly concerned with their own salaries and their own security, but that is comprehensible, given the traditions of their sex, and even compatible with a genuine love of freedom and a genuine hatred of dictatorship. For these gentlemen are, or wish to become, husbands and fathers, and in that case the support of the family will depend upon them. In other words, sir, I take you to mean that the world as it is at present is divided into two services; one the public and the other the private. In one world the sons of educated men work as civil servants, judges, soldiers and are paid for that work; in the other world, the daughters of educated men work as wives, mothers, daughters – but are they not paid for that work? Is the work of a mother, of a wife, of a daughter, worth nothing to the nation in solid cash? That fact, if it be a fact, is so astonishing that we must confirm it by appealing once more to the impeccable Whitaker. Let us turn to his pages again. We may turn them, and turn them again. It seems incredible, yet it seems undeniable. Among all those offices there is no such office as a mother's; among all those salaries there is no such salary as a mother's. The work of an archbishop is worth £15,000 a year to the State;[k] the work of a judge is worth £5,000 a year; the work of a permanent secretary is worth £3,000 a year; the work of an army captain, of a sea captain, of a sergeant of dragoons, of a policeman, of a postman – all these works are worth paying out of the taxes, but wives and mothers and daughters who work all day and every day, without whose work the State would collapse and fall to pieces, without whose work your sons, sir, would cease to exist, are paid nothing whatever. Can it be possible? Or have we convicted Whitaker, the impeccable, of errata?

Ah, you will interpose, here is another misunderstanding. Husband and wife are not only one flesh; they are also one purse. The wife's salary is half the husband's income. The man is paid more than the woman for that very reason – because he has a wife to support. The bachelor then is paid at the same rate as the unmarried woman? It appears not – another queer effect of atmosphere, no doubt; but let it pass. Your statement that the wife's salary is half the husband's income seems to be an equitable arrangement, and no doubt, since it is equitable, it is confirmed by law. Your reply that the law leaves these private matters to be decided privately is less satisfactory, for it means that the wife's half-share of the common income is not paid legally into her hands, but into her husband's. But still a spiritual right may be as binding as a legal right; and if the wife of an educated man has a spiritual right to half her husband's income, then we may assume that the wife of an educated man has as much money to spend, once the common household bills are met, upon any cause that appeals to her as her husband. Now her husband, witness Whitaker, witness the wills in the daily paper, is often not merely well paid by his profession, but is master of a very considerable capital sum. Therefore this lady who asserts that £250 a year is all that a woman can earn to-day in the professions is evading the question; for the profession of marriage in the educated class is a highly paid one, since she has a right, a spiritual right, to half her husband's salary. The puzzle deepens;

the mystery thickens. For if the wives of rich men are themselves rich women, how does it come about that the income of the W.S.P.U. was only £42,000 a year; how does it come about that the honorary treasurer of the college rebuilding fund is still asking for £100,000; how does it come about that the treasurer of a society for helping professional women to obtain employment is asking not merely for money to pay her rent but will be grateful for books, fruit or cast-off clothing? It stands to reason that if the wife has a spiritual right to half her husband's income because her own work as his wife is unpaid, then she must have as much money to spend upon such causes as appeal to her as he has. And since those causes are standing hat in hand a-begging we are forced to conclude that they are causes that do not take the fancy of the educated man's wife. The charge against her is a very serious one. For consider – there is the money – that surplus fund that can be devoted to education, to pleasure, to philanthropy when the household dues are met; she can spend her share as freely as her husband can spend his. She can spend it upon whatever causes she likes; and yet she will not spend it upon the causes that are dear to her own sex. There they are, hat in hand a-begging. That is a terrible charge to bring against her.

But let us pause for a moment before we decide that charge against her. Let us ask what are the causes, the pleasures, the philanthropies upon which the educated man's wife does in fact spend her share of the common surplus fund. And here we are confronted with facts which, whether we like them or not, we must face. The fact is that the tastes of the married woman in our class are markedly virile. She spends vast sums annually upon party funds; upon sport; upon grouse moors; upon cricket and football. She lavishes money upon clubs – Brooks', White's, the Travellers', the Reform, the Athenaeum – to mention only the most prominent. Her expenditure upon these causes, pleasures and philanthropies must run into many millions every year. And yet by far the greater part of this sum is spent upon pleasures which she does not share. She lays out thousands and thousands of pounds upon clubs to which her own sex is not admitted;[15] upon racecourses where she may not ride; upon colleges from which her own sex is excluded. She pays a huge bill annually for wine which she does not drink and for cigars which she does not smoke. In short, there are only two conclusions to which we can come about the educated man's wife – the first is that she is the most altruistic of beings who prefers to spend her share of the common fund upon his pleasures and causes; the second, and more probable, if less creditable, is not that she is the most altruistic of beings, but that her spiritual right to a share of half her husband's income peters out in practice to an actual right to board, lodging and a small annual allowance for pocket money and dress. Either of these conclusions is possible; the evidence of public institutions and subscription lists puts any other out of the question. For consider how nobly the educated man supports his old school, his old college; how splendidly he subscribes to party funds; how munificently he contributes to all those institutions and sports by which he and his sons educate their minds and develop their bodies – the daily papers bear daily witness to those indisputable facts. But the absence of her name from subscription lists, and the poverty of the institutions which educate her mind and her body seem to prove that there is something in the atmosphere of the private house which deflects the wife's spiritual share of the common income impalpably but irresistibly towards those causes which her husband approves and those pleasures which he enjoys. Whether creditable or discreditable, that is the fact. And that is the reason why those other causes stand a-begging.

With Whitaker's facts and the facts of the subscription lists before us, we seem to have arrived at three facts which are indisputable and must have great influence upon our enquiry how we can help you to prevent war. The first is that the daughters of educated men are paid very little from the public funds for their public services; the second is that they are paid nothing at all from the public funds for their private services; and the third is that their share of the husband's income is not a flesh-and-blood share but a spiritual or nominal share, which means that when both are clothed and fed the surplus fund that can be devoted to causes, pleasures or philanthropies gravitates mysteriously but indisputably towards those causes, pleasures and philanthropies which the husband enjoys, and of which the husband approves. It seems that the person to whom the salary is actually paid is the person who has the actual right to decide how that salary shall be spent.

These facts then bring us back in a chastened mood and with rather altered views to our starting point. For we were going, you may remember, to lay your appeal for help in the prevention of war before the women who earn their livings in the professions. It is to them, we said, to whom we must appeal, because it is they who have our new weapon, the influence of an independent opinion based upon an independent income, in their possession. But the facts once more are depressing. They make it clear in the first place that we must rule out, as possible helpers, that large group to whom marriage is a profession, because it is an unpaid profession, and because the spiritual share of half the husband's salary is not, facts seem to show, an actual share. Therefore, her disinterested influence founded upon an independent income is nil. If he is in favour of force, she too will be in favour of force. In the second place, facts seem to prove that the statement 'To earn £250 a year is quite an achievement even for a highly qualified woman with years of experience' is not an unmitigated lie but a highly probable truth. Therefore, the influence which the daughters of educated men have at present from their money-earning power cannot be rated very highly. Yet since it has become more than ever obvious that it is to them that we must look for help, for they alone can help us, it is to them that we must appeal. This conclusion then brings us back to the letter from which we quoted above – the honorary treasurer's letter, the letter asking for a subscription to the society for helping the daughters of educated men to obtain employment in the professions. You will agree, sir, that we have strong selfish motives for helping her – there can be no doubt about that. For to help women to earn their livings in the professions is to help them to possess that weapon of independent opinion which is still their most powerful weapon. It is to help them to have a mind of their own and a will of their own with which to help you to prevent war. But . . . – here again, in those dots, doubts and hesitations assert themselves – can we, considering the facts given above, send her our guinea without laying down very stringent terms as to how that guinea shall be spent?

For the facts which we have discovered in checking her statement as to her financial position have raised questions which make us wonder whether we are wise to encourage people to enter the professions if we wish to prevent war. You will remember that we are using our psychological insight (for that is our only qualification) to decide what kind of qualities in human nature are likely to lead to war. And the facts disclosed above are of a kind to make us ask, before we write our cheque, whether if we encourage the daughters of educated men to enter the professions we shall not be encouraging the very qualities that we wish to prevent? Shall we not be doing our guinea's worth to ensure that in two or three centuries not only the educated men in the professions but the educated women in the professions will be asking – oh, of whom? as the poet says[1] – the very question that you are asking us now: How can we prevent war? If we encourage the daughters to enter the professions without making any conditions as to the way in which the professions are to be practised shall we not be doing our best to stereotype the old tune which human nature, like a gramophone whose needle has stuck, is now grinding out with such disastrous unanimity? 'Here we go round the mulberry tree, the mulberry tree, the mulberry tree. Give it all to me, give it all to me, all to me. Three hundred millions spent upon war.' With that song, or something like it, ringing in our ears we cannot send our guinea to the honorary treasurer without warning her that she shall only have it on condition that she shall swear that the professions in future shall be practised so that they shall lead to a different song and a different conclusion. She shall only have it if she can satisfy us that our guinea shall be spent in the cause of peace. It

is difficult to formulate such conditions; in our present psychological ignorance perhaps impossible. But the matter is so serious,
war is so insupportable, so horrible, so inhuman, that an attempt
must be made. Here then is another letter to the same lady.

'Your letter, Madam, has waited a long time for an answer,
but we have been examining into certain charges made against
you and making certain enquiries. We have acquitted you,
Madam, you will be relieved to learn, of telling lies. It would
seem to be true that you are poor. We have acquitted you
further, of idleness, apathy and greed. The number of causes that
you are championing, however secretly and ineffectively, is in
your favour. If you prefer ice creams and peanuts to roast beef
and beer the reason would seem to be economic rather than
gustatory. It would seem probable that you have not much
money to spend upon food or much leisure to spend upon eating
it in view of the circulars and leaflets you issue, the meetings you
arrange, the bazaars you organize. Indeed, you would appear to
be working, without a salary too, rather longer hours than the
Home Office would approve. But though we are willing to
deplore your poverty and to commend your industry we are not
going to send you a guinea to help you to help women to enter
the professions unless you can assure us that they will practise
those professions in such a way as to prevent war. That, you will
say, is a vague statement, an impossible condition. Still, since
guineas are rare and guineas are valuable you will listen to the
terms we wish to impose if, you intimate, they can be stated
briefly. Well then, Madam, since you are pressed for time, what
with the Pensions Bill,[m] what with shepherding the Peers into
the House of Lords so that they may vote on it as instructed by
you, what with reading Hansard[n] and the newspapers – though
that should not take much time; you will find no mention of
your activities there;[16] a conspiracy of silence seems to be the
rule; what with plotting still for equal pay for equal work in the
Civil Service, while at the same time you are arranging hares and
old coffee-pots so as to seduce people into paying more for them
than they are strictly worth at a bazaar – since, in one word, it is

obvious that you are busy, let us be quick; make a rapid survey; discuss a few passages in the books in your library; in the papers on your table, and then see if we can make the statement less vague, the conditions more clear.

'Let us then begin by looking at the outside of things, at the general aspect. Things have outsides let us remember as well as insides. Close at hand is a bridge over the Thames, an admirable vantage ground for such a survey. The river flows beneath; barges pass, laden with timber, bursting with corn; there on one side are the domes and spires of the city; on the other, Westminster and the Houses of Parliament. It is a place to stand on by the hour, dreaming. But not now. Now we are pressed for time. Now we are here to consider facts; now we must fix our eyes upon the procession – the procession of the sons of educated men.

'There they go, our brothers who have been educated at public schools and universities, mounting those steps, passing in and out of those doors, ascending those pulpits, preaching, teaching, administering justice, practising medicine, transacting business, making money. It is a solemn sight always – a procession, like a caravanserai crossing a desert. Great-grandfathers, grandfathers, fathers, uncles – they all went that way, wearing their gowns, wearing their wigs, some with ribbons across their breasts, others without. One was a bishop. Another a judge. One was an admiral. Another a general. One was a professor. Another a doctor. And some left the procession and were last heard of doing nothing in Tasmania; were seen, rather shabbily dressed, selling newspapers at Charing Cross. But most of them kept in step, walked according to rule, and by hook or by crook made enough to keep the family house, somewhere, roughly speaking, in the West End, supplied with beef and mutton for all, and with education for Arthur. It is a solemn sight, this procession, a sight that has often caused us, you may remember, looking at it sidelong from an upper window, to ask ourselves certain questions. But now, for the past twenty years or so, it is no longer a sight merely, a photograph, or fresco scrawled upon the walls of time, at which we can look with merely an aesthetic appreciation. For there, trapesing along at the tail end of the procession, we go ourselves. And that makes a difference. We who have looked so long at the pageant in books, or from a curtained window watched educated men leaving the house at about nine-thirty to go to an office, returning to the house at about six-thirty from an office, need look passively no longer. We too can leave the house, can mount those steps, pass in and out of those doors, wear wigs and gowns, make money, administer justice. Think – one of these days, you may wear a judge's wig on your head, an ermine cape on your shoulders; sit under the lion and the unicorn; draw a salary of five thousand a year with a pension on retiring. We who now agitate these humble pens may in another century or two speak from a pulpit. Nobody will dare contradict us then; we shall be the mouthpieces of the divine spirit – a solemn thought, is it not? Who can say whether, as time goes on, we may not dress in military uniform, with gold lace on our breasts, swords at our sides, and something like the old family coal-scuttle on our heads, save that that venerable object was never decorated with plumes of white horsehair. You laugh – indeed the shadow of the private house still makes those dresses look a little queer. We have worn private clothes so long – the veil that St Paul recommended. But we have not come here to laugh, or to talk of fashions – men's and women's. We are here, on the bridge, to ask ourselves certain questions. And they are very important questions; and we have very little time in which to answer them. The questions that we have to ask and to answer about that procession during this moment of transition are so important that they may well change the lives of all men and women for ever. For we have to ask ourselves, here and now, do we wish to join that procession, or don't we? On what terms shall we join that procession? Above all, where is it leading us, the procession of educated men? The moment is short; it may last five years; ten years, or perhaps only a matter of a few months longer. But the questions must be answered; and they are so important that if all the

daughters of educated men did nothing, from morning to night, but consider that procession, from every angle, if they did nothing but ponder it and analyse it, and think about it and read about it and pool their thinking and reading, and what they see and what they guess, their time would be better spent than in any other activity now open to them. But, you will object, you have no time to think; you have your battles to fight, your rent to pay, your bazaars to organize. That excuse shall not serve you, Madam. As you know from your own experience, and there are facts that prove it, the daughters of educated men have always done their thinking from hand to mouth; not under green lamps at study tables in the cloisters of secluded colleges. They have thought while they stirred the pot, while they rocked the cradle. It was thus that they won us the right to our brand-new sixpence. It falls to us now to go on thinking; how are we to spend that sixpence? Think we must. Let us think in offices; in omnibuses; while we are standing in the crowd watching Coronations and Lord Mayor's Shows; let us think as we pass the Cenotaph; and in Whitehall; in the gallery of the House of Commons; in the Law Courts; let us think at baptisms and marriages and funerals. Let us never cease from thinking – what is this "civilization" in which we find ourselves? What are these ceremonies and why should we take part in them? What are these professions and why should we make money out of them? Where in short is it leading us, the procession of the sons of educated men?

'But you are busy; let us return to facts. Come indoors then, and open the books on your library shelves. For you have a library, and a good one. A working library, a living library; a library where nothing is chained down and nothing is locked up; a library where the songs of the singers rise naturally from the lives of the livers. There are the poems, here the biographies. And what light, do they throw upon the professions, these biographies? How far do they encourage us to think that if we help the daughters to become professional women we shall discourage war? The answer to that question is scattered all about these volumes; and is legible to anyone who can read plain English. And the answer, one must admit, is extremely queer. For almost every biography we read of professional men in the nineteenth century, to limit ourselves to that not distant and fully documented age, is largely concerned with war. They were great fighters, it seems, the professional men in the age of Queen Victoria. There was the battle of Westminster. There was the battle of the universities. There was the battle of Whitehall. There was the battle of Harley Street. There was the battle of the Royal Academy. Some of these battles, as you can testify, are still in progress. In fact the only profession which does not seem to have fought a fierce battle during the nineteenth century is the profession of literature. All the other professions, according to the testimony of biography, seem to be as bloodthirsty as the profession of arms itself. It is true that the combatants did not inflict flesh wounds;[17] chivalry forbade; but you will agree that a battle that wastes time is as deadly as a battle that wastes blood. You will agree that a battle that costs money is as deadly as a battle that costs a leg or an arm. You will agree that a battle that forces youth to spend its strength haggling in committee rooms, soliciting favours, assuming a mask of reverence to cloak its ridicule, inflicts wounds upon the human spirit which no surgery can heal. Even the battle of equal pay for equal work is not without its timeshed, its spiritshed, as you yourself, were you not unaccountably reticent on certain matters, might agree. Now the books in your library record so many of these battles that it is impossible to go into them all; but as they all seem to have been fought on much the same plan, and by the same combatants, that is by professional men *v.* their sisters and daughters, let us, since time presses, glance at one of these campaigns only and examine the battle of Harley Street, in order that we may understand what effect the professions have upon those who practise them.

'The campaign was opened in the year 1869 under the leadership of Sophia Jex-Blake. Her case is so typical an instance of the great Victorian fight between the victims of the patriarchal system and the patriarchs, of the daughters against the fathers, that it deserves a moment's examination. Sophia's father was an admirable specimen of the Victorian educated man, kindly, cultivated and well-to-do. He was a proctor of Doctors' Commons.⁰ He could afford to keep six servants, horses and carriages, and could provide his daughter not only with food and lodging but with "handsome furniture" and "a cosy fire" in her bedroom. For salary, "for dress and private money", he gave her £40 a year. For some reason she found this sum insufficient. In 1859, in view of the fact that she had only nine shillings and ninepence left to last her till next quarter, she wished to earn money herself. And she was offered a tutorship with the pay of five shillings an hour. She told her father of the offer. He replied, "Dearest, I have only this moment heard that you contemplate being *paid* for the tutorship. It would be quite beneath you, darling, and *I cannot consent to it*." She argued: "Why should I not take it? You as a man did your work and received your payment, and no one thought it any degradation, but a fair exchange . . . Tom is doing on a large scale what I am doing on a small one." He replied: "The cases you cite, darling, are not to the point . . . T. W. . . . feels bound as *a man* . . . to support his wife and family, and his position is a high one, which can only be filled by a first-class man of character, and yielding him nearer two than one thousand a year . . . How entirely different is my darling's case! You want for nothing, and know that (humanly speaking) you will want for nothing. If you married to-morrow – to my liking – and I don't believe you would ever marry otherwise – I should give you a good fortune." Upon which her comment, in a private diary, was: "Like a fool I have consented to give up the fees for this term only – though I am miserably poor. It was foolish. It only defers the struggle."[18]

'There she was right. The struggle with her own father was over. But the struggle with fathers in general, with the patriarchy itself, was deferred to another place and another time. The second fight was at Edinburgh in 1869. She had applied for admission to the Royal College of Surgeons. Here is a newspaper account of the first skirmish. "A disturbance of a very unbecoming nature took place yesterday afternoon in front of the Royal College of Surgeons ... Shortly before four o'clock ... nearly 200 students assembled in front of the gate leading to the building ..." the medical students howled and sang songs. "The gate was closed in their [the women's] faces ... Dr Handyside found it utterly impossible to begin his demonstration ... a pet sheep was introduced into the room" and so on. The methods were much the same as those that were employed at Cambridge during the battle of the Degree. And again, as on that occasion, the authorities deplored those downright methods and employed others, more astute and more effective, of their own. Nothing would induce the authorities encamped within the sacred gates to allow the women to enter. They said that God was on their side, Nature was on their side, Law was on their side, and Property was on their side. The college was founded for the benefit of men only; men only were entitled by law to benefit from its endowments. The usual committees were formed. The usual petitions were signed. The usual humble appeals were made. The usual bazaars were held. The usual questions of tactics were debated. As usual it was asked, ought we to attack now, or is it wiser to wait? Who are our friends and who are our enemies? There were the usual differences of opinion, the usual divisions among the counsellors. But why particularize? The whole proceeding is so familiar that the battle of Harley Street in the year 1869 might well be the battle of Cambridge University at the present moment. On both occasions there is the same waste of strength, waste of temper, waste of time, and waste of money. Almost the same daughters ask almost the same brothers for almost the same privileges. Almost the same gentlemen intone almost the same refusals for almost the same reasons. It seems as if there were no progress in the human race, but only repetition. We can almost hear them, if we listen, singing the same old song, "Here we go round the mulberry tree, the mulberry tree, the mulberry tree" and if we add, "of property, of property, of property", we shall fill in the rhyme without doing violence to the facts.

'But we are not here to sing old songs or to fill in missing rhymes. We are here to consider facts. And the facts which we have just extracted from biography seem to prove that the professions have a certain undeniable effect upon the professors. They make the people who practise them possessive, jealous of any infringement of their rights, and highly combative if anyone dares dispute them. Are we not right then in thinking that if we enter the same professions we shall acquire the same qualities? And do not such qualities lead to war? In another century or so if we practise the professions in the same way, shall we not be just as possessive, just as jealous, just as pugnacious, just as positive as to the verdict of God, Nature, Law and Property as these gentlemen are now? Therefore this guinea, which is to help you to help women to enter the professions, has this condition as a first condition attached to it. You shall swear that you will do all in your power to insist that any woman who enters any profession shall in no way hinder any other human being, whether man or woman, white or black,[9] provided that he or she is qualified to enter that profession, from entering it; but shall do all in her power to help them.

'You are ready to put your hand to that, here and now, you say, and at the same time stretch out that hand for the guinea. But wait. Other conditions are attached to it before it is yours. For consider once more the procession of the sons of educated men; ask yourself once more, where is it leading us? One answer suggests itself instantly. To incomes, it is obvious, that seem, to us at least, extremely handsome. Whitaker puts that beyond a doubt. And besides the evidence of Whitaker, there is the evidence of the daily paper – the evidence of the wills, of the subscription lists that we have considered already. In one issue of one paper, for example, it is stated that three educated men died; and one left £1,193,251; another £1,010,288; another £1,404,132. These are large sums for private people to amass, you will admit. And why should we not amass them too in course of time? Now that the Civil Service is open to us we may well earn from one thousand to three thousand a year; now that the Bar is open to us we may well earn £5,000 a year as judges, and any sum up to forty or fifty thousand a year as barristers. When the Church is open to us we may draw salaries of fifteen thousand, five thousand, three thousand yearly, with palaces and deaneries attached. When the Stock Exchange is open to us we may die worth as many millions as Pierpont Morgan, or as Rockefeller himself.[9] As doctors we may make anything from two thousand to fifty thousand a year. As editors even we may earn salaries that are by no means despicable. One has a thousand a year; another two thousand; it is rumoured that the editor of a great daily paper has a salary of five thousand yearly. All this wealth may in the course of time come our way if we follow the professions. In short, we may change our position from being the victims of the patriarchal system, paid on the truck system,[r] with £30 or £40 a year in cash and board and lodging thrown in, to being the champions of the capitalist system, with a yearly income in our own possession of many thousands which, by judicious investment, may leave us when we die possessed of a capital sum of more millions than we can count.

'It is a thought not without its glamour. Consider what it would mean if among us there were now a woman motor-car manufacturer who, with a stroke of her pen, could endow the women's colleges with two or three hundred thousand pounds apiece. The honorary treasurer of the rebuilding fund, your sister at Cambridge, would have her labours considerably lightened then. There would be no need of appeals and committees, of strawberries and cream and bazaars. And suppose that there were not merely one rich woman, but that rich women were as common as rich men. What could you not do? You could shut up your office at once. You could finance a woman's party in the House of Commons. You could run a daily newspaper committed to a conspiracy, not of silence, but of speech. You could get pensions for spinsters; those victims of the patriarchal system, whose allowance is insufficient and whose board and lodging are no longer thrown in. You could get equal pay for equal work. You could provide every mother with chloroform when her child is born;[19] bring down the maternal death-rate from four in every thousand to none at all, perhaps. In one session you could pass Bills that will now take you perhaps a hundred years of hard and continuous labour to get through the House of Commons. There seems at first sight nothing that you could not do, if you had the same capital at your disposal that your brothers have at theirs. Why not, then, you exclaim, help us to take the first step towards possessing it? The professions are the only way in which we can earn money. Money is the only means by which we can achieve objects that are immensely desirable. Yet here you are, you seem to protest, haggling and bargaining over conditions. But consider this letter from a professional man asking us to help him to prevent war. Look also at the photographs of dead bodies and ruined houses that the Spanish Government sends almost weekly. That is why it is necessary to haggle and to bargain over conditions.

'For the evidence of the letter and of the photographs when combined with the facts with which history and biography provide us about the professions seem together to throw a certain light, a red light, shall we say, upon those same professions. You make money in them; that is true; but how far is money in view of those facts in itself a desirable possession? A great authority upon human life, you will remember, held over two thousand years ago that great possessions were undesirable. To which you reply, and with some heat as if you suspected another excuse for keeping the purse-string tied, that Christ's words[f] about the rich and the Kingdom of Heaven are no longer helpful to those who have to face different facts in a different world. You argue that as things are now in England extreme poverty is less desirable than extreme wealth. The poverty of the Christian who should give away all his possessions produces, as we have daily and abundant proof, the crippled in body, the feeble in mind. The unemployed, to take the obvious example, are not a source of spiritual or intellectual wealth to their country. These are weighty arguments; but consider for a moment the life of Pierpont Morgan. Do you not agree with that evidence before us that extreme wealth is equally undesirable, and for the same reasons? If extreme wealth is undesirable and extreme poverty is undesirable, it is arguable that there is some mean between the two which is desirable. What then is that mean – how much money is needed to live upon in England to-day? How should that money be spent? What is the kind of life, the kind of human being, you propose to aim at if you succeed in extracting this guinea? Those, Madam, are the questions that I am asking you to consider and you cannot deny that those are questions of the utmost importance. But alas, they are questions that would lead us far beyond the solid world of actual fact to which we are here confined. So let us shut the New Testament; Shakespeare, Shelley, Tolstoi and the rest, and face the fact that stares us in the face at this moment of transition – the fact of the procession; the fact that we are trapesing along somewhere in the rear and must consider that fact before we can fix our eyes upon the vision on the horizon.

'There it is then, before our eyes, the procession of the sons of educated men, ascending those pulpits, mounting those steps, passing in and out of those doors, preaching, teaching, administering justice, practising medicine, making money. And it is obvious that if you are going to make the same incomes from the same professions that those men make you will have to accept the same conditions that they accept. Even from an upper window and from books we know or can guess what those conditions are. You will have to leave the house at nine and come back to it at six. That leaves very little time for fathers to know their children. You will have to do this daily from the age of twenty-one or so to the age of about sixty-five. That leaves very little time for friendship, travel or art. You will have to perform some duties that are very arduous, others that are very barbarous. You will have to wear certain uniforms and profess certain loyalties. If you succeed in your professions the words "For God and Empire" will very likely be written, like the address on a dog-collar, round your neck.[20] And if words have meaning, as words perhaps should have meaning, you will have to accept that meaning and do what you can to enforce it. In short, you will have to lead the same lives and profess the same loyalties that professional men have professed for many centuries. There can be no doubt of that.

'If you retaliate, what harm is there in that? Why should we hesitate to do what our fathers and grandfathers have done before us? let us go into greater detail and consult the facts which are nowadays open to the inspection of all who can read their mother tongue in biography. There they are, those innumerable and invaluable works upon the shelves of your own library. Let us glance again rapidly at the lives of professional men who have succeded in their professions. Here is an extract from the life of a great lawyer. "He went to his chambers about half-past nine . . . He took briefs home with him . . . so that he was lucky if he got to bed about one or two o'clock in the morning."[21] That explains why most successful barristers are hardly worth sitting next at dinner – they yawn so. Next, here is a quotation from a famous politician's speech. ". . . since 1914 I have never seen the pageant of the blossom from the first damson to the last apple – never once have I seen that in Worcestershire since 1914, and if that is not a sacrifice I do not know what is."[22] A sacrifice indeed, and one that explains the perennial indifference of the Government to art – why, these unfortunate gentlemen must be as blind as bats. Take the religious profession next. Here is a quotation from the life of a great bishop. "This is an awful mind-and-soul-destroying life. I really do not know how to live it. The arrears of important work accumulate and crush."[23] That bears out what so many people are saying now about the Church and the nation. Our bishops and deans seem to have no soul with which to preach and no mind with which to write. Listen to any sermon in any church; read the journalism of Dean Alington or Dean Inge in any newspaper. Take the doctor's profession next. "I have taken a good deal over £13,000 during the year, but this cannot possibly be maintained, and while it lasts it is slavery. What I feel most is being away from Eliza and the children so frequently on Sundays, and again at Christmas."[24] That is the complaint of a great doctor; and his patient might well echo it, for what Harley Street specialist has time to understand the body, let alone the mind or both in combination, when he is a slave to thirteen thousand a year? But is the life of a professional writer any better? Here is a sample taken from the life of a highly successful journalist. "On another day at this time he wrote a 1,600 words article on Nietzsche, a leader of equal length on the railway strike for the *Standard*, 600 words for the *Tribune* and in the evening was at Shoe Lane."[25t] That explains among other things why the public reads its politics with cynicism, and authors read their reviews with foot-rules – it is the advertisement that counts; praise or blame have ceased to have any meaning. And with one more glance at the politician's life, for his profession after all is the most important practically, let us have done. "Lord Hugh *loitered in the lobby* . . . The Bill [the Deceased Wife's Sister Bill] was in consequence dead, and the further chances of the cause were relegated to the chances and mischances of another year."[26] That not only serves to explain a certain prevalent distrust of politicians, but also reminds us that since you have the Pensions Bill to steer through the lobbies of so just and humane an institution as the House of Commons, we must not loiter too long ourselves among these delightful biographies, but must try to sum up the information which we have gained from them.

'What then do these quotations from the lives of successful professional men prove, you ask? They prove, as Whitaker proves things, nothing whatever. If Whitaker, that is, says that a bishop is paid five thousand a year, that is a fact; it can be checked and verified. But if Bishop Gore says that the life of a bishop is "an awful mind-and-soul-destroying life' he is merely giving us his opinion; the next bishop on the bench may flatly contradict him. These quotations then prove nothing that can be checked and verified; they merely cause us to hold opinions. And those opinions cause us to doubt and criticize and question the value of professional life – not its cash value; that is great; but its spiritual, its moral, its intellectual value. They make us of the opinion that if people are highly successful in their professions they lose their senses. Sight goes. They have no time to look at pictures. Sound goes. They have no time to listen to music. Speech goes. They have no time for conversation. They lose their sense of proportion – the relations between one thing and another. Humanity goes. Money making becomes so important that they must work by night as well as by day. Health goes. And so competitive do they become that they will not share their work with others though they have more than they can do themselves. What then remains of a human being who has lost sight, and sound, and sense of proportion? Only a cripple in a cave.

'That of course is a figure, and fanciful; but that it has some connection with figures that are statistical and not fanciful – with the three hundred millions spent upon arms – seems possible. Such at any rate would seem to be the opinion of disinterested observers whose position gives them every opportunity for judging widely, and for judging fairly. Let us examine two such opinions only. The Marquess of Londonderry said:

> We seem to hear a babel of voices among which direction and guidance are lacking, and the world appears to be marking time ... During the last century gigantic forces of scientific discovery had been unloosed, while at the same time we could discern no corresponding advance in literary or scientific achievement ... The question we are asking ourselves is whether man is capable of enjoying these new fruits of scientific knowledge and discovery, or whether by their misuse he will bring about the destruction of himself and the edifice of civilization.[27]

'Mr Churchill said:

> Certain it is that while men are gathering knowledge and power with ever-increasing and measureless speed, their virtues and their wisdom have not shown any notable improvement as the centuries have rolled. The brain of a modern man does not differ in essentials from that of the human beings who fought and loved

here millions of years ago. The nature of man has remained hitherto practically unchanged. Under sufficient stress – starvation, terror, warlike passion, or even cold intellectual frenzy, the modern man we know so well will do the most terrible deeds, and his modern woman will back him up.[28]

'Those are two quotations only from a great number to the same effect. And to them let us add another, from a less impressive source but worth your reading since it too bears upon our problem, from Mr Cyril Chaventry of North Wembley.

"A woman's sense of values," he writes, "is indisputably different from that of a man. Obviously therefore a woman is at a disadvantage and under suspicion when in competition in a man-created sphere of activity. More than ever to-day women have the opportunity to build a new and better world, but in this slavish imitation of men they are wasting their chance."[29]

'That opinion, too, is a representative opinion, one from a great number to the same effect provided by the daily papers. And the three quotations taken together are highly instructive. The two first seem to prove that the enormous professional competence of the educated man has not brought about an altogether desirable state of things in the civilized world; and the last, which calls upon professional women to use "their different sense of values" to "build a new and better world" not only implies that those who have built that world are dissatisfied with the results, but, by calling upon the other sex to remedy the evil imposes a great responsibility and implies a great compliment. For if Mr Chaventry and the gentlemen who agree with him believe that "at a disadvantage and under suspicion" as she is, with little or no political or professional training and upon a salary of about £250 a year, the professional woman can yet "build a new and better world", they must credit her with powers that might almost be called divine. They must agree with Goethe:

The things that must pass
Are only symbols;
Here shall all failure
Grow to achievement,
Here, the Untellable
Work all fulfilment,
The woman in woman
Lead forward for ever[30]

– another very great compliment, and from a very great poet you will agree.

'But you do not want compliments; you are pondering quotations. And since your expression is decidedly downcast, it seems as if these quotations about the nature of professional life have brought you to some melancholy conclusion. What can it be? Simply, you reply, that we, daughters of educated men, are between the devil and the deep sea. Behind us lies the patriarchal system; the private house, with its nullity, its immorality, its hypocrisy, its servility. Before us lies the public world, the professional system, with its possessiveness, its jealousy, its pugnacity, its greed. The one shuts us up like slaves in a harem; the other forces us to circle, like caterpillars head to tail, round and round the mulberry tree, the sacred tree, of property. It is a choice of evils. Each is bad. Had we not better plunge off the bridge into the river; give up the game; declare that the whole of human life is a mistake and so end it?

'But before you take that step, Madam, a decisive one, unless you share the opinion of the professors of the Church of England that death is the gate of life – *Mors Janua Vitae* is written upon an arch in St Paul's – in which case there is, of course, much to recommend it, let us see if another answer is not possible.

'Another answer may be staring us in the face on the shelves of your own library, once more in the biographies. Is it not possible that by considering the experiments that the dead have made with their lives in the past we may find some help in answering the very difficult question that is now forced upon us? At any rate, let us try. The question that we will now put to biography is this: For reasons given above we are agreed that we must earn money in the professions. For reasons given above those professions seem to us highly undesirable. The question we put to you, lives of the dead, is how can we enter the professions and yet remain civilized human beings; human beings, that is, who wish to prevent war?

'This time let us turn to the lives not of men but of women in the nineteenth century – to the lives of professional women. But there would seem to be a gap in your library, Madam. There are no lives of professional women in the nineteenth century. A Mrs Tomlinson, the wife of a Mr Tomlinson, F.R.S., F.C.S., explains the reason. This lady, who wrote a book "advocating the employment of young ladies as nurses for children", says: ". . . it seemed as if there were no way in which an unmarried lady could earn a living but by taking a situation as governess, for which post she was often unfit by nature and education, or want of education."[31] That was written in 1859 – less than 100 years ago. That explains the gap on your shelves. There were no professional women, except governesses, to have lives written of them. And the lives of governesses, that is the written lives, can be counted on the fingers of one hand. What then can we learn about the lives of professional women from studying the lives of governesses? Happily old boxes are beginning to give up their old secrets. Out the other day crept one such document written about the year 1811. There was, it appears, an obscure Miss Weeton, who used to scribble down her thoughts upon professional life among other things when her pupils were in bed. Here is one such thought. "Oh! how I have burned to learn Latin, French, the Arts, the Sciences, anything rather than the dog trot way of sewing, teaching, writing copies, and washing dishes every day . . . Why are not females permitted to study physics, divinity, astronomy, etc., etc., with their attendants, chemistry, botany, logic, mathematics, &c.?"[32] That comment upon the lives of governesses, that question from the lips of governesses, reaches us from the darkness. It is illuminating, too. But let us go on groping; let us pick up a hint here and a hint there as to the professions as they were practised by women in the nineteenth century. Next we find Anne Clough, the sister of Arthur Clough, pupil of Dr Arnold, Fellow of Oriel, who, though she served without a salary, was the first principal of Newnham, and thus may be called a professional woman in embryo – we find her training for her profession by "doing much of the housework" ... "earning money to pay off what had been lent by their friends", "pressing for leave to keep a small school", reading books her brother lent her, and exclaiming, "If I were a man, I would not work for riches, to make myself a name or to leave a wealthy family behind me. No, I think I would work for my country, and make its people my heirs."[33] The nineteenth-century women were not without ambition it seems. Next we find Josephine Butler, who, though not strictly speaking a professional woman, led the campaign against the Contagious Diseases Act to victory, and then the campaign against the sale and purchase of children "for infamous purposes"[*] – we find Josephine Butler refusing to have a life of herself written, and saying of the women who helped her in those campaigns: "The utter absence in them of any desire for recognition, of any vestige of egotism in any form, is worthy of remark. In the purity of their motives they shine out 'clear as crystal'."[34] That, then, was one of the qualities that the Victorian woman praised and practised – a negative one, it is true; not to be recognized; not to be egotistical; to do the work for the sake of doing the work.[35] An interesting contribution to psychology in its way. And then we come closer to our own time; we find Gertrude Bell, who, though the diplomatic service was and is shut to women, occupied a post in the East which almost entitled her to be called a pseudo-diplomat – we find rather to our surprise that "Gertrude could never go out in London without a female friend or, failing that, a maid . . .[36] when it seemed unavoidable for Gertrude to drive in a hansom with a young man from one tea party to another, she feels obliged to write and confess it to my mother."[37] So they were chaste, the women pseudo-diplomats of the Victorian Age?[38] And not merely in body;

in mind also. Gertrude "was not allowed to read Bourget's *The Disciple*"[v] for fear of contracting whatever disease that book may disseminate. Dissatisfied but ambitious, ambitious but austere, chaste yet adventurous – such are some of the qualities that we have discovered. But let us go on looking – if not at the lines, then between the lines of biography. And we find, between the lines of their husbands' biographies, so many women practising – but what are we to call the profession that consists in bringing nine or ten children into the world, the profession which consists in running a house, nursing an invalid, visiting the poor and the sick, tending here an old father, there an old mother? – there is no name and there is no pay for that profession; but we find so many mothers, sisters and daughters of educated men practising it in the nineteenth century that we must lump them and their lives together behind their husbands' and brothers', and leave them to deliver their message to those who have the time to extract it and the imagination with which to decipher it. Let us ourselves, who as you hint are pressed for time, sum up these random hints and reflections upon the professional life of women in the nineteenth century by quoting once more the highly significant words of a woman who was not a professional woman in the strict sense of the word, but had some nondescript reputation as a traveller nevertheless – Mary Kingsley:

> I don't know if I ever revealed the fact to you that being allowed to learn German was *all* the paid-for education I ever had. £2,000 was spent on my brother's. I still hope not in vain.

'That statement is so suggestive that it may save us the bother of groping and searching between the lines of professional men's lives for the lives of their sisters. If we develop the suggestions we find in that statement, and connect it with the other hints and fragments that we have uncovered, we may arrive at some theory or point of view that may help us to answer the very difficult question, which now confronts us. For when Mary Kingsley says, "... being allowed to learn German was *all* the paid-for education I ever had", she suggests that she had an unpaid-for education. The other lives that we have been examining corroborate that suggestion. What then was the nature of that "unpaid-for education" which, whether for good or for evil, has been ours for so many centuries? If we mass the lives of the obscure behind four lives that were not obscure, but were so successful and distinguished that they were actually written, the lives of Florence Nightingale, Miss Clough, Mary Kingsley and Gertrude Bell, it seems undeniable that they were all educated by the same teachers. And those teachers, biography indicates, obliquely, and indirectly, but emphatically and indisputably none the less, were poverty, chastity, derision, and — but what word covers "lack of rights and privileges"? Shall we press the old word "freedom" once more into service? "Freedom from unreal loyalties", then, was the fourth of their teachers; that freedom from loyalty to old schools, old colleges, old churches, old ceremonies, old countries which all those women enjoyed, and which, to a great extent, we still enjoy by the law and custom of England. We have no time to coin new words, greatly though the language is in need of them. Let "freedom from unreal loyalties" then stand as the fourth great teacher of the daughters of educated men.

'Biography thus provides us with the fact that the daughters of educated men received an unpaid-for education at the hands of poverty, chastity, derision and freedom from unreal loyalties. It was this unpaid-for education, biography informs us, that fitted them, aptly enough, for the unpaid-for professions. And biography also informs us that those unpaid-for professions had their laws, traditions, and labours no less certainly than the paid-for professions. Further, the student of biography cannot possibly doubt from the evidence of biography that this education and these professions were in many ways bad in the extreme, both for the unpaid themselves and for their descendants. The intensive childbirth of the unpaid wife, the intensive money-making of the paid husband in the Victorian age had terrible results, we cannot doubt, upon the mind and body of the present age. To prove it we need not quote once more the famous passage in which Florence Nightingale denounced that education and its results; nor stress the natural delight with which she greeted the Crimean war; nor illustrate from other sources – they are, alas, innumerable – the inanity, the pettiness, the spite, the tyranny, the hypocrisy, the immorality which it engendered as the lives of both sexes so abundantly testify. Final proof of its harshness upon one sex at any rate can be found in the annals of our "great war", when hospitals, harvest fields and munition works were largely staffed by refugees flying from its horrors to their comparative amenity.

'But biography is many-sided; biography never returns a single and simple answer to any question that is asked of it. Thus the biographies of those who had biographies – say Florence Nightingale, Anne Clough, Emily Brontë, Christina Rossetti, Mary Kingsley – prove beyond a doubt that this same education, the unpaid for, must have had great virtues as well as great defects, for we cannot deny that these, if not educated, still were civilized women. We cannot, when we consider the lives of our uneducated mothers and grandmothers, judge education simply by its power to "obtain appointments", to win honour, to make money. We must if we are honest, admit that some who had no paid-for education, no salaries and no appointments were civilized human beings – whether or not they can rightly be called "English" women is matter for dispute; and thus admit that we should be extremely foolish if we threw away the results of that education or gave up the knowledge that we have obtained from it for any bribe or decoration whatsoever. Thus biography, when asked the question we have put to it – how can we enter the professions and yet remain civilized human beings, human beings who discourage war, would seem to reply: If you refuse to be separated from the four great teachers of the daughters of educated men – poverty, chastity, derision and freedom from unreal loyalties – but combine them with some wealth, some knowledge, and some service to real loyalties then you can enter the professions and escape the risks that make them undesirable.

'Such being the answer of the oracle, such are the conditions attached to this guinea. You shall have it, to recapitulate, on condition that you help all properly qualified people, of whatever sex, class or colour, to enter your profession; and further on condition that in the practice of your profession you refuse to be separated from poverty, chastity, derision and freedom from unreal loyalties. Is the statement now more positive, have the conditions been made more clear and do you agree to the terms? You hesitate. Some of the conditions, you seem to suggest, need further discussion. Let us take them, then, in order. By poverty is meant enough money to live upon. That is, you must earn enough to be independent of any other human being and to buy that modicum of health, leisure, knowledge and so on that is needed for the full development of body and mind. But no more. Not a penny more.

'By chastity is meant that when you have made enough to live on by your profession you must refuse to sell your brain for the sake of money. That is you must cease to practise your profession, or practise it for the sake of research and experiment; or, if you are an artist, for the sake of the art; or give the knowledge acquired professionally to those who need it for nothing. But directly the mulberry tree begins to make you circle, break off. Pelt the tree with laughter.

'By derision — a bad word, but once again the English language is much in need of new words — is meant that you must refuse all methods of advertising merit, and hold that ridicule, obscurity and censure are preferable, for psychological reasons, to fame and praise. Directly badges, orders, or degrees are offered you, fling them back in the giver's face.

'By freedom from unreal loyalties is meant that you must rid yourself of pride of nationality in the first place; also of religious pride, college pride, school pride, family pride, sex pride and those unreal loyalties that spring from them. Directly the seducers come with their seductions to bribe you into captivity, tear up the parchments; refuse to fill up the forms.

'And if you still object that these definitions are both too arbitrary and too general, and ask how anybody can tell how much money and how much knowledge are needed for the full development of body and mind, and which are the real loyalties which we must serve and which the unreal which we must despise, I can only refer you – time presses – to two authorities. One is familiar enough. It is the psychometer that you carry on your wrist, the little instrument upon which you depend in all personal relationships. If it were visible it would look something like a thermometer. It has a vein of quicksilver in it which is affected by any body or soul, house or society in whose presence it is exposed. If you want to find out how much wealth is desirable, expose it in a rich man's presence; how much learning is desirable expose it in a learned man's presence. So with patriotism, religion and the rest. The conversation need not be interrupted while you consult it; nor its amenity disturbed. But if you object that this is too personal and fallible a method to employ without risk of mistake, witness the fact that the private psychometer has led to many unfortunate marriages and broken friendships, then there is the other authority now easily within the reach even of the poorest of the daughters of educated men. Go to the public galleries and look at pictures; turn on the wireless and rake down music from the air; enter any of the public libraries which are now free to all. There you will be able to consult the findings of the public psychometer for yourself. To take one example, since we are pressed for time. The *Antigone* of Sophocles has been done into English prose or verse by a man whose name is immaterial.[39] Consider the character of Creon. There you have a most profound analysis by a poet, who is a psychologist in action, of the effect of power and wealth upon the soul. Consider Creon's claim to absolute rule over his subjects. That is a far more instructive analysis of tyranny than any our politicians can offer us. You want to know which are the unreal loyalties which we must despise, which are the real loyalties which we must honour? Consider Antigone's distinction between the laws and the Law. That is a far more profound statement of the duties of the individual to society than any our sociologists can offer us. Lame as the English rendering is,

Antigone's five words are worth all the sermons of all the archbishops.[40] But to enlarge would be impertinent. Private judgement is still free in private; and that freedom is the essence of freedom.

For the rest, though the conditions may seem many and the guinea, alas, is single, they are not for the most part as things are at present very difficult of fulfilment. With the exception of the first – that we must earn enough money to live upon – they are largely ensured us by the laws of England. The law of England sees to it that we do not inherit great possessions; the law of England denies us, and let us hope will long continue to deny us, the full stigma of nationality. Then we can scarcely doubt that our brothers will provide us for many centuries to come, as they have done for many centuries past, with what is so essential for sanity, and so invaluable in preventing the great modern sins of vanity, egotism, and megalomania – that is to say ridicule, censure and contempt.[41] And so long as the Church of England refuses our services – long may she exclude us! – and the ancient schools and colleges refuse to admit us to a share of their endowments and privileges we shall be immune without any trouble on our part from the particular loyalties and fealties which such endowments and privileges engender. Further, Madam, the traditions of the private house, that ancestral memory which lies behind the present moment, are there to help you. We have seen in the quotations given above how great a part chastity, bodily chastity, has played in the unpaid education of our sex. It should not be difficult to transmute the old ideal of bodily chastity into the new ideal of mental chastity – to hold that if it was wrong to sell the body for money it is much more wrong to sell the mind for money, since the mind, people say, is nobler than the body. Then again, are we not greatly fortified in resisting the seductions of the most powerful of all seducers – money – by those same traditions? For how many centuries have we not enjoyed the right of working all day and every day for £40 a year with board and lodging thrown in? And does not Whitaker prove that half the work of educated men's daughters is still unpaid-for work? Finally, honour, fame, consequence – is it not easy for us to resist that seduction, we who have worked for centuries without other honour than that which is reflected from the coronets and badges on our father's or husband's brows and breasts?

'Thus, with law on our side, and property on our side, and ancestral memory to guide us, there is no need of further argument; you will agree that the conditions upon which this guinea is yours are, with the exception of the first, comparatively easy to fulfil. They merely require that you should develop, modify and direct by the findings of the two psychometers the traditions and the education of the private house which have been in existence these 2,000 years. And if you will agree to do that, there can be an end of bargaining between us. Then the guinea with which to pay the rent of your house is yours – would that it were a thousand! For if you agree to these terms then you can join the professions and yet remain uncontaminated by them; you can rid them of their possessiveness, their jealousy, their pugnacity, their greed. You can use them to have a mind of your own and a will of your own. And you can use that mind and will to abolish the inhumanity, the beastliness, the horror, the folly of war. Take this guinea then and use it, not to burn the house down, but to make its windows blaze. And let the daughters of uneducated women dance round the new house, the poor house, the house that stands in a narrow street where omnibuses pass and the street hawkers cry their wares, and let them sing, "We have done with war! We have done with tyranny!" And their mothers will laugh from their graves, "It was for this that we suffered obloquy and contempt! Light up the windows of the new house, daughters! Let them blaze!"

'Those then are the terms upon which I give you this guinea with which to help the daughters of uneducated women to enter the professions. And by cutting short the peroration let us hope that you will be able to give the finishing touches to your bazaar, arrange the hare and the coffee-pot, and receive the Right Honourable Sir Sampson Legend, O.M., K.C.B., LL.D.,

D.C.L., P.C., etc., with that air of smiling deference which befits the daughter of an educated man in the presence of her brother.'

Such then, Sir, was the letter finally sent to the honorary treasurer of the society for helping the daughters of educated men to enter the professions. Those are the conditions upon which she is to have her guinea. They have been framed, so far as possible, to ensure that she shall do all that a guinea can make her do to help you to prevent war. Whether the conditions have been rightly laid down, who shall say? But as you will see, it was necessary to answer her letter and the letter from the honorary treasurer of the college rebuilding fund, and to send them both guineas before answering your letter, because unless they are helped, first to educate the daughters of educated men, and then to earn their livings in the professions, those daughters cannot possess an independent and disinterested influence with which to help you to prevent war. The causes it seems are connected. But having shown this to the best of our ability, let us return to your own letter and to your request for a subscription to your own society.

Three

Here then is your own letter. In that, as we have seen, after asking for an opinion as to how to prevent war, you go on to suggest certain practical measures by which we can help you to prevent it. These are it appears that we should sign a manifesto, pledging ourselves 'to protect culture and intellectual liberty';[1] that we should join a certain society, devoted to certain measures whose aim is to preserve peace; and, finally, that we should subscribe to that society which like the others is in need of funds.[a]

First, then, let us consider how we can help you to prevent war by protecting culture and intellectual liberty, since you assure us that there is a connection between those rather abstract words and these very positive photographs – the photographs of dead bodies and ruined houses.

But if it was surprising to be asked for an opinion how to prevent war, it is still more surprising to be asked to help you in the rather abstract terms of your manifesto to protect culture and intellectual liberty. Consider, Sir, in the light of the facts given above, what this request of yours means. It means that in the year 1938 the sons of educated men are asking the daughters to help them to protect culture and intellectual liberty. And why, you may ask, is that so surprising? Suppose that the Duke of Devonshire, in his star and garter, stepped down into the kitchen and said to the maid who was peeling potatoes with a smudge on her cheek: 'Stop your potato peeling, Mary, and help me to construe this rather difficult passage in Pindar,' would not Mary be surprised and run screaming to Louisa the cook, 'Lawks, Louie, Master must be mad!' That, or something like it, is the cry that rises to our lips when the sons of educated men ask us, their sisters, to protect intellectual liberty and culture. But let us try to translate the kitchenmaid's cry into the language of educated people.

Once more we must beg you, Sir, to look from our angle, from our point of view, at Arthur's Education Fund. Try once more, difficult though it is to twist your head in that direction, to understand what it has meant to us to keep that receptacle filled all these centuries so that some 10,000 of our brothers may be educated every year at Oxford and Cambridge. It has meant that we have already contributed to the cause of culture and intellectual liberty more than any other class in the community. For have not the daughters of educated men paid into Arthur's Education Fund from the year 1262 to the year 1870 all the money that was needed to educate themselves, bating such miserable sums as went to pay the governess, the German teacher, and the dancing master? Have they not paid with their own education for Eton and Harrow, Oxford and Cambridge, and all the great schools and universities on the continent – the Sorbonne and Heidelberg, Salamanca and Padua and Rome? Have they not paid so generously and lavishly if so indirectly, that when at last, in the nineteenth century, they won the right to some paid-for education for themselves, there was not a single woman who had received enough paid-for education to be able to teach them?[2] And now, out of the blue, just as they were hoping that they might filch not only a little of that same university education for themselves but some of the trimmings – travel, pleasure, liberty – for themselves, here is your letter informing them that the whole of that vast, that fabulous sum – for whether counted directly in cash, or indirectly in things done without, the sum that filled Arthur's Education Fund is vast – has been wasted or wrongly applied. With what other purpose were the universities of Oxford and Cambridge founded, save to protect culture and intellectual liberty? For what other object did your sisters go without teaching or travel or luxuries themselves except that with the money so saved their brothers should go to schools and universities and there learn to protect culture and intellectual liberty? But now since you proclaim them in danger and ask us to add our voice to yours, and our sixpence to your guinea, we must assume that the money so spent was wasted and that those societies have failed. Yet, the reflection must intrude, if the public schools and universities with their elaborate machinery for mind-training and body-training have failed, what reason is there to think that your society, sponsored though it is by distinguished names, is going to succeed, or that your manifesto, signed though it is by still more distinguished names, is going to convert? Ought you not, before you lease an office, hire a secretary, elect a committee and appeal for funds, to consider why those schools and universities have failed?

That, however, is a question for you to answer. The question which concerns us is what possible help we can give you in protecting culture and intellectual liberty – we, who have been shut out from the universities so repeatedly, and are only now admitted so restrictedly; we who have received no paid-for education whatsoever, or so little that we can only read our own tongue and write our own language, we who are, in fact, members not of the intelligentsia but of the ignorantsia? To confirm us in our modest estimate of our own culture and to prove that you in fact share it there is Whitaker with his facts. Not a single educated man's daughter, Whitaker says, is thought capable of teaching the literature of her own language at either university. Nor is her opinion worth asking, Whitaker informs us, when it comes to buying a picture for the National Gallery, a portrait for the Portrait Gallery, or a mummy for the British Museum. How then can it be worth your while to ask us to protect culture and intellectual liberty when, as Whitaker proves with his cold facts, you have no belief that our advice is worth having when it comes to spending the money, to which we have contributed, in buying culture and intellectual liberty for the State? Do you wonder that the unexpected compliment takes us by surprise? Still, there is your letter. There are facts in that letter, too. In it you say that war is imminent; and you go on to say, in more languages than one – here is the French version:[3] *Seule la culture désintéressée peut garder le monde de sa ruine* – you go on to say that by protecting intellectual liberty and our inheritance of culture we can help you to prevent war. And since the first statement at least is indisputable and any kitchenmaid even if her French is defective can read and understand the meaning of 'Air Raid Precautions' when written in large letters upon a blank wall, we cannot ignore your request on the plea of ignorance or remain silent on the plea of modesty. Just as any kitchenmaid would attempt to construe a passage in Pindar if told that her life depended on it, so the daughters of educated men, however little their training qualifies them, must consider what they can do to protect culture and intellectual liberty if by so doing they can help you to prevent war. So let us by all means in our power examine this further method of helping you, and see, before we consider your request that we should join your society, whether we can sign this manifesto in favour of culture and intellectual liberty with some intention of keeping our word.

What, then, is the meaning of those rather abstract words? If we are to help you to protect them it would be well to define them in the first place. But like all honorary treasurers you are pressed for time, and to ramble through English literature in search of a definition, though a delightful pastime in its way, might well lead us far. Let us agree, then, for the present, that we know what they are, and concentrate upon the practical question how we can help you to protect them. Now the daily paper with its provision of facts lies on the table; and a single quotation from it may save time and limit our enquiry. 'It was decided yesterday at a conference of head masters that women were not fit teachers for boys over the age of fourteen.' That fact is of instant help to us here, for it proves that certain kinds of help are beyond our reach. For us to attempt to reform the education of our brothers at public schools and universities would be to invite a shower of dead cats, rotten eggs and broken gates from which only street scavengers and locksmiths would benefit, while the gentlemen in authority, history assures us, would survey the tumult from their study windows without taking the cigars from their lips or ceasing to sip, slowly as its bouquet deserves, their admirable claret.[4] The teaching of history, then, reinforced by the teaching of the daily paper, drives us to a more restricted position. We can only help you to defend culture and intellectual liberty by defending our own culture and our own intellectual liberty. That is to say, we can hint, if the treasurer of one of the women's colleges asks us for a subscription, that some change might be made in that satellite body when it ceases to be satellite; or again, if the treasurer of some society for obtaining professional employment for women asks us for a subscription, suggest that some change might be desirable, in the interests of culture and intellectual liberty, in the practice of the professions. But as paid-for education is still raw and young, and as the number of those allowed to enjoy it at Oxford and Cambridge is still strictly limited, culture for the great majority of educated men's daughters must still be that which is acquired outside the sacred gates, in public libraries or in private libraries, whose doors by some unaccountable oversight have been left unlocked. It must still, in the year 1938, largely consist in reading and writing our own tongue. The question thus becomes more manageable. Shorn of its glory it is easier to deal with. What we have to do now, then, Sir, is to lay your request before the daughters of educated men and to ask them to help you to prevent war, not by advising their brothers how they shall protect culture and intellectual liberty, but simply by reading and writing their own tongue in such a way as to protect those rather abstract goddesses themselves.

This would seem, on the face of it, a simple matter, and one that needs neither argument nor rhetoric. But we are met at the outset by a new difficulty. We have already noted the fact that the profession of literature, to give it a simple name, is the only profession which did not fight a series of battles in the nineteenth century. There has been no battle of Grub Street.[b] That profession has never been shut to the daughters of educated men. This was due of course to the extreme cheapness of its professional requirements. Books, pens and paper are so cheap, reading and writing have been, since the eighteenth century at least, so universally taught in our class, that it was impossible for any body of men to corner the necessary knowledge or to refuse admittance, except on their own terms, to those who wished to read books or to write them. But it follows, since the profession of literature is open to the daughters of educated men, that there is no honorary treasurer of the profession in such need of a guinea with which to prosecute her battle that she will listen to our terms, and promise to do what she can to observe them. This places us, you will agree, in an awkward predicament. For how then can we bring pressure upon them – what can we do to persuade them to help us? The profession of literature differs, it would seem, from all the other professions. There is no head of the profession; no Lord Chancellor as in your own case: no official body with the power to lay down rules and enforce them.[5] We cannot debar women from the use of libraries;[6] or forbid them to buy ink and paper; or rule that metaphors shall only be used by one sex, as the male only in art schools was allowed to study from the nude; or rule that rhyme shall be used by one sex only as the male only in Academies of music was allowed to play in orchestras. Such is the inconceivable licence of the profession of letters that any daughter of an educated man may use a man's name – say George Eliot or George Sand – with the result that an editor or a publisher, unlike the authorities in Whitehall, can detect no difference in the scent or savour of a manuscript, or even know for certain whether the writer is married or not.

Thus, since we have very little power over those who earn their livings by reading and writing, we must go to them humbly without bribes or penalties. We must go to them cap in hand, like beggars, and ask them of their goodness to spare time to listen to our request that they shall practise the profession of reading and writing in the interests of culture and intellectual liberty.

And now, clearly, some further definition of 'culture and intellectual liberty' would be useful. Fortunately, it need not be, for our purposes, exhaustive or elaborate. We need not consult Milton, Goethe, or Matthew Arnold; for their definition would apply to paid-for culture – the culture which, in Miss Weeton's definition, includes physics, divinity, astronomy, chemistry, botany, logic and mathematics, as well as Latin, Greek and French. We are appealing in the main to those whose culture is the unpaid-for culture, that which consists in being able to read and write their own tongue. Happily your manifesto is at hand to help us to define the terms further; 'disinterested' is the word you use. Therefore let us define culture for our purposes as the disinterested pursuit of reading and writing the English language. And intellectual liberty may be defined for our purposes as the right to say or write what you think in your own words, and in your own way. These are very crude definitions, but they must serve. Our appeal then might begin: 'Oh, daughters of educated men, this gentleman, whom we all respect, says that war is imminent; by protecting culture and intellectual liberty he says that we can help him to prevent war. We entreat you, therefore, who earn your livings by reading and writing . . .' But here the words falter on our lips, and the prayer peters out into three separate dots because of facts again – because of facts in books, facts in biographies, facts which make it difficult, perhaps impossible, to go on.

What are those facts then? Once more we must interrupt our appeal in order to examine them. And there is no difficulty in finding them. Here, for example, is an illuminating document before us, a most genuine and indeed moving piece of work, the autobiography of Mrs Oliphant, which is full of facts. She was an educated man's daughter who earned her living by reading and writing. She wrote books of all kinds. Novels, biographies, histories, handbooks of Florence and Rome, reviews, newspaper articles innumerable came from her pen. With the proceeds she earned her living and educated her children. But how far did she protect culture and intellectual liberty? That you can judge for yourself by reading first a few of her novels: *The Duke's Daughter, Diana Trelawny, Harry Joscelyn*, say; continue with the lives of Sheridan and Cervantes; go on to the *Makers of Florence and Rome*; conclude by sousing yourself in the innumerable faded articles, reviews, sketches of one kind and another which she contributed to literary papers. When you have done, examine the state of your own mind, and ask yourself whether that reading has led you to respect disinterested culture and intellectual liberty. Has it not on the contrary smeared your mind and dejected your imagination, and led you to deplore the fact that Mrs Oliphant sold her brain, her very admirable brain, prostituted her culture and enslaved her intellectual liberty in order that she might earn her living and educate her children?[7] Inevitably, considering the damage that poverty inflicts upon mind and body, the necessity that is laid upon those who have children to see that they are fed and clothed, nursed and educated, we have to applaud her choice and to admire her courage. But if we applaud the choice and admire the courage of those who do what she did, we can spare ourselves the trouble of addressing our appeal to them, for they will no more be able to protect disinterested culture and intellectual liberty than she was. To ask them to sign your manifesto would be to ask a publican to sign a manifesto in favour of temperance. He may himself be a total abstainer; but since his wife and children depend upon the sale of beer, he must continue to sell beer, and his signature to the manifesto would be of no value to the cause of temperance because directly he had signed it he must be at the counter inducing his customers to drink more beer. So to ask the daughters of educated men who have to earn their livings by reading and writing to sign your manifesto would be of no value to the cause of disinterested culture and intellectual liberty, because directly they had signed it they must be at the desk writing those books, lectures and articles by which culture is prostituted and intellectual liberty is sold into slavery. As an expression of opinion it may have value; but if what you need is not merely an expression of opinion but positive help, you must frame your request rather differently. Then you will have to ask them to pledge themselves not to write anything that defiles culture, or to sign any contract that infringes intellectual liberty. And to that the answer given us by biography would be short but sufficient: Have I not to earn my living?

Thus, Sir, it becomes clear that we must make our appeal only to those daughters of educated men who have enough to live upon. To them we might address ourselves in this wise: 'Daughters of educated men who have enough to live upon . . .' But again the voice falters: again the prayer peters out into separate dots. For how many of them are there? Dare we assume in the face of Whitaker, of the laws of property, of the wills in the newspapers, of facts in short, that 1,000, 500, or even 250 will answer when thus addressed? However that may be, let the plural stand and continue: 'Daughters of educated men who have enough to live upon, and read and write your own language for your own pleasure, may we very humbly entreat you to sign this gentleman's manifesto with some intention of putting your promise into practice?'

Here, if indeed they consent to listen, they might very reasonably ask us to be more explicit – not indeed to define culture and intellectual liberty, for they have books and leisure and can define the words for themselves. But what, they may well ask, is meant by this gentleman's 'disinterested' culture, and how are we to protect that and intellectual liberty in practice? Now as they are daughters, not sons, we may begin by reminding them of a compliment once paid them by a great historian. 'Mary's conduct,' says Macaulay, 'was really a signal instance of that perfect disinterestedness and self-devotion of which man seems to be incapable, but which is sometimes found in women.'[8] Compliments, when you are asking a favour, never come amiss. Next let us refer them to the tradition which has long been honoured in the private house – the tradition of chastity. 'Just as for many centuries, Madam,' we might plead, 'it was thought vile for a woman to sell her body without love, but right to give it to the husband whom she loved, so it is wrong, you will agree, to sell your mind without love, but right to give it to the art which you love.' 'But what,' she may ask, 'is meant by "selling your mind without love"?' 'Briefly,' we might reply, 'to write at the command of another person what you do not want to write for the sake of money. But to sell a brain is worse than to sell a body, for when the body seller has sold her momentary pleasure she takes good care that the matter shall end there. But when a brain seller has sold her brain, its anaemic, vicious and diseased progeny are let loose upon the world to infect and corrupt and sow the seeds of disease in others. Thus we are asking you, Madam, to pledge yourself not to commit adultery of the brain because it is a much more serious offence than the other.' 'Adultery of the brain,' she may reply, 'means writing what I do not want to write for the sake of money. Therefore you ask me to refuse all publishers, editors, lecture agents and so on who bribe me to write or to speak what I do not want to write or to speak for the sake of money?' 'That is so, Madam; and we further ask that if you should receive proposals for such sales you will resent them and expose them as you would resent and expose such proposals for selling your body, both for your own sake and for the sake of others. But we would have you observe that the verb "to adulterate" means, according to the dictionary, "to falsify by admixture of baser ingredients". Money is not the only baser ingredient. Advertisement and publicity are also adulterers. Thus, culture mixed with personal charm, or culture mixed with advertisement and publicity, are also adulter-ated forms of culture. We must ask you to abjure them; not to appear on public platforms; not to lecture; not to allow your private face to be published, or details of your private life; not to avail yourself, in short, of any of the forms of brain prostitution which are so insidiously suggested by the pimps and panders of the brain-selling trade; or to accept any of those baubles and labels by which brain merit is advertised and certified – medals, honours, degrees – we must ask you to refuse them absolutely, since they are all tokens that culture has been prostituted and intellectual liberty sold into captivity.'

Upon hearing this definition, mild and imperfect as it is, of what it means, not merely to sign your manifesto in favour of culture and intellectual liberty, but to put that opinion into practice, even those daughters of educated men who have enough to live upon may object that the terms are too hard for them to keep. For they would mean loss of money which is desirable, loss of fame which is universally held to be agreeable, and censure and ridicule which are by no means negligible. Each would be the butt of all who have an interest to serve or money to make from the sale of brains. And for what reward? Only, in the rather abstract terms of your manifesto, that they would thus 'protect culture and intellectual liberty', not by their opinion but by their practice.

Since the terms are so hard, and there is no body in existence whose ruling they need respect or obey, let us consider what other method of persuasion is left to us. Only, it would seem, to point to the photographs – the photographs of dead bodies and ruined houses. Can we bring out the connection between them and prostituted culture and intellectual slavery and make it so clear that the one implies the other, that the daughters of educated men will prefer to refuse money and fame, and to be the objects of scorn and ridicule rather than suffer themselves, or allow others to suffer, the penalties there made visible? It is difficult in the short time at our disposal, and with the weak weapons in our possession, to make that connection clear, but if what you, Sir, say is true, and there is a connection and a very real one between them, we must try to prove it.

Let us then begin by summoning, if only from the world of imagination, some daughter of an educated man who has enough to live upon and can read and write for her own pleasure and, taking her to be the representative of what may in fact be no class at all, let us ask her to examine the products of that reading and writing which lie upon her own table. 'Look, Madam,' we might begin, 'at the newspapers on your table. Why, may we ask, do you take in three dailies, and three weeklies?' 'Because,' she replies, 'I am interested in politics, and wish to know the facts.' 'An admirable desire, Madam. But why three? Do they differ then about facts, and if so, why?' To which she replies, with some irony, 'You call yourself an educated man's daughter, and yet pretend not to know the facts – roughly that each paper is financed by a board; that each board has a policy; that each board employs writers to expound that policy, and if the writers do not agree with that policy, the writers, as you may remember after a moment's reflection, find themselves unemployed in the street. Therefore if you want to know any fact about politics you must read at least three different papers, compare at least three different versions of the same fact, and come in the end to your own conclusion. Hence the three daily papers on my table.' Now that we have discussed, very briefly, what may be called the literature of fact, let us turn to what may be called the literature of fiction. 'There are such things, Madam,' we may remind her, 'as pictures, plays, music and books. Do you pursue the same rather extravagant policy there – glance at three daily papers and three weekly papers if you want to know the facts about pictures, plays, music and books, because those who write about art are in the pay of an editor, who is in the pay of a board, which has a policy to pursue, so that each paper takes a different view, so that it is only by comparing three different views that you can come to your own conclusion – what pictures to see, what play or concert to go to, which book to order from the library?' And to that she replies, 'Since I am an educated man's daughter, with a smattering of culture picked up from reading, I should no more dream, given the conditions of journalism at present, of taking my opinions of pictures, plays, music or books from the newspapers than I would take my opinion of politics from the newspapers. Compare the views, make allowance for the distortions, and then judge for yourself. That is the only way. Hence the many newspapers on my table.'⁹

So then the literature of fact and the literature of opinion, to make a crude distinction, are not pure fact, or pure opinion, but adulterated fact and adulterated opinion, that is fact and opinion 'adulterated by the admixture of baser ingredients' as the dictionary has it. In other words you have to strip each statement of its money motive, of its power motive, of its advertisement motive, of its publicity motive, of its vanity motive, let alone of all the other motives which, as an educated man's daughter, are familiar to you, before you make up your mind which fact about politics to believe, or even which opinion about art? 'That is so,' she agrees. But if you were told by somebody who had none of those motives for wrapping up truth that the fact was in his or her opinion this or that, you would believe him or her, always allowing of course for the fallibility of human judgement which, in judging works of art, must be considerable? 'Naturally,' she agrees. If such a person said that war was bad, you would believe him; or if such a person said that some picture, symphony, play or poem were good you would believe him? 'Allowing for human fallibility, yes.' Now suppose, Madam, that there were 250, or 50, or 25 such people in existence, people pledged not to commit adultery of the brain, so that it was unnecessary to strip what they said of its money motive, power motive, advertisement motive, publicity motive, vanity motive and so on, before we unwrapped the grain of truth, might not two very remarkable consequences follow? Is it not possible that if we knew the truth about war, the glory of war would be scotched and crushed where it lies curled up in the rotten cabbage leaves of our prostituted fact-purveyors; and if we knew the truth about art instead of shuffling and shambling through the smeared and dejected pages of those who must live by prostituting culture, the enjoyment and practice of art would become so desirable that by comparison the pursuit of war would be a tedious game for elderly dilettantes in search of a mildly sanitary amusement – the tossing of bombs instead of balls over frontiers instead of nets? In short, if newspapers were written by people whose sole object in writing was to tell the truth about politics and the truth about art we should not believe in war, and we should believe in art.

Hence there is a very clear connection between culture and intellectual liberty and those photographs of dead bodies and ruined houses. And to ask the daughters of educated men who have enough to live upon not to commit adultery of the brain is to ask them to help in the most positive way now open to them – since the profession of literature is still that which stands widest open to them – to prevent war.

Thus, Sir, we might address this lady, crudely, briefly it is true; but time presses and we cannot define further. And to this appeal she might well reply, if indeed she exists: 'What you say is obvious; so obvious that every educated man's daughter already knows it for herself, or if she does not, has only to read the newspapers to be sure of it. But suppose she were well enough off not merely to sign this manifesto in favour of disinterested culture and intellectual liberty but to put her opinion into practice, how could she set about it? And do not,' she may reasonably add, 'dream dreams about ideal worlds behind the stars; consider actual facts in the actual world.' Indeed, the actual world is much more difficult to deal with than the dream world. Still, Madam, the private printing press is an actual fact, and not beyond the reach of a moderate income. Typewriters and duplicators are actual facts and even cheaper. By using these cheap and so far unforbidden instruments you can at once rid yourself of the pressure of boards, policies and editors. They will speak your own mind, in your own words, at your own time, at your own length, at your own bidding. And that, we are agreed, is our definition of 'intellectual liberty'. 'But,' she may say, '"the public"? How can that be reached without putting my own mind through the mincing machine and turning it into sausage?' '"The public", Madam,' we may assure her, 'is very like ourselves; it lives in rooms; it walks in streets, and is said moreover to be tired of sausage. Fling leaflets down basements; expose them on stalls; trundle them along streets on barrows to be sold for a penny or given away. Find out new ways of approaching "the public"; single it into separate people instead of massing it into one monster, gross in body, feeble in mind. And then reflect – since you have enough to live on, you have a room, not necessarily "cosy" or "handsome" but still silent, private; a room where safe from publicity and its poison you could, even asking a reasonable fee for the service, speak the truth to artists, about pictures, music, books, without fear of affecting their sales, which are exiguous, or wounding their vanity, which is prodigious.[10] Such at least was the criticism that Ben Jonson gave Shakespeare at the Mermaid and there is no reason to suppose, with *Hamlet* as evidence, that literature suffered in consequence. Are not the best critics private people, and is not the only criticism worth having spoken criticism? Those then are some of the active ways in which you, as a writer of your own tongue, can put your opinion into practice. But if you are passive, a reader, not a writer, then you must adopt not active but passive methods of protecting culture and intellectual liberty.' 'And what may they be?' she will ask. 'To abstain, obviously. Not to subscribe to papers that encourage intellectual slavery; not to attend lectures that prostitute culture; for we are agreed that to write at the command of another what you do not want to write is to be enslaved, and to mix culture with personal charm or advertisement is to prostitute culture. By these active and passive measures you would do all in your power to break the ring, the vicious circle, the dance round and round the mulberry tree, the poison tree of intellectual harlotry. The ring once broken, the captives would be freed. For who can doubt that once writers had the chance of writing what they enjoy writing they would find it so much more pleasurable that they would refuse to write on any other terms; or that readers once they had the chance of reading what writers enjoy writing, would find it so much more nourishing than what is written for money that they would refuse to be palmed off with the stale substitute any longer? Thus the slaves who are now kept hard at work piling words into books, piling words into articles, as the old slaves piled stones into pyramids, would shake the manacles from their wrists and give up their loathsome labour. And "culture", that amorphous bundle, swaddled up as she now is in insincerity, emitting half truths from her timid lips, sweetening and diluting her message with whatever sugar or water serves to swell the writer's fame or his master's purse, would regain her shape and become, as Milton, Keats and other great writers assure us that she is in reality, muscular, adventurous, free. Whereas now, Madam, at the very mention of culture the head aches, the eyes close, the doors shut, the air thickens; we are in a lecture room, rank with the fumes of stale print, listening to a gentleman who is forced to lecture or to write every Wednesday, every Sunday, about Milton or about Keats, while the lilac shakes its branches in the garden free, and the gulls, swirling and swooping, suggest with wild laughter that such stale fish might with advantage be tossed to them. That is our plea to you, Madam; those are our reasons for urging it. Do not merely sign this manifesto in favour of culture and intellectual liberty; attempt at least to put your promise into practice.'

Whether the daughters of educated men who have enough to live upon and read and write their own tongue for their own pleasure will listen to this request or not, we cannot say, Sir. But if culture and intellectual liberty are to be protected, not by opinions merely but by practice, this would seem to be the way. It is not an easy way, it is true. Nevertheless, such as it is, there are reasons for thinking that the way is easier for them than for their brothers. They are immune, through no merit of their own, from certain compulsions. To protect culture and intellectual liberty in practice would mean, as we have said, ridicule and chastity, loss of publicity and poverty. But those, as we have seen, are their familiar teachers. Further, Whitaker with his facts is at hand to help them; for since he proves that all the fruits of professional culture – such as directorships of art galleries and museums, professorships and lectureships and editorships – are still beyond their reach, they should be able to take a more purely disinterested view of culture than their brothers, without for a moment claiming, as Macaulay asserts, that they are by nature more disinterested. Thus helped by tradition and by facts as they are, we have not only some right to ask them to help us to break the circle, the vicious circle of prostituted culture, but some hope that if such people exist they will help us. To return then to your manifesto: we will sign it if we can keep these terms; if we cannot keep them, we will not sign it.

Now that we have tried to see how we can help you to prevent war by attempting to define what is meant by protecting culture and intellectual liberty let us consider your next and inevitable request: that we should subscribe to the funds of your society. For you, too, are an honorary treasurer, and like the other honorary treasurers in need of money. Since you, too, are asking for money it might be possible to ask you, also, to define your aims, and to bargain and to impose terms as with the other honorary treasurers. What then are the aims of your society? To prevent war, of course. And by what means? Broadly speaking, by protecting the rights of the individual; by opposing dictatorship; by ensuring the democratic ideals of equal opportunity for all. Those are the chief means by which as you say, 'the lasting peace of the world can be assured.' Then, Sir, there is no need to bargain or to haggle. If those are your aims, and if, as it is impossible to doubt, you mean to do all in your power to achieve them, the guinea is yours – would that it were a million! The guinea is yours; and the guinea is a free gift, given freely.

But the word 'free' is used so often, and has come, like used words, to mean so little, that it may be well to explain exactly, even pedantically, what the word 'free' means in this context. It means here that no right or privilege is asked in return. The giver is not asking you to admit her to the priesthood of the Church of England; or to the Stock Exchange; or to the Diplomatic Service. The giver has no wish to be 'English' on the same terms that you yourself are 'English'. The giver does not claim in return for the gift admission to any profession; any honour, title, or medal; any professorship or lectureship; any seat upon any society, committee or board. The gift is free from all such conditions because the one right of paramount importance to all human beings is already won. You cannot take away her right to earn a living. Now then for the first time in English history an educated man's daughter can give her brother one guinea of her own making at his request for the purpose specified above without asking for anything in return. It is a free gift, given without fear, without flattery, and without conditions. That, Sir, is so momentous an occasion in the history of civilization that some celebration seems called for. But let us have done with the old ceremonies – the Lord Mayor, with turtles and sheriffs in attendance, tapping nine times with his mace upon a stone while the Archbishop of Canterbury in full canonicals invokes a blessing. Let us invent a new ceremony for this new occasion. What more fitting than to destroy an old word, a vicious and corrupt word that has done much harm in its day and is now obsolete? The word 'feminist' is the word indicated. That word, according to the dictionary, means 'one who champions the rights of women.' Since the only right, the right to earn a living, has been won, the word no longer has a meaning. And a word without a meaning is a dead word, a corrupt word. Let us therefore celebrate this occasion by cremating the corpse. Let us write that word in large black letters on a sheet of foolscap; then solemnly apply a match to the paper. Look, how it burns! What a light dances over the world! Now let us bray the ashes in a mortar with a goose-feather pen, and declare in unison singing together that anyone who uses that word in future is a ring-the-bell-and-run-away man,[11] a mischief maker, a groper among old bones, the proof of whose defilement is written in a smudge of dirty water upon his face. The smoke has died down; the word is destroyed. Observe, Sir, what has happened as the result of our celebration. The word 'feminist' is destroyed; the air is cleared; and in that clearer air what do we see? Men and women working together for the same cause. The cloud has lifted from the past too. What were they working for in the nineteenth century – those queer dead women in their poke bonnets and shawls? The very same cause for which we are working now. 'Our claim was no claim of women's rights only' – it is Josephine Butler who speaks – 'it was larger and deeper; it was a claim for the rights of all – all men and women – to the respect in their persons of the great principles of Justice and Equality and Liberty.' The words are the same as yours; the claim is the same as yours. The daughters of educated men who were called, to their resentment, 'feminists' were in fact the advance guard of your own movement. They were fighting the same enemy that you are fighting and for the same reasons. They were fighting the tyranny of the patriarchal state as you are fighting the tyranny of the Fascist state. Thus we are merely carrying on the same fight that our mothers and grandmothers fought; their words prove it; your words prove it. But now with your letter before us we have your assurance that you are fighting with us, not against us. That fact is so inspiring that another celebration seems called for. What could be more fitting than to write more dead words, more corrupt words, upon more sheets of paper and burn them – the words, Tyrant, Dictator, for example? But, alas, those words are not yet obsolete. We can still shake out eggs from newspapers; still smell a peculiar and unmistakable odour in the region of Whitehall and Westminster. And abroad the monster has come more openly to the surface. There is no mistaking him there. He has widened his scope. He is interfering now with your liberty; he is dictating how you shall live; he is making distinctions not merely between the sexes, but between the races. You are feeling in your own persons what your mothers felt when they were shut out, when they were shut up, because they were women. Now you are being shut out, you are being shut up, because you are Jews, because you are democrats, because of race, because of religion. It is not a photograph that you look upon any longer; there you go, trapesing along in the procession yourselves. And that makes a difference. The whole iniquity of dictatorship, whether in Oxford or Cambridge, in Whitehall or Downing Street, against Jews or against women, in England, or in Germany, in Italy or in Spain is now apparent to you. But now we are fighting together. The daughters and sons of educated men are fighting side by side. That fact is so inspiring, even if no celebration is yet possible, that if this one guinea could be multiplied a million times all those guineas should be at your service without any other conditions than those that you have imposed upon yourself. Take this one guinea then and use it to assert 'the rights of all – all men and women – to the respect in their persons of the great principles of Justice and Equality and Liberty'. Put this penny candle in the window of your new society, and may we live to see the day when in the blaze of our common freedom the words tyrant and dictator shall be burnt to ashes, because the words tyrant and dictator shall be obsolete.

That request then for a guinea answered, and the cheque signed, only one further request of yours remains to be considered – it is that we should fill up a form and become members of your society. On the face of it that seems a simple request, easily granted. For what can be simpler than to join the society to which this guinea has just been contributed? On the face of it, how easy, how simple; but in the depths, how difficult, how complicated . . . What possible doubts, what possible hesitations can those dots stand for? What reason or what emotion can make us hesitate to become members of a society whose aims we approve, to whose funds we have contributed? It may be neither reason nor emotion, but something more profound and fundamental than either. It may be difference.ᶜ Different we are, as facts have proved, both in sex and in education. And it is from that difference, as we have already said, that our help can come, if help we can, to protect liberty, to prevent war. But if we sign this form which implies a promise to become active members of your society, it would seem that we must lose that difference and therefore sacrifice that help. To explain why this is so is not easy, even though the gift of a guinea has made it possible (so we have boasted), to speak freely without fear or flattery. Let us then keep the form unsigned on the table before us while we discuss, so far as we are able, the reasons and the emotions which make us hesitate to sign it. For those reasons and emotions have their origin deep in the darkness of ancestral memory; they have grown together in some confusion; it is very difficult to untwist them in the light.

To begin with an elementary distinction: a society is a conglomeration of people joined together for certain aims; while you, who write in your own person with your own hand are single. You the individual are a man whom we have reason to respect; a man of the brotherhood, to which, as biography proves, many brothers have belonged. Thus Anne Clough, describing her brother, says: 'Arthur is my best friend and adviser . . . Arthur is the comfort and joy of my life; it is for him, and from him, that I am incited to seek after all that is lovely and of good report.' To which William Wordsworth, speaking of his sister but answering the other as if one nightingale called to another in the forests of the past, replies:

> The Blessing of my later years
> Was with me when a Boy:
> She gave me eyes, she gave me ears;
> And humble cares, and delicate fears;
> A heart, the fountain of sweet tears;
> And love, and thought, and joy.[12]

Such was, such perhaps still is, the relationship of many brothers and sisters in private, as individuals. They respect each other and help each other and have aims in common. Why then, if such can be their private relationship, as biography and poetry prove, should their public relationship, as law and history prove, be so very different? And here, since you are a lawyer, with a lawyer's memory, it is not necessary to remind you of certain decrees of English law from its first records to the year 1919 by way of proving that the public, the society relationship of brother and sister has been very different from the private. The very word 'society' sets tolling in memory the dismal bells of a harsh music: shall not, shall not, shall not. You shall not learn; you shall not earn; you shall not own; you shall not— such was the society relationship of brother to sister for many centuries. And though it is possible, and to the optimistic credible, that in time a new society may ring a carillon of splendid harmony, and your letter heralds it, that day is far distant. Inevitably we ask ourselves, is there not something in the conglomeration of people into societies that releases what is most selfish and violent, least rational and humane in the individuals themselves? Inevitably we look upon society, so kind to you, so harsh to us, as an ill-fitting form that distorts the truth; deforms the mind; fetters the will. Inevitably we look upon societies as conspiracies that sink the private brother, whom many of us have reason to respect, and inflate in his stead a monstrous male, loud of voice, hard of fist, childishly intent upon scoring the floor of the earth with chalk marks, within whose mystic boundaries human beings are penned, rigidly, separately, artificially; where, daubed red and gold, decorated like a savage with feathers he goes through mystic rites and enjoys the dubious pleasures of power and dominion while we, 'his' women, are locked in the private house without share in the many societies of which his society is composed. For such reasons compact as they are of many memories and emotions – for who shall analyse the complexity of a mind that holds so deep a reservoir of time past within it? – it seems both wrong for us rationally and impossible for us emotionally to fill up your form and join your society. For by so doing we should merge our identity in yours; follow and repeat and score still deeper the old worn ruts in which society, like a gramophone whose needle has stuck, is grinding out with intolerable unanimity 'Three hundred millions spent upon arms.' We should not give effect to a view which our own experience of 'society' should have helped us to envisage. Thus, Sir, while we respect you as a private person and prove it by giving you a guinea to spend as you choose, we believe that we can help you most effectively by refusing to join your society; by working for our common ends – justice and equality and liberty for all men and women – outside your society, not within.

But this, you will say, if it means anything, can only mean that you, the daughters of educated men, who have promised us your positive help, refuse to join our society in order that you may make another of your own. And what sort of society do you propose to found outside ours, but in co-operation with it, so that we may both work together for our common ends? That is a question which you have every right to ask, and which we must try to answer in order to justify our refusal to sign the form you send. Let us then draw rapidly in outline the kind of society which the daughters of educated men might found and join outside your society but in co-operation with its ends. In the first place, this new society, you will be relieved to learn, would have no honorary treasurer, for it would need no funds. It would have no office, no committee, no secretary; it would call no meetings; it would hold no conferences. If name it must have, it could be called the Outsiders' Society. That is not a resonant name, but it has the advantage that it squares with facts – the facts of history, of law, of biography; even, it may be, with the still hidden facts of our still unknown psychology. It would consist of educated men's daughters working in their own class – how indeed can they work in any other?[13] – and by their own methods for liberty, equality and peace. Their first duty, to which they would bind themselves not by oath, for oaths and ceremonies have no part in a society which must be anonymous and elastic before everything, would be not to fight with arms. This is easy for them to observe, for in fact, as the papers inform us, 'the Army Council have no intention of opening recruiting for any women's corps.'[14] The country ensures it. Next they would refuse in the event of war to make munitions or nurse the wounded. Since in the last war both these activities were mainly discharged by the daughters of working men, the pressure upon them here too would be slight, though probably disagreeable. On the other hand the next duty to which they would pledge themselves is one of considerable difficulty, and calls not only for courage and initiative, but for the special knowledge of the educated man's daughter. It is, briefly, not to incite their brothers to fight, or to dissuade them, but to maintain an attitude of complete indifference. But the attitude expressed by the word 'indifference' is so complex and of such importance that it needs even here further definition. Indifference in the first place must be given a firm footing upon fact. As it is a fact that she cannot understand what instinct compels him, what glory, what interest, what manly satisfaction fighting provides for him – 'without war there would be no outlet for the manly qualities which fighting develops' – as fighting thus is a sex characteristic which she cannot share, the counterpart some claim of the maternal instinct which he cannot share, so is it an instinct which she cannot judge. The outsider therefore must leave him free to deal with this instinct by himself, because liberty of opinion must be respected, especially when it is based upon an instinct which is as foreign to her as centuries of tradition and education can make it.[15] This is a fundamental and instinctive distinction upon which indifference may be based. But the outsider will make it her duty not merely to base her indifference upon instinct, but upon reason. When he says, as history proves that he has said, and may say again, 'I am fighting to protect our country' and thus seeks to rouse her patriotic emotion, she will ask herself, 'What does "our country" mean to me an outsider?' To decide this she will analyse the meaning of patriotism in her own case. She will inform herself of the position of her sex and her class in the past. She will inform herself of the amount of land, wealth and property in the possession of her own sex and class in the present – how much of 'England' in fact belongs to her. From the same sources she will inform herself of the legal protection which the law has given her in the past and now gives her. And if he adds that he is fighting to protect her body, she will reflect upon the degree of physical protection that she now enjoys when the words 'Air Raid Precaution' are written on blank walls. And if he says that he is fighting to protect England from foreign rule, she will reflect that for her there are no 'foreigners', since by law she becomes a foreigner if she marries a foreigner. And she will do her best to make this a fact, not by forced fraternity, but by human sympathy. All these facts will convince her reason (to put it in a nutshell) that her sex and class has very little to thank England for in the past; not much to thank England for in the present; while the security of her person in the future is highly dubious. But probably she will have imbibed, even from the governess, some romantic notion that Englishmen, those fathers and grandfathers whom she sees marching in the picture of history, are 'superior' to the men of other countries. This she will consider it her duty to check by comparing French historians with English; German with French; the testimony of the ruled – the Indians or the Irish, say – with the claims made by their rulers. Still some 'patriotic' emotion, some ingrained belief in the intellectual superiority of her own country over other countries may remain. Then she will compare English painting with French painting; English music with German music; English literature with Greek literature, for translations abound. When all these comparisons have been faithfully made by the use of reason, the outsider will find herself in possession of very good reasons for her indifference. She will find that she has no good reason to ask her brother to fight on her behalf to protect 'our' country. '"Our country",' she will say, 'throughout the greater part of its history has treated me as a slave; it has denied me education or any share in its possessions. "Our" country still ceases to be mine if I marry a foreigner. "Our" country denies me the means of protecting myself, forces me to pay others a very large sum annually to protect me, and is so little able, even so, to protect me that Air Raid precautions are written on the wall. Therefore if you insist upon fighting to protect me, or "our" country, let it be understood, soberly and rationally between us, that you are fighting to gratify a sex instinct which I cannot share; to procure benefits which I have not shared and probably will not share; but not to gratify my instincts, or to protect either myself or my country. For,' the outsider will say, 'in fact, as a woman, I have no country. As a woman I want no country. As a woman my country is the whole world.' And if, when reason has said its say, still some obstinate emotion[d] remains, some love of England dropped into a child's ears by the cawing of rooks in an elm tree, by the splash of waves on a beach, or by English voices murmuring nursery rhymes, this drop of pure, if irrational, emotion she will make serve her to give to England first what she desires of peace and freedom for the whole world.

Such then will be the nature of her 'indifference' and from this indifference certain actions must follow. She will bind herself to take no share in patriotic demonstrations; to assent to no form of national self-praise; to make no part of any claque or audience that encourages war; to absent herself from military displays, tournaments, tattoos, prize-givings and all such ceremonies as

encourage the desire to impose 'our' civilization or 'our' dominion upon other people. The psychology of private life, moreover,
warrants the belief that this use of indifference by the daughters
of educated men would help materially to prevent war. For
psychology would seem to show that it is far harder for human
beings to take action when other people are indifferent and
allow them complete freedom of action, than when their actions
are made the centre of excited emotion. The small boy struts and
trumpets outside the window: implore him to stop; he goes on;
say nothing; he stops. That the daughters of educated men then
should give their brothers neither the white feather of cowardice
nor the red feather of courage, but no feather at all; that they
should shut the bright eyes that rain influence, or let those eyes
look elsewhere when war is discussed – that is the duty to which
outsiders will train themselves in peace before the threat of death
inevitably makes reason powerless.

Such then are some of the methods by which the society, the
anonymous and secret Society of Outsiders would help you, Sir,
to prevent war and to ensure freedom. Whatever value you may
attach to them you will agree that they are duties which your
own sex would find it more difficult to carry out than ours; and
duties moreover which are specially appropriate to the daughters
of educated men. For they would need some acquaintance with
the psychology of educated men, and the minds of educated men
are more highly trained and their words subtler than those of
working men.[16] There are other duties, of course – many have
already been outlined in the letters to the other honorary treasurers. But at the risk of some repetition let us roughly and rapidly
repeat them, so that they may form a basis for a society of
outsiders to take its stand upon. First, they would bind themselves to earn their own livings. The importance of this as a
method of ending war is obvious; sufficient stress has already
been laid upon the superior cogency of an opinion based upon
economic independence over an opinion based upon no income
at all or upon a spiritual right to an income to make further
proof unnecessary. It follows that an outsider must make it her

business to press for a living wage in all the professions now open to her sex; further that she must create new professions in which she can earn the right to an independent opinion. Therefore she must bind herself to press for a money wage for the unpaid worker in her own class – the daughters and sisters of educated men who, as biographies have shown us, are now paid on the truck system, with food, lodging and a pittance of £40 a year. But above all she must press for a wage to be paid by the State legally to the mothers of educated men. The importance of this to our common fight is immeasurable; for it is the most effective way in which we can ensure that the large and very honourable class of married women shall have a mind and a will of their own, with which, if his mind and will are good in her eyes, to support her husband, if bad to resist him, in any case to cease to be 'his woman' and to be her self. You will agree, Sir, without any aspersion upon the lady who bears your name, that to depend upon her for your income would effect a most subtle and undesirable change in your psychology. Apart from that, this measure is of such importance directly to yourselves, in your own fight for liberty and equality and peace, that if any condition were to be attached to the guinea it would be this: that you should provide a wage to be paid by the State to those whose profession is marriage and motherhood. Consider, even at the risk of a digression, what effect this would have upon the birth-rate, in the very class where the birth-rate is falling, in the very class where births are desirable – the educated class. Just as the increase in the pay of soldiers has resulted, the papers say, in additional recruits to the force of arm-bearers, so the same inducement would serve to recruit the child-bearing force, which we can hardly deny to be as necessary and as honourable, but which, because of its poverty, and its hardships, is now failing to attract recruits. That method might succeed where the one in use at present – abuse and ridicule – has failed. But the point which, at the risk of further digression, the outsiders would press upon you is one that vitally concerns your own lives as educated men and the honour and vigour of your professions. For if your wife were paid for her work, the work of bearing and bringing up children, a real wage, a money wage, so that it became an attractive profession instead of being as it is now an unpaid profession, an unpensioned profession, and therefore a precarious and dishonoured profession,[17] your own slavery would be lightened. No longer need you go to the office at nine-thirty and stay there till six. Work could be equally distributed. Patients could be sent to the patientless. Briefs to the briefless. Articles could be left unwritten. Culture would thus be stimulated. You could see the fruit trees flower in spring. You could share the prime of life with your children. And after that prime was over no longer need you be thrown from the machine on to the scrap heap without any life left or interests surviving to parade the environs of Bath or Cheltenham in the care of some unfortunate slave. No longer would you be the Saturday caller, the albatross on the neck of society, the sympathy addict, the deflated work slave calling for replenishment; or, as Herr Hitler puts it, the hero requiring recreation, or, as Signor Mussolini puts it, the wounded warrior requiring female dependants to bandage his wounds.[18] If the State paid your wife a living wage for her work which, sacred though it is, can scarcely be called more sacred than that of the clergyman, yet as his work is paid without derogation so may hers be – if this step which is even more essential to your freedom than to hers were taken the old mill in which the professional man now grinds out his round, often so wearily, with so little pleasure to himself or profit to his profession, would be broken; the opportunity of freedom would be yours; the most degrading of all servitudes, the intellectual servitude, would be ended; the half-man might become whole. But since three hundred millions or so have to be spent upon the arms-bearers, such expenditure is obviously, to use a convenient word supplied by the politicians, 'impracticable' and it is time to return to more feasible projects.

The outsiders then would bind themselves not only to earn their own livings, but to earn them so expertly that their refusal to earn them would be a matter of concern to the work master.

They would bind themselves to obtain full knowledge of professional practices, and to reveal any instance of tyranny or abuse in their professions. And they would bind themselves not to continue to make money in any profession, but to cease all competition and to practise their profession experimentally, in the interests of research and for love of the work itself, when they had earned enough to live upon. Also they would bind themselves to remain outside any profession hostile to freedom, such as the making or the improvement of the weapons of war. And they would bind themselves to refuse to take office or honour from any society which, while professing to respect liberty, restricts it, like the universities of Oxford and Cambridge. And they would consider it their duty to investigate the claims of all public societies to which, like the Church and the universities, they are forced to contribute as taxpayers as carefully and fearlessly as they would investigate the claims of private societies to which they contribute voluntarily. They would make it their business to scrutinize the endowments of the schools and universities and the objects upon which that money is spent. As with the educational, so with the religious profession. By reading the New Testament in the first place and next those divines and historians whose works are all easily accessible to the daughters of educated men, they would make it their business to have some knowledge of the Christian religion and its history. Further they would inform themselves of the practice of that religion by attending Church services, by analysing the spiritual and intellectual value of sermons; by criticizing the opinions of men whose profession is religion as freely as they would criticize the opinions of any other body of men. Thus they would be creative in their activities, not merely critical. By criticizing education they would help to create a civilized society which protects culture and intellectual liberty. By criticizing religion they would attempt to free the religious spirit from its present servitude and would help, if need be, to create a new religion based, it might well be, upon the New Testament, but, it might well be, very different from the religion now erected upon that basis. And in all this, and in much more than we have time to particularize, they would be helped, you will agree, by their position as outsiders, that freedom from unreal loyalties, that freedom from interested motives which are at present assured them by the State.

It would be easy to define in greater number and more exactly the duties of those who belong to the Society of Outsiders, but not profitable. Elasticity is essential; and some degree of secrecy, as will be shown later, is at present even more essential. But the description thus loosely and imperfectly given is enough to show you, Sir, that the Society of Outsiders has the same ends as your society — freedom, equality, peace; but that it seeks to achieve them by the means that a different sex, a different tradition, a different education, and the different values which result from those differences have placed within our reach. Broadly speaking, the main distinction between us who are outside society and you who are inside society must be that whereas you will make use of the means provided by your position — leagues, conferences, campaigns, great names, and all such public measures as your wealth and political influence place within your reach — we, remaining outside, will experiment not with public means in public but with private means in private. Those experiments will not be merely critical but creative. To take two obvious instances: — the outsiders will dispense with pageantry not from any puritanical dislike of beauty. On the contrary, it will be one of their aims to increase private beauty; the beauty of spring, summer, autumn; the beauty of flowers, silks, clothes; the beauty which brims not only every field and wood but every barrow in Oxford Street; the scattered beauty which needs only to be combined by artists in order to become visible to all. But they will dispense with the dictated, regimented, official pageantry, in which only one sex takes an active part — those ceremonies, for example, which depend upon the deaths of kings, or their coronations to inspire them. Again, they will dispense with personal distinctions — medals, ribbons, badges, hoods, gowns — not from any dislike of personal adornment, but because of the obvious effect of such distinctions to constrict, to stereotype and to destroy. Here, as so often, the example of the Fascist States is at hand to instruct us – for if we have no example of what we wish to be, we have, what is perhaps equally valuable, a daily and illuminating example of what we do not wish to be. With the example then, that they give us of the power of medals, symbols, orders and even, it would seem, of decorated ink-pots[19] to hypnotize the human mind it must be our aim not to submit ourselves to such hypnotism. We must extinguish the coarse glare of advertisement and publicity, not merely because the limelight is apt to be held in incompetent hands, but because of the psychological effect of such illumination upon those who receive it. Consider next time you drive along a country road the attitude of a rabbit caught in the glare of a head-lamp – its glazed eyes, its rigid paws. Is there not good reason to think without going outside our own country, that the 'attitudes', the false and unreal positions taken by the human form in England as well as in Germany, are due to the limelight which paralyses the free action of the human faculties and inhibits the human power to change and create new wholes much as a strong head-lamp paralyses the little creatures who run out of the darkness into its beams? It is a guess; guessing is dangerous; yet we have some reason to guide us in the guess that ease and freedom, the power to change and the power to grow, can only be preserved by obscurity; and that if we wish to help the human mind to create, and to prevent it from scoring the same rut repeatedly, we must do what we can to shroud it in darkness.

But enough of guessing. To return to facts – what chance is there, you may ask, that such a Society of Outsiders without office, meetings, leaders or any hierarchy, without so much as a form to be filled up, or a secretary to be paid, can be brought into existence, let alone work to any purpose? Indeed it would have been waste of time to write even so rough a definition of the Outsiders' Society were it merely a bubble of words, a covert form of sex or class glorification, serving, as so many such expressions do, to relieve the writer's emotion, lay the blame elsewhere, and then burst. Happily there is a model in being, a model from which the above sketch has been taken, furtively it is true, for the model, far from sitting still to be painted, dodges and disappears. That model then, the evidence that such a body, whether named or unnamed, exists and works is provided not yet by history or biography, for the outsiders have only had a positive existence for twenty years – that is since the professions were opened to the daughters of educated men. But evidence of their existence is provided by history and biography in the raw – by the newspapers that is, sometimes openly in the lines, sometimes covertly between them. There, anyone who wishes to verify the existence of such a body, can find innumerable proofs. Many, it is obvious, are of dubious value. For example, the fact that an immense amount of work is done by the daughters of educated men without pay or for very little pay need not be taken as a proof that they are experimenting of their own free will in the psychological value of poverty. Nor need the fact that many daughters of educated men do not 'eat properly'[20] serve as a proof that they are experimenting in the physical value of undernourishment. Nor need the fact that a very small proportion of women compared with men accept honours be held to prove that they are experimenting in the virtues of obscurity. Many such experiments are forced experiments and therefore of no positive value. But others of a much more positive kind are coming daily to the surface of the Press. Let us examine three only, in order that we may prove our statement that the Society of Outsiders is in being. The first is straightforward enough.

Speaking at a bazaar last week at the Plumstead Common Baptist Church the Mayoress (of Woolwich) said: '. . . I myself would not even do as much as darn a sock to help in a war.' These remarks are resented by the majority of the Woolwich public, who hold that the Mayoress was, to say the least, rather tactless. Some 12,000 Woolwich electors are employed in Woolwich Arsenal on armament making.[21]

There is no need to comment upon the tactlessness of such a

statement made publicly, in such circumstances; but the courage can scarcely fail to command our admiration, and the value of the experiment, from a practical point of view, should other mayoresses in other towns and other countries where the electors are employed in armament making follow suit may well be immeasurable. At any rate, we shall agree that the Mayoress of Woolwich, Mrs Kathleen Rance, has made a courageous and effective experiment in the prevention of war by not knitting socks. For a second proof that the outsiders are at work let us choose another example from the daily paper, one that is less obvious, but still you will agree an outsider's experiment, a very original experiment, and one that may be of great value to the cause of peace.

> Speaking of the work of the great voluntary associations for the playing of certain games, Miss Clarke [Miss E. R. Clarke of the Board of Education] referred to the women's organizations for hockey, lacrosse, netball, and cricket, and pointed out that under the rules there could be no cup or award of any kind to a successful team. The 'gates' for their matches might be a little smaller than for the men's games, but their players played the game for the love of it, and they seemed to be proving that cups and awards are not necessary to stimulate interest for each year the numbers of players steadily continued to increase.[22]

That, you will agree, is an extraordinarily interesting experiment, one that may well bring about a psychological change of great value in human nature, and a change that may be of real help in preventing war. It is further of interest because it is an experiment that outsiders, owing to their comparative freedom from certain inhibitions and persuasions, can carry out much more easily than those who are necessarily exposed to such influences inside. That statement is corroborated in a very interesting way by the following quotation:

> Official football circles here [Wellingborough, Northants] regard with anxiety the growing popularity of girls' football. A secret meeting of the Northants Football Association's consultative com-

mittee was held here last night to discuss the playing of a girls'
match on the Peterborough ground. Members of the Committee
are reticent . . . One member, however, said to-day: 'The Northants
Football Association is to forbid women's football. This popularity
of girls' football comes when many men's clubs in the country are
in a parlous state through lack of support. Another serious aspect
is the possibility of grave injury to women players.'[23]

There we have proof positive of those inhibitions and persuasions which make it harder for your sex to experiment freely in
altering current values than for ours; and without spending time
upon the delicacies of psychological analysis even a hasty glance
at the reasons given by this Association for its decision will
throw a valuable light upon the reasons which lead other and
even more important associations to come to their decisions. But
to return to the outsiders' experiments. For our third example let
us choose what we may call an experiment in passivity.

A remarkable change in the attitude of young women to the
Church was discussed by Canon F. R. Barry, vicar of St Mary the
Virgin (the University Church), at Oxford last night . . . The task
before the Church, he said, was nothing less than to make civilization moral, and this was a great co-operative task which demanded
all that Christians could bring to it. It simply could not be carried
through by men alone. For a century, or a couple of centuries,
women had predominated in the congregations in roughly the
ratio of 75 per cent. to 25 per cent. The whole situation was now
changing, and what the keen observer would notice in almost any
church in England was the paucity of young women . . . Among
the student population the young women were, on the whole,
farther away from the Church of England and the Christian faith
than the young men.[24]

That again is an experiment of very great interest. It is, as we
have said, a passive experiment. For while the first example was
an outspoken refusal to knit socks in order to discourage war,
and the second was an attempt to prove whether cups and
awards are necessary to stimulate interest in games, the third is
an attempt to discover what happens if the daughters of educated

men absent themselves from church. Without being in itself more valuable than the others, it is of more practical interest because it is obviously the kind of experiment that great numbers of outsiders can practise with very little difficulty or danger. To absent yourself – that is easier than to speak aloud at a bazaar, or to draw up rules of an original kind for playing games. Therefore it is worth watching very carefully to see what effect the experiment of absenting oneself has had – if any. The results are positive and they are encouraging. There can be no doubt that the Church is becoming concerned about the attitude to the Church of educated men's daughters at the universities. The report of the Archbishops' Commission on the Ministry of Women is there to prove it. This document, which costs only one shilling and should be in the hands of all educated men's daughters, points out that 'one outstanding difference between men's colleges and women's colleges is the absence in the latter of a chaplain.' It reflects that 'It is natural that in this period of their lives they [the students] exercise to the full their critical faculties.' It deplores the fact that 'Very few women coming to the universities can now afford to offer continuous voluntary service either in social or in directly religious work.' And it concludes that 'There are many special spheres in which such services are particularly needed, and the time has clearly come when the functions and position of women within the Church require further determination.'[25] Whether this concern is due to the empty churches at Oxford, or whether the voices of the 'older schoolgirls' at Isleworth expressing 'very grave dissatisfaction at the way in which organized religion was carried on'[26] have somehow penetrated to those august spheres where their sex is not supposed to speak, or whether our incorrigibly idealistic sex is at last beginning to take to heart Bishop Gore's warning, 'Men do not value ministrations which are gratuitous,'[27] and to express the opinion that a salary of £150 a year – the highest that the Church allows her daughters as deaconesses – is not enough – whatever the reason, considerable uneasiness at the attitude of educated men's daughters is apparent; and this experiment in passivity, whatever our belief in the value of the Church of England as a spiritual agency, is highly encouraging to us as outsiders. For it seems to show that to be passive is to be active; those also serve who remain outside. By making their absence felt their presence becomes desirable. What light this throws upon the power of outsiders to abolish or modify other institutions of which they disapprove, whether public dinners, public speeches, Lord Mayors' banquets and other obsolete ceremonies are pervious to indifference and will yield to its pressure, are questions, frivolous questions, that may well amuse our leisure and stimulate our curiosity. But that is not now the object before us. We have tried to prove to you, Sir, by giving three different examples of three different kinds of experiment that the Society of Outsiders is in being and at work. When you consider that these examples have all come to the surface of the newspaper you will agree that they represent a far greater number of private and submerged experiments of which there is no public proof. Also you will agree that they substantiate the model of the society given above, and prove that it was no visionary sketch drawn at random but based upon a real body working by different means for the same ends that you have set before us in your own society. Keen observers, like Canon Barry, could, if they liked, discover many more proofs that experiments are being made not only in the empty churches of Oxford. Mr Wells even might be led to believe if he put his ear to the ground that a movement is going forward, not altogether imperceptibly, among educated men's daughters against the Nazi and the Fascist. But it is essential that the movement should escape the notice even of keen observers and of famous novelists.

Secrecy is essential. We must still hide what we are doing and thinking even though what we are doing and thinking is for our common cause. The necessity for this, in certain circumstances, is not hard to discover. When salaries are low, as Whitaker proves that they are, and jobs are hard to get and keep, as everybody knows them to be, it is, 'to say the least, rather tactless', as the newspaper puts it, to criticize your master. Still,

in country districts, as you yourself may be aware, farm labourers
will not vote Labour. Economically, the educated man's daughter
is much on a level with the farm labourer. But it is scarcely
necessary for us to waste time in searching out what reason it is
that inspires both his and her secrecy. Fear is a powerful reason;
those who are economically dependent have strong reasons for
fear. We need explore no further. But here you may remind us of
a certain guinea, and draw our attention to the proud boast that
our gift, small though it was,ᵉ but to speak freely without fear or
flattery. The boast it seems had an element of brag in it. Some
fear, some ancestral memory prophesying war, still remains, it
seems. There are still subjects that educated people, when they
are of different sexes, even though financially independent, veil,
or hint at in guarded terms and then pass on. You may have
observed it in real life; you may have detected it in biography.
Even when they meet privately and talk, as we have boasted,
about 'politics and people, war and peace, barbarism and civilization', yet they evade and conceal. But it is so important to
accustom ourselves to the duties of free speech, for without
private there can be no public freedom, that we must try to
uncover this fear and to face it. What then can be the nature of
the fear that still makes concealment necessary between educated
people and reduces our boasted freedom to a farce? . . . Again
there are three dots; again they represent a gulf – of silence this
time, of silence inspired by fear. And since we lack both the
courage to explain it and the skill, let us lower the veil of St Paul
between us, in other words take shelter behind an interpreter.
Happily we have one at hand whose credentials are above
suspicion. It is none other than the pamphlet from which quotation has already been made, the report of the Archbishops'
Commission on the Ministry of Women – a document of the
highest interest for many reasons. For not only does it throw
light of a searching and scientific nature upon this fear, but it
gives us an opportunity to consider that profession which, since
it is the highest of all may be taken as the type of all, the

profession of religion, about which, purposely, very little has yet
been said. And since it is the type of all it may throw light upon
the other professions about which something has been said. You
will pardon us therefore if we pause here to examine this report
in some detail.

The Commission was appointed by the Archbishops of Canterbury and York 'in order to examine any theological or other
relevant principles which have governed or ought to govern the
Church in the development of the Ministry of Women.'[28] Now
the profession of religion, for our purposes the Church of
England, though it seems on the surface to resemble the others
in certain respects – it enjoys, Whitaker says, a large income,
owns much property, and has a hierarchy of officials drawing
salaries and taking precedence one of the other – yet ranks above
all the other professions. The Archbishop of Canterbury precedes
the Lord High Chancellor; the Archbishop of York precedes the
Prime Minister. And it is the highest of all the professions
because it is the profession of religion. But what, we may ask, is
'religion'? What the Christian religion is has been laid down
once and for all by the founder of that religion in words that can
be read by all in a translation of singular beauty; and whether or
not we accept the interpretation that has been put on them, we
cannot deny them to be words of the most profound meaning. It
can thus safely be said that whereas few people know what
medicine is, or what law is, everyone who owns a copy of the
New Testament knows what religion meant in the mind of its
founder. Therefore, when in the year 1935 the daughters of
educated men said that they wished to have the profession of
religion opened to them, the priests of that profession, who
correspond roughly to the doctors and barristers in the other
professions, were forced not merely to consult some statute or
charter which reserves the right to practise that profession
professionally to the male sex; they were forced to consult the
New Testament. They did so; and the result, as the Commissioners point out, was that they found that 'the Gospels show us that
our Lord regarded men and women alike as members of the

same spiritual kingdom, as children of God's family, and as
possessors of the same spiritual capacities . . .' In proof of this
they quote: 'There is neither male nor female: for ye are all one
in Christ Jesus' (Gal. iii, 28). It would seem then that the
founder of Christianity believed that neither training nor sex was
needed for this profession. He chose his disciples from the
working class from which he sprang himself. The prime qualification was some rare gift which in those early days was bestowed
capriciously upon carpenters and fishermen, and upon women
also. As the Commission points out there can be no doubt that
in those early days there were prophetesses – women upon
whom the divine gift had descended. Also they were allowed to
preach. St Paul, for example, lays it down that women, when
praying in public, should be veiled. 'The implication is that if
veiled a woman might prophesy [i.e. preach] and lead in prayer.'
How then can they be excluded from the priesthood since they
were thought fit by the founder of the religion and by one of his
apostles to preach? That was the question, and the Commission
solved it by appealing not to the mind of the founder, but to the
mind of the Church. That, of course, involved a distinction. For
the mind of the Church had to be interpreted by another mind,
and that mind was St Paul's mind; and St Paul, in interpreting
that mind, changed his mind. For after summoning from the
depths of the past certain venerable if obscure figures – Lydia
and Chloe, Euodia and Syntyche, Tryphoena and Tryphosa and
Persis, debating their status, and deciding what was the difference
between a prophetess and presbyteress, what the standing of a
deaconess in the pre-Nicene Church and what in the post-Nicene
Church, the Commissioners once more have recourse to St Paul,
and say: 'In any case it is clear that the author of the Pastoral
Epistles, be he St Paul or another, regarded woman as being
debarred on the ground of her sex from the position of an
official "teacher" in the Church, or from any office involving
the exercise of a governmental authority over a man (1 Tim. ii,
12).' That, it may frankly be said, is not so satisfactory as it
might be; for we cannot altogether reconcile the ruling of St

Paul, or another, with the ruling of Christ himself who 'regarded men and women alike as members of the same spiritual kingdom . . . and as possessors of the same spiritual capacities.' But it is futile to quibble over the meaning of words, when we are so soon in the presence of facts. Whatever Christ meant, or St Paul meant, the fact was that in the fourth or fifth century the profession of religion had become so highly organized that 'the deacon (unlike the deaconess) may, "after serving unto well-pleasing the ministry committed unto him," aspire to be appointed eventually to higher offices in the Church; whereas for the deaconess the Church prays simply that God "would grant unto her the Holy Spirit . . . that she may worthily accomplish the work committed to her."' In three or four centuries, it appears, the prophet or prophetess whose message was voluntary and untaught became extinct; and their places were taken by the three orders of bishops, priests and deacons, who are invariably men, and invariably, as Whitaker points out, paid men, for when the Church became a profession its professors were paid. Thus the profession of religion seems to have been originally much what the profession of literature is now.[29] It was originally open to anyone who had received the gift of prophecy. No training was needed; the professional requirements were simple in the extreme – voice and a market-place, a pen and paper. Emily Brontë, for instance, who wrote

> No coward soul is mine,
> No trembler in the world's storm-troubled sphere;
> I see Heaven's glories shine,
> And faith shines equal, arming me from fear.
>
> O God within my breast,
> Almighty, ever-present Deity!
> Life – that in me has rest,
> As I – undying Life – have power in Thee!

though not worthy to be a priest in the Church of England, is the spiritual descendant of some ancient prophetess, who prophesied when prophecy was a voluntary and unpaid occupation.

But when the Church became a profession, required special knowledge of its prophets and paid them for imparting it, one sex remained inside; the other was excluded. 'The deacons rose in dignity – partly no doubt from their close association with the bishops – and become subordinate ministers of worship and of the sacraments; but the deaconess shared only in the preliminary stages of this evolution.' How elementary that evolution has been is proved by the fact that in England in 1938 the salary of an archbishop is £15,000; the salary of a bishop is £10,000 and the salary of a dean is £3,000. But the salary of a deaconess is £150; and as for the 'parish worker', who 'is called upon to assist in almost every department of parish life,' whose 'work is exacting and often solitary . . .' she is paid from £120 to £150 a year; nor is there anything to surprise us in the statement that 'prayer needs to be the very centre of her activities.' Thus we might even go further than the Commissioners and say that the evolution of the deaconess is not merely 'elementary', it is positively stunted; for though she is ordained, and 'ordination . . . conveys an indelible character, and involves the obligation of lifelong service,' she must remain outside the Church; and rank beneath the humblest curate. Such is the decision of the Church. For the Commission, having consulted the mind and tradition of the Church, reported finally: 'While the Commission as a whole would not give their positive assent to the view that a woman is inherently incapable of receiving the grace of Order, and consequently to admission to any of the three Orders, we believe that the general mind of the Church is still in accord with the continuous tradition of a male priesthood.'

By thus showing that the highest of all the professions has many points of similarity with the other professions our interpreter, you will admit, has thrown further light upon the soul or essence of those professions. We must now ask him to help us, if he will, to analyse the nature of that fear which still, as we have admitted, makes it impossible for us to speak freely as free people should. Here again he is of service. Though identical in many respects, one very profound difference between the religious profession and the other professions has been noted above: the Church being a spiritual profession has to give spiritual and not merely historical reasons for its actions; it has to consult the mind, not the law. Therefore when the daughters of educated men wished to be admitted to the profession of the Church it seemed advisable to the Commissioners to give psychological and not merely historical reasons for their refusal to admit them. They therefore called in Professor Grensted, D.D., the Nolloth Professor of the Philosophy of the Christian Religion in the University of Oxford, and asked him 'to summarize the relevant psychological and physiological material', and to indicate 'the grounds for the opinions and recommendations put forward by the Commission.' Now psychology is not theology; and the psychology of the sexes, as the Professor insisted, and 'its bearing upon human conduct, is still a matter for specialists ... and ... its interpretation remains controversial and in many respects obscure.' But he gave his evidence for what it was worth, and it is evidence that throws so much light upon the origin of the fear which we have admitted and deplored that we can do no better than follow his words exactly.

'It was represented,' he said, 'in evidence before the Commission that man has a natural precedence of woman. This view, in the sense intended, cannot be supported psychologically. Psychologists fully recognize the fact of male dominance, but this must not be confused with male superiority, still less with any type of precedence which could have a bearing upon questions as to the admissibility of one sex rather than the other to Holy Orders.'

The psychologist, therefore, can only throw light upon certain facts. And this was the first fact that he investigated.

It is clearly a fact of the very greatest practical importance that strong feeling is aroused by any suggestion that women should be admitted to the status and functions of the threefold Order of the Ministry. The evidence before the Commission went to show that this feeling is predominantly hostile to such proposals ... This strength of feeling, conjoined with a wide variety of rational explanations, is clear evidence of the presence of powerful and widespread subconscious motive. In the absence of detailed analytical material, of which there seems to be no record in this particular connection, it nevertheless remains clear that infantile fixation plays a predominant part in determining the strong emotion with which this whole subject is commonly approached.

The exact nature of this fixation must necessarily differ with different individuals, and suggestions which can be made as to its origin can only be general in character. But whatever be the exact value and interpretation of the material upon which theories of the 'oedipus complex' and the 'castration complex' have been founded, it is clear that the general acceptance of male dominance, and still more of feminine inferiority, resting upon subconscious ideas of woman as 'man manqué', has its background in infantile conceptions of this type. These commonly, and even usually, survive in the adult, despite their irrationality, and betray their presence, below the level of conscious thought, by the strength of the emotions to which they give rise. It is strongly in support of this view that the admission of women to Holy Orders, and especially to the ministry of the sanctuary, is so commonly regarded as something shameful. This sense of shame cannot be regarded in any other light than as a non-rational sex-taboo.

Here we can skip; we can take the Professor's word for it that he has sought, and found, 'ample evidence of these unconscious forces', both in Pagan religions and in the Old Testament, and so follow him to his conclusion:

At the same time it must not be forgotten that the Christian conception of the priesthood rests not upon these subconscious emotional factors, but upon the institution of Christ. It thus not only fulfils but supersedes the priesthoods of paganism and the Old Testament. So far as psychology is concerned there is no theoretical reason why this Christian priesthood should not be exercised by women as well as by men and in exactly the same sense. The difficulties which the psychologist foresees are emotional and practical only.[30]

With that conclusion we may leave him.

The Commissioners, you will agree, have performed the delicate and difficult task that we asked them to undertake. They have acted as interpreters between us. They have given us an admirable example of a profession in its purest state; and shown us how a profession bases itself upon mind and tradition. They have further explained why it is that educated people when they are of different sexes do not speak openly upon certain subjects. They have shown why the outsiders, even when there is no question of financial dependence, may still be afraid to speak freely or to experiment openly. And, finally, in words of scientific precision, they have revealed to us the nature of that fear. For as Professor Grensted gave his evidence, we, the daughters of educated men, seemed to be watching a surgeon at work – an impartial and scientific operator, who, as he dissected the human mind by human means laid bare for all to see what cause, what root lies at the bottom of our fear. It is an egg. Its scientific name is 'infantile fixation'.∫ We, being unscientific, have named it wrongly. An egg we called it; a germ. We smelt it in the atmosphere; we detected its presence in Whitehall, in the universities, in the Church. Now undoubtedly the Professor has defined it and described it so accurately that no daughter of an educated man, however uneducated she may be, can miscall it or misinterpret it in future. Listen to the description. 'Strong feeling is aroused by any suggestion that women be admitted' – it matters not to which priesthood; the priesthood of medicine or the priesthood of science or the priesthood of the Church. Strong feeling, she can corroborate the Professor, is undoubtedly shown should she ask to be admitted. 'This strength of feeling is clear evidence of the presence of powerful and subconscious motive.' She will take the Professor's word for that, and even supply him with some motives that have escaped him. Let us draw attention to two only. There is the money motive for excluding her, to put it plainly. Are not salaries motives now, whatever they may have been in the time of Christ? The archbishop has £15,000, the deaconess £150; and the Church, so the Commissioners say, is poor. To pay women more would be to pay men less. Secondly, is there not a motive, a psychological motive, for excluding her, hidden beneath what the Commissioners call a 'practical consideration'? 'At present a married priest,' they tell us, 'is able to fulfil the requirements of the ordination service "to forsake and set aside all worldly cares and studies" largely because his wife can undertake the care of the household and the family . . .'[31] To be able to set aside all worldly cares and studies and lay them upon another person is a motive, to some of great attractive force; for some undoubtedly wish to withdraw and study, as theology with its refinements, and scholarship with its subtleties, prove; to others, it is true, the motive is a bad motive, a vicious motive, the cause of that separation between the Church and the people; between literature and the people; between the husband and the wife which has had its part in putting the whole of our Commonwealth out of gear. But whatever the powerful and subconscious motives may be that lie behind the exclusion of women from the priesthoods, and plainly we cannot count them, let alone dig to the roots of them here, the educated man's daughter can testify from her own experience that they 'commonly, and even usually, survive in the adult and betray their presence, below the level of conscious thought, by the strength of the emotions to which they give rise.' And you will agree that to oppose strong emotion needs courage; and that when courage fails, silence and evasion are likely to manifest themselves.

But now that the interpreters have performed their task, it is time for us to raise the veil of St Paul and to attempt, face to face, a rough and clumsy analysis of that fear and of the anger which causes that fear; for they may have some bearing upon the question you put us, how we can help you to prevent war. Let us suppose, then, that in the course of that bi-sexual private conversation about politics and people, war and peace, barbarism and civilization, some question has cropped up, about admitting, shall we say, the daughters of educated men to the Church or the Stock Exchange or the diplomatic service. The question is adumbrated merely; but we on our side of the table become aware at once of some 'strong emotion' on your side 'arising from some motive below the level of conscious thought' by the ringing of an alarm bell within us; a confused but tumultuous clamour: You shall not, shall not, shall not ... The physical symptoms are unmistakable. Nerves erect themselves; fingers automatically tighten upon spoon or cigarette; a glance at the private psychometer shows that the emotional temperature has risen from ten to twenty degrees above normal. Intellectually, there is a strong desire either to be silent; or to change the conversation; to drag in, for example, some old family servant, called Crosby, perhaps, whose dog Rover has died ...⁸ and so evade the issue and lower the temperature.

But what analysis can we attempt of the emotions on the other side of the table – your side? Often, to be candid, while we are talking about Crosby, we are asking questions – hence a certain flatness in the dialogue – about you. What are the powerful and subconscious motives that are raising the hackles on your side of the table? Is the old savage who has killed a bison asking the other old savage to admire his prowess? Is the tired professional man demanding sympathy and resenting competition? Is the patriach calling for the siren? Is dominance craving for submission? And, most persistent and difficult of all the questions that our silence covers, what possible satisfaction can dominance give to the dominator?[32] Now, since Professor Grensted has said that the psychology of the sexes is 'still a matter for specialists', while 'its interpretation remains controversial and in many respects obscure,' it would be politic perhaps to leave these questions to be answered by specialists. But since, on the other hand, if common men and women are to be free they must learn to speak freely, we cannot leave the psychology of the sexes to the charge of specialists. There are two good reasons why we must try to analyse both our fear and your anger; first, because such fear and anger prevent real freedom in the private house; second, because such fear and anger may prevent real freedom in the public world: they may have a positive share in causing war. Let us then grope our way amateurishly enough among these very ancient and obscure emotions which we have known ever since the time of Antigone and Ismene and Creon at least; which St Paul himself seems to have felt; but which the Professors have only lately brought to the surface and named 'infantile fixation', 'Oedipus complex', and the rest.[b] We must try, however feebly, to analyse those emotions since you have asked us to help you in any way we can to protect liberty and to prevent war.

Let us then examine this 'infantile fixation', for such it seems is the proper name, in order that we may connect it with the question you have put to us. Once more, since we are generalists not specialists, we must rely upon such evidence as we can collect from history, biography, and from the daily paper – the only evidence that is available to the daughters of educated men. We will take our first example of infantile fixation from biography, and once more we will have recourse to Victorian biography because it is only in the Victorian age that biography becomes rich and representative. Now there are so many cases of infantile fixation as defined by Professor Grensted in Victorian biography that we scarcely know which to choose. The case of Mr Barrett of Wimpole Street is, perhaps, the most famous and the best authenticated. Indeed, it is so famous that the facts scarcely bear repetition. We all know the story of the father who would allow neither sons nor daughters to marry; we all know in greatest detail how his daughter Elizabeth was forced to conceal her lover from her father; how she fled with her lover from the house in Wimpole Street; and how her father never forgave her for that act of disobedience. We shall agree that Mr Barrett's emotions were strong in the extreme; and their strength makes it obvious that they had their origin in some dark place below the level of conscious thought. That is a typical, a classical case of infantile fixation which we can all bear in mind. But there are others less famous which a little investigation will bring to the surface and show to be of the same nature. There is the case of the Rev. Patrick Brontë. The Rev. Arthur Nicholls was in love with his daughter, Charlotte; 'What his words were,' she wrote, when Mr Nicholls proposed to her, 'you can imagine; his manner you can hardly realize nor can I forget it . . . I asked if he had spoken to Papa. He said he dared not.' Why did he dare not? He was strong and young and passionately in love; the father was old. The reason is immediately apparent. 'He [the Rev. Patrick Brontë] always disapproved of marriages, and constantly talked against them. But he more than disapproved this time; he could not bear the idea of this attachment of Mr Nicholls to his daughter. Fearing the consequences . . . she made haste to give her father a promise that, on the morrow, Mr Nicholls should have a distinct refusal.'[33] Mr Nicholls left Haworth; Charlotte remained with her father. Her married life – it was to be a short one – was shortened still further by her father's wish.

For a third example of infantile fixation let us choose one that is less simple, but for that reason more illuminating. There is the case of Mr Jex-Blake. Here we have the case of a father who is not confronted with his daughter's marriage but with his daughter's wish to earn her living. That wish also would seem to have aroused in the father a very strong emotion and an emotion which also seems to have its origin in the levels below conscious thought. Again with your leave we will call it a case of infantile fixation. The daughter, Sophia, was offered a small sum for teaching mathematics; and she asked her father's permission to take it. That permission was instantly and heatedly refused. 'Dearest, I have only this moment heard that you contemplate being *paid* for the tutorship. It would be quite beneath you, darling, and I *cannot consent* to it.' [The italics are the father's.] 'Take the post as one of honour and usefulness, and I shall be glad . . . But to be *paid* for the work would be to alter the thing *completely*, and would lower you sadly in the eyes of almost everybody.' That is a very interesting statement. Sophia, indeed, was led to argue the matter. Why was it beneath her, she asked, why should it lower her? Taking money for work did not lower Tom in anybody's eyes. That, Mr Jex-Blake explained, was quite a different matter; Tom was a man; Tom 'feels bound as a *man* . . . to support his wife and family'; Tom had therefore taken

'the *plain path* of duty'. Still Sophia was not satisfied. She argued
– not only was she poor and wanted the money; but also she felt
strongly 'the honest, and I believe perfectly justifiable pride of
earning'. Thus pressed Mr Jex-Blake at last gave, under a semi-
transparent cover, the real reason why he objected to her taking
money. He offered to give her the money himself if she would
refuse to take it from the College. It was plain, therefore, that he
did not object to her taking money; what he objected to was her
taking money from another man. The curious nature of his
proposal did not escape Sophia's scrutiny. 'In that case,' she said,
'I must say to the Dean, not "I am willing to work without
payment," but "My Father prefers that I should receive payment
from *him*, not from the College," and I think the Dean would
think us both ridiculous, or at least foolish.' Whatever interpretation the Dean might have put upon Mr Jex-Blake's behaviour,
we can have no doubt what emotion was at the root of it. He
wished to keep his daughter in his own power. If she took
money from him she remained in his power; if she took it from
another man not only was she becoming independent of Mr Jex-
Blake, she was becoming dependent upon another man. That he
wished her to depend upon him, and felt obscurely that this
desirable dependence could only be secured by financial dependence is proved indirectly by another of his veiled statements. 'If
you married to-morrow to my liking – and I don't believe you
would ever marry otherwise – I should give you a good fortune.'[34] If she became a wage-earner, she could dispense with the
fortune and marry whom she liked. The case of Mr Jex-Blake is
very easily diagnosed, but it is a very important case because it is
a normal case, a typical case. Mr Jex-Blake was no monster of
Wimpole Street; he was an ordinary father; he was doing what
thousands of other Victorian fathers whose cases remain un-
published were doing daily. It is a case, therefore, that explains
much that lies at the root of Victorian psychology – that
psychology of the sexes which is still, Professor Grensted tells
us, so obscure. The case of Mr Jex-Blake shows that the daughter
must not on any account be allowed to make money because if

she makes money she will be independent of her father and free to marry any man she chooses. Therefore the daughter's desire to earn her living rouses two different forms of jealousy. Each is strong separately; together they are very strong. It is further significant that in order to justify this very strong emotion which has its origin below the levels of conscious thought Mr Jex-Blake had recourse to one of the commonest of all evasions; the argument which is not an argument but an appeal to the emotions. He appealed to the very deep, ancient and complex emotion which we may, as amateurs, call the womanhood emotion. To take money was beneath her he said; if she took money she would lower herself in the eyes of almost everybody. Tom being a man would not be lowered; it was her sex that made the difference. He appealed to her womanhood.

Whenever a man makes that appeal to a woman he rouses in her, it is safe to say, a conflict of emotions of a very deep and primitive kind which it is extremely difficult for her to analyse or to reconcile. It may serve to transmit the feeling if we compare it with the confused conflict of manhood emotions that is roused in you, Sir, should a woman hand you a white feather.[35i] It is interesting to see how Sophia, in the year 1859, tried to deal with this emotion. Her first instinct was to attack the most obvious form of womanhood, that which lay uppermost in her consciousness and seemed to be responsible for her father's attitude – her ladyhood. Like other educated men's daughters Sophia Jex-Blake was what is called 'a lady'. It was the lady who could not earn money; therefore the lady must be killed. 'Do you honestly, father, think,' she asked, 'any lady lowered by the mere act of receiving money? Did you think the less of Mrs Teed because you paid her?' Then, as if aware that Mrs Teed, being a governess, was not on a par with herself who came of an upper middle-class family, 'whose lineage will be found in *Burke's Landed Gentry*,' she quickly called in to help her to kill the lady 'Mary Jane Evans ... one of the proudest families of our relations,' and then Miss Wodehouse, 'whose family is better and older than mine' – they both thought her right in wishing to earn money. And not only did Miss Wodehouse think her right in wishing to earn money; Miss Wodehouse 'showed she agreed with my opinions by her actions. She sees no meanness in earning, but in those that think it mean. When accepting Maurice's school, she said to him, most nobly, I think, "If you think it better that I should work as a paid mistress, I will take any salary you please; if not, I am willing to do the work freely and for nothing."' The lady, sometimes, was a noble lady; and that lady it was hard to kill; but killed she must be, as Sophia realized, if Sophia were to enter that Paradise where 'lots of girls walk about London when and where they please', that 'Elysium upon earth', which is (or was), Queen's College, Harley Street, where the daughters of educated men enjoy the happiness not of ladies 'but of Queens – Work and independence!'[36] Thus Sophia's first instinct was to kill the lady;[37] but when the lady was killed the woman still remained. We can see her, concealing and excusing the disease of infantile fixation, more clearly in the other two cases. It was the woman, the human being whose sex made it her sacred duty to sacrifice herself to the father, whom Charlotte Brontë and Elizabeth Barrett had to kill. If it was difficult to kill the lady, it was even more difficult to kill the woman. Charlotte found it at first almost impossible. She refused her lover. '. . . thus thoughtfully for her father, and unselfishly for herself [she] put aside all consideration of how she should reply, excepting as he wished.' She loved Arthur Nicholls; but she refused him. '. . . she held herself simply passive, as far as words and actions went, while she suffered acute pain from the strong expressions which her father used in speaking of Mr Nicholls.' She waited; she suffered; until 'the great conqueror Time,' as Mrs Gaskell puts it, 'achieved his victory over strong prejudice and human resolve.' Her father consented. The great conqueror, however, had met his match in Mr Barrett; Elizabeth Barrett waited; Elizabeth suffered; at last Elizabeth fled.

The extreme force of the emotions to which the infantile fixation gives rise is proved by these three cases. It is remarkable, we may agree. It was a force that could quell not only Charlotte Brontë but Arthur Nicholls; not only Elizabeth Barrett but Robert Browning. It was a force thus that could do battle with the strongest of human passions – the love of men and women; and could compel the most brilliant and the boldest of Victorian sons and daughters to quail before it; to cheat the father, to deceive the father, and then to fly from the father. But to what did it owe this amazing force? Partly, as these cases make clear, to the fact that the infantile fixation was protected by society. Nature, law and property were all ready to excuse and conceal it. It was easy for Mr Barrett, Mr Jex-Blake and the Rev. Patrick Brontë to hide the real nature of their emotions from themselves. If they wished that their daughter should stay at home, society agreed that they were right. If the daughter protested, then nature came to their help. A daughter who left her father was an unnatural daughter; her womanhood was suspect. Should she persist further, then law came to his help. A daughter who left her father had no means of supporting herself. The lawful professions were shut to her. Finally, if she earned money in the one profession that was open to her, the oldest profession of all, she unsexed herself.*/* There can be no question – the infantile fixation is powerful, even when a mother is infected. But when the father is infected it has a threefold power; he has nature to protect him, law to protect him; and property to protect him. Thus protected it was perfectly possible for the Rev. Patrick Brontë to cause 'acute pain' to his daughter Charlotte for several months, and to steal several months of her short married happiness without incurring any censure from the society in which he practised the profession of a priest of the Church of England; though had he tortured a dog, or stolen a watch, that same society would have unfrocked him and cast him forth. Society it seems was a father, and afflicted with the infantile fixation too.

Since society protected and indeed excused the victims of the infantile fixation in the nineteenth century, it is not surprising that the disease, though unnamed, was rampant. Whatever biography we open we find almost always the familiar symptoms – the father is opposed to his daughter's marriage; the father is opposed to his daughter's earning her living. Her wish either to marry, or to earn her living, rouses strong emotion in him; and he gives the same excuses for that strong emotion; the lady will debase her ladyhood; the daughter will outrage her womanhood. But now and again, very rarely, we find a father who was completely immune from the disease. The results are then extremely interesting. There is the case of Mr Leigh Smith.[38] This gentleman was contemporary with Mr Jex-Blake, and came of the same social caste. He, too, had property in Sussex; he, too, had horses and carriages; and he, too, had children. But there the resemblance ends. Mr Leigh Smith was devoted to his children; he objected to schools; he kept his children at home. It would be interesting to discuss Mr Leigh Smith's educational methods; how he had masters to teach them; how, in a large carriage built like an omnibus, he took them with him on long journeys yearly all over England. But like so many experimentalists, Mr Leigh Smith remains obscure; and we must content ourselves with the fact that he 'held the unusual opinion that daughters should have an equal provision with sons.' So completely immune was he from the infantile fixation that 'he did not adopt the ordinary plan of paying his daughter's bills and giving them an occasional present, but when Barbara came of age in 1848 he gave her an allowance of £300 a year.' The results of that immunity from the infantile fixation were remarkable. For 'treating her money as a power to do good, one of the first uses to which Barbara put it was educational.' She founded a school; a school that was open not only to different sexes and different classes, but to different creeds; Roman Catholics, Jews and 'pupils from families of advanced free thought' were received in it. 'It was a most unusual school,' an outsiders' school. But that was not all that she attempted upon three hundred a year. One thing led to another. A friend, with her help, started a co-operative evening class for ladies 'for drawing from an undraped model.' In 1858 only one life class in London was open to ladies. And then a petition was got up to the Royal Academy; its schools were actually, though as so often happens only nominally, opened to women in 1861;[39] next Barbara went into the question of the laws concerning women; so that actually in 1871 married women were allowed to own their property; and finally she helped Miss Davies to found Girton. When we reflect what one father who was immune from infantile fixation could do by allowing one daughter £300 a year we need not wonder that most fathers firmly refused to allow their daughters more than £40 a year with bed and board thrown in.

The infantile fixation in the fathers then was, it is clear, a strong force, and all the stronger because it was a concealed force. But the fathers were met, as the nineteenth century drew on, by a force which had become so strong in its turn that it is much to be hoped that the psychologists will find some name for it. The old names as we have seen are futile and false. 'Feminism', we have had to destroy. 'The emancipation of women' is equally inexpressive and corrupt. To say that the daughters were inspired prematurely by the principles of anti-Fascism is merely to repeat the fashionable and hideous jargon of the moment.[k] To call them champions of intellectual liberty and culture is to cloud the air with the dust of lecture halls and the damp dowdiness of public meetings. Moreover, none of these tags and labels express the real emotions that inspired the daughters' opposition to the infantile fixation of the fathers, because, as biography shows, that force had behind it many different emotions, and many that were contradictory. Tears were behind it, of course — tears, bitter tears: the tears of those whose desire for knowledge was frustrated. One daughter longed to learn chemistry; the books at home only taught her alchemy. She 'cried bitterly at not being taught things'. Also the desire for an open and rational love was behind it. Again there were tears — angry tears. 'She flung herself on the bed in tears ... "Oh," she said, "Harry is on the roof." "Who's Harry?" said I; "which roof? Why?" "Oh, don't be silly," she said; "he had to go."'[40] But again the desire not to love, to lead a rational existence without love, was behind it. 'I make the confession humbly ... I know nothing myself of love,'[41] wrote one of them. An odd confession from one of the class whose only profession for so many centuries had been marriage; but significant. Others wanted to travel; to explore Africa; to dig in Greece and Palestine. Some wanted to learn music, not to tinkle domestic airs, but to compose — operas, symphonies, quartets. Others wanted to paint, not ivy-clad cottages, but naked bodies. They all wanted — but what one word can sum up the variety of the things that they wanted, and had wanted, consciously or subconsciously, for so long? Josephine Butler's[j] label — Justice, Equality, Liberty — is a fine one; but it is only a label, and in our age of innumerable labels, of multi-coloured labels, we have become suspicious of labels; they kill and constrict. Nor does the old word 'freedom' serve, for it was not freedom in the sense of license that they wanted; they wanted, like Antigone, not to break the laws, but to find the law.[42] Ignorant as we are of human motives and ill supplied with words, let us then admit that no one word expresses the force which in the nineteenth century opposed itself to the force of the fathers. All we can safely say about that force was that it was a force of tremendous power. It forced open the doors of the private house. It opened Bond Street and Piccadilly; it opened cricket grounds and football grounds; it shrivelled flounces and stays; it made the oldest profession in the world (but Whitaker supplies no figures) unprofitable. In fifty years, in short, that force made the life lived by Lady Lovelace and Gertrude Bell[m] unlivable, and almost incredible. The fathers, who had triumphed over the strongest emotions of strong men, had to yield.

If that full stop were the end of the story, the final slam of the door, we could turn at once to your letter, Sir, and to the form which you have asked us to fill up. But it was not the end; it was the beginning. Indeed though we have used the past, we shall soon find ourselves using the present tense. The fathers in private, it is true, yielded; but the fathers in public, massed together in societies, in professions, were even more subject to the fatal disease than the fathers in private. The disease had acquired a motive, had connected itself with a right, a conception, which made it still more virulent outside the house than within. The desire to support wife and children – what motive could be more powerful, or deeply rooted? For it was connected with manhood itself – a man who could not support his family failed in his own conception of manliness. And was not that conception as deep in him as the conception of womanhood in his daughter? It was those motives, those rights and conceptions that were now challenged. To protect them, and from women, gave, and gives, rise it can scarcely be doubted to an emotion perhaps below the level of conscious thought but certainly of the utmost violence. The infantile fixation develops, directly the priest's right to practise his profession is challenged, to an aggravated and exacerbated emotion to which the name sex taboo is scientifically applied. Take two instances; one private, the other public. A scholar has 'to mark his disapproval of the admission of women to his university by refusing to enter his beloved college or city'.[43] A hospital has to decline an offer to endow a scholarship because it is made by a woman on behalf of women.[44] Can we doubt that both actions are inspired by that sense of shame which, as Professor Grensted says 'cannot be regarded in any other light than as a non-rational sex taboo?' But since the emotion itself had increased in strength it became necessary to invoke the help of stronger allies to excuse and conceal it. Nature was called in; Nature it was claimed who is not only omniscient but unchanging, had made the brain of woman of the wrong shape or size. 'Anyone,' writes Bertrand Russell, 'who desires amusement may be advised to look up the tergiversations of eminent craniologists in their attempts to prove from brain measurements that women are stupider than men.'[45] Science, it would seem, is not sexless; she is a man, a father, and infected too. Science, thus infected, produced measurements to order: the brain was too small to be examined. Many years were spent waiting before the sacred gates of the universities and hospitals for permission to have the brains that the professors said that Nature had made incapable of passing examinations examined. When at last permission was granted the examinations were passed. A long and dreary list of those barren if necessary triumphs lies presumably along with other broken records[46] in college archives, and harassed head mistresses still consult them, it is said, when desiring official proof of impeccable mediocrity. Still Nature held out. The brain that could pass examinations was not the creative brain; the brain that can bear responsibility and earn the higher salaries. It was a practical brain, a pettifogging brain, a brain fitted for routine work under the command of a superior. And since the professions were shut, it was undeniable – the daughters had not ruled Empires, commanded fleets, or led armies to victory; only a few trivial books testified to their professional ability, for literature was the only profession that had been open to them. And, moreover, whatever the brain might do when the professions were opened to it, the body remained. Nature, the priests said, in her infinite wisdom, had laid down the unalterable law that man is the creator. He enjoys; she only passively endures. Pain was more beneficial than pleasure to the body that endures. 'The views of medical men on pregnancy, childbirth, and lactation were until fairly recently,' Bertrand Russell writes, 'impregnated with sadism. It required, for example, more evidence to persuade them that anaesthetics may be used in childbirth than it would have required to persuade them of the opposite.' So science argued, so the professors agreed. And when at last the daughters interposed, But are not brain and body affected by training? Does not the wild rabbit differ from the rabbit in the hutch? And must we not, and do we not change this unalterable nature? By setting a match to a fire frost is defied; Nature's decree of death is postponed. And the breakfast egg, they persisted, is it all the work of the cock? Without yolk, without white, how far would your breakfasts, oh priests and professors, be fertile? Then the priests and professors in solemn unison intoned: But childbirth itself, that burden you cannot deny, is laid upon woman alone. Nor could they deny it, nor wish to renounce it. Still they declared, consulting the statistics in books, the time occupied by woman in childbirth is under modern conditions – remember we are in the twentieth century now – only a fraction.[47] Did that fraction incapacitate us from working in Whitehall, in fields and factories, when our country was in danger? To which the fathers replied: The war is over; we are in England now.

And if, Sir, pausing in England now, we turn on the wireless of the daily press we shall hear what answer the fathers who are infected with infantile fixation now are making to those questions now. 'Homes are the real places of the women . . . Let them go back to their homes . . . The Government should give work to men . . . A strong protest is to be made by the Ministry of Labour . . . Women must not rule over men . . . There are two worlds, one for women, the other for men . . . Let them learn to cook our dinners . . . Women have failed . . . They have failed . . . They have failed . . .'

Even now the clamour, the uproar that infantile fixation is making even here is such that we can hardly hear ourselves speak; it takes the words out of our mouths; it makes us say what we have not said. As we listen to the voices we seem to hear an infant crying in the night, the black night that now covers Europe, and with no language but a cry, Ay, ay, ay, ay . . . But it is not a new cry, it is a very old cry. Let us shut off the wireless and listen to the past. We are in Greece now; Christ has not been born yet, nor St Paul either. But listen:

'Whomsoever the city may appoint, that man must be obeyed, in little things and great, in just things and unjust . . . disobedience is the worst of evils . . . We must support the cause of order, and in no wise suffer a woman to worst us . . . They must be women, and not range at large. Servants, take them within.' That is the voice of Creon, the dictator. To whom Antigone, who was to have been his daughter, answered, 'Not such are the laws set among men by the justice who dwells with the gods below.' But she had neither capital nor force behind her. And Creon said: 'I will take her where the path is loneliest, and hide her, living, in a rocky vault.' And he shut her not in Holloway or in a concentration camp," but in a tomb. And Creon we read brought ruin on his house, and scattered the land with the bodies of the dead. It seems, Sir, as we listen to the voices of the past, as if we were looking at the photograph again, at the picture of dead bodies and ruined houses that the Spanish Government sends us almost weekly. Things repeat themselves it seems. Pictures and voices are the same to-day as they were 2,000 years ago.

Such then is the conclusion to which our enquiry into the nature of fear has brought us – the fear which forbids freedom in the private house. That fear, small, insignificant and private as it is, is connected with the other fear, the public fear, which is neither small nor insignificant, the fear which has led you to ask us to help you to prevent war. Otherwise we should not be looking at the picture again. But it is not the same picture that caused us at the beginning of this letter to feel the same emotions – you called them 'horror and disgust'; we called them horror and disgust. For as this letter has gone on, adding fact to fact, another picture has imposed itself upon the foreground. It is the figure of a man; some say, others deny, that he is Man himself,[480] the quintessence of virility, the perfect type of which all the others are imperfect adumbrations. He is a man certainly. His eyes are glazed; his eyes glare. His body, which is braced in an unnatural position, is tightly cased in a uniform. Upon the breast of that uniform are sewn several medals and other mystic symbols. His hand is upon a sword. He is called in German and Italian Führer or Duce; in our own language Tyrant or Dictator. And behind him lie ruined houses and dead bodies – men, women and children. But we have not laid that picture before you in order to excite once more the sterile emotion of hate. On the contrary it is in order to release other emotions such as the human figure, even thus crudely in a coloured photograph, arouses in us who are human beings. For it suggests a connection and for us a very important connection. It suggests that the public and the private worlds are inseparably connected; that the tyrannies and servilities of the one are the tyrannies and servilities of the other.[p] But the human figure even in a photograph suggests other and more complex emotions. It suggests that we cannot dissociate ourselves from that figure but are ourselves that figure. It suggests that we are not passive spectators doomed to unresisting obedience but by our thoughts and actions can ourselves change that figure. A common interest unites us; it is one world, one life. How essential it is that we should realize that unity the dead bodies, the ruined houses prove. For such will be our ruin if you, in the immensity of your public abstractions forget the private figure, or if we in the intensity of our private emotions forget the public world. Both houses will be ruined, the public and the private, the material and the spiritual, for they are inseparably connected. But with your letter before us we have reason to hope. For by asking our help you recognize that connection; and by reading your words we are reminded of other connections that lie far deeper than the facts on the surface. Even here, even now your letter tempts us to shut our ears to these little facts, these trival details, to listen not to the bark of the guns and the bray of the gramophones but to the voices of the poets, answering each other, assuring us of a unity that rubs out divisions as if they were chalk marks only; to discuss with you the capacity of the human spirit to overflow boundaries and make unity out of multiplicity. But that would be to dream – to dream the recurring dream that has haunted the human mind since the beginning of time; the dream of peace, the dream of freedom. But, with the sound of the guns in your ears you have not asked us to dream. You have not asked us what peace is; you have asked us how to prevent war. Let us then leave it to the poets to tell us what the dream is; and fix our eyes upon the photograph again: the fact.

Whatever the verdict of others may be upon the man in uniform – and opinions differ – there is your letter to prove that to you the picture is the picture of evil. And though we look upon that picture from different angles our conclusion is the same as yours – it is evil. We are both determined to do what we can to destroy the evil which that picture represents, you by your methods, we by ours. And since we are different, our help must be different. What ours can be we have tried to show –

how imperfectly, how superficially there is no need to say.[49] But as a result the answer to your question must be that we can best help you to prevent war not by repeating your words and following your methods but by finding new words and creating new methods. We can best help you to prevent war not by joining your society but by remaining outside your society but in co-operation with its aim. That aim is the same for us both. It is to assert 'the rights of all − all men and women − to the respect in their persons of the great principles of Justice and Equality and Liberty.' To elaborate further is unnecessary, for we have every confidence that you interpret those words as we do. And excuses are unnecessary, for we can trust you to make allowances for those deficiencies which we foretold and which this letter has abundantly displayed.

To return then to the form that you have sent and ask us to fill up: for the reasons given we will leave it unsigned. But in order to prove as substantially as possible that our aims are the same as yours, here is the guinea, a free gift, given freely, without any other conditions than you choose to impose upon yourself. It is the third of three guineas; but the three guineas, you will observe, though given to three different treasurers are all given to the same cause, for the causes are the same and inseparable.

Now, since you are pressed for time, let me make an end; apologising three times over to the three of you, first for the length of this letter, second for the smallness of the contribution, and thirdly for writing at all. The blame for that however rests upon you, for this letter would never have been written had you not asked for an answer to your own.

Notes and References

1. *The Life of Mary Kingsley*, by Stephen Gwynn, p. 15. It is difficult to get exact figures of the sums spent on the education of educated men's daughters. About £20 or £30 presumably covered the entire cost of Mary Kingsley's education (*b*. 1862; *d*. 1900). A sum of £100 may be taken as about the average in the nineteenth century and even later. The women thus educated often felt the lack of education very keenly. 'I always feel the defects of my education most painfully when I go out,' wrote Anne J. Clough, the first Principal of Newnham. (*Life of Anne J. Clough*, by B. A. Clough, p. 60.) Elizabeth Haldane, who came, like Miss Clough, of a highly literate family, but was educated in much the same way, says that when she grew up, 'My first conviction was that I was not educated, and I thought of how this could be put right. I should have loved going to college, but college in those days was unusual for girls, and the idea was not encouraged. It was also expensive. For an only daughter to leave a widowed mother was indeed considered to be out of the question, and no one made the plan seem feasible. There was in those days a new movement for carrying on correspondence classes . . .' (*From One Century to Another*, by Elizabeth Haldane, p. 73.) The efforts of such uneducated women to conceal their ignorance were often valiant, but not always successful. 'They talked agreeably on current topics, carefully avoiding controversial subjects. What impressed me was their ignorance and indifference concerning anything outside their own circle . . . no less a personage than the mother of the Speaker of the House of Commons believed that California belonged to us, part of our Empire!' (*Distant Fields*, by H. A. Vachell, p. 109.) That

ignorance was often simulated in the nineteenth century owing to the current belief that educated men enjoyed it is shown by the energy with which Thomas Gisborne, in his instructive work *On the Duties of Women* (p. 278), rebuked those who recommend women 'studiously to refrain from discovering to their partners in marriage the full extent of their abilities and attainments'. 'This is not discretion but art. It is dissimulation, it is deliberate imposition ... It could scarcely be practised long without detection.'

But the educated man's daughter in the nineteenth century was even more ignorant of life than of books. One reason for that ignorance is suggested by the following quotation: 'It was supposed that most men were not "virtuous", that is, that nearly all would be capable of accosting and annoying – or worse – any unaccompanied young woman whom they met.' ('Society and the Season', by Mary, Countess of Lovelace, in *Fifty Years*, 1882–1932, p. 37.) She was therefore confined to a very narrow circle; and her 'ignorance and indifference' to anything outside it was excusable. The connection between that ignorance and the nineteenth century conception of manhood, which – witness the Victorian hero – made 'virtue' and virility incompatible is obvious. In a well-known passage Thackeray complains of the limitations which virtue and virility between them imposed upon his art.

2. Our ideology is still so inveterately anthropocentric that it has been necessary to coin this clumsy term – educated man's daughter – to describe the class whose fathers have been educated at public schools and universities. Obviously, if the term 'bourgeois' fits her brother, it is grossly incorrect to use it of one who differs so profoundly in the two prime characteristics of the bourgeoisie – capital and environment.

3. The number of animals killed in England for sport during the past century must be beyond computation. 1,212 head of game is given as the average for a day's shooting at Chats-

worth in 1909. (*Men, Women and Things*, by the Duke of Portland, p. 251.) Little mention is made in sporting memoirs of women guns; and their appearance in the hunting field was the cause of much caustic comment. 'Skittles', the famous nineteenth-century horsewoman, was a lady of easy morals. It is highly probable that there was held to be some connection between sport and unchastity in women in the nineteenth century.

4. *Francis and Riversdale Grenfell*, by John Buchan, pp. 189, 205.

5. *Antony (Viscount Knebworth)*, by the Earl of Lytton, p. 355.

6. *The Poems of Wilfred Owen*, edited by Edmund Blunden, pp. 25, 41.

7. Lord Hewart, proposing the toast of 'England' at the banquet of the Society of St George at Cardiff.

8. and 9. *The Daily Telegraph*, February 5th, 1937.

10. There is of course one essential that the educated woman can supply: children. And one method by which she can help to prevent war is to refuse to bear children. Thus Mrs Helena Normanton is of opinion that 'The only thing that women in any country can do to prevent war is to stop the supply of "cannon fodder".' (Report of the Annual Council for Equal Citizenship, *Daily Telegraph*, March 5th, 1937.) Letters in the newspapers frequently support this view. 'I can tell Mr Harry Campbell why women refuse to have children in these times. When men have learnt how to run the lands they govern so that wars shall hit only those who make the quarrels, instead of mowing down those who do not, then women may again feel like having large families. Why should women bring children into such a world as this one is to-day?' (Edith Maturin-Porch, in the *Daily Telegraph*, September 6th, 1937.) The fact that the birth rate in the educated class is falling would seem to show that educated women are taking Mrs Normanton's advice. It was offered them in very similar circumstances over two thousand years ago by Lysistrata.[a]

11. There are of course innumerable kinds of influence besides

those specified in the text. It varies from the simple kind described in the following passage: 'Three years later . . . we find her writing to him as Cabinet Minister to solicit his interest on behalf of a favourite parson for a Crown living . . .' (*Henry Chaplin, a Memoir*, by Lady Londonderry, p. 57) to the very subtle kind exerted by Lady Macbeth upon her husband. Somewhere between the two lies the influence described by D. H. Lawrence: 'It is hopeless for me to try to do anything without I have a woman at the back of me . . . I daren't sit in the world without I have a woman behind me . . . But a woman that I love sort of keeps me in direct communication with the unknown, in which otherwise I am a bit lost' (*Letters of D. H. Lawrence*, pp. 93–4), with which we may compare, though the collocation is strange, the famous and very similar definition given by the ex-King Edward VIII upon his abdication.[b] Present political conditions abroad seem to favour a return to the use of interested influence. For example: 'A story serves to illustrate the present degree of women's influence in Vienna. During the past autumn a measure was planned to further diminish women's professional opportunities. Protests, pleas, letters, all were of no avail. Finally, in desperation, a group of well-known ladies of the city . . . got together and planned. For the next fortnight, for a certain number of hours per day, several of these ladies got on to the telephone to the Ministers they knew personally, ostensibly to ask them to dinner at their homes. With all the charm of which the Viennese are capable, they kept the Ministers talking, asking about this and that, and finally mentioning the matter that distressed them so much. When the Ministers had been rung up by several ladies, all of whom they did not wish to offend, and kept from urgent State affairs by this manoeuvre, they decided on compromise – and so the measure was postponed.' (*Women Must Choose*, by Hilary Newitt, p. 129.) Similar use of influence was often deliberately made during the battle for the franchise. But women's influence is said to be impaired by the possession of a vote. Thus Marshal von Bieberstein was of opinion that 'Women led men always . . . but he did not wish them to vote.' (*From One Century to Another*, by Elizabeth Haldane, p. 258.)

12. English women were much criticized for using force in the battle for the Franchise. When in 1910 Mr Birrell had his hat 'reduced to pulp' and his shins kicked by suffragettes, Sir Almeric Fitzroy commented, 'an attack of this character upon a defenceless old man by an organized band of "janissaries" will, it is hoped, convince many people of the insane and anarchical spirit actuating the movement.' (*Memoirs of Sir Almeric Fitzroy*, Vol. II, p. 425.) These remarks did not apply apparently to the force in the European War. The vote indeed was given to English women largely because of the help they gave to Englishmen in using force in that war. 'On 14th August [1916], Mr Asquith himself gave up his opposition [to the Franchise]. "It is true," he said, "[that women] cannot fight in the sense of going out with rifles and so forth, but . . . they have aided in the most effective way in the prosecution of the war."' ('*The Cause*', by Ray Strachey, p. 354.) This raises the difficult question whether those who did not aid in the prosecution of the war, but did what they could to hinder the prosecution of the war, ought to use the vote to which they are entitled chiefly because others 'aided in the prosecution of the war'? That they are stepdaughters, not full daughters, of England is shown by the fact that they change nationality on marriage. A woman, whether or not she helped to beat the Germans, becomes a German if she marries a German. Her political views must then be entirely reversed, and her filial piety transferred.

13. *Sir Ernest Wild, K.C.*, by Robert J. Blackburn, pp. 174–5.

14. That the right to vote has not proved negligible is shown by the facts published from time to time by the National Union of Societies for Equal Citizenship. 'This publication (*What the Vote Has Done*) was originally a single-page leaflet; it has now (1927) grown to a six-page pamphlet, and has to be

constantly enlarged.' (*Josephine Butler*, by M. G. Fawcett and
E. M. Turner, note, p. 101.)

15. There are no figures available with which to check facts that
must have a very important bearing upon the biology and
psychology of the sexes. A beginning might be made in this
essential but strangely neglected preliminary by chalking on
a large-scale map of England property owned by men, red;
by women, blue. Then the number of sheep and cattle
consumed by each sex must be compared; the hogsheads of
wine and beer; the barrels of tobacco; after which we must
examine carefully their physical exercises; domestic employments; facilities for sexual intercourse, etc. Historians are of
course mainly concerned with war and politics; but sometimes throw light upon human nature. Thus Macaulay,
dealing with the English country gentleman in the seventeenth century, says: 'His wife and daughter were in tastes
and acquirements below a housekeeper or still room maid of
the present day. They stitched and spun, brewed gooseberry
wine, cured marigolds, and made the crust for the venison
pasty.'

Again, 'The ladies of the house, whose business it had commonly been to cook the repast, retired as soon as the dishes
had been devoured, and left the gentlemen to their ale and
tobacco.' (Macaulay, *History of England*, Chapter Three.) But
the gentlemen were still drinking and the ladies were still
withdrawing a great deal later. 'In my mother's young days
before her marriage, the old hard-drinking habits of the
Regency and of the eighteenth century still persisted. At
Woburn Abbey it was the custom for the trusted old family
butler to make his nightly report to my grandmother in the
drawing-room. "The gentlemen have had a good deal to-
night; it might be as well for the young ladies to retire," or,
"The gentlemen have had very little to-night," was announced according to circumstances by this faithful family
retainer. Should the young girls be packed off upstairs, they
liked standing on an upper gallery of the staircase to watch

the shouting, riotous crowd issuing from the dining-room.'
(*The Days Before Yesterday*, by Lord F. Hamilton, p. 322.) It
must be left to the scientist of the future to tell us what
effect drink and property have had upon chromosomes.

16. The fact that both sexes have a very marked though dissim-
ilar love of dress seems to have escaped the notice of the
dominant sex owing largely it must be supposed to the
hypnotic power of dominance. Thus the late Mr Justice
MacCardie, in summing up the case of Mrs Frankau, remarked: 'Women cannot be expected to renounce an essential
feature of femininity or to abandon one of nature's solaces
for a constant and insuperable physical handicap . . . Dress,
after all, is one of the chief methods of women's self-
expression . . . In matters of dress women often remain
children to the end. The psychology of the matter must not
be overlooked. But whilst bearing the above matters in
mind the law has rightly laid it down that the rule of
prudence and proportion must be observed.' The Judge
who thus dictated was wearing a scarlet robe, an ermine
cape, and a vast wig of artificial curls. Whether he was
enjoying 'one of nature's solaces for a constant and insuperable physical handicap', whether again he was himself observing 'the rule of prudence and proportion' must be doubtful.
But 'the psychology of the matter must not be overlooked';
and the fact that the singularity of his own appearance
together with that of Admirals, Generals, Heralds, Life
Guards, Peers, Beefeaters, etc., was completely invisible to
him so that he was able to lecture the lady without any
consciousness of sharing her weakness, raises two questions:
how often must an act be performed before it becomes
traditional, and therefore venerable; and what degree of
social prestige causes blindness to the remarkable nature of
one's own clothes? Singularity of dress, when not associated
with office, seldom escapes ridicule.

17. In the New Year's Honours List for 1937, 147 men accepted
honours as against seven women. For obvious reasons this

cannot be taken as a measure of their comparative desire for such advertisement. But that it should be easier, psychologically, for a woman to reject honours than for a man seems to be indisputable. For the fact that intellect (roughly speaking) is man's chief professional asset, and that stars and ribbons are his chief means of advertising intellect, suggests that stars and ribbons are identical with powder and paint, a woman's chief method of advertising her chief professional asset: beauty. It would therefore be as unreasonable to ask him to refuse a Knighthood as to ask her to refuse a dress. The sum paid for a Knighthood in 1901 would seem to provide a very tolerable dress allowance: '21st April (Sunday) – To see Meynell, who was as usual full of gossip. It appears that the King's debts have been paid off privately by his friends, one of whom is said to have lent £100,000, and satisfies himself with £25,000 in repayment plus a Knighthood.' (*My Diaries*, Wilfrid Scawen Blunt, Part II, p. 8.)

18. What the precise figures are it is difficult for an outsider to know. But that the incomes are substantial can be conjectured from a delightful review some years ago by Mr J. M. Keynes in *The Nation* of a history of Clare College, Cambridge. The book 'it is rumoured cost six thousand pounds to produce'. Rumour has it also that a band of students returning at dawn from some festivity about that time saw a cloud in the sky; which as they gazed assumed the shape of a woman; who, being supplicated for a sign, let fall in a shower of radiant hail the one word 'Rats'. This was interpreted to signify what from another page of the same number of *The Nation* would seem to be the truth; that the students of one of the women's colleges suffered greatly from 'cold gloomy ground floor bedrooms overrun with mice'. The apparition, it was supposed, took this means of suggesting that if the gentlemen of Clare wished to do her honour a cheque for £6,000 payable to the Principal of — would celebrate her better than a book even though 'clothed in the finest dress of paper and black buckram . . .' There is

nothing mythical, however, about the fact recorded in the same number of *The Nation* that 'Somerville received with pathetic gratitude the £7,000 which went to it last year from the Jubilee gift and a private bequest.'[c]

19. A great historian has thus described the origin and character of the universities, in one of which he was educated: 'The schools of Oxford and Cambridge were founded in a dark age of false and barbarous science; and they are still tainted by the vices of their origin ... The legal incorporation of these societies by the charters of popes and kings had given them a monopoly of public instruction; and the spirit of monopolists is narrow, lazy, and oppressive: their work is more costly and less productive than that of independent artists; and the new improvements so eagerly grasped by the competition of freedom, are admitted with slow and sullen reluctance in those proud corporations, above the fear of a rival, and below the confession of an error. We may scarcely hope that any reformation will be a voluntary act; and so deeply are they rooted in law and prejudice, that even the omnipotence of parliament would shrink from an inquiry into the state and abuses of the two universities.' (Edward Gibbon, *Memoirs of My Life and Writings*.) 'The omnipotence of Parliament' did however institute an inquiry in the middle of the nineteenth century 'into the state of the University [of Oxford], its discipline, studies, and revenues. But there was so much passive resistance from the Colleges that the last item had to go by the board. It was ascertained however that out of 542 Fellowships in all the Colleges of Oxford only twenty-two were really open to competition without restrictive conditions of patronage, place or kin ... The Commissioners ... found that Gibbon's indictment had been reasonable ...' (*Herbert Warren of Magdalen*, by Laurie Magnus, pp. 47–49.) Nevertheless the prestige of a university education remained high; and Fellowships were considered highly desirable. When Pusey became a Fellow of Oriel, 'The bells of the parish church at Pusey expressed the

satisfaction of his father and family.' Again, when Newman was elected a Fellow, 'all the bells of the three towers [were] set pealing – at Newman's expense.' (*Oxford Apostles*, by Geoffrey Faber, pp. 131, 69.) Yet both Pusey and Newman were men of a distinctly spiritual nature.

20. *The Crystal Cabinet*, by Mary Butts, p. 138. The sentence in full runs: 'For just as I was told that desire for learning in woman was against the will of God, so were many innocent freedoms, innocent delights, denied in the same Name' – a remark which makes it desirable that we should have a biography from the pen of an educated man's daughter of the Deity in whose Name such atrocities have been committed. The influence of religion upon women's education, one way or another can scarcely be overestimated. 'If, for example,' says Thomas Gisborne, 'the uses of music are explained, let not its effect in heightening devotion be overlooked. If drawing is the subject of remark, let the student be taught habitually to contemplate in the works of creation the power, the wisdom and the goodness of their Author.' (*The Duties of the Female Sex*, by Thomas Gisborne, p. 85.) The fact that Mr Gisborne and his like – a numerous band – base their educational theories upon the teaching of St Paul would seem to hint that the female sex was to be 'taught habitually to contemplate in the works of creation, the power and wisdom and the goodness,' not so much of the Deity, but of Mr Gisborne. And from that we are led to conclude that a biography of the Deity would resolve itself into a Dictionary of Clerical Biography.

21. *Mary Astell*, by Florence M. Smith. 'Unfortunately, the opposition to so new an idea (a college for women) was greater than the interest in it, and came not only from the satirists of the day, who, like the wits of all ages, found the progressive woman a source of laughter and made Mary Astell the subject of stock jokes in comedies of the *Femmes Savantes* types, but from churchmen, who saw in the plan an attempt to bring back popery. The strongest opponent of

the idea was a celebrated bishop, who, as Ballard asserts, prevented a prominent lady from subscribing £10,000 to the plan. Elizabeth Elstob gave to Ballard the name of this celebrated bishop in reply to an inquiry from him. "According to Elizabeth Elstob ... it was Bishop Burnet that prevented that good design by dissuading that lady from encouraging it."' (Op. cit., pp. 21–2.) 'That lady' may have been Princess Ann, or Lady Elizabeth Hastings; but there seems reason to think that it was the Princess. That the Church swallowed the money is an assumption, but one perhaps justified by the history of the Church.

22. *Ode for Music*, performed in the Senate House at Cambridge, July 1st, 1769.

23. 'I assure you I am not an enemy of women. I am very favourable to their employment as *labourers* or in other *menial* capacity. I have, however, doubts as to the likelihood of their succeeding in business as capitalists. I am sure the nerves of most women would break down under the anxiety, and that most of them are utterly destitute of the disciplined reticence necessary to every sort of co-operation. Two thousand years hence you may have changed it all, but the present women will only flirt with men, and quarrel with one another.' Extract from a letter from Walter Bagehot to Emily Davies, who had asked his help in founding Girton.

24. *Recollections and Reflections*, by Sir J.J. Thomson, pp. 86–8, 296–7.

25. 'Cambridge University still refuses to admit women to the full rights of membership; it grants them only titular degrees and they have therefore no share in the government of the University.' (*Memorandum on the Position of English Women in Relation to that of English Men*, by Philippa Strachey, p. 26. (1935.)) Nevertheless, the Government makes a 'liberal grant' from public money to Cambridge University.

26. 'The total number of students at recognized institutions for the higher education of women who are receiving instruction in the University or working in the University laboratories

or museums shall not at any time exceed five hundred.' (*The Student's Handbook to Cambridge*, 1934–5, p. 616.) Whitaker[d] informs us that the number of male students who were in residence at Cambridge in October 1935 was 5,328. Nor would there appear to be any limitation.

27. The men's scholarship list at Cambridge printed in *The Times* of December 20th, 1937, measures roughly thirty-one inches; the women's scholarship list at Cambridge measures roughly five inches. There are, however, seventeen colleges for men and the list here measured includes only eleven. The thirty-one inches must therefore be increased. There are only two colleges for women; both are here measured.

28. Until the death of Lady Stanley of Alderley, there was no chapel at Girton. 'When it was proposed to build a chapel, she objected, on the ground that all the available funds should be spent on education. "So long as I live, there shall be no chapel at Girton," I heard her say. The present chapel was built immediately after her death.' (*The Amberley Papers*, Patricia and Bertrand Russell, Vol. I, p. 17.) Would that her ghost had possessed the same influence as her body! But ghosts, it is said, have no cheque books.

29. "I have also a feeling that girls' schools have, on the whole, been content to take the general lines of their education from the older-established institutions for my own, the weaker sex. My own feeling is that the problem ought to be attacked by some original genius on quite different lines . . .' (*Things Ancient and Modern*, by C. A. Alington, pp. 216–17.) It scarcely needs genius or originality to see that 'the lines', in the first place, must be cheaper. But it would be interesting to know what meaning we are to attach to the word 'weaker' in the context. For since Dr Alington is a former head master of Eton he must be aware that his sex has not only acquired, but retained the vast revenues of that ancient foundation – a proof, one would have thought, not of sexual weakness but of sexual strength. That Eton is not 'weak', at least from the material point of view, is shown by the

following quotation from Dr Alington: 'Following out the suggestion of one of the Prime Minister's Committees on Education, the Provost and Fellows in my time decided that all scholarships at Eton should be of a fixed value, capable of being liberally augmented in case of need. So liberal has been this augmentation that there are several boys in College whose parents pay nothing towards either their board or education.' One of the benefactors was the late Lord Rosebery. 'He was a generous benefactor to the school,' Dr Alington informs us, 'and endowed a history scholarship, in connection with which a characteristic episode occurred. He asked me whether the endowment was adequate, and I suggested that a further £200 would provide for the payment to the examiner. He sent a cheque for £2,000: his attention was called to the discrepancy, and I have in my scrap book the reply in which he said that he thought a good round sum would be better than a fraction.' (Op. cit., pp. 163, 186.) The entire sum spent at Cheltenham College for Girls in 1854 upon salaries and visiting teachers was £1,300; 'and the accounts in December showed a deficit of £400.' (*Dorothea Beale of Cheltenham*, by Elizabeth Raikes, p. 91.)

30. The words 'vain and vicious' require qualification. No one would maintain that all lecturers and all lectures are 'vain and vicious';[e] many subjects can only be taught with diagrams and personal demonstration. The words in the text refer only to the sons and daughters of educated men who lecture their brothers and sisters upon English literature; and for the reasons that it is an obsolete practice dating from the Middle Ages when books were scarce; that it owes its survival to pecuniary motives; or to curiosity; that the publication in book form is sufficient proof of the evil effect of an audience upon the lecturer intellectually; and that psychologically eminence upon a platform encourages vanity and the desire to impose authority. Further, the reduction of English literature to an examination subject must be viewed with suspicion by all who have firsthand knowledge of the

difficulty of the art, and therefore of the very superficial value of an examiner's approval or disapproval; and with profound regret by all who wish to keep one art at least out of the hands of middlemen and free, as long as may be, from all association with competition and money making. Again, the violence with which one school of literature is now opposed to another, the rapidity with which one school of taste succeeds another, may not unreasonably be traced to the power which a mature mind lecturing immature minds has to infect them with strong, if passing, opinions, and to tinge those opinions with personal bias. Nor can it be maintained that the standard of critical or of creative writing has been raised. A lamentable proof of the mental docility to which the young are reduced by lecturers is that the demand for lectures upon English literature steadily increases (as every writer can bear witness) and from the very class which should have learnt to read at home – the educated. If, as is sometimes urged in excuse, what is desired by college literary societies is not knowledge of literature but acquaintance with writers, there are cocktails, and there is sherry; both better unmixed with Proust. None of this applies of course to those whose homes are deficient in books. If the working class finds it easier to assimilate English literature by word of mouth they have a perfect right to ask the educated class to help them thus. But for the sons and daughters of that class after the age of eighteen to continue to sip English literature through a straw, is a habit that seems to deserve the terms vain and vicious; which terms can justly be applied with greater force to those who pander to them.

31. It is difficult to procure exact figures of the sums allowed the daughters of educated men before marriage. Sophia Jex-Blake had an allowance of from £30 to £40 annually; her father was an upper-middle-class man. Lady M. Lascelles, whose father was an Earl, had, it seems, an allowance of about £100 in 1860; Mr Barrett, a rich merchant, allowed his daughter Elizabeth 'from forty to forty-five pounds ...

every three months, the income tax being first deducted'.
But this seems to have been the interest upon £8,000, 'or
more or less . . . it is difficult to ask about it,' which she had
'in the funds', 'the money being in two different per cents.',
and apparently, though belonging to Elizabeth, under Mr
Barrett's control. But these were unmarried women. Married
women were not allowed to own property until the passing
of the Married Woman's Property Act in 1870.ʃ Lady St
Helier records that since her marriage settlements had been
drawn up in conformity with the old law, 'What money I
had was settled on my husband, and no part of it was
reserved for my private use . . . I did not even possess a
cheque book, nor was I able to get any money except by
asking my husband. He was kind and generous, but he
acquiesced in the position then existing that a woman's
property belonged to her husband . . . he paid all my bills,
he kept my bank book, and gave me a small allowance for
my personal expenses.' (*Memories of Fifty Years*, by Lady St
Helier, p. 341.) But she does not say what the exact sum
was. The sums allowed to the sons of educated men were
considerably larger. An allowance of £200 was considered to
be only just sufficient for an undergraduate at Balliol, 'which
still had traditions of frugality', about 1880. On that allowance 'they could not hunt and they could not gamble . . .
But with care, and with a home to fall back on in the
vacations, they could make this do.' (*Anthony Hope and His
Books*, by Sir C. Mallet, p. 38.) The sum that is now needed
is considerably more. Gino Watkins 'never spent more than
the £400 yearly allowance with which he paid all his college
and vacation bills'. (*Gino Watkins*, by J. M. Scott, p. 59.)
This was at Cambridge, a few years ago.

32. How incessantly women were ridiculed throughout the nineteenth century for attempting to enter their solitary profession, novel readers know, for those efforts provide half the
stock-in-trade of fiction. But biography shows how natural
it was, even in the present century, for the most enlightened

of men to conceive of all women as spinsters, all desiring marriage. Thus: '"Oh dear, what is to happen to them?" he [G. L. Dickinson] once murmured sadly as a stream of aspiring but uninspiring spinsters flowed round the front court of King's; "I don't know and they don't know." And then in still lower tones as if his bookshelves might overhear him, "Oh dear! What they want is a husband!"' (*Goldsworthy Lowes Dickinson* by E. M. Forster, p. 106.) 'What they wanted' might have been the Bar, the Stock Exchange or rooms in Gibbs's Buildings, had the choice been open to them. But it was not; and therefore Mr Dickinson's remark was a very natural one.

33. 'Now and then, at least in the larger houses, there would be a set party, selected and invited long beforehand, and over these always one idol dominated – the pheasant. Shooting had to be used as a lure. At such times the father of the family was apt to assert himself. If his house was to be filled to bursting, his wines drunk in quantities, and his best shooting provided, then for that shooting he would have the best guns possible. What despair for the mother of daughters to be told that the one guest whom of all others she secretly desired to invite was a bad shot and totally inadmissible!' ('Society and the Season', by Mary, Countess of Lovelace, in *Fifty Years*, 1882–1932, p. 29.)

34. Some idea of what men hoped that their wives might say and do, at least in the nineteenth century, may be gathered from the following hints in a letter 'addressed to a young lady for whom he had a great regard a short time before her marriage' by John Bowdler. 'Above all, avoid everything which has the *least tendency* to indelicacy or indecorum. Few women have *any idea* how much men are disgusted at the slightest approach to these in any female, and especially in one to whom they are attached. By attending the nursery, or the sick bed, women are too apt to acquire a habit of conversing on such subjects in language which men of delicacy are shocked at.' (*Life of John Bowdler*, p. 123.) But

though delicacy was essential, it could, after marriage, be disguised. 'In the seventies of last century, Miss Jex-Blake and her associates were vigorously fighting the battle for admission of women to the medical profession, and the doctors were still more vigorously resisting their entry, alleging that it must be improper and demoralizing for a woman to have to study and deal with delicate and intimate medical questions. At that time, Ernest Hart, the Editor of the *British Medical Journal*, told me that the majority of the contributions sent to him for publication in the *Journal* dealing with delicate and intimate medical questions were in the handwriting of the doctors' wives, to whom they had obviously been dictated. There were no typewriters or stenographers available in those days.' (*The Doctor's Second Thoughts*, by Sir J. Crichton-Browne, pp. 73, 74.)

The duplicity of delicacy was observed long before this, however. Thus Mandeville in *The Fable of the Bees* (1714) says: '. . . I would have it first consider'd that the Modesty of Women is the result of Custom and Education, by which all unfashionable Denudations and filthy Expressions are render'd frightful and abominable to them, and that notwithstanding this, the most Virtuous Young Woman alive will often, in spite of her Teeth, have Thoughts and confus'd Ideas of Things arise in her Imagination, which she would not reveal to some People for a Thousand Worlds.'

TWO

1. To quote the exact words of one such appeal: 'This letter is to ask you to set aside for us garments for which you have no further use . . . Stockings, of every sort, no matter how worn, are also most acceptable . . . The Committee find that by offering these clothes at bargain prices . . . they are performing a really useful service to women whose professions require that they should have presentable day and evening dresses which they can ill afford to buy.' (Extract

from a letter received from the London and National Society for Women's Service. (1938.))

2. *The Testament of Joad*, by C. E. M. Joad, pp. 210–11. Since the number of societies run directly or indirectly by English-women in the cause of peace is too long to quote (see *The Story of the Disarmament Declaration*, p. 15, for a list of the peace activities of professional, business and working-class women) it is unnecessary to take Mr Joad's criticism seriously, however illuminating psychologically.

3. *Experiment in Autobiography*, by H. G. Wells, p. 486. The men's 'movement to resist the practical obliteration of their freedom by Nazis or Fascists' may have been more perceptible. But that it has been more successful is doubtful. 'Nazis now control the whole of Austria' (Daily paper, March 12th, 1938).

4. 'Women, I think, ought not to sit down to table with men; their presence ruins conversation, tending to make it trivial and genteel, or at best merely clever.' (*Under the Fifth Rib*, by C. E. M. Joad, p. 58.) This is an admirably outspoken opinion, and if all who share Mr Joad's sentiments were to express them as openly, the hostess's dilemma – whom to ask, whom not to ask – would be lightened and her labour saved. If those who prefer the society of their own sex at table would signify the fact, the men, say, by wearing a red, the women by wearing a white rosette, while those who prefer the sexes mixed wore parti-coloured buttonholes of red and white blended, not only would much inconvenience and misunderstanding be prevented, but it is possible that the honesty of the buttonhole would kill a certain form of social hypocrisy now all too prevalent. Meanwhile Mr Joad's candour deserves the highest praise, and his wishes the most implicit observance.

5. According to Mrs H. M. Swanwick, the W.S.P.U. had 'an income from gifts, in the year 1912, of £42,000.'[a] (*I Have Been Young*, by H. M. Swanwick, p. 189.) The total spent in 1912 by the Women's Freedom League was £26,772 12s. 9d.

('*The Cause*', by Ray Strachey, p. 311.) Thus the joint income of the two societies was £68,772 12s. 9d. But the two societies were, of course, opposed.

6. 'But, exceptions apart, the general run of women's earnings is low, and £250 a year is quite an achievement, even for a highly qualified woman with years of experience.' (*Careers and Openings for Women*, by Ray Strachey, p. 70.) Nevertheless 'The numbers of women doing professional work have increased very fast in the last twenty years, and were about 400,000 in 1931, in addition to those doing secretarial work or employed in the Civil Service.' (Op cit., p. 44.)

7. The income of the Labour Party in 1936 was £50,153. (*Daily Telegraph*, September 1937.)

8. *The British Civil Service. The Public Service*, by William A. Robson, p. 16.

Professor Ernest Barker suggests that there should be an alternative Civil Service Examination for 'men and women of an older growth' who have spent some years in social work and social service. 'Women candidates in particular might benefit. It is only a very small proportion of women students who succeed in the present open competition: indeed very few compete. On the alternative system here suggested it is possible, and indeed probable, that a much larger proportion of women would be candidates. Women have a genius and a capacity for social work and service. The alternative form of competition would give them a chance of showing that genius and that capacity. It might give them a new incentive to compete for entry into the administrative service of the state in which their gifts and their presence are needed.' (*The British Civil Servant*. 'The Home Civil Service', by Professor Ernest Barker, p. 41.) But while the home service remains as exacting as it is at present, if is difficult to see how any incentive can make women free to give 'their gifts and their presence' to the service of the state, unless the state will undertake the care of elderly parents; or make it a penal offence for elderly people of either sex to require the services of daughters at home.

9. Mr Baldwin, speaking at Downing Street, at a meeting on behalf of Newnham College Building Fund, March 31st, 1936.

10. The effect of a woman in the pulpit is thus defined in *Women and the Ministry, Some Considerations on the Report of the Archbishops' Commission on the Ministry of Women* (1936), p. 24. 'But we maintain that the ministration of women ... will tend to produce a lowering of the spiritual tone of Christian worship, such as is not produced by the ministrations of men before congregations largely or exclusively female. It is a tribute to the quality of Christian womanhood that it is possible to make this statement; but it would appear to be a simple matter of fact that in the thoughts and desires of that sex the natural is more easily made subordinate to the supernatural, the carnal to the spiritual than is the case with men; and that the ministrations of a male priesthood do not normally arouse that side of female human nature which should be quiescent during the times of the adoration of almighty God. We believe, on the other hand, that it would be impossible for the male members of the average Anglican congregation to be present at a service at which a woman ministered without becoming unduly conscious of her sex.'

In the opinion of the Commissioners, therefore, Christian women are more spiritually minded than Christian men – a remarkable, but no doubt adequate, reason for excluding them from the priesthood.

11. *Daily Telegraph*, January 20th, 1936.

12. *Daily Telegraph*, 1936.

13. *Daily Telegraph*, January 22nd, 1936.

14. 'There are, so far as I know, no universal rules on this subject [i.e. sexual relations between civil servants]; but civil servants and municipal officers of both sexes are certainly expected to observe the conventional proprieties and to avoid conduct which might find its way into the newspapers and there be described as 'scandalous'. Until recently sexual relations between men and women officers of the Post

Office were punishable with immediate dismissal of both parties ... The problem of avoiding newspaper publicity is a fairly easy one to solve so far as court proceedings are concerned: but official restriction extends further so as to prevent women civil servants (who usually have to resign on marriage) from cohabiting openly with men if they desire to do so. The matter, therefore, takes on a different complexion.' (*The British Civil Servant. The Public Service*, by William A. Robson, pp. 14, 15.)

15. Most men's clubs confine women to a special room, or annexe, and exclude them from other apartments, whether on the principle observed at St Sofia that they are impure, or whether on the principle observed at Pompeii that they are too pure, is matter for speculation.

16. The power of the Press to burke discussion of any undesirable subject was, and still is, very formidable. It was one of the 'extraordinary obstacles' against which Josephine Butler had to fight in her campaign against the Contagious Diseases Act.[b] 'Early in 1870 the London Press began to adopt that policy of silence with regard to the question, which lasted for many years, and called forth from the Ladies' Association the famous "Remonstrance against the Conspiracy of Silence", signed by Harriet Martineau and Josephine E. Butler, which concluded with the following words: "Surely, while such a conspiracy of silence is possible and practised among leading journalists, we English greatly exaggerate our privileges as a free people when we profess to encourage a free press, and to possess the right to hear both sides in a momentous question of morality and legislation."' (*Personal Reminiscences of a Great Crusade*, by Josephine E. Butler, p. 49.) Again, during the battle for the vote the Press used the boycott with great effect. And so recently as July 1937 Miss Philippa Strachey in a letter headed 'A Conspiracy of Silence', printed (to its honour) by the *Spectator* almost repeats Mrs Butler's words: 'Many hundreds and thousands of men and women have been participating in an endeavour to induce

the Government to abandon the provision in the new Contributory Pensions Bill for the black-coated workers which for the first time introduces a differential income limit for men and women entrants . . . In the course of the last month the Bill has been before the House of Lords, where this particular provision has met with strong and determined opposition from all sides of the Chamber . . . These are events one would have supposed to be of sufficient interest to be recorded in the daily Press. But they have been passed over in complete silence by the newspapers from *The Times* to the *Daily Herald* . . . The differential treatment of women under this Bill has aroused a feeling of resentment among them such as has not been witnessed since the granting of the franchise . . . How is one to account for this being completely concealed by the Press?'

17. Flesh wounds were of course inflicted during the battle of Westminster. Indeed the fight for the vote seems to have been more severe than is now recognized. Thus Flora Drummond says: 'Whether we won the vote by our agitation, as I believe, or whether we got it for other reasons, as some people say, I think many of the younger generation will find it hard to believe the fury and brutality aroused by our claim for votes for women less than thirty years ago.' (Flora Drummond in the *Listener*, August 25th, 1937.) The younger generation is presumably so used to the fury and brutality that claims for liberty arouse that they have no emotion available for this particular instance. Moreover, that particular fight has not yet taken its place among the fights which have made England the home, and Englishmen the champions, of liberty. The fight for the vote is still generally referred to in terms of sour deprecation: '. . . and the women . . . had not begun that campaign of burning, whipping, and picture-slashing which was finally to prove to both Front Benches their eligibility for the Franchise.' (*Reflections and Memories*, by Sir John Squire, p. 10.) The younger generation therefore can be excused if they believe that there was

nothing heroic about a campaign in which only a few windows were smashed, shins broken, and Sargent's portrait of Henry James damaged, but not irreparably, with a knife. Burning, whipping and picture-slashing only it would seem become heroic when carried out on a large scale by men with machine-guns.

18. *The Life of Sophia Jex-Blake*, by Margaret Todd, M.D., p. 72.

19. 'Much has lately been said and written of the achievements and accomplishments of Sir Stanley Baldwin during his Premierships and too much would be impossible. Might I be permitted to call attention to what Lady Baldwin has done? When I first joined the committee of this hospital in 1929, analgesics (pain deadeners) for normal maternity cases in the wards were almost unknown, now their use is ordinary routine and they are availed of in practically 100 per cent. of cases, and what is true of this hospital is true virtually for all similar hospitals. This remarkable change in so short a time is due to the inspiration and the tireless efforts and encouragement of Mrs Stanley Baldwin, as she then was . . .' (Letter to *The Times* from C. S. Wentworth Stanley, Chairman House Committee, The City of London Maternity Hospital, 1937.) Since chloroform was first administered to Queen Victoria on the birth of Prince Leopold in April 1853, 'normal maternity cases in the wards' have had to wait for seventy-six years and the advocacy of a Prime Minister's wife to obtain this relief.

20. According to *Debrett* the Knights and Dames of the Most Excellent Order of the British Empire wear a badge consisting of 'a cross patonce, enamelled pearl, fimbriated or, surmounted by a gold medallion with a representation of Britannia seated within a circle gules inscribed with the motto "For God and the Empire".' This is one of the few orders open to women, but their subordination is properly marked by the fact that the ribbon in their case is only two inches and one-quarter in breadth; whereas the ribbon of the Knights is three inches and three-quarters in breadth. The

stars also differ in size. The motto, however, is the same for both sexes, and must be held to imply that those who thus ticket themselves see some connection between the Deity and the Empire, and hold themselves prepared to defend them. What happens if Britannia seated within a circle gules is opposed (as is conceivable) to the other authority whose seat is not specified on the medallion, *Debrett* does not say, and the Knights and Dames must themselves decide.

21. *Life of Sir Ernest Wild, K.C.*, by R. J. Rackham, p. 91.

22. Lord Baldwin, speech reported in *The Times*, April 20th, 1936.

23. *Life of Charles Gore*, by G. L. Prestige, D.D., pp. 240–1.

24. *Life of Sir William Broadbent, K.C.V.O., F.R.S.*, edited by his daughter, M. E. Broadbent, p. 242.

25. *The Lost Historian, a Memoir of Sir Sidney Low*, by Desmond Chapman-Huston, p. 198.

26. *Thoughts and Adventures*, by the Rt. Hon. Winston Churchill, p. 57.

27. Speech at Belfast by Lord Londonderry, reported in *The Times*, July 11th, 1936.

28. *Thoughts and Adventures*, by the Rt. Hon. Winston Churchill, p. 279.

29. *Daily Herald*, February 13th, 1935.

30. Goethe's *Faust*, translated by Melian Stawell and G. L. Dickinson.

31. *The Life of Charles Tomlinson*, by his niece, Mary Tomlinson, p. 30.

32. *Miss Weeton, Journal of a Governess*, 1807–1811, edited by Edward Hall, pp. 14, xvii.

33. *A Memoir of Anne Jemima Clough*, by B. A. Clough, p. 32.

34. *Personal Reminiscences of a Great Crusade*, by Josephine Butler, p. 189.

35. 'You and I know that it matters little if we have to be the out-of-sight piers driven deep into the marsh, on which the visible ones are carried, that support the bridge. We do not mind if, hereafter, people forget that there *are* any low down

at all; if some have to be used up in trying experiments, before the best way of building the bridge is discovered. We are quite willing to be among these. The bridge is what we care for, and not our place in it; and we believe that, to the end, it may be kept in remembrance that this is alone to be our object.' (Letter from Octavia Hill to Mrs N. Senior, September 20th, 1874. *The Life of Octavia Hill*, by C. Edmund Maurice, pp. 307–8.)

Octavia Hill (1838–1912) initiated the movement for 'securing better homes for the poor and open spaces for the public ... The "Octavia Hill System" has been adopted over the whole planned extension of [Amsterdam]. In January 1928 no less than 28,648 dwellings had been built.' (*Octavia Hill*, from letters edited by Emily S. Maurice, pp. 10–11.)

36. The maid played so important a part in English upper-class life from the earliest times until the year 1914, when the Hon. Monica Grenfell went to nurse wounded soldiers accompanied by a maid [*Bright Armour*, by Monica Salmond, p. 20], that some recognition of her services seems to be called for. Her duties were peculiar. Thus she had to escort her mistress down Piccadilly 'where a few club men might have looked at her out of a window', but was unnecessary in Whitechapel, 'where malefactors were possibly lurking round every corner'. But her office was undoubtedly arduous. Wilson's part in Elizabeth Barrett's private life is well known to readers of the famous letters. Later in the century (about 1889–92) Gertrude Bell 'went with Lizzie, her maid, to picture exhibitions; she was fetched by Lizzie from dinner parties; she went with Lizzie to see the Settlement in Whitechapel where Mary Talbot was working ...' (*Early Letters of Gertrude Bell*, edited by Lady Richmond.) We have only to consider the hours she waited in cloak rooms, the acres she toiled in picture galleries, the miles she trudged along West End pavements to conclude that if Lizzie's day is now almost over, it was in its day a long one. Let us hope that the thought that she was putting into practice the

commands laid down by St Paul in his Letters to Titus and the Corinthians, was a support; and the knowledge that she was doing her utmost to deliver her mistress's body intact to her master a solace. Even so in the weakness of the flesh and in the darkness of the beetle-haunted basement she must sometimes have bitterly reproached St Paul on the one hand for his chastity, and the gentlemen of Piccadilly on the other for their lust. It is much to be regretted that no lives of maids, from which a more fully documented account could be constructed, are to be found in the *Dictionary of National Biography*.

37. *The Earlier Letters of Gertrude Bell*, collected and edited by Elsa Richmond, pp. 217–18.

38. The question of chastity, both of mind and body, is of the greatest interest and complexity. The Victorian, Edwardian and much of the Fifth Georgian conception of chastity was based, to go no further back, upon the words of St Paul. To understand their meaning we should have to understand his psychology and environment – no light task in view of his frequent obscurity and the lack of biographical material. From internal evidence it seems clear that he was a poet and a prophet, but lacked logical power, and was without that psychological training which forces even the least poetic or prophetic nowadays to subject their personal emotions to scrutiny. Thus his famous pronouncement on the matter of veils, upon which the theory of women's chastity seems to be based, is susceptible to criticism from several angles. In the Letter to the Corinthians his argument that a woman must be veiled when she prays or prophesies is based upon the assumption that to be unveiled 'is one and the same thing as if she were shaven'. That assumption granted, we must ask next, What shame is there in being shaven? Instead of replying, St Paul proceeds to assert, 'For a man indeed ought not to have his head veiled, forasmuch as he is the image and glory of God': from which it appears that it is not being shaven in itself that is wrong; but to be a woman and

to be shaven. It is wrong, it appears, for the woman because 'the woman is the glory of the man.' If St Paul had said openly that he liked the look of women's long hair many of us would have agreed with him, and thought the better of him for saying so. But other reasons appeared to him preferable, as appears from his next remark: 'For the man is not of the woman; but the woman of the man; for neither was the man created for the woman; but the woman for the man: for this cause ought the woman to have a sign of authority on her head, because of the angels.' What view the angels took of long hair we have no means of knowing; and St Paul himself seems to have been doubtful of their support or he would not think it necessary to drag in the familiar accomplice nature. 'Doth not even nature itself teach you, that, if a man have long hair, it is a dishonour to him? But if a woman have long hair, it is a glory to her: for her hair is given her for a covering. But if any man seemeth to be contentious, we have no such custom, neither the churches of God.' The argument from nature may seem to us suscep- tible of amendment; nature, when allied with financial advantage, is seldom of divine origin; but if the basis of the argument is shifty, the conclusion is firm. 'Let the women keep silence in the churches: for it is not permitted unto them to speak; but let them be in subjection, as also saith the law.' Having thus invoked the familiar but always suspect trinity of accomplices, Angels, nature and law, to support his personal opinion, St Paul reaches the conclusion which has been looming unmistakably ahead of us: 'And if they would learn anything, let them ask their own husbands at home: for it is shameful for a woman to speak in the church.' The nature of that 'shame', which is closely con- nected with chastity has, as the letter proceeds, been consider- ably alloyed. For it is obviously compounded of certain sexual and personal prejudices. St Paul, it is obvious, was not only a bachelor (for his relations with Lydia see Renan, *Saint Paul*, p. 149. 'Est-il cependant absolument impossible que Paul ait contracté avec cette soeur une union plus intime? On ne saurait l'affirmer');ᶜ and, like many bachelors, suspicious of the other sex; but a poet and like many poets preferred to prophesy himself rather than to listen to the prophecies of others. Also he was of the virile or dominant type, so familiar at present in Germany, for whose gratification a subject race or sex is essential. Chastity then as defined by St Paul is seen to be a complex conception, based upon the love of long hair; the love of subjection; the love of an audience; the love of laying down the law, and, subconsciously, upon a very strong and natural desire that the woman's mind and body shall be reserved for the use of one man and one only. Such a conception when supported by the Angels, nature, law, custom and the Church, and enforced by a sex with a strong personal interest to enforce it, and the economic means, was of undoubted power. The grip of its white if skeleton fingers can be found upon whatever page of history we open from St Paul to Gertrude Bell. Chastity was invoked to prevent her from studying medicine; from painting from the nude; from reading Shakespeare; from playing in orchestras; from walking down Bond Street alone. In 1848 it was 'an unpardonable solecism' for the daughters of a gardener to drive down Regent Street in a hansom cab (*Paxton and the Bachelor Duke*, by Violet Markham, p. 288); that solecism became a crime, of what magnitude theologians must decide, if the flaps were left open. In the beginning of the present century the daughter of an ironmaster (for let us not flout distinctions said to-day to be of prime importance), Sir Hugh Bell, had 'reached the age of 27 and married without ever having walked alone down Piccadilly . . . Gertrude, of course, would never have dreamt of doing that . . .' The West End was the contaminated area. 'It was one's own class that was taboo . . .' (*The Earlier Letters of Gertrude Bell*, collected and edited by Elsa Richmond, pp. 217–18.) But the complexities and inconsistencies of chastity were such that the same girl who had to be veiled, i.e. accompanied by a male or a maid, in Piccadilly, could visit Whitechapel, or Seven Dials, then haunts of vice and disease, alone and with her parents' approval. This anomaly did not altogether escape comment. Thus Charles Kingsley as a boy exclaimed: '. . . and the girls have their heads crammed full of schools, and district visiting, and baby linen, and penny clubs. Confound!!! and going about among the most abominable scenes of filth and wretchedness, and indecency to visit the poor and read the Bible to them. My own mother says that the places they go into are fit for no girl to see, and that they should not know such things exist.' (*Charles Kingsley*, by Margaret Farrand Thorp, p. 12.) Mrs Kingsley, however, was exceptional. Most of the daughters of educated men saw such 'abominable scenes', and knew that such things existed. That they concealed their knowledge, is probable; what effect that concealment had psychologically it is impossible here to inquire. But that chastity, whether real or imposed, was an immense power, whether good or bad, it is impossible to doubt. Even to-day it is probable that a woman has to fight a psychological battle of some severity with the ghost of St Paul, before she can have intercourse with a man other than her husband. Not only was the social stigma strongly exerted on behalf of chastity, but the Bastardy Act did its utmost to impose chastity by financial pressure. Until women had the vote in 1918, 'the Bastardy Act of 1872 fixed the sum of 5s. a week as the maximum which a father, whatever his wealth, could be made to pay towards the maintenance of his child.' (*Josephine Butler*, by M. G. Fawcett and E. M. Turner, note, p. 101.) Now that St Paul and many of his apostles have been unveiled themselves by modern science chastity has undergone considerable revision. Yet there is said to be a reaction in favour of some degree of chastity for both sexes. This is partly due to economic causes; the protection of chastity by maids is an expensive item in the bourgeois budget. The psychological argument in favour of chastity is

well expressed by Mr Upton Sinclair: 'Nowadays we hear a
great deal about mental troubles caused by sex repression; it
is the mood of the moment. We do not hear anything about
the complexes which may be caused by sex indulgence. But
my observation has been that those who permit themselves
to follow every sexual impulse are quite as miserable as
those who repress every sexual impulse. I remember a class-
mate in College; I said to him: "Did it ever occur to you to
stop and look at your own mind? Everything that comes to
you is turned into sex." He looked surprised, and I saw that
it was a new idea to him; he thought it over, and said: "I
guess you are right."' (*Candid Reminiscences*, by Upton Sinclair, p. 63.) Further illustration is supplied by the following
anecdote: 'In the splendid library of Columbia University
were treasures of beauty, costly volumes of engravings, and
in my usual greedy fashion I went at these, intending to
learn all there was to know about Renaissance art in a week
or two. But I found myself overwhelmed by this mass of
nakedness; my senses reeled, and I had to quit.' (Op. cit.
pp. 62–3.)

39. The translation here used is by Sir Richard Jebb (*Sophocles,
the Plays and Fragments*, with critical notes, commentary and
translation in English prose.) It is impossible to judge any
book from a translation, yet even when thus read *The
Antigone* is clearly one of the great masterpieces of dramatic
literature. Nevertheless, it could undoubtedly be made, if
necessary, into anti-Fascist propaganda. Antigone herself
could be transformed either into Mrs Pankhurst, who broke
a window and was imprisoned in Holloway; or into Frau
Pommer, the wife of a Prussian mines official at Essen, who
said: '"The thorn of hatred has been driven deep enough
into the people by the religious conflicts, and it is high time
that the men of to-day disappeared." . . . She has been
arrested and is to be tried on a charge of insulting and
slandering the State and the Nazi movement.' (*The Times*,
August 12th, 1935.) Antigone's crime was of much the same

nature and was punished in much the same way. Her words, 'See what I suffer, and from whom, because I feared to cast away the fear of heaven! . . . And what law of heaven have I transgressed? Why, hapless one, should I look to the gods any more – what ally should I invoke – when by piety I have earned the name of impious?' could be spoken either by Mrs Pankhurst, or by Frau Pommer; and are certainly topical. Creon, again, who 'thrust the children of the sunlight to the shades, and ruthlessly lodged a living soul in the grave'; who held that 'disobedience is the worst of evils', and that 'whomsoever the city may appoint, that man must be obeyed, in little things and great, in just things and unjust' is typical of certain politicians in the past, and of Herr Hitler and Signor Mussolini in the present. But though it is easy to squeeze these characters into up-to-date dress, it is impossible to keep them there. They suggest too much; when the curtain falls we sympathize, it may be noted, even with Creon himself. This result, to the propagandist undesirable, would seem to be due to the fact that Sophocles (even in a translation) uses freely all the faculties that can be possessed by a writer; and suggests, therefore, that if we use art to propagate political opinions, we must force the artist to clip and cabin his gift to do us a cheap and passing service. Literature will suffer the same mutilation that the mule has suffered; and there will be no more horses.

40. The five words of Antigone are: οὔτοι συνέχθειν, ἀλλὰ συνφιλεῖν ἔφυν. 'Tis not my nature to join in hating, but in loving. (*Antigone*, line 523 (Jebb).) To which Creon replied: 'Pass, then, to the world of the dead, and, if thou must needs love, love them. While I live, no woman shall rule me.'

41. Even at a time of great political stress like the present it is remarkable how much criticism is still bestowed upon women. The announcement, 'A shrewd, witty and provocative study of modern woman,' appears on an average three

times yearly in publishers' lists. The author, often a doctor of letters is invariably of the male sex; and 'to mere man,' as the blurb puts it (see *Times Lit. Sup.*, March 12th, 1938), 'this book will be an eye-opener.'

THREE

1. It is to be hoped that some methodical person has made a collection of the various manifestos and questionnaires issued broadcast during the years 1936–7. Private people of no political training were invited to sign appeals asking their own and foreign governments to change their policy; artists were asked to fill up forms stating the proper relations of the artist to the State, to religion, to morality; pledges were required that the writer should use English grammatically and avoid vulgar expressions; and dreamers were invited to analyse their dreams. By way of inducement it was generally proposed to publish the results in the daily or weekly Press. What effect this inquisition has had upon governments it is for the politician to say. Upon literature, since the output of books is unstaunched, and grammar would seem to be neither better nor worse, the effect is problematical. But the inquisition is of great psychological and social interest. Presumably it originated in the state of mind suggested by Dean Inge (The Rickman Godlee Lecture, reported in *The Times*, November 23rd, 1937), 'whether in our own interests we were moving in the right direction. If we went on as we were doing now, would the man of the future be superior to us or not? . . . Thoughtful people were beginning to realize that before congratulating ourselves on moving fast we ought to have some idea where we were moving to': a general self-dissatisfaction and desire 'to live differently'. It also points, indirectly, to the death of the Siren, that much ridiculed and often upper-class lady who by keeping open house for the aristocracy, plutocracy, intelligentsia, ignorantsia, etc, tried to provide all classes with a talking-ground or

scratching-post where they could rub up minds, manners and morals more privately, and perhaps as usefully. The part that the Siren played in promoting culture and intellectual liberty in the eighteenth century is held by historians to be of some importance. Even in our own day she had her uses. Witness W. B. Yeats – 'How often I have wished that he (Synge) might live long enough to enjoy that communion with idle, charming cultivated women which Balzac in one of his dedications calls "the chief consolation of genius"!' (*Dramatis Personae*, W. B. Yeats, p. 127.) Lady St Helier who, as Lady Jeune, preserved the eighteenth-century tradition, informs us, however, that 'Plovers' eggs at 2s. 6d. apiece, forced strawberries, early asparagus, *petits poussins* . . . are now considered almost a necessity by anyone aspiring to give a good dinner' (1909); and her remark that the reception day was 'very fatiguing . . . how exhausted I felt when half-past seven came, and how gladly at eight o'clock I sat down to a peaceful *tête-à-tête* dinner with my husband!' (*Memories of Fifty Years*, by Lady St Helier, pp. 3, 5, 182) may explain why such houses are shut, why such hostesses are dead, and why therefore the intelligentsia, the ignorantsia, the aristocracy, the bureaucracy, the bourgeoisie, etc., are driven (unless somebody will revive that society on an economic basis) to do their talking in public. But in view of the multitude of manifestos and questionnaires now in circulation it would be foolish to suggest another into the minds and motives of the Inquisitors.

2. 'He did begin however on May 13th (1844) to lecture weekly at Queen's College[a] which Maurice and other professors at King's had established a year before, primarily for the examination and training of governesses. Kingsley was ready to share in this unpopular task because he believed in the higher education of women.' (*Charles Kingsley*, by Margaret Farrand Thorp, p. 65.)

3. The French, as the above quotation shows, are as active as the English in issuing manifestos. That the French, who

refuse to allow the women of France to vote, and still inflict upon them laws whose almost medieval severity can be studied in *The Position of Women in Contemporary France*, by Frances Clark, should appeal to English women to help them to protect liberty and culture must cause surprise.

4. Strict accuracy, here slightly in conflict with rhythm and euphony, requires the word 'port'. A photograph in the daily Press[b] of 'Dons in a Senior Common Room after dinner' (1937) shows 'a railed trolley in which the port decanter travels across a gap between diners at the fireplace, and thus continues its round without passing against the sun.' Another picture shows the 'sconce' cup in use. 'This old Oxford custom ordains that mention of certain subjects in Hall shall be punished by the offender drinking three pints of beer at one draught . . .' Such examples are by themselves enough to prove how impossible it is for a woman's pen to describe life at a man's college without committing some unpardonable solecism. But the gentlemen whose customs are often, it is to be feared, travestied, will extend their indulgence when they reflect that the female novelist, however reverent in intention, works under grave physical drawbacks. Should she wish, for example, to describe a Feast at Trinity, Cambridge, she has to 'listen through the peephole in the room of Mrs Butler (the Master's wife) to the speeches taking place at the Feast which was held in Trinity College'. Miss Haldane's observation was made in 1907, when she reflected that 'The whole surroundings seemed mediaeval.' (*From One Century to Another*, by E. Haldane, p. 235.)

5. According to Whitaker there is a Royal Society of Literature and also the British Academy, both presumably, since they have offices and officers, official bodies, but what their powers are it is impossible to say, since if Whitaker had not vouched for their existence it would scarcely have been suspected.

6. Women were apparently excluded from the British Museum

Reading-Room in the eighteenth century. Thus: '*Miss Chud-leigh* solicits permission to be received into the reading-room. The only female student who as yet has honoured us was *Mrs Macaulay*; and your Lordship may recollect what an untoward event offended her delicacy.' (Daniel Wray to Lord Harwicke, October 22nd, 1768. Nichols, *Literary Anec-dotes of the Eighteenth Century*, Vol. I, p. 137.) The editor adds in a footnote: 'This alludes to the indelicacy of a gentleman there, in *Mrs Macaulay's* presence; of which the particulars will not bear to be repeated.'

7. *The Autobiography and Letters of Mrs M. O. W. Oliphant*, arranged and edited by Mrs Harry Coghill. Mrs Oliphant (1825–97) 'lived in perpetual embarrassment owing to her undertaking education and maintenance of her widowed brother's children in addition to her own two sons . . .' (*Dictionary of National Biography*.)

8. Macaulay's *History of England*, Vol. III, p. 278 (standard edi-tion).

9. Mr Littlewood, until recently dramatic critic of the *Morning Post*, described the condition of Journalism at Present at a dinner given in his honour, December 6th, 1937. Mr Little-wood said: 'that he had in season and out of season fought for more space for the theatre in the columns of the London daily papers. It was Fleet Street where, between eleven and half-past twelve, not to mention before and after, thousands of beautiful words and thoughts were systematically mas-sacred. It had been his lot for at least two out of his four decades to return to that shambles every night with the sure and certain prospect of being told that the paper was already full with important news, and that there was no room for any sanguinary stuff about the theatre. It had been his luck to wake up the next morning to find himself answerable for the mangled remains of what was once a good notice . . . It was not the fault of the men in the office. Some of them put the blue pencil through with tears in their eyes. The real culprit was that huge public who knew nothing about the

theatre and could not be expected to care.' *The Times*, December 6th, 1937.

Mr Douglas Jerrold describes the treatment of politics in the Press. 'In those few brief years [between 1928–33] truth had fled from Fleet Street. You could never tell all the truth all the time. You never will be able to do so. But you used at least to be able to tell the truth about other countries. By 1933, you did it at your peril. In 1928 there was no direct political pressure from advertisers. To-day it is not only direct but effective.'

Literary criticism would seem to be in much the same case and for the same reason: 'There are no critics in whom the public have any more confidence. They trust, if at all, to the different Book Societies, and the selections of individual newspapers, and on the whole they are wise ... The Book Society are frankly book sellers, and the great national newspapers cannot afford to puzzle their readers. They must all choose books which have, at the prevailing level of public taste, a potentially large sale.' (*Georgian Adventure*, by Douglas Jerrold, pp. 282, 283, 298.)

10. While it is obvious that under the conditions of journalism at present the criticism of literature must be unsatisfactory, it is also obvious that no change can be made, without changing the economic structure of society and the psychological structure of the artist. Economically, it is necessary that the reviewer should herald the publication of a new book with his town-crier's shout 'O yez, O yez, O yez, such and such a book has been published; its subject is this, that or the other.' Psychologically, vanity and the desire for 'recognition' are still so strong among artists that to starve them of advertisement and to deny them frequent if contrasted shocks of praise and blame would be as rash as the introduction of rabbits into Australia: the balance of nature would be upset and the consequences might well be disastrous. The suggestion in the text is not to abolish public criticism; but to supplement it by a new service based on the

example of the medical profession. A panel of critics recruited from reviewers (many of whom are potential critics of genuine taste and learning) would practise like doctors and in strictest privacy. Publicity removed, it follows that most of the distractions and corruptions which inevitably make contemporary criticism worthless to the writer would be abolished; all inducement to praise or blame for personal reasons would be destroyed; neither sales nor vanity would be affected; the author could attend to criticism without considering the effect upon public or friends; the critic could criticize without considering the editor's blue pencil or the public taste. Since criticism is much desired by the living, as the constant demand for it proves, and since fresh books are as essential for the critic's mind as fresh meat for his body, each would gain; literature even might benefit. The advantages of the present system of public criticism are mainly economic; the evil effects psychologically are shown by the two famous *Quarterly* reviews of Keats and Tennyson. Keats was deeply wounded; and 'the effect . . . upon Tennyson himself was penetrating and prolonged. His first act was at once to withdraw from the press *The Lover's Tale* . . . We find him thinking of leaving England altogether, of living abroad.' (*Tennyson*, by Harold Nicolson, p. 118.) The effect of Mr Churton Collins upon Sir Edmund Gosse was much the same: 'His self-confidence was undermined, his personality reduced . . . was not everyone watching his struggles and regarding him as doomed? . . . His own account of his sensations was that he went about feeling that he had been flayed alive.' (*The Life and Letters of Sir Edmund Gosse*, by Evan Charteris, p. 196.)

11. 'A ring-the-bell-and-run-away-man.' This word has been coined in order to define those who make use of words with the desire to hurt but at the same time to escape detection. In a transitional age when many qualities are changing their value, new words to express new values are much to be desired. Vanity, for example, which would seem to lead to

severe complications of cruelty and tyranny, judging from evidence supplied abroad, is still masked by a name with trivial associations. A supplement to the *Oxford English Dictionary* is indicated.

12. *Memoir of Anne J. Clough*, by B. A. Clough, pp. 38, 67.
"The Sparrow's Nest," by William Wordsworth.

13. In the nineteenth century much valuable work was done for the working class by educated men's daughters in the only way that was then open to them. But now that some of them at least have received an expensive education, it is arguable that they can work much more effectively by remaining in their own class and using the methods of that class to improve a class which stands much in need of improvement. If on the other hand the educated (as so often happens) renounce the very qualities which education should have bought – reason, tolerance, knowledge – and play at belonging to the working class and adopting its cause, they merely expose that cause to the ridicule of the educated class, and do nothing to improve their own. But the number of books written by the educated about the working class would seem to show that the glamour of the working class and the emotional relief afforded by adopting its cause, are to-day as irresistible to the middle class as the glamour of the aristocracy was twenty years ago (see *A La Recherche du Temps Perdu*). Meanwhile it would be interesting to know what the true-born working man or woman thinks of the playboys and playgirls of the educated class who adopt the working-class cause without sacrificing middle-class capital, or sharing working-class experience. 'The average housewife,' according to Mrs Murphy, Home Service Director of the British Commercial Gas Association 'washed an acre of dirty dishes, a mile of glass and three miles of clothes and scrubbed five miles of floor yearly.' (*Daily Telegraph*, September 29th, 1937.) For a more detailed account of working-class life, see *Life as We Have Known It*, by Co-operative working women, edited by Margaret Llewelyn Davies. The *Life of*

Joseph Wright also gives a remarkable account of working class life at first hand and not through pro-proletarian spectacles.

14. 'It was stated yesterday at the War Office that the Army Council have no intention of opening recruiting for any women's corps.' (*The Times*, October 22nd, 1937.) This marks a prime distinction between the sexes. Pacifism is enforced upon women. Men are still allowed liberty of choice.

15. The following quotation shows, however, that if sanctioned the fighting instinct easily develops. 'The eyes deeply sunk into the sockets, the features acute, the amazon keeps herself very straight on the stirrups at the head of her squadron ... Five English parlementaries look at this woman with the respectful and a bit restless admiration one feels for a "fauve" of an unknown species ...

—Come nearer Amalia—orders the commandant. She pushes her horse towards us and salutes her chief with the sword.

—Sergeant Amalia Bonilla—continues the chief of the squadron—how old are you?—Thirty-six—Where were you born?—In Granada—Why have you joined the army—My two daughters were militiawomen. The younger has been killed in the Alto de Leon. I thought I had to supersede her and to avenge her.—And how many enemies have you killed to avenge her?—You know it, commandant, five. The sixth is not sure.—No, but you have taken his horse. The amazon Amalia rides in fact a magnificent dapple-grey horse, with glossy hair, which flatters like a parade horse ... This woman who has killed five men—but who feels not sure about the sixth—was for the envoys of the House of Commons an excellent introducer to the Spanish war.' (*The Martyrdom of Madrid*, Inedited Witnesses, by Louis Delaprée, pp. 34, 5, 6. Madrid, 1937.)

16. By way of proof, an attempt may be made to elucidate the reasons given by various Cabinet Ministers in various Parliaments from about 1870 to 1918 for opposing the Suffrage

Bill. An able effort has been made by Mrs Oliver Strachey (see chapter 'The Deceitfulness of Politics' in her 'The Cause').

17. 'We have had women's civil and political status before the League only since 1935.' From reports sent in as to the position of the woman as wife, mother and home maker, 'the sorry fact was discovered that her economic position in many countries (including Great Britain) was unstable. She is entitled neither to salary nor wages and has definite duties to perform. In England, though she may have devoted her whole life to husband and children, her husband, no matter how wealthy, can leave her destitute at his death and she has no legal redress. We must alter this – by legislation . . .' (Linda P. Littlejohn, reported in the Listener, November 10th, 1937.)

18. This particular definition of woman's task comes not from an Italian but from a German source. There are so many versions and all are so much alike that it seems unnecessary to verify each separately. But it is curious to find how easy it is to cap them from English sources. Mr Gerhardi for example writes: 'Never yet have I committed the error of looking on women writers as serious fellow artists. I enjoy them rather as spiritual helpers who, endowed with a sensitive capacity for appreciation, may help the few of us afflicted with genius to bear our cross with good grace. Their true role, therefore, is rather to hold out the sponge to us, cool our brow, while we bleed. If their sympathetic understanding may indeed be put to a more romantic use, how we cherish them for it!' (Memoirs of a Polyglot, by William Gerhardi, pp. 320, 321.) This conception of woman's role tallies almost exactly with that quoted above.

19. To speak accurately, 'a large silver plaque in the form of the Reich eagle . . . was created by President Hindenburg for scientists and other distinguished civilians . . . It may not be worn. It is usually placed on the writing-desk of the recipient.' (Daily paper, April 21st, 1936.)

20. 'It is a common thing to see the business girl contenting

herself with a bun or a sandwich for her midday meal; and though there are theories that this is from choice . . . the truth is that they often cannot afford to eat properly.' (*Careers and Openings for Women*, by Ray Strachey, p. 74.) Compare also Miss E. Turner: '. . . many offices had been wondering why they were unable to get through their work as smoothly as formerly. It had been found that junior typists were fagged out in the afternoons because they could afford only an apple and a sandwich for lunch. Employers should meet the increased cost of living by increased salaries.' (*The Times*, March 28th, 1938.)

21. The Mayoress of Woolwich (Mrs Kathleen Rance) speaking at a bazaar, reported in *Evening Standard*, December 20th, 1937.

22. Miss E. R. Clarke, reported in *The Times*, September 24th, 1937.

23. Reported in *Daily Herald*, August 15th, 1936.

24. Canon F. R. Barry, speaking at conference arranged by Anglican Group at Oxford, reported in *The Times*, January 10th, 1933.

25. *The Ministry of Women. Report of the Archbishops' Commission.* VII. Secondary Schools and Universities, p. 65.

26. 'Miss D. Carruthers, Head Mistress of the Green School, Isleworth, said there was a "very grave dissatisfaction" among older schoolgirls at the way in which organized religion was carried on. "The Churches seem somehow to be failing to supply the spiritual needs of young people," she said. "It is a fault that seems common to all churches."' (*Sunday Times*, November 21st, 1937.)

27. *Life of Charles Gore*, by G. L. Prestige, D.D., p. 353.

28. *The Ministry of Women. Report of the Archbishops' Commission, passim.*

29. Whether or not the gift of prophecy and the gift of poetry were originally the same, a distinction has been made between those gifts and professions for many centuries. But the fact that the Song of Songs, the work of a poet, is

included among the sacred books, and that propagandist poems and novels, the works of prophets, are included among the secular, points to some confusion. Lovers of English literature can scarcely be too thankful that Shakespeare lived too late to be canonized by the Church. Had the plays been ranked among the sacred books they must have received the same treatment as the Old and the New Testaments; we should have had them doled out on Sundays from the mouths of priests in snatches; now a soliloquy from *Hamlet*; now a corrupt passage from the pen of some drowsy reporter; now a bawdy song; now half a page from *Antony and Cleopatra*, as the Old and New Testaments have been sliced up and interspersed with hymns in the Church of England service; and Shakespeare would have been as unreadable as the Bible. Yet those who have not been forced from childhood to hear it thus dismembered weekly assert that the Bible is a work of the greatest interest, much beauty, and deep meaning.

30. *The Ministry of Women*, Appendix I. 'Certain Psychological and Physiological Considerations,' by Professor Grensted, D.D., pp. 79–87.

31. 'At present a married priest is able to fulfil the requirements of the ordination service, "to forsake and set aside all worldly cares and studies," largely because his wife can undertake the care of the household and the family . . .' (*The Ministry of Women*, p. 32.)

The Commissioners are here stating and approving a principle which is frequently stated and approved by the dictators. Herr Hitler and Signor Mussolini have both often in very similar words expressed the opinion that 'There are two worlds in the life of the nation, the world of men and the world of women'; and proceeded to much the same definition of the duties. The effect which this division has had upon the woman; the petty and personal nature of her interests; her absorption in the practical; her apparent incapacity for the poetical and adventurous – all this has been made the staple of so many novels, the target for so much satire, has confirmed so many theorists in the theory that by the law of nature the woman is less spiritual than the man, that nothing more need be said to prove that she has carried out, willingly or unwillingly, her share of the contract. But very little attention has yet been paid to the intellectual and spiritual effect of this division of duties upon those who are enabled by it 'to forsake all worldly cares and studies'. Yet there can be no doubt that we owe to this segregation the immense elaboration of modern instruments and methods of war; the astonishing complexities of theology; the vast deposit of notes at the bottom of Greek, Latin and even English texts; the innumerable carvings, chasings and unnecessary ornamentations of our common furniture and crockery; the myriad distinctions of *Debrett* and *Burke*; and all those meaningless but highly ingenious turnings and twistings into which the intellect ties itself when rid of 'the cares of the household and the family'. The emphasis which both priests and dictators place upon the necessity for two worlds is enough to prove that it is essential to their domination.

32. Evidence of the complex nature of satisfaction of dominance is provided by the following quotation: 'My husband insists that I call him "Sir",' said a woman at the Bristol Police Court yesterday, when she applied for a maintenance order. 'To keep the peace I have complied with his request,' she added. 'I also have to clean his boots, fetch his razor when he shaves, and speak up promptly when he asks me questions.' In the same issue of the same paper Sir E. F. Fletcher is reported to have 'urged the House of Commons to stand up to dictators.' (*Daily Herald*, August 1st, 1936.) This would seem to show that the common consciousness which includes husband, wife and House of Commons is feeling at one and the same moment the desire to dominate, the need to comply in order to keep the peace, and the necessity of dominating the desire for dominance – a psychological conflict which serves to explain much that appears inconsistent

and turbulent in contemporary opinion. The pleasure of dominance is of course further complicated by the fact that it is still, in the educated class, closely allied with the pleasures of wealth, social and professional prestige. Its distinction from the comparatively simple pleasures – e.g. the pleasure of a country walk – is proved by the fear of ridicule which great psychologists, like Sophocles, detect in the dominator; who is also peculiarly susceptible according to the same authority either to ridicule or defiance on the part of the female sex. An essential element in this pleasure therefore would seem to be derived not from the feeling itself but from the reflection of other people's feelings, and it would follow that it can be influenced by a change in those feelings. Laughter as an antidote to dominance is perhaps indicated.

33. *The Life of Charlotte Brontë*, by Mrs Gaskell.

34. *The Life of Sophia Jex-Blake*, by Margaret Todd, pp. 67–9, 70–1, 72.

35. External observation would suggest that a man still feels it a peculiar insult to be taunted with cowardice by a woman in much the same way that a woman feels it a peculiar insult to be taunted with unchastity by a man. The following quotation supports this view. Mr Bernard Shaw writes: 'I am not forgetting the gratification that war gives to the instinct of pugnacity and admiration of courage that are so strong in women ... In England on the outbreak of war civilized young women rush about handing white feathers to all young men who are not in uniform. This,' he continues, 'like other survivals from savagery is quite natural,' and he points out that 'in old days a woman's life and that of her children depended on the courage and killing capacity of her mate.' Since vast numbers of young men did their work all through the war in offices without any such adornment, and the number of 'civilized young women' who stuck feathers in coats must have been infinitesimal compared with those who did nothing of the kind, Mr Shaw's exaggeration is

sufficient proof of the immense psychological impression that fifty or sixty feathers (no actual statistics are available) can still make. This would seem to show that the male still preserves an abnormal susceptibility to such taunts; therefore that courage and pugnacity are still among the prime attributes of manliness; therefore that he still wishes to be admired for possessing them; therefore that any derision of such qualities would have a proportionate effect. That 'the manhood emotion' is also connected with economic independence seems probable. 'We have never known a man who was not, openly or secretly, proud of being able to support women; whether they were his sisters or his mistresses. We have never known a woman who did not regard the change from economic independence on an employer to economic dependence on a man, as an honourable promotion. What is the good of men and women lying to each other about these things? It is not we that have made them' – (*A. H. Orage*, by Philip Mairet, vii) – an interesting statement, attributed by G. K. Chesterton to A. H. Orage.

36. Until the beginning of the 'eighties, according to Miss Haldane, the sister of R. B. Haldane, no lady could work. 'I should, of course, have liked to study for a profession, but that was an impossible idea unless one were in the sad position of "having to work for one's bread" and that would have been a terrible state of affairs. Even a brother wrote of the melancholy fact after he had been to see Mrs Langtry act. "She was a lady and acted like a lady, but what a sad thing it was that she should have to do so!"' (*From One Century to Another*, by Elizabeth Haldane, pp. 73–4). Harriet Martineau earlier in the century was delighted when her family lost its money, for thus she lost her 'gentility' and was allowed to work.

37. *Life of Sophia Jex-Blake*, by Margaret Todd, pp. 69, 70.

38. For an account of Mr Leigh Smith, see *The Life of Emily Davies*, by Barbara Stephen. Barbara Leigh Smith became Madame Bodichon.

39. How nominal that opening was is shown by the following account of the actual conditions under which women worked in the R.A. Schools about 1900. 'Why the female of the species should never be given the same advantages as the male it is difficult to understand. At the R.A. Schools we women had to compete against men for all the prizes and medals that were given each year, and we were only allowed half the amount of tuition and less than half their opportunities for study . . . No nude model was allowed to be posed in the women's painting room at the R.A. Schools . . . The male students not only worked from nude models, both male and female, during the day, but they were given an evening class as well, at which they could make studies from the figure, the visiting R.A. instructing.' This seemed to the women students 'very unfair indeed'; Miss Collyer had the courage and the social standing necessary to beard first Mr Frank Dicksee, who argued that since girls marry, money spent on their teaching is money wasted; next Lord Leighton; and at length the thin edge of the wedge, that is the undraped figure, was allowed. But 'the advantages of the night class we never did succeed in obtaining . . .' The women students therefore clubbed together and hired a photographer's studio in Baker Street. 'The money that we, as the committee, had to find, reduced our meals to near starvation diet.' (*Life of an Artist*, by Margaret Collyer, pp. 79–81, 82.) The same rule was in force at the Nottingham Art School in the twentieth century. 'Women were not allowed to draw from the nude. If the men worked from the living figure I had to go into the Antique Room . . . the hatred of those plaster figures stays with me till this day. I never got any benefit out of their study.' (*Oil Paint and Grease Paint*, by Dame Laura Knight, p. 47.) But the profession of art is not the only profession that is thus nominally open. The profession of medicine is 'open,' but '. . . nearly all the Schools attached to London Hospitals are barred to women students, whose training in London is mainly carried

on at the London School of Medicine.' (*Memorandum on the Position of English Women in Relation to that of English Men*, by Philippa Strachey (1935), p. 26.) 'Some of the girl "medicals" at Cambridge University have formed themselves into a group to ventilate the grievance.' (*Evening News*, March 25th, 1937.) In 1922 women students were admitted to the Royal Veterinary College, Camden Town. '. . . since then the profession has attracted so many women that the number has recently been restricted to 50.' (*Daily Telegraph*, October 1st, 1937.)

40. and 41. *The Life of Mary Kingsley*,^c by Stephen Gwyn, pp. 18, 26. In a fragment of a letter Mary Kingsley writes: 'I am useful occasionally, but that is all – very useful a few months ago when on calling on a friend she asked me to go up to her bedroom and see her new hat – a suggestion that staggered me, I knowing her opinion of mine in such matters.' 'The letter,' says Mr Gwyn, 'did not complete this adventure of an unauthorised *fiancé*, but I am sure she got him off the roof and enjoyed the experience riotously.'

42. According to Antigone there are two kinds of law, the written and the unwritten, and Mrs Drummond^d maintains that it may sometimes be necessary to improve the written law by breaking it. But the many and varied activities of the educated man's daughter in the nineteenth century were clearly not simply or even mainly directed towards breaking the laws. They were, on the contrary, endeavours of an experimental kind to discover what are the unwritten laws; that is the private laws that should regulate certain instincts, passions, mental and physical desires. That such laws exist, and are observed by civilized people, is fairly generally allowed; but it is beginning to be agreed that they were not laid down by 'God', who is now very generally held to be a conception, of patriarchal origin, valid only for certain races, at certain stages and times; nor by nature, who is now known to vary greatly in her commands and to be largely under control;^e but have to be discovered afresh by successive

generations, largely by their own efforts of reason and imagination. Since, however, reason and imagination are to some extent the product of our bodies, and there are two kinds of body, male and female, and since these two bodies have been proved within the past few years to differ fundamentally, it is clear that the laws that they perceive and respect must be differently interpreted. Thus Professor Julian Huxley says: '. . . from the moment of fertilization onwards, man and woman differ in every cell of their body in regard to the number of their chromosomes – those bodies which, for all the world's unfamiliarity, have been shown by the last decade's work to be the bearers of heredity, the determiners of our characters and qualities.' In spite of the fact, therefore, that 'the superstructure of intellectual and practical life is potentially the same in both sexes,' and that 'The recent Board of Education Report of the Committee on the Differentiation of the Curriculum for Boys and Girls in Secondary Schools (London, 1923), has established that the intellectual differences between the sexes are very much slighter than popular belief allows,' (*Essays in Popular Science*, by Julian Huxley, pp. 62–3), it is clear that the sexes now differ and will always differ. If it were possible not only for each sex to ascertain what laws hold good in its own case, and to respect each other's laws; but also to share the results of those discoveries, it might be possible for each sex to develop fully and improve in quality without surrendering its special characteristics. The old conception that one sex must 'dominate' another would then become not only obsolete, but so odious that if it were necessary for practical purposes that a dominant power should decide certain matters, the repulsive task of coercion and dominion would be relegated to an inferior and secret society, much as the flogging and execution of criminals is now carried out by masked beings in profound obscurity. But this is to anticipate.*f*

43. From *The Times* obituary notice of H. W. Greene, fellow of

Magdalen College, Oxford, familiarly called 'Grugger', February 6th, 1933.

44. 'In 1747 the quarterly court (of the Middlesex Hospital) decided to set apart some of the beds for lying-in cases under rules which precluded any woman from acting as midwife. The exclusion of women has remained the traditional attitude. In 1861 Miss Garrett, afterwards Dr Garrett Anderson, obtained permission to attend classes ... and was permitted to visit the wards with the resident officers, but the students protested and the medical officers gave way. The Board declined an offer from her to endow a scholarship for women students.' *The Times*, May 17th, 1935.

45. 'There is, in the modern world, a great body of well-attested knowledge ... but as soon as any strong passion intervenes to warp the expert's judgement he becomes unreliable, whatever scientific equipment he may possess.' (*The Scientific Outlook*, by Bertrand Russell, p. 17.)

46. One of the record-breakers, however, gave a reason for record-breaking which must compel respect: 'Then, too, there was my belief that now and then women should do for themselves what men have already done – and occasionally what men have not done – thereby establishing themselves as persons, and perhaps encouraging other women towards greater independence of thought and action ... When they fail, their failure must be a challenge to others.' (*The Last Flight*, by Amelia Earhart, pp. 21, 65.)

47. 'In point of fact this process [childbirth] actually disables women only for a very small fraction in most of their lives – even a woman who has six children is only necessarily laid up for twelve months out of her whole lifetime.' (*Careers and Openings for Women*, by Ray Strachey, pp. 47–8.) At present, however, she is necessarily occupied for much longer. The bold suggestion has been made that the occupation is not exclusively maternal, but could be shared by both parents to the common good.

48. The nature of manhood and the nature of womanhood are

frequently defined both by Italian and German dictators. Both repeatedly insist that it is the nature of man and indeed the essence of manhood to fight. Hitler, for example, draws a distinction between 'a nation of pacifists and a nation of men.' Both repeatedly insist that it is the nature of womanhood to heal the wounds of the fighter. Nevertheless a very strong movement is on foot towards emancipating man from the old 'natural and eternal law' that man is essentially a fighter; witness the growth of pacifism among the male sex to-day. Compare further Lord Knebworth's statement 'that if permanent peace were ever achieved, and armies and navies ceased to exist, there would be no outlet for the manly qualities which fighting developed,' with the following statement by another young man of the same social caste a few months ago: '. . . it is not true to say that every boy at heart longs for war. It is only other people who teach it us by giving us swords and guns, soldiers and uniforms to play with.' (*Conquest of the Past*, by Prince Hubertus Loewenstein, p. 215.) It is possible that the Fascist States by revealing to the younger generation at least the need for emancipation from the old conception of virility are doing for the male sex what the Crimean and the European wars did for their sisters. Professor Huxley, however, warns us that 'any considerable alteration of the hereditary constitution is an affair of millennia, not of decades.' On the other hand, as science also assures us that our life on earth is 'an affair of millennia, not of decades,' some alteration in the hereditary constitution may be worth attempting.

49. Coleridge however expresses the views and aims of the outsiders with some accuracy in the following passage: 'Man must be *free* or to what purpose was he made a Spirit of Reason, and not a Machine of Instinct? Man must *obey*; or wherefore has he a conscience? The powers, which create this difficulty, contain its solution likewise; for *their* service is perfect freedom. And whatever law or system of law compels any other service, disennobles our nature, leagues

itself with the animal against the godlike, kills in us the very principle of joyous well-doing, and fights against humanity ... If therefore society is to be under a *rightful* constitution of government, and one that can impose on rational Beings a true and moral obligation to obey it, it must be framed on such principles that every individual follows his own Reason, while he obeys the laws of the constitution, and performs the will of the state while he follows the dictates of his own Reason. This is expressly asserted by Rousseau, who states the problem of a perfect constitution of government in the following words: Trouver une forme d'Association – par laquelle chacun s'unisant a tous, n'obeisse pourtant qu'à lui même, et reste aussi libre qu'auparavant, i.e. To find a form of society according to which each one uniting with the whole shall yet obey himself only and remain as free as before.' (*The Friend*, by S. T. Coleridge, Vol. I, pp. 333, 334, 335, edition 1818.) To which may be added a quotation from Walt Whitman:

'Of Equality – as if it harm'd me, giving others the same chances and rights as myself – as if it were not indispensable to my own rights that others possess the same.'

And finally the words of a half-forgotten novelist, George Sand, are worth considering:

'Toutes les existences sont solidaires les unes des autres, et tout être humain qui présenterait la sienne isolément, sans la rattacher à celle de ses semblables, n'offrirait qu'une énigme à débrouiller ... Cette individualité n'a par elle seule ni signification ni importance aucune. Elle ne prend un sens quelconque qu'en devenant une parcelle de la vie générale, en se fondant avec l'individualité de chacun de mes semblables, et c'est par là qu'elle devient de l'histoire.'[8] (*Histoire de ma Vie*, par George Sand, pp. 240–1).

Editor's Notes

a. *Mary Kingsley is not speaking for herself alone*: Mary Kingsley (1862–1900) was an explorer and travel writer. Woolf was very conscious of her own lack of a formal education. See, for example, her essay 'On Not Knowing Greek' in *WE*, pp. 93–106.

b. *the Pastons to the Pendennises*: Woolf had written an essay on 'The Pastons and Chaucer', published in the first series of *The Common Reader; Pendennis* is a novel by Thackeray (*The History of Pendennis*, 1848–50); the accumulation of Arthur's Education Fund, logged in John Pendennis's accounts as 'A.E.F', is described in chapter xviii.

c. *K.C.*: King's Counsel (in modern British parlance therefore QC), a title given to eminent barristers and also referred to in the profession as 'taking silk' (i.e. having the right to wear a silk gown). Woolf is clarifying that her addressee is a lawyer.

d. *the year 1919*: in 1919 the professions in Britain were opened to women through the passing of the Sex Disqualification (Removal) Act.

e. *European war*: the First World War.

f. *Scarborough Conference . . . of working men*: refers to the locations of the Conservative and Labour party annual conferences of 1937.

g. *photographs . . . Spanish Government*: the Spanish Civil War (1936–9) was a conflict between supporters and opponents of the socialist Spanish republic, founded in 1931. The Republicans (then in government) were aided by the USSR and the International Brigades; Woolf's nephew Julian Bell volunteered as an ambulance driver and was killed there in 1937, aged twenty-nine. (*TG* can be read as a painful argument between Woolf and Julian Bell – see introduction for discussion.) The 'Nationalist' insurgents, led by Franco and supported by fascist Italy and Germany, won the war. Virginia and Leonard Woolf were among liberals supporting the republican cause: in June 1937, for example, they joined other notable figures on the platform at an Albert Hall meeting organized by the National Joint Committee for Spanish Relief. Woolf's diary note was typical:

325

'To the Albert Hall meeting last night. The last I swear ... All very stagey empty and unreal' (*Diary*, V, pp. 98–9). The photographs themselves do not appear in *TG* (and do not appear to have survived in the Woolf archives). Woolf received them on 14 November 1936 according to a letter written to Julian Bell at the time (*Letters*, VI, p.85). Presumably they were sent by the republican government to sympathizers abroad, for purposes of political persuasion and raising financial support.

h. *one guinea*: a guinea was worth 21/- (twenty-one shillings), the current UK sterling equivalent being £1.05 (not adjusted for inflation).

i. *as before in France*: Woolf refers again to the First World War.

j. *our position is still ... of the slightest*: later in the text Woolf elaborates this argument. Since 1938 the position of women in the professions in Britain has changed. As of 1992, it is as follows: the Army and Navy do not accept women as combatants, only in supporting roles; the first woman member of the Stock Exchange has been admitted recently; the established church has approved the ordination of women priests, since 1992; the press is entirely owned and almost entirely controlled by men; the civil service is very sharply segregated, less than 10 per cent of 'career grade' employees are women; an increasing proportion of qualifying barristers are women, but there are very few women in the judiciary.

k. *Mrs Carlyle*: Jane Baillie Welsh Carlyle (1801–66), noted for her astringency and shrewd wit. Woolf is probably referring to her letters, a new collection of which had been published in 1931. The many names referred to in this paragraph are well-known hostesses of the eighteenth and nineteenth centuries (Duchess of Devonshire–Lady Ashburton), male politicians (Pitt–Gladstone), male writers (Sheridan–Carlyle) and female writers (Jane Austen–George Eliot).

l. *the franchise*: universal female suffrage had been won in 1929, and the vote for women over thirty (the male age was twenty-one) in 1918 in Britain. The suffrage movement had been divided over the use of militancy, constitutionalists being called suffragists and only the more violent Women's Social and Political Union being known as suffragettes. Woolf had a period of activism in support of this cause, circa 1910. In *TG* she uses the authoritative work by Ray Strachey, *The Cause: A Short History of the Women's Movement in Great Britain* (1928; still in print in 1992) as a source.

m. prostitutes . . . under the lamps of Piccadilly Circus: known at that time as a base for London prostitutes. Woolf's argument here is reminiscent of the view of Friedrich Engels, that the middle-class financially dependent wife differed from the common courtesan only in so far as she did not sell her body at piecework rates but 'once and for all' in marriage (Engels, *The Origin of the Family, Private Property and the State*, 1884). In *Mrs Dalloway* 'those poor girls in Piccadilly' are invoked in an outburst against the hypocrisies of the middle-class, patriarchal family (1925; Penguin Books, 1992, p. 80).

n. an Act which unbarred the professions: see Note *d.*

o. sixpence: currently equivalent to 2½p.

p. first brief: first commission for a barrister. They are briefed by solicitors, traditionally by means of a parchment document tied with red ribbon.

q. St Paul: St Paul had said that women should cover their heads when praying or prophesying: '. . . for a man indeed ought not to cover his head, forasmuch as he is the image and glory of God: but the woman is the glory of the man' (1 Cor., 11: 7).

r. your finest clothes are those that you wear as soldiers: Woolf took press, cuttings on the subject of soldiers' dress; see the example 'New Uniforms for Army' in Appendix I.

s. we can refuse all such distinctions: Woolf herself refused honorary degrees from universities and one of the state's highest honours, the Companion of Honour (see introduction for discussion).

t. money with which to rebuild a women's college: Woolf had received a letter in 1936 from Pernel Strachey, then Principal of Newnham College, Cambridge, asking her to act as a patron of the college and assist their appeal for building funds.

u. an outsider: note Woolf's use of this term, which is built up as the argument progresses.

v. the English tripos: the Cambridge term for degree examinations.

TWO

a. a society to help . . . obtain employment in the professions: Woolf is referring to the National Society for Women's Service, whose London branch she had addressed in 1931. The speech is printed in *The Pargiters* (ed. Mitchell Leaska, Hogarth Press, 1978). The organization was more lively than it sounded: Vera Brittain commented wryly that it 'somehow captures exciting visitors who will not so much as put their distinguished noses into the offices of other associations' (*Nation*, 31 Jan. 1931). Subsequently Woolf tried (unsuccessfully) to sell the manuscript of *A ROO* to support this organization.

b. *her sister at Cambridge*: Woolf is making a joke for insiders here. Her two letters had come from Pernel and Philippa Strachey, both sisters of her friend Lytton Strachey. Pernel was the Principal of Newnham College, Cambridge, and Philippa the Secretary of the National Society for Women's Service.

c. *Mr Joad and Mr Wells*: C. E. M. Joad (1891–1953) was an English philosopher whose books were relatively popular; H. G. Wells (1866–1946) was a novelist and political commentator.

d. *W.S.P.U.*: the Women's Social and Political Union was the militant wing of the women's suffrage movement.

e. *Cleopatra's needle*: an obelisk (and well-known landmark) on London's river embankment. When it was erected in 1878 a copy of *Whitaker's Almanack* was buried beneath it as part of a time capsule.

f. *five shillings in the pound*: i. e. an income tax rate of 25 per cent.

g. *Mr Baldwin*: Stanley Baldwin (1867–1947), the leader of the Conservative Party at the time. He is featured in the photograph of an academic procession (p. 143) in his role as Chancellor of Cambridge University. Just after *TG* was published Woolf's friend Tom (T. S.) Eliot was given an honorary degree by him; Woolf commented in her diary on him walking in a procession with the other bigwigs '. . . if anyone reads it, the illustration is pat to hand' (*Diary*, V, 11 June 1938, pp. 149–50).

h. *boards and divisions*: these are civil service categories: boards are committees, divisions are grades of staff.

i. *Whitehall excludes it entirely*: Whitehall, in London, is the centre of the British civil service. Woolf is referring to the civil service 'marriage bar', according to which a woman civil servant was obliged to resign if she married.

j. *the other in German*: the words quoted are Adolf Hitler's, from the *Sunday Times* (13 Sept. 1936). In Woolf's notes to chapter three of *TG* she declares, in relation to Italian and German fascist definitions of women's tasks, that 'there are so many versions and all are so much alike that it seems unnecessary to verify each separately' (p. 312, Note 18). In practice, many of the quotations cited in the text can be found in the press cuttings Woolf took from the daily papers and pasted into her scrapbooks (see Appendix I).

k. *the work of an archbishop is worth £15,000 to the state*: several readers wrote to Woolf to complain about the inaccuracy of this remark. Although the Church of England was and is the established church, clergy salaries are not a drain on the taxpayer.

l. *as the poet says*: Woolf is probably referring to Shelley's 'The Question', line 40, which she had quoted in *The Waves* and *The Years*: '. . . present them – oh, to whom?'

m. *the Pensions Bill*: Philippa Strachey, whom Woolf seems to be addressing at this point, was active in the campaign against different income limits for pensions for women and men, as proposed in the government's new bill (1937).

n. *Hansard*: the official record of proceedings in the British Houses of Parliament.

o. *a proctor of Doctors' Commons*: an officer of an association for legal practitioners.

p. *white or black*: this condition gives the lie to the view of Woolf as unthinkingly racist in her attitudes.

q. *Morgan or Rockefeller himself*: the two best-known millionaires of the day. John Pierpoint Morgan Jr (1867–1943) was the son of the American financier whose family helped to establish the Metropolitan Museum of Art and the Pierpoint Morgan Library in New York; John Jr gave the library to the public in 1924. J. D. Rockefeller (1839–1937) was an industrialist and the founder of the Standard Oil Company in 1870, from which he retired in 1911, devoting the rest of his life to good causes.

r. *the truck system*: paying employees their wages in forms other than money (abolished in 1831).

s. *Christ's words*: 'It is easier for a camel to go through the eye of a needle than for a rich man to enter into the kingdom of God' (Matt., 19:24).

t. *Shoe Lane*: off London's Fleet Street, therefore signifying that he was at his office in the evening.

u. *for infamous purposes*: as well as spearheading the fight against the contagious diseases legislation, Josephine Butler was instrumental in bringing about the exposure and banning of child prostitution. The controversy caused by W. T. Stead's 'The Maiden Tribute of Modern Babylon' was written up in Ray Strachey's *The Cause*.

v. Bourget's The Disciple: *The Disciple* depicted the effects of atheism and was the first successful novel by Paul Bourget (1852–1935), a French novelist who engaged in psychological explorations of moral issues.

THREE

a. society ... in need of funds: Woolf was a member of a group For Intellectual Liberty, which had been founded in December 1935 as an English equivalent to a French organization of anti-fascist intellectuals, the *Comité de Vigilance*. In her diary and letters she records many instances of being asked to involve herself in such good causes.

b. Grub Street: once a London street inhabited by low-grade writers, it has now come to stand for literary hacks.

c. It may be difference: Woolf's use of the term 'difference' is significant here. Within the text it shows how contradictory her impulse was to burn the word 'feminism': feminism cannot be redundant, but must return to the centre of things if difference between women and men is, after all, allowed. In terms of Woolf's thought as a whole, *TG* makes a case for a feminism based on the perception of difference, which *AROO* had used the concept of androgyny to deny (see the introduction for discussion).

d. some obstinate emotion: see introduction for examples of irrational emotion of this type from Woolf's own life.

e. to burn a certain corrupt word: Woolf means feminism (cf. Note *c*).

f. infantile fixation: although Woolf refers to this concept as scientific in comparison with the eggs and smells that she uses as symbols or leitmotifs of atavistic male dominance, it is not clear exactly what she means by it. The obvious inference is that it is a psychoanalytic concept, and certainly the cases she goes on to cite in her elaboration of 'infantile fixation' are ones involving an element of unconscious as well as conscious motivation. In practice she uses the term to refer to strong emotions whose origins are 'below' conscious thought. She applies it to societies as well as to individuals. In psychoanalysis fixation is usually thought of as a consequence of the repression of a particular stage of development, but the term can also refer more generally to the 'mode of inscription of certain ideational contents (experiences, imagos, phantasies) which persist in the unconscious in unchanging fashion and to which the instinct remains bound' (J. Laplanche and J.-B. Pontalis, *The Language of Psycho-Analysis*, pp. 162–5). It is often assumed that since the Hogarth Press published Freud in Britain at an early stage, Virginia Woolf must have been very well-versed in his theories; this is, perhaps, unwarranted. There are references in her diaries to points at which she was reading Freud, and also to her meeting with him in London (see introduction for discussion).

g. *Crosby . . . whose dog Rover*: Woolf refers to a character in her novel, *The Years* (1937).

h. *Antigone . . . 'Oedipus complex', and the rest*: Woolf's reference to Antigone, Ismene and Creon is to the story of Antigone, a daughter of Oedipus, whose tragedy was written by Sophocles. (King Creon forbade her to bury the body of her brother, she disobeyed him and did so, he ordered her to be buried alive as punishment, she committed suicide first; Ismene was her sister.) Oedipus, who in ignorance of his parentage had married and fathered four children by his own mother (Jocasta), was taken by Freud as a key symbolic figure in his theories about infantile sexuality and the unconscious.

i. *a white feather*: a symbol of cowardice; Woolf's Note 35 to chapter three (p. 316) outlines its significance at the outbreak of the First World War.

j. *the oldest profession of all, she unsexed herself*: Woolf refers to prostitution; her use of the word 'unsexed' in this connection is typically unexpected.

k. *hideous jargon of the moment*: Woolf's hostile and critical language here is very strong: feminism, the emancipation of women and antifascism were all causes that she herself espoused. As this passage makes clear, she often drew a distinction between 'real' emotions and superficial political activism. See the introduction for discussion of her ambivalence about political action.

l. *Josephine Butler*: a key figure in British nineteenth-century feminism. Ray Strachey said, 'When Mrs Butler came forward in the cause, a double moral standard was not only tolerated but widely upheld; before she had been working a year that comfortable assumption was upset' (*The Cause*, p. 204). Cf. Note *u*, chapter two.

m. *Lady Lovelace and Gertrude Bell*: on Lady Lovelace see Woolf's notes 1 and 33 to chapter one; on Gertrude Bell see Woolf's notes 36 and 38 to chapter two.

n. Holloway or in a concentration camp: Holloway prison in London is where the suffragettes were not only held, but also forcibly fed in violent attempts by the state to break their will. The modern meaning of concentration camp has been changed for ever by the experience of the holocaust; Woolf's usage in 1938 is uncannily apposite, in the context of her argument about fascism.

o. Man himself: Woolf's argument here shows her as one of the earliest thinkers to make a connection between the ideology and iconography of fascism and exaggerated stereotypes of masculinity and femininity.

p. tyrannies and servilities of the other: Woolf anticipates one of the characteristic slogans of the feminism that was to arise in the West in the 1960s and 70s: 'the personal is political'.

VIRGINIA WOOLF'S NOTES TO CHAPTER ONE

a. Lysistrata: in the play by Aristophanes Lysistrata argued that women should refuse sexual relations with men as a strategy to pressurize them to end war.

b. Edward VIII upon his abdication: King Edward VIII abdicated in 1936 in order to marry Mrs Wallis Simpson, who was not eligible to become queen nor morganatic consort as she had already been married and divorced (twice). In a speech broadcast on radio he said that he could not face his high office 'without the help and support of the woman I love'. Woolf was very interested in the politics of the abdication, which was the outcome of a constitutional crisis, and refers to it several times in her diaries and letters.

c. Clare College . . . a private bequest: Woolf's treatment of the issues raised by the conjunction of these two pieces in the *Nation* is very light compared with her more unguarded first response. In the text of her speech to the Women's Service League she cites the Keynes review in the context of her anger that Clare College had spent so much money on a book. Had the book been sent to her for review, she continued, she would have written very differently.

O you old humbugs. I should have begun. O you who have enjoyed for all these centuries comfort and prosperity – O you who profess devotion to the lady of Clare and love for the Sentiment of colleges, would it not be better to spend your six thousand pounds not upon a book, clothed in the finest dress of paper and buckram, but upon a girl, whose dress allowance is very meagre, and who tries to do her work, as you will read if you turn the very next page in the Nation, in one cold gloomy ground floor bedroom which faces due north and is overrun with mice. (Somerville it seems is very hard up.) ('Speech of 21 January 1931', reprinted in *The Pargiters*, p. xxxiv).

Woolf's remarks are slightly confusing, as Somerville is a women's college at Oxford. The *Nation and Athenaeum* was a liberal magazine, with which the Woolfs were associated; it was subsequently incorporated into the *New Statesman*.

d. *Whitaker*: Woolf refers to the reference book, *Whitaker's Almanac*, which she used when compiling the data for *TG*.

e. *vain and vicious*: Woolf's argument has found recent scholarly support. See, for example, Pierre Bourdieu and Jean-Claude Passeron, *Reproduction in Education, Society and Culture* (Sage, 1977), where it is argued that conventions such as the lecture form are designed to occlude the imposition of arbitrary authority and legitimate symbolic violence.

f. *Married Women's Property Act in 1870*: strictly speaking, Woolf is wrong here about property. The right of married women to keep their own earnings, only, was secured in 1870 (the full property bill having been truncated in the House of Lords), and it was not until 1882 that it was extended to cover wealth as well as income.

VIRGINIA WOOLF'S NOTES TO CHAPTER TWO

a. *Mrs Swanwick . . . £42,000*: Mrs Swanwick subsequently wrote to Woolf, pointing out that she had misquoted her: it was not the militant WSPU but the constitutionalist National Union of Women's Suffrage Societies (run by Mrs Fawcett rather than Mrs Pankhurst) that had the income of £42,000.

b. *Contagious Diseases Act*: this legislation forced prostitutes to submit to medical examinations for venereal disease; it provoked heated controversy and was eventually repealed.

c. *St Paul . . . On ne saurait l'affirmer*: 'Is it absolutely impossible, then, that Paul had contracted a greater intimacy with this sister? One could not be certain of it.'

VIRGINIA WOOLF'S NOTES TO CHAPTER THREE

a. *Queen's College*: King's College, London, had established Queen's College in Harley Street, with a view to educating governesses.

b. *a photograph in the daily Press*: this part of Woolf's copy of the press feature is reproduced in Appendix I.

c. *The Life of Mary Kingsley*: this is the only example in the text where Woolf's note does not explain her text adequately. The implication is that Harry was chosen by Mary Kingsley's friend but rejected by her parents and was hence paying a clandestine visit.

d. *Mrs Drummond*: Woolf's scrapbooks for *TG* contain a cutting from the *Listener* (25 August 1937, pp. 405–7) by Flora Drummond, describing the women's suffrage movement.

e. *God ... under control*: Woolf's argument here is extremely sophisticated, presaging much later feminist arguments. Note especially the witty demolition of religion (of patriarchal origin and only sometimes valid), and of biologism and appeals to nature (now known to vary greatly in her commands and to be largely under control).

f. *But this is to anticipate*: Woolf does indeed here 'anticipate' Michel Foucault's analysis of the shift from public exemplary spectacles of punishment to the private surveillance characteristic of modern Western societies. See Foucault, *Discipline and Punish* (Penguin Books, 1975).

g. *George Sand ... l'histoire*: the passage from George Sand reads:

> All human lives are interdependent on one another, and any human being who presents his existence in isolation, without attaching it to his fellow creatures, offers only an enigma to be resolved ... This individuality has neither meaning nor importance in itself. It assumes some sort of meaning only in becoming part of life in general, in blending with the individualities of all my fellow creatures, and it is by this means that it enters into history (trans., Morag Schiach).

Appendix I

THE *THREE GUINEAS* SCRAPBOOKS

Readers of *Three Guineas* may be interested in the following illustration of Virginia Woolf's methods of collecting the data that she used in her argument. As was explained in the introduction to this edition, she spent several years working on the theme of the book before deciding to publish it in its present form. During that period she kept files and notebooks of material that seemed relevant, starting in the early 1930s.

In *A Room of One's Own* Woolf refers to a 'cock a doodle dum' book, in which one would collect bits and pieces. In her own notes to *Three Guineas* she hoped that 'some methodical person' would make a collection of all the manifestos and questionnaires circulated in 1936–7: as has been widely recognized, Woolf herself had done this.

The three *Three Guineas* scrapbooks are in the collection of Monks House Papers in the library of the University of Sussex. They are listed and itemized in Brenda R. Silver's *Virginia Woolf's Reading Notebooks* (Princeton University Press, 1983).

The scrapbooks are very interesting to look at, as they show the materiality of a writer's preparation and process. On some pages Woolf has made marginal comments or calculations. There is no doubt, however, that the most striking aspect of these scrapbooks is the extraordinary connections that she made between items, by simple juxtaposition. On many pages of the books we find two press cuttings, frequently of different dates, arranged side by side to make a point – usually a theme that can also be found in the book itself. Many of these are very funny. In fact, these scrapbooks illustrate a sense of humour little appreciated in the enormous literature on Virginia Woolf. There is a dry and ironic spirit at work in these arrangements, as well as a woman angered by a frightening increase in dictatorship.

1. This is the cover of Scrapbook I. The scrapbooks were kept in marbled boards, the spines having now disintegrated. On the cover Woolf attached a rough list of contents. On this one we can see various items used in the text, for example: Joad and women dining; Bagehot on Girton college; Lady Lovelace; Mary Kingsley; and the Cost of War.

2. This is an early example, dated February 1932. Woolf has clipped two similar stories about complaints and resignations being made over the appointment of women to jobs obviously previously considered the province of men. Note that when she had no tape or paste to hand she simply turned a variety of sticky labels to the job of fixing cuttings to the page.

n a Tunnel

WHITEHALL STORM OVER A WOMAN

SHOULD SHE CONTROL BIG LABOUR EXCHANGE?

MINISTRY STAFF VIEW

A STRONG protest is to be made by certain grades of the Ministry of Labour clerical staff against the appointment of Miss K. M. Walls to the management of the Shoreditch Labour Exchange.

Miss Walls is the first woman to be appointed in complete control of a great Labour Exchange for both sexes.

In an interview with the "Evening Standard" on March 12 she said:

"The development is the natural sequel to the recommendations of the report of the Royal Commission that women in the Civil Service should be given a fair field and no favour."

Resolutions of protest have been submitted by various branches of the Ministry of Labour Staff Association, and it is expected that the Minister of Labour will be asked to receive a deputation on the subject.

FULLY COMPETENT

The situation was explained to the "Evening Standard" to-day by Mr. R. D. Cook, secretary of the Staff Association. He said:

"In the first place I want to make it clear that our protest has nothing to do with the efficiency or otherwise of Miss Walls. We believe that she is fully competent, but we do not think it desirable that a woman should be appointed to the charge of a Labour Exchange which deals with a bigger percentage of men than women.

"Shoreditch is an exchange which deals with male industries.

"Although the bulk of the members of our association consist of women, they are as much opposed to the idea as the men.

"The appointment of Miss Walls does not mean that any additional post has been created for a woman, but it is an experiment of trying a woman manager. The women do not get the same pay as the men—they receive about 15 per cent. less; but no question of economy can be involved, as the total numbers of men and women remain respectively the same.

"The Royal Commission on the Civil Service made a remark about giving women a fair field and no favour, but in our view this is a fair field and favour.

"It is probable that we shall ask the Minister to receive a deputation on the subject."

The game can not interfered with

WOMAN APPOINTED LIBRARIAN

ELEVEN COMMITTEE MEMBERS RESIGN

FROM OUR OWN CORRESPONDENT

WOLVERHAMPTON, Saturday.

A sensation has been caused here by the resignation of eleven members, including the chairman, of the Wolverhampton Art Gallery and Public Library Committee.

The members' action follows a dispute with the General Purposes Committee concerning the appointment of a librarian at the new branch library at Heath Town.

The Gallery and Library Committee had appointed a fully-qualified woman, with twelve years' experience, to the post, but the General Purposes Committee rejected the appointment, stating they wished a male librarian to occupy the office.

Only three members of the Library Committee now remain. Two are also members of the Council, while the third is a co-opted member.

At a meeting of the Council on Monday, the General Purposes Committee will recommend that the resignations tendered be accepted, and that other members be elected to the Library Committee.

3. This illustrates Woolf's quirky sense of humour, given her antipathy to state honours. The reference to Hitler and Mussolini, 'whose turn for embalming may come', is noteworthy.

PRESERVERS OF LENIN'S BODY

PERMANENT TASK OF TWO SCIENTISTS

METHODS A SECRET

FROM OUR OWN CORRESPONDENT

MOSCOW, Monday.

Yesterday—the tenth anniversary of Lenin's death—Professors Vosobief and Zbarski were awarded the "Order of Lenin" for their "exceptional services in the cause of preserving Lenin's body."

For the last ten years these two scientists have devoted themselves entirely to keeping the corpse of the founder of Bolshevism in a lifelike state in its tomb in Red Square, Moscow. It is visited there by hundreds of thousands of earnest pilgrims—and many foreign sensation-hunters.

When they first worked on the body, they told me to-day, they only aimed at keeping it for three months. But now, as it has been kept for so long, they do not see why it should not remain perfectly preserved for ever, provided that constant precautions are taken against damp and changes of temperature.

A steady temperature of 64-65deg. Fahrenheit must be maintained. That is why visiting hours are restricted.

LIKE A SICK MAN

Some time ago I attended a private view of the frail, puny body of the great man. It lies, dressed in a khaki tunic, decorated with the Order of the Red Star, and with the legs concealed by a dark red silk coverlet, on a sloping bier, beneath a glass canopy. Hidden flesh-coloured lights give the face the appearance of that of a very sick man, rather than that of a corpse.

After carefully sending away the Red Guard, who stands at attention day and night in the vault, Prof. Vorobief demonstrated to me the perfection of his work.

The two scientists refuse to reveal their secret method in this age of Duces and Führers, whose turn for embalming may come. But they told me that if they had to work over Lenin again they could now make their work still more perfect.

The right hand does not entirely please them. One of its fingernails is blackened. "When, in 1932, Viscountess Astor saw the body, she exclaimed: "What an aristocrat—just look at those fine hands." "Yes," retorted Mr. Bernard Shaw, who was with her, "those hands have not worked for years."

MEAT TRADE MERGER

4. A vintage example. Woolf has selected an article from the *Evening Standard* (5 Feb. 1937) on the dangers of pacifism as perceived by the church, and juxtaposed it with one of the many accounts given in *The Times* (17 Feb. 1937) of what dress codes would prevail at the coronation of King Edward VIII. Many of the themes of *Three Guineas* are neatly encapsulated.

If We Had Been Pacifists In 1914—

"HITLER WOULD BE IN WHITEHALL"

Good Samaritan Might Have Laid About Him

THE Church Assembly, meeting in London to-day, passed a resolution deploring general world rearmament, welcoming the declared policy of the Government to adhere to the Covenant of the League, and stating:

"This assembly recognises the right of the Government to maintain such force as the Imperial Parliament deem necessary for the pursuance of this policy, and believes that so long as this policy is maintained Christian citizens may bear arms in the service of their country."

It was also decided by a large majority to adopt the following addendum put forward by the Bishop of Southwark (Dr. R. G. Parsons):

"The Assembly affirms the responsibility of Christian people to support, criticise, or oppose all defence programmes in the light of Christian principles and in relation to their advancement of the Kingdom of God."

During the debate the **Bishop of London** (Dr. Winnington-Ingram) said:

"The real dangers to the peace of the world to-day are the pacifists.

"There is no great danger of war if we are strong enough to be policemen with a trun-

The Bishop of London   The Archbishop of York

cheon to keep order, but the policeman must have his truncheon—otherwise he is no good.

"If we had taken the view of the pacifists in 1914, either the German Emperor or Hitler would now be in Whitehall.

"The German plan was first to swallow France and then go on to Great Britain. This little island in the silver sea would be a German province.

"Coming to later times, I should have thought that Abyssinia would have cured every pacifist in the world.

"If we have no force at our disposal the dictators of the world will triumph over the democracies of the world."

Bombs on Children

Dr. Winnington-Ingram referred to the speech made yesterday by the Bishop of Birmingham (Dr. Barnes).

(Dr. Barnes described himself as an "extreme pacifist," and said: "I cannot see myself that war can be regarded as consonant with the spirit of Christ.")

"I hate opposing the Bishop of Birmingham," Dr. Winnington-Ingram said, "because I have a great affection and admiration for him.

"I would rather die than see bombs dropping on the children and burning

(Continued on PAGE FIVE)

19lb CLOTHES AT CORONATION

WHAT SOME PEERS MUST WEAR

NEW COIFFURE FOR PEERESSES

FROM A SPECIAL CORRESPONDENT

Peeresses attending the Coronation who—as revealed in THE DAILY TELEGRAPH yesterday—will each have to wear robes weighing more than 19lb. will be fortunate compared with men at the ceremony. Their robes and uniforms will weigh many pounds heavier.

A West End firm making robes and uniforms for peers, Ministers and officers gave me the following weights of the robes:

Full dress coatee of a first-class Minister	8lb 8oz
Peer's robe	6lb
Full court dress	2lb 8oz
Court-knickers	1lb
Court shoes	1lb 8oz
Dress sword	1lb 8oz
White silk satin waistcoat	8oz
Cocked hat	10oz

First-class Ministers who are also peers will wear clothes weighing about 19lb. nearly twice as heavy as the robes worn by the average peeress.

HEAVY SWORDS

Many other peers will wear a 6lb robe, which is 2lb heavier than the corresponding train and cape of the peeress. A peer's appurtenances will weigh more, and he will also carry a sword and a heavier coronet.

I was told that men wish to keep to tradition in their robes, while women prefer to have them adapted to present-day fashions. Peeresses, while abiding by the rules laid down by the Earl Marshal, are demanding some conformity to the latest mode.

The difficulty of perching coronets on the modern coiffure has been overcome by a new hair-dressing style. This Coronation coiffure will consist of a sleek top waving, with side and neck curls to support the coronet.

MARCH TO BE

5.   Another instance of an ostensibly 'light' item on clothes, illustrating Woolf's view that they symbolize the rank of their male wearers, set alongside a more serious account of the social and political consequences for women of the Nazi regime in Germany (*The Times*, 14 and 16 Dec. 1937). The latter includes the passage: 'It was the aim of National-Socialism to let men's work be done by men and not by women. To believe that a woman's principal work was family life and bringing up the young generation was simply to return to natural and eternal law.'

NEW UNIFORMS FOR ARMY

SMARTER "WALKING OUT" DRESS

EQUIPMENT TO BE LIGHTER

FROM A SPECIAL CORRESPONDENT

Soldiers are to have smarter walking-out uniforms. The whole question of clothing and equipment is now being considered by a special War Office Committee, as it is hoped that before the next training season a decision will be reached.

The authorities have come to the conclusion that smartness in dress and bearing, which are bound up with tradition, influence greatly the potential recruit.

For ceremonial duty and " walking out " therefore the soldier is promised a more distinctive, better fitting and smarter uniform.

For training and manœuvre a more hygienic and loose-fitting dress has been designed, and a lighter and more comfortable equipment recommended by specialists after years of study and experiment.

It is not intended to return to the traditional full dress of scarlet and blue. The expense involved, it is said, would be prohibitive. In addition, the equipment of the modern soldier has undergone changes which, in a large measure, dictate the dress to be worn.

UNPOPULAR BLUE

The blue dress, issued only to troops taking part in the Coronation parade, has not been popular either with soldiers or the public. The main objections to it are that it is not sufficiently distinctive.

There are certain exceptions. In the Cavalry, Artillery and other Royal Regiments the cap-bands of the blue uniform are coloured and the trousers have coloured stripes.

Rifle regiments wear green instead of blue, but the other infantry regiments of the line complain that practically all their distinctive emblems have been eliminated and that they " do not look like soldiers." There is little discrimination between the various regiments and corps.

Modifications are also recommended in the khaki service dress. This is now generally worn by all regiments except the Household Cavalry and the Brigade of Guards, who, with the bandsmen of other regiments, retain the colourful regimental full dress.

The problem of finding a suitable working dress has engaged the attention of experts for the past 10 years. Recently, experiments have been carried out in the field with the object of returning to " light " Infantry.

LIFE IN MODERN GERMANY

DR. WOERMANN ON THE STATE'S AIMS

STATUS OF WOMEN

Dr. E. Woermann, Counsellor of the German Embassy, gave a lecture on present-day Germany at the Royal United Service Institution yesterday. He described the chief National-Socialist institutions by following the life of a typical German, from birth to early manhood, under the continuous influence of those institutions.

The new German State, Dr. Woermann said, had taken its shape out of the two guiding principles of German Nationalism and German Socialism. Nationalism in Germany was not conceived in the same terms as Chauvinism. Since the War the implications of Nationalism had become much deeper for Germans, yet at the same time it implied respect for foreign countries. What it meant was that they should do their utmost to uphold their race, because they believed that whatever they could achieve had to grow out of their national qualities; it could not come out of an ill-conceived and ill-defined internationalism. But that did not mean they were not prepared for international cooperation. Socialism, as they saw it, had nothing to do with Marxism or Bolshevism, nor could their Socialist State be created just by abolishing capitalists.

CONFIDENCE IN THE LEADER

Germany, Dr. Woermann continued, was not, as was so often said in England, a dictatorship, for they had democratic control by means of frequent plebiscites, but it was certainly not a democracy in the old sense. Germany was a State directed by a Leader who enjoyed the full confidence of the entire nation.

After describing the restrictions imposed by the Versailles Treaty on Germany and the successive steps by which Herr Hitler, after unavailing attempts to secure equality of treaty rights, overthrew those restrictions, Dr. Woermann expressed his belief that Germany in re-establishing her equality of rights had rendered a service to the peace of Europe. History had taught them that the cowards and the weak were the targets of aggression from other people. Only the brave and the strong could subsist, and only strong nations could maintain the peace of the world.

The Four Years' Plan was concerned to some extent with defence, but its true purpose was to give permanent work to German workers. He believed that by the completion of the plan the general standard of living in Germany would rise, and that a greater exchange of goods with foreign countries would result from the improved standard of living.

DUTY TO FAMILY

In some foreign countries fantastic ideas were current about the position of women in Germany to-day. Nothing could be more ridiculous and stupid than the assertion that National-Socialism looked on women only as breeding-machines. There were millions of German women working in all kinds of professions. It was the aim of National-Socialism to let man's work be done by men and not by women. To believe that a woman's principal work was family life and bringing up the young generation was simply to return to natural and eternal law.

Numerous questions were answered by Dr. Woermann. Regarding concentration camps, he said there were two types in Germany, one for unsocial elements, several times convicted for certain crimes. The other for political offenders. He assured them that the treatment of these political offenders was reasonable. There were also some people who did not deal with their employees in the right manner. If their offence was serious they went to a concentration camp for a time to learn better.

" We have not a free Press in Germany," Dr. Woermann said to another inquirer. He added, amid laughter and some applause : " It is not so bad not to have a free Press sometimes." What they wanted was not only news value but other values, and the main value was not to disturb the life of Germany and not to disturb international relations.

The CHAIRMAN (General Sir Felix Ready), thanking Dr. Woermann for his lecture, said in this country there had been always a great admiration for the powers of organization of the German people and for the great thoroughness with which they dealt with their social problems. After what they had heard they would agree that this admiration had not been misplaced.

6. A third example of what became a common pattern in the scrapbooks as the threat of war increased: men's desire for smart and hierarchically differentiated dress is put alongside a debate of a major issue for women's independence, in this instance whether to support a pronatalist position. Note that one of the speakers against the campaign to increase the birth rate argued that this was 'in line with what Hitler and Mussolini wanted', but that the pronatalist view won the day.

POSTMEN WANT TO BE SMARTER

UNION'S DEMAND TO POSTMASTER-GENERAL

IMPROVEMENTS IN CUT SUGGESTED

By An INDUSTRIAL CORRESPONDENT

Smartly-cut uniforms for postal workers are being demanded by the Union of Postal Workers.

A request is to be made to Major G. C. Tryon, the Postmaster-General, for the appointment of a joint committee to consider improvements for all grades on the grounds that the thousands of uniform-wearing officials are constantly in the public eye and should present the smartest possible appearance.

The Post Office has already agreed to make some changes in time for the Coronation, but the Union is of the opinion that still further improvements can be made.

Some of the suggestions of the Union are:
    Style and cut to be of the best kind and appropriate to the nature of duty;
    Postmen's caps to be straw-crowned for summer wear, and officers to be allowed, after obtaining permission, to increase the number of ventilation holes;
    Button-hole in lapel of tunic;
    Deeper pockets in vest;
    Watch pocket in trousers;
    Abolition of breast badge.

The Union is also asking for "more suitable headgear of smarter design" for boy messengers.

"DISREPUTABLE APPEARANCE."

Mr. H. W. Wallace, assistant secretary of the Union, said yesterday that he believed the attitude of the present Post Office administration to suggestions for smarter uniforms was sympathetic.

"Owing to the economies which lengthened the period of service of uniforms, the appearance of our men in the streets was disreputable," he added. "It will be greatly improved in May, when we shall resume the old order of two suits a year.

"We want to go further and are prepared to spend money to assist the Post Office in a search for a uniform of the finest possible style, quality and fitting.

£100,000 GIFT TO MANCHESTER

NEW DENTAL HOSPITAL

Plans for a new dental ...

WOMEN DIVIDED ON 'MORE BABIES' CAMPAIGN

'CANNON FODDER FOR NEXT WAR'

FAMILY ALLOWANCE PROPOSAL

Vigorous arguments for and against a campaign to increase the birth rate were put forward yesterday by women delegates at the annual meeting of the National Council for Equal Citizenship at Millicent Fawcett Hall, Westminster.

A resolution, moved by Mrs. E. M. Hubback, on behalf of the executive committee, urged that a campaign should be undertaken to check the declining population. She advocated:

    The establishment of family allowances.
    The provision of such an increase in social services as would make the economic position of people with children at least as favourable as that of those without.
    The provision of a more adequate maternity service.

Several delegates protested against the resolution on the ground that it was advocating enormous families to provide "cannon fodder" for the next war.

"EXAGGERATED PROPHECIES"

Mrs. N. Shackleton, of Liverpool, speaking in favour of the resolution, said that they should make use of the schools to bring home to girls their responsibilities as future citizens and to educate them to expect a good standard of conditions for their children.

Mrs. Helena Normanton, of London, senior practising woman barrister of the English Bar, strongly opposed the proposal, saying that she distrusted it terribly. She felt that this resolution, together with the whole agenda of the conference, was in line with what Hitler and Mussolini wanted.

"I think all these prophecies about what is going to happen as a result of the decline in the birth rate are very exaggerated," she added. "The only thing that women in any country can do to prevent war is to stop the supply of 'cannon fodder.'"

The resolution was carried by 29 votes to 12.

SOCIALIST VOTE

7. Woolf clipped a large feature on the Oxford appeal, including a picture of the 'sconce cup' mentioned in *Three Guineas*. The railed trolley, which passes the port across the fireplace so that post-prandial dons don't have to get out of their chairs to circulate it, is just discernible in this press photograph. Note the scale of Lord Nuffield's donations mentioned in the caption, more than three million pounds, in comparison with the poverty of the women's colleges.

4

THE OXFORD APPEAL COMMITTEE—Following Lord Nuffield's first gift—£2,000,000 for medical research—Oxford, needing extensions in other departments, had decided to issue a public appeal for money, for the first time in its history. In picture No. 3 the Committee, over which Mr. A. D. Lindsay, the Vice-Chancellor, is presiding, is framing the appeal. It was following this that Lord Nuffield made his second donation of £1,300,000. 4—DONS in a Senior Common Room after dinner. The contrivance shown is a railed trolley in which the port decanter travels across the gap between diners at the fireplace, and thus continues its round without passing against the sun. 5—THE "SCONCE" cup in use. This old Oxford custom ordains that mention of certain subjects in Hall shall be punished by the offender drinking three pints of beer at one draught, or, failing this, to buy enough for the whole table.

8.   This cutting (*The Times*, 12 Aug. 1935) provided Woolf with the source for the point she stresses throughout the book, that Hitler explicitly counterposes pacifism and masculinity, claiming them to be incompatible.

"A NATION OF MEN"

THE FÜHRER'S BOAST

SPEECH TO NAZI OLD GUARD

FROM OUR OWN CORRESPONDENT

BERLIN, AUG. 11

Herr Hitler made an unexpected appearance and speech to-day at the celebration of the fifteenth anniversary of the Rosenheim branch of the National-Socialist Party, the second oldest in Germany. Addressing the assembled " old guard," Herr Hitler recalled his first speech in the town 15 years ago—15 years " filled with a wonderful struggle, such as had never before been waged for the heart and the soul of the German nation." In apparent reference to opponents at home, Herr Hitler said :—

In battle we have won the German Reich, and in battle we shall maintain and guard it. Those who are against us need not deceive themselves. We have never shrunk from the combat. If they want it they can have it. We shall crush them in such a way that they will abandon for the next 14 years all idea of continuing the struggle.

Recalling " the heavy trials of the movement in the last 15 years," Herr Hitler said :—

If fate is to put it to the test again, we should be really hardened by the hammer-blows of Providence. The years since 1918 have taught us: " Woe to the people which is unprepared to take its liberty and independence under its own protection." Nobody will deny that in the last two and a half years Germany has attained a different position in the world. I am convinced that nobody in the world can attack our Reich again. We want peace and reconstruction, but just as we want peace so the other nations ought to want peace. He who wishes to disturb our peace will no longer fight against a nation of pacifists but against a nation of men. This fact alone will contribute more to peace than all the speeches.

HEROIC

9. Taken from the same paper as the previous cutting, and juxtaposed with it in the scrapbook, is this account of the arrest of a woman for anti-Nazi talk. Woolf, who was married to a Jew, would have a particular response to the line 'as long as one does not cohabit with a Jew one can safely buy from him' as an example of an insufficiently anti-semitic attitude.

"THE THORN OF HATRED"

OUTSPOKEN ESSEN WOMAN ARRESTED

FROM OUR OWN CORRESPONDENT
BERLIN, Aug. 11

Frau Pommer, the wife of a Prussian mines official at Essen, has been arrested and is to be tried on a charge of insulting and slandering the State and the Nazi movement.

Frau Pommer told the girl behind the counter of a confectioner's shop that if her favourite brand of chocolate was not in stock she would have to go to another shop which she mentioned. The girl replied, with some pertness, it may be imagined, that the other shop was " pure Jewish." Frau Pommer is then alleged to have said : —

I and my husband are and remain German Nationalists ; but as long as one does not cohabit with a Jew one can safely buy from him. The thorn of hatred has been driven deep enough into the people by the religious conflicts and it is high time that the men of to-day disappeared.

10. A certain amount of the scrapbooks consists of Woolf's typewritten observations and summaries of what she has read, and here is an interesting example. Many of these snippets found their way into the final text of *Three Guineas*. The entry on dictators is perhaps the most succinct, following the reference to standing up to dictators, nationally, with an instance of petty domestic dictatorship. Woolf's standard of typing was not good, as can be seen here.

Party funds. Honours.

Blunt Diaries. Part 2. 21st April 1901
To see Meynell.... It appears that the Kings debts have been
paid private y by his freinds, one of whomis said to have
lent £100, 000 and satisfies himself with £25,000 in repay
ment plus a knighthood.

Horror of Church

I have often been asked what I think of Cathedral
establishments, and aft havi g lived in one for 40 years
perhaps I have had some means of judging. I think and say
this deliberately, ten years after my departure, that they
are wasteful institutions, causing much idleness, makinh
for spiritual pride; inducing much quarrelling and bad
feeling and a horrible waste of time. The daily services
cut up the day and keep a whole set of able-bodied men
idle.
                    dale
        Sohia Lonsadle. complied n Violet Mattineau. 103

Dictaors.
Sir E.F. Fletcher urged the House of Commons to "stand up
to dictators" reported in D.H. Aug. 1st 1936
"My husband insists that I call him "Sir", said a woman at
the Bristol Police Court yestderday, when she applied for
a maintenece order. To keep the peace I have complied
with his request" she added. "I also have t clean his
boots, fetch his razor when she shaves, and speak up promptly
when he asks one questions."

Disinterestedness.
Marys conduct was really a signal instance of that pe fect
disinter stedness and self-devotion of which man seems to be
incapable, but whi h is somtimes found in women.
            Macaulay. Hist. Vol. 3. 278

Porfessional writing
                                a
On another day at this time he wrote one thousand six hundred
words article on Nietzsche, a leader of equal length
on the "ailway Strike for the Standard , six hundred
words for the tribune and, in the evening was at Shoe ane.
    The lost Historian A memoir of Sir Sidney Low. Desmond
Xxxxkxx Chapman- Huston. 198   1936

Notes on Cambridge

Endowments of the Unive sity of Cambridge by JW Clark.
Gunnings Rems. of the Uni. Town and County of C. 1854
Trinity and John the rich coleges.

PROFESSIONS FOR WOMEN

Woolf read this lecture to the National Society for Women's
Service on 21 January 1931.

When your secretary invited me to come here, she told me that your
Society is concerned with the employment of women and she suggested
that I might tell you something about my own professional experiences.
It is true I am a woman; it is true I am employed; but what professional
experiences have I had? It is difficult to say. My profession is literature;
and in that profession there are fewer experiences for women than in
any other, with the exception of the stage – fewer, I mean, that are
peculiar to women. For the road was cut many years ago – by Fanny
Burney, by Aphra Behn, by Harriet Martineau, by Jane Austen, by
George Eliot – many famous women, and many more unknown and
forgotten, have been before me, making the path smooth, and regulating
my steps. Thus, when I came to write, there were very few material
obstacles in my way. Writing was a reputable and harmless occupation.
The family peace was not broken by the scratching of a pen. No
demand was made upon the family purse. For ten and sixpence one can
buy paper enough to write all the plays of Shakespeare – if one has a
mind that way. Pianos and models, Paris, Vienna and Berlin, masters
and mistresses, are not needed by a writer. The cheapness of writing
paper is, of course, the reason why women have succeeded as writers
before they have succeeded in the other professions.

But to tell you my story – it is a simple one. You have only got to
figure to yourselves a girl in a bedroom with a pen in her hand. She
had only to move that pen from left to right – from ten o'clock to one.
Then it occurred to her to do what is simple and cheap enough after all
– to slip a few of those pages into an envelope, fix a penny stamp in the
corner, and drop the envelope into the red box at the corner. It was
thus that I became a journalist; and my effort was rewarded on the first
day of the following month – a very glorious day it was for me – by a
letter from an editor containing a cheque for one pound ten shillings
and sixpence. But to show you how little I deserve to be called a

professional woman, how little I know of the struggles and difficulties of such lives, I have to admit that instead of spending that sum upon bread and butter, rent, shoes and stockings, or butcher's bills, I went out and bought a cat – a beautiful cat, a Persian cat, which very soon involved me in bitter disputes with my neighbours.

What could be easier than to write articles and to buy Persian cats with the profits? But wait a moment. Articles have to be about something. Mine, I seem to remember, was about a novel by a famous man. And while I was writing this review, I discovered that if I were going to review books I should need to do battle with a certain phantom. And the phantom was a woman, and when I came to know her better I called her after the heroine of a famous poem, The Angel in the House. It was she who used to come between me and my paper when I was writing reviews. It was she who bothered me and wasted my time and so tormented me that at last I killed her. You who come of a younger and happier generation may not have heard of her – you may not know what I mean by the Angel in the House. I will describe her as shortly as I can. She was intensely sympathetic. She was immensely charming. She was utterly unselfish. She excelled in the difficult arts of family life. She sacrificed herself daily. If there was chicken, she took the leg; if there was a draught she sat in it – in short she was so constituted that she never had a mind or a wish of her own, but preferred to sympathize always with the minds and wishes of others. Above all – I need not say it – she was pure. Her purity was supposed to be her chief beauty – her blushes, her great grace. In those days – the last of Queen Victoria – every house had its Angel. And when I came to write I encountered her with the very first words. The shadow of her wings fell on my page; I heard the rustling of her skirts in the room. Directly, that is to say, I took my pen in my hand to review that novel by a famous man, she slipped behind me and whispered: 'My dear, you are a young woman. You are writing about a book that has been written by a man. Be sympathetic; be tender; flatter; deceive; use all the arts and wiles of our sex. Never let anybody guess that you have a mind of your own. Above all, be pure.' And she made as if to guide my pen. I now record the one act for which I take some credit to myself, though the credit rightly belongs to some excellent ancestors of mine who left me a certain sum of money – shall we say five hundred pounds a year? – so that it was not necessary for me to depend solely on charm for my living. I turned upon her and caught her by the throat. I did my best to kill her. My excuse, if I were to be had up in a court of law, would be that I acted in self-defence. Had I not killed her she would have killed me. She would have plucked the heart out of my writing. For, as I found, directly I put pen to paper, you cannot review even a novel without having a mind of your own, without expressing what you think to be the truth about human relations, morality, sex. And all these questions, according to the Angel of the House, cannot be dealt with freely and openly by women; they must charm, they must conciliate, they must – to put it bluntly – tell lies if they are to succeed. Thus, whenever I felt the shadow of her wing or the radiance of her halo upon my page, I took up the inkpot and flung it at her. She died hard. Her fictitious nature was of great assistance to her. It is far harder to kill a phantom than a reality. She was always creeping back when I thought I had despatched her. Though I flatter myself that I killed her in the end, the struggle was severe; it took much time that had better have been spent upon learning Greek grammar; or in roaming the world in search of adventures. But it was a real experience; it was an experience that was bound to befall all women writers at that time. Killing the Angel in the House was part of the occupation of a woman writer.

But to continue my story. The Angel was dead; what then remained? You may say that what remained was a simple and common object – a young woman in a bedroom with an inkpot. In other words, now that she had rid herself of falsehood, that young woman had only to be herself. Ah, but what is 'herself'? I mean, what is a woman? I assure you, I do not know. I do not believe that you know. I do not believe that anybody can know until she has expressed herself in all the arts and professions open to human skill. That indeed is one of the reasons why I have come here – out of respect for you, who are in process of showing us by your experiments what a woman is, who are in process of providing us, by your failures and successes, with that extremely important piece of information.

But to continue the story of my professional experiences. I made one pound ten and six by my first review; and I bought a Persian cat with the proceeds. Then I grew ambitious. A Persian cat is all very well, I said; but a Persian cat is not enough. I must have a motor car. And it was thus that I became a novelist – for it is a very strange thing that people will give you a motor car if you will tell them a story. It is a still stranger thing that there is nothing so delightful in the world as telling stories. It is far pleasanter than writing reviews of famous novels. And yet, if I am to obey your secretary and tell you my professional experiences as a novelist, I must tell you about a very strange experience that befell me as a novelist. And to understand it you must try first to imagine a novelist's state of mind. I hope I am not giving away professional secrets if I say that a novelist's chief desire is to be as unconscious as possible. He has to induce in himself a state of perpetual lethargy. He wants life to proceed with the utmost quiet and regularity. He wants to see the same faces, to read the same books, to do the same things day after day, month after month, while he is writing, so that nothing may break the illusion in which he is living – so that nothing may disturb or disquiet the mysterious nosings about, feelings round, darts, dashes and sudden discoveries of that very shy and illusive spirit, the imagination. I suspect that this state is the same both for men and women. Be that as it may, I want you to imagine me writing a novel in a state of trance. I want you to figure to yourselves a girl sitting with a pen in her hand, which for minutes, and indeed for hours, she never dips into the inkpot. The image that comes to my mind when I think of this girl is the image of a fisherman lying sunk in dreams on the verge of a deep lake with a rod held out over the water. She was letting her imagination sweep unchecked round every rock and cranny of the world that lies submerged in the depths of our unconscious being. Now came the experience, the experience that I believe to be far commoner with women writers than with men. The line raced through the girl's fingers. Her imagination had rushed away. It had sought the pools, the depths, the dark places where the largest fish slumber. And then there was a smash. There was an explosion. There was foam and confusion. The imagination had dashed itself against something hard. The girl was roused from her dream. She was indeed in a state of the most acute and difficult distress. To speak without figure she had thought of something, something about the body, about the passions which it was unfitting for her as a woman to say. Men, her reason told her, would be shocked. The consciousness of what men will say of a woman who speaks the truth about her passions had roused her from her artist's state of unconsciousness. She could write no more. The trance was over. Her imagination could work no longer. This I believe to be a very common experience with women writers – they are impeded by the extreme conventionality of the other sex. For though men sensibly allow themselves great freedom in these respects, I doubt that they realize or can control the extreme severity with which they condemn such freedom in women.

These then were two very genuine experiences of my own. These were two of the adventures of my professional life. The first – killing the Angel in the House – I think I solved. She died. But the second, telling the truth about my own experiences as a body, I do not think I solved. I doubt that any woman has solved it yet. The obstacles against her are still immensely powerful – and yet they are very difficult to define. Outwardly, what is simpler than to write books? Outwardly, what obstacles are there for a woman rather than for a man? Inwardly, I think, the case is very different; she has still many ghosts to fight, many prejudices to overcome. Indeed it will be a long time still, I think, before a woman can sit down to write a book without finding a phantom to be slain, a rock to be dashed against. And if this is so in literature, the freest of all professions for women, how is it in the new professions which you are now for the first time entering?

Those are the questions that I should like, had I time, to ask you. And indeed, if I have laid stress upon these professional experiences of mine, it is because I believe that they are, though in different forms, yours also. Even when the path is nominally open – when there is nothing to prevent a woman from being a doctor, a lawyer, a civil servant – there are many phantoms and obstacles, as I believe, looming in her way. To discuss and define them is I think of great value and importance; for thus only can the labour be shared, the difficulties be solved. But besides this, it is necessary also to discuss the ends and the aims for which we are fighting, for which we are doing battle with these formidable obstacles. Those aims cannot be taken for granted; they must be perpetually questioned and examined. The whole position, as I see it – here in this hall surrounded by women practising for the first time in history I know not how many different professions – is one of extraordinary interest and importance. You have won rooms of your own in the house hitherto exclusively owned by men. You are able, though not without great labour and effort, to pay the rent. You are earning your five hundred pounds a year. But this freedom is only a beginning; the room is your own, but it is still bare. It has to be furnished; it has to be decorated; it has to be shared. How are you going to furnish it, how are you going to decorate it? With whom are you going to share it, and upon what terms? These, I think are questions of the utmost importance and interest. For the first time in history you are able to ask them; for the first time you are able to decide for yourselves what the answers should be. Willingly would I stay and discuss those questions and answers – but not to-night. My time is up; and I must cease.

Appendix III

As with most of Woolf's texts, there are quite a large number of minor differences between the first British and the first American editions, and in this case there are also a few major ones: these consist of extra sentences, or in one case a paragraph, added to the notes in the American edition; Woolf seems to have treated the writing of the notes as an ongoing process. The following list records differences of wording, and, in addition, a number of changes in punctuation adopted from the American edition for reasons of sense or consistency. In general, the American edition is slightly more heavily punctuated than the British – for example, it uses commas more frequently and all longer quotations in the American edition are set inside double inverted commas; most of those in the British text are not. Page and line numbers given below refer to this edition, the first entry being from the British first edition, the second from the American first edition; variants adopted in this text are indicated by an asterisk.

121.4   by us; and it is difficult   ]   by us; it is difficult

129.29   profession, the late Sir Ernest Wild.   ]   profession, the last Sir Ernest Wild.

130.19   the right to vote,[14] in itself by no means negligible,   ]   the right to vote, in itself by no means negligible,[14]*

131.3   Through that light we may guess everything she saw   ]   Through that light everything she saw

131.9   And if checking imagination   ]   And if, checking imagination*

134.24   others, three, four, five or six.   ]   others three, four or five.

137.4   Apart from the ceremonies such decorative   ]   Apart from the ceremonies, such decorative*

142.4   both have bridges, too, for us   ]   both have bridges, for us

156.32   some festival, a bazaar presumably, 'but we have to   ]   some festival, 'fire off your rhetoric, but we have to

158.20   we are offered offices and honours for ourselves   ]   we are offered honours and degrees for ourselves

362

162.29 and the quickest way to understand them] and the way to understand them

163.19 if she is poor, as poor as she pretends] if she is as poor as she pretends

190.33 hear them if we listen singing] hear them, if we listen, singing*

192.27 of strawberries and cream and bazaars.] of bazaars and strawberries and cream.

193.1 is born;[19] bring down the maternal death-rate] is born;[19] you could bring down the maternal death-rate

194.5 England to-day? How should that] England today? And how should that

194.33 If you succeed in your professions the words 'For God and Empire'] If you succeed in those professions the words 'For God and the Empire'

197.10 lost sight, and sound, and sense of] lost sight, sound, and sense of

198.16 wasting their chance.'] wasting their chance.'[29]

202.1 'Gertrude was not allowed] Gertrude 'was not allowed*

203.11 derision, and – but what word covers] derision, and – what word however covers

209.1 P.C., etc., with that] P.C., etc., etc., with that

209.5 professions. Those are the conditions upon which she is to have her guinea. They have been framed, so far as possible, to ensure that she shall do all that a guinea can make her do to help you to prevent war. Whether the conditions have been rightly laid down, who shall say? But as] professions. In it such influence as a guinea can exert has been framed so far as our psychological competence allows to ensure that she shall do all that is in her power to help you to prevent war. Whether the terms have been rightly defined it is impossible to say. But as

216.33 a few of her novels; The Duke's Daughter,] a few of her novels: The Duke's Daughter,*

220.1 loss of money, which is desirable,] loss of money which is desirable,*

232.13 elastic before everything would be not to] elastic before everything, would be not to*

234.21 to protect either myself or my country.] to protect myself or my country.

237.5   dishonoured profession, your own slavery would be light-
enened.[17]] dishonoured profession,[17] your own slavery
would be lightened.*

237.30   upon the arm-bearers, such] upon the arms-bearers, such*

238.34   based it might well be upon] based, it might well be,
upon*

241.9   raw – by the newspapers that is, sometimes] raw – by the
newspapers that is – sometimes

242.26   human nature, and a change that may be of real help] human nature, and be of real help

250.22   in interpreting that mind, changed his mind.] in interpreting the other mind, changed his own mind.

251.21   the gift of prophesy.] the gift of prophecy.*

251.35   and unpaid occupation.] and unpaid for occupation.

252.23   reported finally; 'While] reported finally: 'While*

253.16   remains controversial in many respects obscure.'] remains
controversial and in many respects obscure.'*

254.23   Here we can take the Professor's word] Here we can skip;
we can take the Professor's word*

258.21   the facts scarcely bear repetition.] the facts scarcely require
repetition.

264.27   She founded a school;] She started a school;

265.2   1861;[39] next Barbara went into] 1861;[39] then Barbara went
into

268.12   only profession that had been open] only profession that
was open

269.15   Even now the clamour, the uproar that infantile fixation is
making even here is such that] Even here, even now, the
clamour, the uproar that infantile fixation is making is such
that

283.24   in founding Girton.] in founding Girton. But compare Mr
Baldwin at Downing St (March 31st, 1926.)

289.25   for a Thousand Worlds.'] for a Thousand Worlds.' The
real nature of delicacy and the real nature of chastity (let alone
the real nature of marriage) are still therefore highly conjec-
tural.

303.27   [The Greek in the English edition is inaccurate in minor
respects, in the American edition incorrect.]

304.4   'this book will be an eye-opener.'] 'this book will be an eye-opener.' Presumably the need for a scapegoat is largely responsible, and the role is traditionally a woman's. (See Genesis.) It is a curious fact that although the 'practical obliteration' of her freedom is assured if certain characteristics generally if erroneously associated with aggravated masculinity remain unchecked, the educated woman not only accepts criticism, but if publishers' lists are to be taken as evidence, makes no attempt to return it. This may be attributed to poverty which, as the poet says, makes cowards of us all. On the other hand, a statement in the *Times* (Sept. 1st, 1937) that 'in the last few years women have developed a great taste for oysters' suggests that an increase of spending power may in time develop the critical faculty as well as the sensual.

310.31   Gas Association' washed an acre of dirty dishes,] Gas Association 'washed an acre of dirty dishes,*

313.26   carried on. The Churches seem somehow] carried on. 'The Churches seem somehow*

321.33   the occupation is not exclusively maternal, but could be shared by both parents to the common good.] the occupation is not necessarily maternal, but should be shared by both parents. And actually an English Member of Parliament has resigned in order to be with his children.

READ MORE IN PENGUIN

In every corner of the world, on every subject under the sun, Penguin represents quality and variety – the very best in publishing today.

For complete information about books available from Penguin – including Puffins, Penguin Classics and Arkana – and how to order them, write to us at the appropriate address below. Please note that for copyright reasons the selection of books varies from country to country.

In the United Kingdom: Please write to *Dept. EP, Penguin Books Ltd, Bath Road, Harmondsworth, West Drayton, Middlesex UB7 ODA*

In the United States: Please write to *Consumer Sales, Penguin Putnam Inc., P.O. Box 12289 Dept. B, Newark, New Jersey 07101-5289.* VISA and MasterCard holders call 1-800-788-6262 to order Penguin titles

In Canada: Please write to *Penguin Books Canada Ltd, 10 Alcorn Avenue, Suite 300, Toronto, Ontario M4V 3B2*

In Australia: Please write to *Penguin Books Australia Ltd, P.O. Box 257, Ringwood, Victoria 3134*

In New Zealand: Please write to *Penguin Books (NZ) Ltd, Private Bag 102902, North Shore Mail Centre, Auckland 10*

In India: Please write to *Penguin Books India Pvt Ltd, 11 Community Centre, Panchsheel Park, New Delhi 110017*

In the Netherlands: Please write to *Penguin Books Netherlands bv, Postbus 3507, NL-1001 AH Amsterdam*

In Germany: Please write to *Penguin Books Deutschland GmbH, Metzlerstrasse 26, 60594 Frankfurt am Main*

In Spain: Please write to *Penguin Books S. A., Bravo Murillo 19, 1° B, 28015 Madrid*

In Italy: Please write to *Penguin Italia s.r.l., Via Benedetto Croce 2, 20094 Corsico, Milano*

In France: Please write to *Penguin France, Le Carré Wilson, 62 rue Benjamin Baillaud, 31500 Toulouse*

In Japan: Please write to *Penguin Books Japan Ltd, Kaneko Building, 2-3-25 Koraku, Bunkyo-Ku, Tokyo 112*

In South Africa: Please write to *Penguin Books South Africa (Pty) Ltd, Private Bag X14, Parkview, 2122 Johannesburg*

BY THE SAME AUTHOR

'Woolf is modern ... With Joyce and Eliot she has shaped a literary century' Jeanette Winterson, *The Times*

Mrs Dalloway

Clarissa Dalloway, elegant and vivacious, is preparing for a party and remembering those she once loved. In another part of London, Septimus Warren Smith is shell-shocked and on the brink of madness. Smith's day interweaves with that of Clarissa and her friends, their lives converging as the party reaches its glittering climax. Past, present and future are brought together one momentous June day in 1923.

The Waves

Tracing the lives of a group of friends, *The Waves* follows their development from childhood to youth and middle age. The novel is remarkable for the rich poetic language that conveys the inner life of its characters: their aspirations, their triumphs and regrets, their awareness of unity and isolation. Separately and together, they query the relationship of past to present, and the meaning of life itself.

Orlando

Written for Virginia Woolf's intimate friend Vita Sackville-West, *Orlando* is a playful mock 'biography' of a chameleon-like historical figure who changes sex and identity at will. First masculine, then feminine, Orlando begins life as a young sixteenth-century nobleman, then gallops through three centuries to end up as a woman writer in Virginia Woolf's present day.

also published:

Between the Acts	**The Crowded Dance of Modern Life**
Flush	**Jacob's Room**
Night and Day	**Selected Short Stories**
To the Lighthouse	**The Voyage Out**
A Woman's Essays	**The Years**

The Diary of Virginia Woolf Volumes 1–5